"BETRAYAL...."

Barac watched Rael add the word to the facts she had just obtained from his mind. He saw reluctant conviction settle small lines around the edges of her mouth. "Yes. You're right, of course," Rael said slowly. "How else could such attacks be timed? But who? The Council may use pawns like Kurr or Dorsen, you or I. But not Sira. I can't believe they'd risk her in any way."

"You know what they're capable of, Rael," Barac argued. "What would they do if she was escaping them?"

Rael drew in a startled breath. "What do you see that I don't? What do you think has happened to Sira?"

A THOUSAND WORDS FOR STRANGER

"A wonderfully entertaining SF adventure with fascinating, well-developed characters. A must read!"
—Josepha Sherman,
author of STAR TREK: *Vulcan's Forge*

"Julie Czerneda has resurrected the classic SF themes of Norton, Heinlein, and Moore—the young amnesiac protagonist searching for her identity in a universe of spaceships, exotic alien races, and high adventure—with a distinctly modern sensibility."
—S. M. Stirling,
coauthor of *The City Who Fought*

"A wonderful new voice in science fiction—sure to be one of the fastest-rising stars of the new millennium."
—Robert J. Sawyer,
author of *Frameshift*

A THOUSAND WORDS FOR STRANGER

Julie E. Czerneda

DAW BOOKS, INC.
DONALD A. WOLLHEIM, FOUNDER
375 Hudson Street, New York, NY 10014

ELIZABETH R. WOLLHEIM
SHEILA E. GILBERT
PUBLISHERS

For Joy Starink

Well, Mom, this is what happens when you give a kid who complains about the ending of a book a handful of blank paper and that challenging raised eyebrow of yours. I only wish you and Stan could have stayed around to read this one. Thanks again, with all my love.

ACKNOWLEDGMENTS

Can't do it. I've been given so much support in birthing my first book that there isn't room to name you all. I humbly hope you'll know who you are and that you know I really do thank you for your help, whether it came as critical comment or a bottle of dragon wine.

Here goes the list I can fit: Thank you Linda Heier, for being the first to read and believe. Thank you Trudy Rising, for making me pull this manuscript out of its home in my drawer. Thanks also to Roxanne Hubbard and Jonathan Bocknek, for your support and wonderful editing. Thank you Jan and Steve Stirling, for being both mentors and incredible friends. And thank you, Josepha Sherman, for taking me under your falcon's wing every time it looked like doomsday!

My thanks to the Ontario Arts Council for its kind support during the early stages of this new venture.

Thank you, Sheila Gilbert, for your insightful comments that helped me pull the last loose pieces together. (And for letting me have as many pages as I wanted!)

Thank you, Jennifer and Scott, for your patience and encouragement. Well, kids, now you can find out what Mom's been doing after supper! Hope you like it.

Last, but first as well, thank you, Roger. It just wouldn't have happened without you. Maybe that's because I've never had to look very far for a hero.

PRELUDE

THE sign was rain-smeared and had never been overly straight. P'tr wit 'Whix spared one eye to read it as he passed, then chuckled to himself: "Fabulous Embassy Row? Tours daily?" Then again, he thought, why not? After all, Embassy Row was about the only thing worth touring on Auord.

The necessities of a shared government meant interspecies embassies on every Trade Pact world, no matter how insignificant the world—or the species. And convenience clustered the embassies together, hence Embassy Row, a street along which building styles ranged from the unlikely fluted domes of the Skenkran, barely anchored to the ground, to the lumps of plas-coated imported mud favored by ambassadors from Ret 7.

Tonight, however, the tour cars sat as empty as the street itself. The first rains of the season had arrived early, setting up a cheerful cacophony from the chimes Auordians strung from every lamppost and door, whether allowed to or not. But a chill wind had slipped in with the rain, and the benefits of seeing and being seen were apparently not enough for most to brave the cold dampness.

Which was a shame, 'Whix thought. He himself was not fond of uncontrolled water, yet he appreciated that other beings would find the effect quite attractive. Reflected lights sparkled over the buildings and their grounds, lifting each from the dark. Along the avenue itself, the lamps lining the walkways on either side cast circles of brightness that danced across the wet pavement, transforming its surface into a mosaic of gems.

'Whix's momentary fancy quickly turned to a muted but shrill curse in his native tongue, as his three-clawed foot landed with a splash in one of those light-begemmed puddles.

It would have to rain on his shift, not his partner's. It had to be 'Whix out in the drizzle, feeling water flattening the feathers of his crest; 'Whix the one with icy drops sliding under the upraised collar of his uniform, soaking the feathers of his back.

Muscles twitched maddeningly in a reflex, and 'Whix shuddered with the effort not to shake out the moisture. He knew from experience his magnificent crest would only stick out wildly in all directions, like a chick's, until the rain matted it against his head again.

Proper grooming was the only answer, combined with a good rub under a dryer and probably some of his hoarded supply of bertwee oil. All things considered, there was a lot to be said for a space assignment.

'Whix rolled down one eye to check his wrist chrono, keeping his other eye faithfully fixed on the pair he followed. His vision, even under these conditions, was keen enough to let him keep a block and a half behind the two—which was why night surveillance fell to him and not his Human partner, Russell Terk.

The walkway lights were spaced to provide convenient pools of darkness between them, room enough for packages to be exchanged unnoticed, or for a walking couple to slip in and out of sight. 'Whix swung both his eyes forward, and details of the two ahead jumped into clear focus.

Reflected light played over the female's elaborately jeweled headpiece—an alluring object of apparel, 'Whix decided, as well as practical. The headpiece covered most of the female's face as well as her hair. Her male companion was bareheaded—caught, like 'Whix, without protection from the change in weather. His hair was either black or darkened by the rain. The richly dressed pair could have passed for Human, if 'Whix hadn't known they were Clan.

Which was why he trailed them. And why he trailed them at a distance. The Clan were not members of the Trade Pact, being uninterested in alliances of any kind. No Clan Embassy sparkled here in the dark; not surprisingly, since there was no Clan world to represent. The few Clan known to live within Trade Pact space kept to themselves and by themselves, living alone on their isolated estates on Human worlds, preferring the established inner systems where their wealth could be spent in privacy. The latest estimate, doubtless as inaccurate as it was secret, placed their number at a mere thousand.

So to see one of the Clan on a fringe world like Auord was unusual. To see two together sent alarms ringing through any Trade Pact Enforcer who knew them. 'Whix clicked his beaked mouthparts together thoughtfully. His commander knew the Clan better than most. Which was why applicants to her personal staff were offered a choice: accept a still-experimental mind-shield implant or work elsewhere. 'Whix had to admit the surgeon had done an excellent job of preserving his feathers. It remained to be proved whether the device could protect him from the Clan.

True telepaths were rare among Humans, scarce at best among the three other Trade Pact species who claimed that power, and completely absent in most. The Clan, rumor had it, were all telepaths of extraordinary ability. Rumor also said that they disdained mental contact with any species other than their own. 'Whix hoped that was true. But like any rumor, the source was suspect.

Trailing at a distance did have its disadvantages. When a tight group of figures boiled from the darkness of a side street, 'Whix was too far away to do more than bleat a bulletin into his throat com as he started running. Almost as suddenly, he hesitated, slowed to a walk. His orders were specific: to observe the Clan, not interfere.

But it was hard to only watch.

'Whix made out six assailants closing in on the two, now halted under one of the streetlamps. The attackers seemed unarmed, but he doubted it. At a minimum, each probably carried one or more impact clubs, the easily concealed but deadly device popular among hit-and-run criminals on Auord.

'Whix saw the Clansman step quickly in front of his companion, drawing a force blade from his belt. He waved its blazing tip slowly, expertly. For a moment, all was frozen and silent except for the rain drumming on the sidewalk and the drops hissing to steam on the white hot blade.

'Whix admired the Clansman's choice of defense.

Knowing the Clan's avowed dislike of technology, the
blade was a nice compromise. And most criminals of
'Whix's experience vastly preferred a stunner headache to
losing body parts. Still, force blades were uncommon—
their use took skill, not to mention that they were illegal
on most worlds. 'Whix found himself looking forward to
the battle.

A cry from the darkness cracked the tableau and launched
the attack. Four figures moved toward the Clansman while
two others tried to dodge past to reach the Clanswoman he
protected. Screams echoed amid the snap-crack of clubs.

A groundcar, sirens whining, wheeled around the corner. Port Authority, 'Whix knew immediately, not his
backup. Commander Bowman would not be pleased if the
locals interfered. 'Whix clicked his beak, thought longingly of hot oil, and broke into a run, spreading his arms
for balance.

Meanwhile, the battle was hardly one-sided. Four
bodies already sprawled amid the pools of light, blood
spreading to mingle with the puddles and rain. The Clansman stood facing the remaining two, his blade lifted like
a dare.

Something rose, hung for an instant in the air, then
plunged toward the Clansman. 'Whix squawked a warning as he threw himself flat. A sear of heat, accompanied
by a whomp of sound, signaled the explosion of the blast
globe.

'Whix cautiously tried each of his joints. The Port Authority car slid to a stop beside him. He ignored the shouts
from its occupants as they spotted him and ordered him to
wait. Their waving lights made a distracting flicker along
the dome of his eye lens.

'Whix tossed his head, feeling his blast-dried feathers
lift and settle into their proper regal positioning. Shame it
was still raining. He made sure his Pact insignia was in
his hand as he trotted over to the heap of scorched and
broken bodies. No ground authority would interfere with
a Pact Enforcer—in theory, at least. The Trade Pact, and
its Enforcers, protected the rights of all signatory sentient species. But Auord's Port Authority was known to be
touchy.

The blast had been confined, relatively minor, which
made sense if capture, not murder, was the intent. It had,

however, killed the two who had—to that point—survived the Clansman. The Clansman himself, remarkably intact, lay half under one of those bodies.

The attackers were all native Auordians, 'Whix noticed without surprise, Auord being a world where morals rarely put food on the table. He sniffed delicately. Tolians had lousy noses, if truth be told, except for a fine sensitivity to dead flesh, fresh or rotten—a talent the Tolians wisely chose to keep to themselves when offplanet.

He swung his head up, catching the sound of doubled footsteps echoing in the distance—the globe-tosser and accomplice making their escape.

'Whix immediately dismissed the notion of giving chase. He knew what Bowman would have to say if he left the Clansman for Port Authority.

'Whix eased back on his haunches to pick up a scrap of something that caught the light. It was the jeweled headdress the Clanswoman had worn. But where was she? 'Whix straightened, looked around, but saw no body, or piece of a body, that belonged with the jewels in his hand.

Wait. His eyes swung forward, straining to see. There she was, down the street, a small figure just visible through the sheets of rain. Somehow she must have escaped the worst of the explosion, possibly thrown or pushed clear. 'Whix watched her until she stumbled into a side street and was gone. He activated his com again.

The two corpsmen bustled up, hoods pulled up against the rain. "We'll take over, Enforcer."

'Whix didn't answer until he had finished transmitting his message. "Trade Pact jurisdiction," he said then, his trill automatically translated into a tinny Comspeak that issued from a device embedded beneath the feathers of his throat.

The two from Port Authority exchanged glances before looking at 'Whix again. One, a stocky Auordian, actually put her hand on the stunner strapped to her leg. "This looks local to us," she said in a no-nonsense voice. "You know something we don't, I suggest you share it. Otherwise, head back to the shipcity where you belong, flyboy."

'Whix rocked back on his powerful haunches, ready for action, his long clawed feet on either side of the now-groaning Clansman, although this meant stepping in a spreading pool of warm red. "This is a Trade Pact matter," he repeated.

"Prove it."

"He doesn't have to, Corpsman," said a harsh voice from above their heads. 'Whix didn't bother looking up, slightly exasperated, as usual, by his Human partner's dramatics. No need to wonder about Terk's timing; he loved a grand entrance. It was part of what Bowman referred to as Terk's exceptional gift for annoying the local law. 'Whix was supposed to use his cool, methodical approach to balance his partner's excitable nature. After five years, 'Whix hadn't so much made progress as learned to cope.

The aircar, a sleeker and far more deadly vehicle than anything permitted Port Authority, touched the sidewalk in a master's landing. Terk hit the floods before disembarking, driving back all the shadows and forcing the corpsmen to shade their eyes.

Their dismissal was complete when Terk waved a strip of plas under their noses. "Here's our permit to take these beings into our custody," the big man announced. "I'll be sure to mention your helpfulness to our commander."

Once the disgruntled pair drove away, Terk prowled over to his partner. His apparent size was deceiving. Shorter by a handspan than the slender Tolian, Terk's mass was bundled up in a deep chest and shoulders wide enough to need a custom-fitted uniform. Even so, he always looked as though his clothes pinched. "A simple surveillance," the Human said with disgust. "This is quite the foul-up, 'Whix. Any of them alive to take into custody?"

'Whix had already begun sorting the injured from the dead. He tagged the Clansman and one of the assailants with med signals and watched the stabilizing field encompass the injured beings within its purple glow. "These two. Forensics can have the others."

Terk nodded, taking a moment to use his wrist com to summon the med transport and a forensic team. Then he considered his partner. "You're a mess. Want to head in? I can take this from here."

'Whix dipped his beak to each of his shoulders in turn, his approximation of a Human shaking his head. "No. I'll dry out when I make my report." He focused both eyes on the unconscious face of the Clansman. "I am concerned,

Partner Terk. I think our commander may be wrong about this one."

"Don't bet on it," Terk grunted. "They always look Human, but looks aren't everything."

"If he's Clan, why didn't he use his Talent to stop the attack or to escape?" 'Whix argued.

"Maybe he'd spotted you. They don't like to be caught at work." Terk grinned. "Anyway, we can't take the chance. Just think what interesting changes of mind our Clansman might have given those Port Jellies when he woke up. Want to lay odds they wouldn't even remember seeing him?"

'Whix tried to lower his crest in disapproval, but it was already flattened by the rain. "As always, you show a distressing lack of respect for other law keepers, partner Terk. You should not refer to them as Jellies."

Terk grinned, rubbing a piece of plas between his thick fingers. "When I can chase them off with a road map, they deserve whatever name I call them."

'Whix clicked his beak, far from amused. One day, Terk's blatant actions were going to land them both in trouble—trouble he, for one, did not deserve. But he knew the futility of arguing with someone with a crest lifted in triumph (if Terk had one instead of a mass of pale-colored and always limp hair). "I was not observed by the Clansman." 'Whix said instead. "Therefore, I see no reason for him not to use his Talent to save himself and his companion. Or hers, for that matter. Given this," 'Whix continued with patience, despite the fact that Terk's attention was obviously wandering, "I must conclude—"

Terk put a finger to his lips. 'Whix was uncertain whether this was because he wished to cut short their discussion—which happened regularly—or something else. Ah, something else, 'Whix heard the throb of more than one aircar heading their way.

Time to talk of less secret things.

"Do you know if there's a dryer in the commander's office?" he asked with a mournful chirp.

Chapter 1

I STARED at the hand pressed near my cheek. It had five fingers, tipped with small, blunt nails, one broken. There were smudges of dirt on the palm and back; the clean skin was paler, except where a spiderweb of red marked the edges of a cut. It was mine, I decided, confused by the delay in recognition.

I shuddered, stumbling away from the damp wall. A flicker of movement caught my eye. A nearby window had lost part of its covering shutter, exposing a dirty slice of glass and curtain to the street. Something looked out at me. Cautiously, I tilted my head to see, then lurched back as the pale something did the same.

My feet landed in the small river that currently passed for a gutter at the same instant I realized I'd been startled by my own reflection. Sheepishly, I stepped closer to the window again. Was I that wet or was it the water running down the glass itself that made me look like a swimmer underwater, blurring my hair and clothes into the same dark mass? My face appeared as little more than two eyes stuck on a disk of white. Old and puzzled eyes. Maybe it was another trick of the rain-smeared glass. I wasn't old.

Then was I a child? I didn't think so. But what? Lost and wet. Humanoid. Those were easy. Male or female? The reflection kept mute on that interesting detail. I was definitely unwilling to strip in the rain to satisfy my curiosity. I patted my hands over my body, discovering water, but little else in the pockets and creases of my clothing. I continued my self-exploration. Nothing of me felt male, but nothing felt particularly female either.

A shout. Only an echo of a voice, probably the next street away, but enough to startle me back into myself, to force my feet to move. The rain struck harder as I left the partial shelter of the overhanging eaves; I hesitated, distracted by the taste of it in my mouth.

My mind suddenly turned inside out, filling with thoughts I knew weren't mine, compulsions rippling like muscle, gripping me with needs and purposes I didn't understand. *Find the starships. One ship,* a trailing wisp of thought corrected, *"his" ship.*

Numb under the impact of imposed ideas, all I could do was look along the narrow street, empty of all but two parked groundcars on the other side. What ship?

More thoughts pushed their way to the surface, each dragging fear like something hooked to a line. *Danger. Leave this world. Stay hidden, stay safe.* I whimpered to myself, then glanced about to be sure no one had heard.

The compulsions gradually faded, leaving echoes that burned into my mind: *Find the ship, leave this world, stay hidden.* As I came back to myself, I realized my feet were walking, already carrying me somewhere. I stopped, my mouth dry despite the rain.

For the first time, I really looked at my surroundings. Both sides of the street were lined with a chaotic assortment of buildings, most at least three stories high, their upper floors leaning together as if in conversation. Away from the streetlamps, the strident colors of the walls sank into a dull assortment of grays. Rain collecting on the roofs channeled down in noisy waterfalls to feed the gutters. As if this weren't enough, metal chimes hung everywhere, transmuting the tinkling of raindrops into a full orchestra.

Great, I said to myself, glaring at the buildings, all peacefully asleep and probably dry inside. If I was supposed to find a ship, I was certainly in the wrong place. This had to be somewhere in the All Sapients' District, the maze of haphazard streets and alleyways between the native portion of Auord's Port City and the shipcity itself. At least keeping hidden wasn't a problem. Finding my way out would be.

More vital information spun away from my thoughts, quicksilver and slippery as I tried to hold it. My wet clothes slapped heavily against my legs as I began to walk again. Walking was progress, even if I didn't know which way to go.

The alleyway I turned into next twisted so I couldn't see the end. The pavement was stained and littered with lumps the rain had tried to wash away but had only pounded flat around the edges. I wrinkled my nose at the smell of spoiled food. Maybe the servos had been kept away by the rainstorm; more likely someone hadn't paid their taxes. This last thought surprised me. It was as if a resonance had briefly rippled through my mind, colliding to reveal a tidy node of knowledge.

Glimpsing the consequences of tax evasion wasn't exactly helpful in my present situation. I picked my way through the debris until I reached an area where the bundles of trash were heaped shoulder-high on both sides, with gaps only at each barred and locked rear door. Waste disposal by the heave-ho method, I decided, imagining the nightly routine of opened doors, tossed bags, and slammed locks.

The foul smell began to settle at the back of my throat, as if the dampness of the air helped it stick. Cans tumbled loose in an odd counterpoint to the rain. I stopped and peered into the shadows. One of the piles moved again.

Another sound—this time a word. An impossibly filthy face glared up at me as its owner shoved away a covering of shredded plas and rotting fruit. More words, followed by a spit in my direction. The language was strange. No. It was tantalizingly familiar. Another resonance; the sentence re-formed. I understood.

"—this here's my spot, scum. Get lost—"

"I am lost," I said politely, pleasantly surprised by the fluency of my own Comspeak. I moved closer to better examine the being, feeling no threat despite its words. *Stay hidden, be safe,* whispered that something beneath my thoughts, but I found I could push it away. Ah. The blue wattle under its chin was crusted with unshed skin, but still distinctive. A Neblokan. How wonderful to have a name for something. I felt under my own chin. It was smooth. "I am not one of you," I admitted, disappointed.

"Brain-dead Human pest. Go away and leave me in peace." The creature rolled up his eyes, a very rude gesture for one of his kind, then turned his back on me and settled his bulk more comfortably amid the bags of garbage.

I blinked raindrops out of my eyes. The Neblokan had almost disappeared again under his trash cover. I couldn't understand what he now muttered, but then, he seemed to be talking to himself, and in no pleasant tone either. I wrinkled up my nose again, trying to decide if the fishy being smelled worse than the garbage. Could I convince him to talk to me again? Might he know even more about me?

A new sound began, this time from the way I had just come, quickly growing to a shrill whine. I winced at the sudden pain in my ears. The Neblokan lunged up and past me, scattering soggy bits and pieces as he moved with unexpected speed. I turned toward the sound, judging it harmless enough. But the Neblokan was already scurrying in the opposite direction as fast as his stubby legs could take him, uttering more of those incomprehensible sounds as his feet slipped in the puddles.

Should I do the same?

The noise stopped as suddenly as it had started, then began again, only this time ahead of where the creature was running. I crouched away from a light that appeared from nowhere to transfix the Neblokan. He stopped in mid-stride, shoulders folding back in a defeated shrug. The sound closed in, then stopped.

"Credit check," said one of two figures who came striding up the alley. One carried the source of the light, the edge of its beam catching a small cone the other held in his hands, likely the source of the sound. I put my hands on the slick pavement and carefully wiggled my way into the shadow of the Neblokan's hole in the trash. I peered out.

"My credit's good—" the Neblokan offered, but weakly. His wattle shook and his wide-mouthed face was wrinkled in distress. Raindrops collected on the ridges of his eyebrows, running off the ends like tears.

"Mind if we don't take your word for it?" said one of the figures, I couldn't tell which. His tone was bored. "You offworlders think everything insystem is as free as the air."

"You want to live here, you've got to pay. What's it to be?" the second one demanded. I shivered and crouched lower. His voice had a pleased anticipation to it.

The Neblokan spread his empty hands. "I'll get a ship today—"

"You certainly will." The cone-sound keened again,

this time in a brief burst, muffled because the tip had been pressed against the Neblokan's head. The creature dropped to the ground in a heap, looking like little more than another of the piles of waste that a moment ago had been his refuge.

"Even with this fratling rain, it's been a good night, Enex." This from the light carrier as he set his lamp on a crate. I could see them both now, Auordian males, one with blue luck beads braided in his hair and the other, yellow. Otherwise, they were alike enough to be twins, with a well-fed smugness to their pudgy faces. They busied themselves for a moment around the fallen figure. When they stood, the Neblokan's body rose with them, supported by a grav belt.

"It's always good here," replied Enex, the one with the blue beads. "Best place in the sector to get skilled labor. Downed spacers go broke—"

"And nobody cares but us." This brought a laugh from both of them, laughter that faded away with their steps.

Recruiters. I watched them go, for the first time wishing not to understand. It could have been me they took away, to be sent offworld, my life to be spent as bonded labor to some colony world or station that lacked the technical resources to support servos. Sold and forgotten.

It was happening to the poor Neblokan. I pushed myself out of the pile, forcing away self-pity. At least I had a purpose. Find my ship, stay hidden. Staying hidden would have helped the Neblokan. I wondered why he hadn't listened to his own inner voice.

Didn't he have one?

Choosing the direction opposite to the one the recruiters had taken, I ended up facing a barrier of boxes and plas crates. It was climbable, barely. I found I could squeeze up one side as long as I was careful where I put my feet and clung to anything that stayed put. I didn't look down, or dare to think how easily I might be spotted as I climbed. At the top, I paused to catch my breath and look for the best way down the other side.

Spotting a glimpse of rain-gray fabric, I grabbed for it, scrabbling for purchase among the slippery plas and broken metal. The object came free reluctantly. Hugging my prize, I slid down the other side of the rubble barrier into the safety of deeper shadows.

I straightened the fabric, letting the rain soften the en-crusting dirt so I could pull out the legs. The cloth smelled like something called home by several generations of small rodents, but at least there were no holes. Quickly I stripped, waddling up the wet mass of my own cloth-ing and shoving it beneath the nearest pile. My shoes followed.

I shivered as the rain raised gooseflesh on my bare skin. Something dark washed down my arm with the drips. I followed its trail with a finger to the top of my shoulder. The dark liquid was welling up in irregular drops over a patch of blackened skin. I touched this, felt pain, and withdrew my fingers quickly. At least now I knew why my arm ached.

There should be fasteners. As my mind faltered, my fin-gers worked, opening the front so I could push in my feet. The thing was delightfully dry inside, though my toes en-countered a large prickly mass of fibers in one leg that I quickly removed without looking at it. I hoped no one was home. I struggled for a moment to get the garment over my wounded shoulder, then scowled down at myself. I could rent out space in here.

A moment later, clothed in what had once been a blue coverall, with a ridiculous amount of excess fabric bunched through the side straps, I strode out of the shadows hold-ing my head high. Of course, this served to keep my nose a bit farther from my clothing, but that was hardly the point. I looked and felt like a real spacer, one of the elite who arrogantly defended their right to come and go from such backwater worlds as Auord. I would go to my ship. I would not tolerate any more interference.

What odd thoughts I was having. I shook my head and waited for the eddies in my brain to subside. Wasn't I the one supposed to be hiding? And the recruiters could still be prowling around.

So much for being a spacer. I pulled my head back down between my shoulders and kept to the rain-swept shadows.

I walked for what seemed hours, my new foot-gear less than a bargain. Although my feet were blissfully warm and dry, they slipped constantly from side to side within the too-large shoes, forcing me to plant each step with care. I should have kept the nest and used it to stuff the toes.

Each time I came to an intersection, I would hesitate, then take whichever alley or street looked less traveled or more shadowed. It was one way to deal with the fact that I had no idea where I wanted to go. If I'd been in any shape to wonder, I'd have seriously doubted my sanity. Shadowy streets were also preferred by predators; I carried no weapon. Another wisp floated to my mind as I plodded along in my oversized spacer gear—I hadn't always been helpless.

At some point, I found I could make my feet stop moving. I rested in shadows deeper than most, grateful for a wall that prevented me from sagging to the pavement. The rain had also stopped, although drips continued to slide from the rooftops, usually on my head. The chimes sang softly to themselves. Over those same rooftops, the rising sun was melting away the storm clouds, gilding the spires beyond them with gold. Those spires. I puzzled over their irregular, narrow shapes for a moment; they couldn't belong to buildings. It took several heartbeats before I allowed myself to believe I was looking at the tips of starships. Now, I knew the direction of the shipcity. The question was, which set of twisting alleyways would take me there?

Considering that my mind was almost empty, I was almost grateful for the compulsions trying to pass themselves as my thoughts.

Find my ship.

Leave Auord.

Stay hidden.

Perhaps I'd made those decisions but couldn't remember my reasoning. They gave me a purpose I accepted without questioning—yet. But more and more I wondered what was missing from my mind. The universe, and my place in it, could not have begun last night. The piles of old litter in the streets proved that much.

But as I tried to concentrate, to think about myself, my mind grew fuzzy, unfocused. I quickly tired of the effort; it was like trying to pull a hair out of syrup. I'd work on survival, and think about regaining my place in the universe later. My stomach growled its agreement and I knew it was time to move again. But where?

As if yanked by a thread, my head turned without my deciding it, scraping my cheek against cool, wet stone. I blinked, unsure of what had attracted my attention.

I was looking along another of the All Sapients' District's narrow winding walkways. I was alone. Doors, some sporting colored and, to me, incomprehensible signs in the local language, others firmly barred and forbidding, lined the walls on one side. Where I stood was an unbroken depth of shadows, with the still-shuttered windows of living quarters beginning on the upper floors. As I watched, rooted in place by some anticipation I didn't understand, a door burst open across from me.

"Sleep it off on your ship, Outsystem Dregs!" This bellow in accented Comspeak was warning enough—I wasn't surprised when a figure was propelled out of the doorway. I winced at the smack as it hit the pavement and slid into a pile of waste. The door slammed shut. I moved, thinking to help the unfortunate creature, then froze—the impulse checked by the clattering of a shutter above. *Stay hidden,* I reminded myself.

Two pairs of arms, one pair glittering with golden paint and the other striped in green, waved from the open window. They were female arms, slender and adorned with bracelets. The man, for once he pushed himself up to a stand I could see him plainly, glared at the now-closed door before bowing gallantly to the occupants of the window above.

He then began to stagger away. As he did so, he set his foot down carelessly and twisted about in a full circle. This brought titters of laughter from the window, but I drew back, startled. As he spun around, the seeming drunkard had raked his surroundings with eyes of vivid blue—eyes which found me unerringly and which were anything but clouded by drug or drink. Then, to all other observers a fool ending a binge, the fascinating man wandered off, his path weaving toward the shipcity.

Another tug on the thread—this time stronger. Shrugging my shoulders, which hurt my arm, I began following him, unable to refuse that urging and wishing I knew how. True, the man was dressed as a spacer, with coveralls not much better than my own. Significantly cleaner, I added to myself honestly.

He has a ship, something inside of me gloated.

Fine. But how did I know his ship was the one I had to find? His exit from the inn could almost have been planned, as if he needed to deceive any watchers. Maybe he was a smuggler—or worse, one of the pirates who made their living preying upon the space traffic of fringe systems like Auord's. A normal, sane person would avoid this man.

But a ship was a ship. And I understood enough of my fragmented thoughts to know I was hardly normal, though I hoped I was at least sane. If the mysterious figure ahead, whose clumsy steps miraculously avoided the more odorous litter underfoot, could lead me to a starship, to transport off Auord, maybe I could silence the compulsions drumming in my head long enough to think for myself. With the utmost care, I kept my spacer just in sight.

Abruptly, he was gone! I gasped, instantly and unreasonably desperate. I hurried forward, turned a corner too sharply, and was roughly grabbed from the side. Frantically, though silently, I kicked and twisted.

"Stop," a voice breathed in my ear as my body was given a quelling shake. "What were you planning, thief, a knife in my back?" Then, as if considering a new, more unpleasant possibility: "Or were you sent to follow me?"

"I'm no thief. Let go of me," I said, thoroughly disgusted. His grip pulled me into the shadow of a nearby doorway, then released me.

I rubbed my bruised arms and eyed the spacer warily. There was equal suspicion in the tanned, plain-featured face glaring down at mine. His clear, shockingly blue eyes were cold and hard. "If you're no thief, then perhaps you're worse—a runner for ~~**~~." My surprise at the chirping whistle emitted by his pursed lips must have been plain enough. He frowned, a trace of puzzlement raising one dark brow. "Stop looking so desperate, chit. I won't hurt you. But you'll tell me who set you on my back."

He made it sound as though he had some unknown means to force such information from me. I stifled an urge to laugh. "I followed you because I need transport," I said truthfully, though I doubted he'd believe it. "Back there, I heard him say you had a ship."

For the first time, the man seemed to notice the spacer clothing I wore, so like his own despite its present unwashed state and odd size. His nose wrinkled. "Who are your kin?" he demanded. I realized with a rush of hope that he was becoming troubled.

Kin? A word possibly with meaning for another me; an empty space here and now. "Do you have a ship or not? I need to leave Auord."

"I don't need crew," he said, his expression making it plain that he'd rather be somewhere else too. But he hesitated.

'We're both spacers," I pleaded. "You can't leave me stranded."

He was silent for a moment, blue eyes hooded. I could hear a distant murmur—voices. We were close to the market. Louder was the pounding of my heart, counting each second in double time.

Then: "I'm sorry, chit," and there seemed an honest regret in his voice. "I'm booked for lift already. Your kin must really be down on their luck. Spacers should stick by their own. Especially on this dirtball of a planet." He paused and then shrugged as though he was doing something against his better judgment. "Here." One hand dug into a pocket and pulled out a crumpled handful of what appeared to be local currency. He pressed it into my unresisting fingers. "Next street over you can flag yourself a groundcar. Go to the north gate and ask at traffic control for Thel Masim. Got that?"

"Thel Masim, north gate," I repeated without understanding.

"Tell her Morgan of the *Fox* sent you. Thel's got a soft spot for youngsters. That's the best I can do."

I raised my chin. "I don't need her help. I need to get off this planet. I must leave. Please . . ." then, although I didn't plan it, my voice failed me. Waves of exhaustion and pain roared in my ears. I leaned back against the doorway.

The spacer, Morgan, had already assumed an absentminded air that I knew meant he was done with me. "I've been grounded myself a few times, chit; happens to everyone," he said briskly. "Start taking care of yourself, though, or no ship will take you. Get a wash and a good meal . . . you'll feel better."

Suddenly, I was looking at his back. He was leaving.

And I would have to follow, whether I wanted to or not, even if I had to crawl.

I tried to call after him, but my voice lost itself somewhere in my throat. He turned a corner and was out of sight. I shivered, dropping the currency heedlessly to the ground. One thing I couldn't do was lose him.

The compulsion to follow was strong enough to push me away from the doorway's support, when I couldn't have done it alone. I had to get to my ship. I had to follow Morgan.

I had only taken a couple of unsteady steps when a familiar sound whined out of the rain, exploding against my skull to drag me like an anchor into total blackness.

* * *

INTERLUDE

"He's coming around."

Barac sud Sarc, First Scout, Third Level Adept of the Clan, and current owner of a body that was one giant ache, allowed himself a small groan before making the effort to open his puffed-shut eyes. The strange voice had been a warning. Barac peered up at the two uniformed figures bending over him and carefully hid his dismay. "Ah, Enforcers. It's to you I owe my rescue," he said hoarsely. He could think of a lot of better places to be at the moment. Almost anywhere, in fact.

There was a quick shuffle of feet as the curious officers backed away and a short, heavyset woman took their place. She wore her uniform casually, its sleeves, with their insignia of a full commander, pushed up to reveal thick, tanned forearms. There was, however, nothing casual about the look in her sharp eyes. "I've seen the others, Hom Barac sud Sarc," she responded briskly. "Or what's left of them. Force blades are illegal on Auord."

Feeling acutely at a disadvantage, Barac tried his most charming smile, but his face hurt too much to hold it. What had happened since his assailants resorted to the unfair tactic of a blast globe? What was he doing here, flat on his back, held by blanketing that could more bluntly be called a restraint? He gathered himself. "Hopefully," he said, "attacking an innocent tourist is also illegal on Auord, Commander . . . ?"

"Bowman. Commander Lydis Bowman," she supplied readily. Her voice was deceptively friendly. "Chief Investigator for the Board of Interspecies Commerce—the Trade Pact—in this quadrant, Hom sud Sarc. These are members of my staff, Constables Terk and 'Whix." Barac probed delicately for her thoughts, then for those of the others, only to recoil from the blank nothingness where they should be. Shielded. How quaint. Useful no doubt as a barrier against their own feeble Human telepaths.

Barac opened his mind, allowing the merest edge of his thoughts to enter the M'hir. Some Clan scholars argued that the M'hir was a construct formed by Clan thoughts over generations of use. Others, with equal passion, described the M'hir as another dimension, in which disciplined Clan thoughts slipped like needles through thread, bypassing normal space.

Most Clan, like Barac, ignored both arguments. What truly mattered was that the ability to enter the M'hir belonged only to the Clan. The M'hir gave Clan thoughts the ability to transcend distance, to transport matter, to touch layers of thought in other minds—such as those of Humans—believed unreachable.

Barac remembered how his link with the M'hir had grown each time he entered it, starting with childhood dreams of that darkness filled with the passage of power. His adult ability in the M'hir might not be as great as some of the Clan, but it was respectable for a sud. Barac was sure he could bypass Bowman's shielding as he focused his strength in the M'hir.

What was this? A taint of metal, of nonlife, opposed his inner sense, obstructed the flow of power through the M'hir around each of the Humans and the Tolian. Impossible. No other species even suspected the existence of the M'hir; how could these have a device to affect it?

Bowman's mind-deadening device must be something totally new. The Clan routinely planted false reports, sabotaged research. Yet here was the proof of the Humans' stubborn persistence. There were too many of them to control.

And so the Humans had at last achieved more than they should, Barac realized, vastly uneasy as he pulled his thoughts back to normal space. He could only hope they didn't know.

"We've managed to keep life in one of your assailants, Hom sud Sarc," Bowman had continued, unaware of Barac's probing—or its failure. "She's yet to speak to us." Unspoken, but understood, was the inevitability of that conversation.

Barac blinked slowly, marshalling his thoughts with feverish haste. "What can the criminal tell you? Nothing you don't already know," he predicted. "They were taking advantage of a fool out in the storm." Recognizing this sounded less than gracious, Barac tried his smile again. It usually worked with Humans. "I'm truly grateful for your rescue. I'm certain they meant to kill me."

"I'm sure they did," Bowman agreed too cheerfully, waving a hand. One of the uniformed officers, Constable Terk, brought her a stool. Barac had to twist his neck to keep her in sight. "But you proved very stubborn," Bowman continued. "Let's see: five dead, one just about. And how many got away, 'Whix?"

"I heard at least two running after the explosion, Commander, likely the ones responsible," the Tolian replied quickly, russet-and-gold feathers fluttering delicately as each word of Comspeak left the tiny speaker on his throat. Barac disapproved of Tolians in general, especially at the moment. They had a depressingly thorough approach to things. "I also saw Hom sud Sarc's companion run in another direction," the Enforcer continued. "It was my duty to stay with the wounded." There was a faint note of regret in the dry voice, audible even through the speaking device.

"My thanks for that," Barac said truthfully, feeling some of his tense muscles relax. So Sira had gotten away—somehow. For once, these lackeys of the Trade Pact had been of some use. Usually they were a minor irritation, to be distracted as necessary by lower-rank adepts such as himself, or avoided altogether. He concentrated for a moment, assessing the damage to his body. Cracked ribs, burns, bruises, nothing worse.

Bowman wasn't telepathic, but her instincts were good. "You were lucky, indeed, Hom sud Sarc. Our meds say you'll be up and about very soon. But first, I've a few questions for you."

"Your attention is flattering, Commander," Barac said. "But surely this is a matter for local authorities. What interest can it have for Pact Enforcers?"

Bowman leaned forward, eyes narrowed. "When local assassins are using classified Pact equipment, it is a matter for us, Hom sud Sarc." Bowman held up three connected disks of dull brown, the small two attached to the larger by a hair-thin wire. "We recovered one from each of your attackers."

She paused. "These are mind-shields, in case you don't recognize the effect. Quite impenetrable, aren't they?" Bowman lifted the hair from the back of her head, turning so Barac could see the small, shaved half circle where her neck and skull met—an unnecessary confirmation of what his mind had sensed.

Barac remained silent, feeling this was the safest course. Bowman regarded him thoughtfully for a moment, choosing her next words with care. "You haven't told me the whole truth, Hom sud Sarc. Why did your attackers need mind-shields? Why take the risk of stealing equipment from us? As if that weren't enough, these so-called common thieves of yours also underwent surgical implantation—which I'll confess to you is very dangerous indeed. Which makes me wonder if all their precautions were necessary for protection—from you."

Barac sud Sarc coolly raised a brow, then winced as the movement irritated the bruises which marred one side of his lean, handsome face. He avoided looking directly at the disks. "I don't know what you're implying, Commander," he said. "I was the one attacked, remember?"

Bowman apparently reached a decision. "Leave us," she ordered her subordinates. Once the door had closed behind them, she continued. "I imply nothing, Hom sud Sarc—Clansman."

"My ident is on record, Commander," Barac said. "I'm sure you've also verified my travel clearance." Who was she? he wondered furiously. How much did she know? How fortunate she sent out her guards, a darker thought intruded.

"Yours. But let's talk about your companion. Her records are, let's say, less than helpful. No name. No planet of origin. According to Port Authority, you were walking alone last night, Clansman."

"We comply with your obsession with record keeping when convenient," Barac countered. "The Clan—"

"—is not bound by Pact regulations. Yes. I know." Bowman smiled. "Well, enough of this. Do you want to see your companion now?"

"Do not try your tricks with me, Human," Barac tried not to snarl. "She has gone her way—as would any Clan. One of us here," he glared around the room, "is more than you deserve in your net."

"Net? I'm not your enemy, Clansman. In fact, my people were watching out for just such an incident." Bowman hadn't lost her smile. "You see, I communicate regularly with the High Councillor of Camos Cluster, Jarad di Sarc. A familiar name, I'm sure, since he also happens to be your uncle—and Spokesman of the Clan Council."

Barac felt a familiar frustrated anger. How typical of the Council to include this—this Human!—in its intricate web of strategy while leaving the true risk-takers in the dark. "We are not under your authority, nor do I claim your aid," he snapped, finished with evasions. This Human pet of Jarad's was the last straw.

"Ah, but these devices were stolen from this facility before you arrived on Auord. Someone else was expecting you, Clansman. Someone with a healthy respect for your—abilities."

"Your toys are your problem, Commander Bowman," Barac said testily. "Not mine. I object to your insistence that the Clan has some strange mental power. This kind of rumor-mongering is why we refuse to join your Pact."

Bowman's smile tightened. "You may decide differently, Clansman Sarc. You see, I also want to talk to you about something that has nothing to do with last night—at least as far as I know." She stood and walked ponderously to the end of Barac's bed, her movements giving the impression of someone finding planet gravity a nuisance.

Bowman produced a compact image box and aimed it midway between them. "What do you know about this, Barac sud Sarc?" she asked, activating the device.

Barac craned his head forward, staring at the image hovering above his waist. It showed the interior of a standard stateroom, the type common on intersystem transports. A figure in blue and yellow lay upon the floor in a hunched, tormented position. Barac heard the sudden roar of blood in his ears as a distant thing, a sign of the body's ability to react to pain before the mind dares admit the truth.

He drove a questing thought into the M'hir, seeking a familiar channel through its nothingness, the effect close to draining his reserve of energy, heedless of all but the contact he sought. There was no answer, no anchor drawing him to the comforting strength of that other mind. There was nothing at all.

With all the disinterest he could muster, Barac shrugged and lay back against the pillows. "Why do you expect me to know anything about this? I've never seen that man before."

Bowman pressed another control. Instantly the image shifted, spun dizzyingly larger until only the left hand of the dead man and a portion of the deck showed. "I expect you to tell me something about this, Barac sud Sarc," she said, her eyes never leaving his face. The carpet beneath the hand had been burned away down to the dull shine of metal. The metal itself was incised with tiny, irregular but plain letters. "That is your name, isn't it?" Bowman added unnecessarily, just as the door to the room opened.

Barac ignored the too-convenient return of the two Enforcers, meeting her gaze steadily. "I do not have to answer your questions, Human," he said. "Or are you planning to hold me here?"

"That won't be necessary, Clansman Barac." Bowman's voice held a hint of smugness. "Let's say, for once, our interests may run together. I have a murder to solve, a murder which took place on Pact commercial shipping. I can't imagine how your name was written by that man— suffice it to say that it's one of your kind's more interesting secrets. But I intend to learn how he died—and your involvement." She paused, her expression hardening.

"The room was locked from within," the commander

went on. "The crew of the ship have been thoroughly mind-searched by our people, and are innocent. My willingness to oblige the High Councillor or the Clan will not extend to unknown lethal weapons—or to Clan wars in my space."

"Kurr." Saying the name made it real. His power ached for a target, but there was none. Yet.

"What did you say?" she said blankly.

"Whatever name was on the manifest, the dead man is . . . was Kurr di Sarc. And before you ask, yes, he was my brother, Commander Bowman." Barac faltered, trying to restore calm to his voice. "All I can tell you is what you must have already guessed: Kurr left my name so that I would be contacted. He must have been desperate if he had to rely on Humans to relay his message." A heavy silence. "When did it happen?"

Bowman decided to look sympathetic, an effort which fell short of credible, but then Clan never relied on Human expressions. "I had no way of—"

"When. Where." Barac had almost succeeded in burying his own emotions under a cold detachment. The discipline of a scout had its uses.

"Three days ago. He was last seen alive when they went insystem in Acranam. The body was discovered the next day enroute to Letis VI." She paused. "The ship and all aboard are being held at the Letis Pact facility. Will you want the body?"

Barac ignored her question, with its Human assumption. To the Clan, what remained after death was a shell, dropped from the M'hir, of no significance to the living. "What killed him? Who?"

Bowman's eyes glittered, her sympathetic air discarded. "We don't know. And that is why you'll stay and talk with me, Barac sud Sarc, Clansman and focus of trouble. I'll have no more of your Clan business leaving bodies in Pact territory. I want answers."

Barac nodded slowly. "I understand, And in return for passing Kurr's dying message to me, I'd honestly like to help you. But I haven't time to search out Kurr's murderer now." His handsome face might have been carved from ice, its bruises stones embedded beneath the surface. "I have someone else to find—" And before Bowman could open her mouth to dispute this, Barac's body shimmered and disappeared. The white blanket slumped flat with a surprised sigh of air.

"Damn," Bowman said to the empty bed, annoyed she had driven him away. Then she consoled herself—who'd have guessed the injured man could summon such power? She activated her implanted communicator with a twitch of one eyebrow. "Med-com. Did you get anything unusual just now on your scopes?"

"Your guest left the room, sir. I don't have scanners in the hall. Is that what you meant?"

Bowman sighed. Still, it was always worth trying. "Any more from the prisoner?"

The whisper in her ear was apologetic. "Just what you know already, Commander." A pause. "I don't think we can keep her alive much longer."

Bowman tapped her brow with one stubby finger; the new implant was supposedly sensitive enough to control with an unobtrusive twitch of muscle, but she'd rather be sure the wretched thing was really off. She pursed her lips thoughtfully, glancing with approval at the pair waiting patiently for her commands, their composed faces too well-trained to show any reaction to Barac's startling departure.

The feathered Tolian, P'tr wit 'Whix, and his partner, the dour-faced Terk, were the most senior of Bowman's personal staff. They had been together long enough to know when to wait and when to speak. Almost.

Terk scowled. "So we forget this one, too? Diplomacy." The word might have been a curse.

Bowman's lips curled. It wasn't a smile. "I forget none of it. What you continue to forget, Terk, is that we're not law keepers—or diplomats. I know how you feel," she said more gently. "It's a thankless task, keeping everyone's feet, flippers, or whatever, off everyone else's anatomy." More sharply. "But as Enforcers, we have nothing to do with justice—get used to that. We enforce the treaty rights of Pact member species. The Clan aren't Pact, not yet. But so long as they live on Pact worlds we'll watch them."

"What use is watching?" Terk went on, not cowed. His face was all angles and planes, with harsh lines running from mouth to nose and framing eyes that even his few friends found uncomfortable to meet. When happy, his voice was a low, heavily accented growl. Now it rumbled like so much thunder. "Seems to me they do pretty much what they like."

"As long as they keep it to themselves, that's fine," Bowman said with sudden weariness. "God knows, there's enough to do without disturbing the peaceful ones. I just need to know if the Clan are beginning to push at the Pact."

"Then what?"

"You know as well as I do. We push back. We damp the pendulum. Then we leave them alone." A decision was needed, urgently, and Bowman was no longer in a mood to hesitate. "We'll begin with what we know so far," she said.

Terk shook his head. "Which is a lot of nothing."

P'tr wit 'Whix fluttered disagreement. Unfortunately, the effect was lost while most of his iridescent feathers were covered by his uniform. He raised a slim four-fingered hand in emphasis instead. "Right after the explosion, I saw Sarc's companion go west on West Central Street, grid coordinates 140-5D," the being said firmly. "She wore clothing similar to the Clansman—a detail confirmed by our less-than-healthy prisoner. Thus we have time, place, and description. You are always too quick to say it cannot be, Partner Terk."

Terk muttered something under his breath that sounded like: "Featherhead."

Bowman stood, paced a few steps, then turned to look at them. "Things are happening among the Clan," she said, heavily. "Dangerous things. The key is Barac's mysterious companion."

"He's gone to find her," Terk rumbled, unaffected by his partner's optimism. "Probably teleported right to her." For a moment, he looked wistful.

Bowman shook her head, eyes bright. "I know them, Terk. I know how they think. Barac had put aside his brother's murder because of this woman. Why is she so important? Someone arranged an almost foolproof attack. Who was the target—Sarc, or was it her? While we've no proof they can all teleport, certainly Barac has that ability. So why didn't he use this ability when attacked? Was it because of the woman?

"No," Bowman continued, "I think our Clansman, for whatever reason, is worried that he won't be able to find her easily. That's going to be to our advantage."

"What do you want us to do, Commander?" 'Whix asked.

"Want?" Bowman's smile grew predatory. "I want you to find her first."

Chapter 2

VOICES brought me back to myself, anxious voices arguing in heated whispers so close I could smell ammonia on the breath of one. "—gonna get caught. This was a stupid idea."

"You worry too much."

"And you're a greedy fool. I told you to make sure you doped 'em all before shipment. So what do you do with this one? What do you think will happen when Smegard finds out?"

"He won't find out. Dregs die in sleep passage all the time. Come on, we don't have much time." I kept limp as rough careless hands picked me up, not daring to open my eyes. The voices were familiar—the recruiters from the alleyway. I somehow doubted they'd believe me if I protested I had no skills to sell. Or care.

They dropped me onto some flat surface and I bit back a cry. Something heavy and dusty was thrown over me. I remained limp, opening one eye a tiny crack only to be met by total darkness. The surface under me began to move slowly, with a rhythmic mutter of machinery. I felt around cautiously, stretching out the fingers of one hand in slow motion. Where were the Auordians now?

And where was the spacer, Morgan? Had he watched me being collected like so much trash from the street, while he stood by, protected by his weapons and wealth? I tried to work up some anger, but fear didn't leave much room for it. At least being afraid seemed to diminish the power of those commanding whispers in my head: *Find your ship, leave Auord, stay safe*. They faded to a frustrated chattering.

It was quiet, except for the monotonous throbbing of

my pulse and the machine beneath me. Minutes crawled past. I couldn't stand it any longer. I had to risk lifting a corner of my cover. As I did, just a bit, a wave of cooler air slid underneath, taking some of the heat from my face.

A sudden series of bone-jarring bumps bounced me back against a yielding, warm object. I reached, touched bare skin, and shrank away in horror. After a long moment, I gathered enough courage to gently, then more desperately, shake what felt like an arm, hoping for a response. None. I squeezed the arm once, then slowly pulled my fingers away, knowing there was nothing more I could do.

All was quiet. I bit my lip, tucking my legs up bit by bit until I thought I could spring. Then, before I could hesitate, I threw myself off the moving platform and rolled as fast as I could, dragging the cover off with me.

It was not quite the graceful, swift maneuver I had planned. Thoroughly tangled in the blanket, I landed heavily—and painfully—on a hard floor. Immediately, I struggled to get free, only to bite off a shocked scream as something struck my backside with the force of a kick. I decided not to move anymore, though my head and body were completely covered.

"Forget to dope your s-sscrapss again, Enex-ss?" a new voice said in an amused hiss that sent shivers down my spine. "Didn't sSsmegard warn you you'd get your own berth outssysstem next time?"

Enex's voice was shrill. "The dose was right, Hom Captain. I don't underst—" A sodden thud ended Enex's desperate pleading. Feeling considerably safe huddled beneath my blanket, I waited through a thick, ominous silence. *My turn*, I thought numbly. Seconds stretched to an eternity. Dust tickled my nose and I sneezed.

Abruptly light blinded me as my shelter was torn away. I had time to focus on a reptilian snout, see two yellow slit-pupiled eyes peer close before what felt like servo-claws fastened on my arm. The creature's painful grip pulled me to my feet.

I stared at it. Our bodies were similar in size and plan, but I knew I wasn't the least bit terrifying. It was. A pair of thin, tall crests rose from its snout to forehead, curling like a frame behind each forward-pointing eye. The crests were a mottled purple and yellow, the colors more like stains than natural pigmentation. The scaled snout bore irregular knuckle-sized knobs along its length. Each eye was bigger than my fist, with jet-black pupils slicing their gleaming yellow in half. I looked away quickly.

We were standing inside a gigantic warehouse, probably one that served the shipcity itself. Canyons of piled plas crates stretched to distant points of darkness, while the sounds of unseen machines echoed from a ceiling high enough to allow air travel.

The portion of wide aisle where the recruiters' train had stopped was overhung by hovering portlights obediently waiting for the halted procession of machines to move forward again. Seven of the waist-high transport platforms were shrouded by a wrapping; the last, mine, was open to the air—on it a naked body lay unconscious, flaccid upon its gray surface, breathing peacefully.

Another body, this one incapable of breathing, was crumpled next to my foot. The face was a smear of red topped by blue-beaded braids. Enex's luck. I pressed my lips together, taking several quick shallow breaths through my nose to subdue the urgings of my stomach.

Three other natives, including the one I recognized from the alley as Enex's partner, stood clustered to one side of the transports.

"Gsst." The irritated sound drew my attention back to the reptile holding me in its claws. "Awake and alert both. You are fortunate this-ss occurred before you were placssed into a trip box-ss, s-ssoft flesssh."

I shuddered, my imagination readily painting for me a death comprised of unanswered screams and suffocation. A wave of a clawed hand sent the remaining Auordians scurrying back to the servos, the cover I had pulled off thrown over the body of my former companion. Enex's partner warily crouched by the corpse to cut the luck beads from Enex's hair and tuck them into a pocket. I couldn't guess why.

The little passenger train with its Auordian guides resumed its journey. All but one of the lights went as well, turning the aisle into a cave walled by darkness. I tried not to wince at the grip still holding me in place.

The creature, ignoring me for the present, turned to the Human male at its side. "I want the *Torquad* ready to lift by moonrissse."

The slender, bejeweled Human turned dead eyes to me for a moment before replying coolly: "A wish shared by Port Authority, Captain Roraqk, but repairs take time—"

I felt two of three claws penetrate my skin and flinched. "Do not annoy me, Kort," Roraqk said. "s-Ssee what can be left. sSSurely there are better facilities-ss and attitudes-ss than on this-ss backworld."

A short bow. "Shall I dispose of this, Captain?" I was uncomfortably certain of what he meant.

"s-Sseeing me was-ss a misstake," Roraqk explained to me, as if instructing a wayward child. "It is-ss expenssive and difficult to remove memory from a s-ssapient—sso often the whole is-ss losst."

Was that what had happened to me? I wondered. Cold comfort that I had nothing worth remembering left to lose. "Why would I give your face to Port Authority, Captain?" I tried to be polite, my voice level and calm, despite the feel of my own blood dripping warmly over wrist and hand. "You just saved my life."

I swallowed, but before I could figure out what to say next, a compulsion pushed through my thoughts, bullying aside my fear for an instant along with my will. "Perhaps we can help each other," I heard myself say boldly. "I need to find a spacer called Morgan. His ship is the *Fox*."

Roraqk made a hissing sound. "Morgan, is-ss it? You remember our good friend Morgan, don't you, Kort?"

The strange darkness in Kort's pale eyes made me shiver slightly. Or was I mistaken? He smiled slowly. "Morgan of Karolus. The *Silver Fox*. The wheel makes an interesting turn today, Captain."

I knew they were playing with me, amused, but for how long? My eyes avoided the corpse. "Help me find Morgan," I insisted. "He owes me. I could pay for transport offworld once I get back what's mine." I only hoped the reptile's greed would make my bluff work.

Roraqk lowered his snout, slit-pupiled eyes impossible to read and unsettling to meet. "What makes-ss you believe you could retrieve your property?"

"Tell me where to find Morgan," I repeated, voice trembling. Maybe they'd think it was righteous rage.

"But Morgan and his-ss s-sspeedy s-sship are valuable to me, s-ssoft flesssh. I wouldn't want you to hurt him." Roraqk's jaws began clattering, moving so rapidly that tiny froths of spittle appeared and trickled under his jutting chin. Kort's laugh was even less human: a dry, silent shaking that didn't touch his lifeless eyes.

I drooped, at last admitting defeat. A black sliver of a tongue darted out from the random gaps between Roraqk's teeth, collecting the froth as though it were precious. "You go offworld, primate," he hissed at me. "And s-sspeedily. With me."

"Captain?" There was a frown on Kort's thin face, drawing the skin into fine white lines.

"What is-ss it?" Roraqk glared at his counterpart with a sideways twist of his heavily-jawed head.

"Enex wasn't a total fool. He would have added her to the transport's records. If we remove her from the shipment, Smegard will notice—"

The alien's jaw hung half-open, a predator's anticipation rather than a smile. "This-ss partnersship of s-Ssmegard's-ss is-ss beginning to bore me, as-ss is-ss his-ss trafficking in live mammals-ss. Be careful I do not tire of a fangless-ss firsst mate."

Not one of the recruiters, I thought, and reclassified Roraqk as a pirate, then wondered how the difference could possibly matter at the moment.

The pirate captain examined his claw tips. "Ah, Kort. You musst realiz-sse your value, or you would not always be s-sso difficult. Certainly in this-ss casse, you are better equipped to keep her alive than I." He spared a moment to send me a malignant flash of yellow eyes. "There is-ss s-ssomething familiar about this-ss one. And of coursse, we mussst take proper care of all shipments-ss that involve our old acquaintancsse, Captain Morgan."

Kort nodded curtly, accepting this explanation, licking his lips in unconscious mimicry of his leader. With a practiced twist, Roraqk freed his claws from the fabric of my coveralls, as well as my skin, and shoved me toward his subordinate.

"Take her to the Tulis-ss," Roraqk said as he strode away, the last portlight following behind one shoulder.

A lamp flashed to life in Kort's hand, creating a false intimacy. "As you may have noticed, commodity," Kort, a faceless shadow behind the lamp, informed me coldly, "the captain is not very fond of us warm-bloods—unless served on a tray. You'd best prove of value." The man came to a decision, shrugging in a gesture which set his necklaces of light-touched silver jingling softly. "Put this under the greedy fool." Kort held out a green-marbled sphere, indicating the corpse with a casual flicker from his light.

The pirate was tall but bone-thin, a fragile-looking thug. I considered my chances against him: none. About all I could accomplish at the moment was to maybe keep what was in my stomach in its proper place. I took the small sphere and pushed it beneath Enex's still-warm body. When I stood, I found myself rubbing at the hand that had touched the dead man.

"Back," Kort ordered. An instant later, there was a blinding flash and I flung my arm up to protect my eyes from the brightness. When I dropped my arm again and looked, Enex's body was sagging into itself, a clear liquid starting to ooze from underneath. A sweet, corrupt smell filled the air. "Come." I obeyed that order readily enough, having no wish to linger and see what would be left.

Kort led the way down a maze of echoing corridors. There was an endless sameness to the place. I didn't know how Kort chose our path, unless he used the cargo codes stamped on the crates. I lost my sense of direction almost immediately. My guiding compulsions were silent for once; I wondered sourly if that meant my current predicament satisfied the noises in my head.

I almost collided with Kort when he stopped. We were at the end of one of the narrow intersecting aisles that subdivided the immense warehouse, standing in the gap between the building's wall and the ranks of waiting cargo crates. I glanced from Kort to the blank wall in front of us. A small portlight floated from its resting shelf to shed a courteous spot of brightness. Kort turned off his lamp.

As if that had been a signal, a portion of the otherwise unremarkable wall split open soundlessly, revealing two stocky humanoids waiting in what was now a wide, low doorway. The beings were furred: a soft gray pelt that was short and lay flat to the skin. Long, white tufts of hair made striking flashes above each of three large pale eyes. Broader than tall, they wore only wide belts from which hung various small instruments and tools. These had to be Roraqk's Tulis. Odd-looking things.

"Captain Roraqk wants the usual tests on this one," Kort ordered, without any preamble. I scowled at him, then at the Tulis. The Tuli on the right made an intricate gesture with stubby fingers. If it was a protest, I heartily agreed. Kort snorted, pushing me forward with a rough hand. "It's the captain that orders it," he said firmly. "And we're booked for lift, so none of your delays."

"Tests?" I said, balking.

"Tests," Kort confirmed, one side of his mouth sliding upward in an unpleasant smile. "And their results better be interesting, or we won't see each other again. Now go with the Tulis. They won't harm you," a raised brow, "unless you provoke them."

I reluctantly began walking through the doorway. One Tuli waited until I passed then took my elbow. I felt a sharp prick in my upper arm and twisted around, struggling against its hold. "What was that?" I shouted. "What did it do to me?" I couldn't take my eyes from the now-empty syringe in the Tuli's hand, my erratic memory supplying me with an appalling list of exotic drugs.

Kort's head came forward, a clinical interest giving a false sparkle to his lackluster eyes. "Captain's standing orders," he said with distinct relish. "Roraqk hates mind-crawlers. He has all our *guests* given a little something that numbs that particular gift. Ask me, waste of good money, especially for port trash. But I don't argue the point, you understand." A Tuli put its dry furred hand into mine, urging me farther into the room with an impatient, though gentle, tug. "Don't worry," Kort added as the door began to slide closed. "Hasn't killed any being—yet."

The door shut between us with a whisper, becoming a wall again in a room barely large enough to accommodate the Tulis and myself. Fortunately, we didn't have to share it with any furniture. As I looked around, the floor beneath my feet began to sink, and I yelped with surprise.

My silent escorts paid no attention to me, standing motionless, one on either side. Well, not quite motionless; their broad noses twitched furiously. I'd forgotten the smell of my clothing long ago.

The lift opened into a long hall, its walls pierced by openings aglow with the bronze transparency of force fields. I could hear sobbing, quickly muffled. My mouth went dry and the steadying breath I drew caught in my throat. A hand pressed my back. I stepped out.

I walked ahead of the Tulis, leading our small procession the length of that dreadful corridor, trying not to wince as we passed each cell. Each held its captive; few were young, and more than half nonhumanoid. I didn't see the Neblokan and wasn't sure what that meant about his fate. Some of the prisoners looked up with dulled incurious stares as we passed; none spoke beyond the occasional hushed complaint.

I wasn't given time to ponder their future or my own. The corridor widened into a bulb of a room, lined with sophisticated equipment, the walls broken at regular intervals by closed doors. A Tuli opened one of these and handed me the same white robe worn by the wretches in the cells. Eyeing the muscular shoulders and impassive faces of my captors, I entered meekly enough, to reemerge stripped save for the loose garment. My treasured coveralls were tossed into a disposal chute, and I thought the Tuli who did it looked relieved. I nursed what small strength of rebellion I had as gooseflesh rose on my arms, even though the room was too warm.

One of the Tulis pointed to a bench positioned under a complex machine. It was the bravest thing I remembered doing—to climb up and lie there, waiting.

* * *

INTERLUDE

The feel of a warm sharpness along one's throat was a decidedly unpleasant way to end a deserved moment of peace, Barac decided, holding his mind and body motionless. He opened his eyes with a careful lack of haste. Now what?

"An unexpected pleasure, Clansman." Jason Morgan's piercing eyes met Barac's—their expression scarcely less icy than that low voice. "I trust you've been enjoying yourself."

"I've slept better," Barac countered, shoving away the Human's unresisting knife hand. The Clansman tipped his chair upright and glared. "Hell of a way to wake a guest."

The knife caught a gleam of light before Morgan turned off the blade and made the handle disappear up the right sleeve of his faded blue coveralls. "Considering I locked the *Fox* up tight, you can't blame me for being a bit surprised myself, old friend." He moved past the Clansman to enter his choice at the galley's servo panel. The Human didn't bother to ask how Barac had bested Port Authority to enter his ship; he knew well enough.

Barac resisted the urge to feel the still-tender skin of his throat. Instead he stretched, the movement drawing an involuntary hiss of pain from his lips.

Cup in hand, Morgan put a foot up onto a chair and leaned his arms on his knee. His expression was openly suspicious. "Hurt," he observed. "And probably in hiding, too. You've got a bad habit of making yourself at home whenever you're in trouble, Barac."

"I could use a favor," Barac admitted.

Morgan snorted with disgust and took a sip of his drink before answering. "Who've you stirred up now—Clan or the Trade Pact?"

Barac couldn't quite smile. "Both. That's why I've come to you."

Morgan scowled but only said: "Hungry? I'd be a poor host to throw you out before feeding you." He tossed a nutritious but decidedly tasteless package of c-cubes on the table.

"Your galley can do better than that," Barac commented less than tactfully.

"I'm sure you know," the Human said dryly. "But I'm booked to lift and eating slowly is a luxury I can't afford. Neither is your roundabout approach to things, Barac. What do you want?"

As usual, Barac found himself wishing Morgan didn't possess such strong natural shielding. The Human's thoughts were simply impossible to touch. *Like Bowman's,* Barac thought with sudden suspicion. He opened his mind to the M'hir, focusing on Morgan, searching for the telltale disturbance. Nothing. No device, but no exposed thoughts.

What had he expected? Barac asked himself with scorn. No Human mind had ever penetrated the M'hir, at least not since the Clan had first begun monitoring the layer for intrusion. It was believed Humans were incapable of the power needed to push thought into the layer or to hold against its remorseless currents. That belief might change, Barac thought grimly, once he reported how the Humans had built a device that could disturb the M'hir.

But here and now, the M'hir's turbulence was soothingly familiar. There was no detectable alteration in it within Barac's range. Barac pulled free, relieved. Perhaps Morgan was what he seemed, a curiosity, an unreadable Human.

Or perhaps he was more. Morgan had always amused Kurr, as had Barac's insistence on shielding their thoughts from the Human. But First Scouts survived by trusting no preconceptions.

And Kurr was dead.

"I sometimes wonder why I don't report you to the Council and have you erased," Barac said with some exasperation. "I should, you know."

Morgan looked unconcerned, having heard this before; the Sarcs had been steady customers over the years. "You enjoy defying them, Barac," the Human said. "And, as long as you don't owe me credits, I see no reason to twitch the curiosity of any Pact Enforcers."

Barac grimaced. "I've already accomplished that. Another day, Jason," he added, seeing the curiosity that sharpened Morgan's gaze. "As you've said, your time is short. Mine is also. I have to leave Auord immediately."

Morgan sighed. "If a lift's what you're after, why didn't you say so? Stow your gear—but be quick."

"No. Not that I don't enjoy your unique way of waking guests. I need you to do something for me in the Port City."

Morgan stood, gathering up his unfinished cubes and tucking them into a pocket with a spacer's absentminded tidiness. "Then you need someone else. I've a schedule to keep."

Barac lunged across the narrow table, wincing as his torn rib muscles protested, but managing to grasp Morgan's arm. "There's no one else I can reach in time."

With an easy movement, the Human shrugged free of Barac's grip. But he stood still. "I'm listening."

"That's all I ask." Barac sat down again, his hands wrapped tightly around his middle to hide their trembling. It also helped hold together the ribs which were again grating each time he drew a breath. "I need you to find someone. I had a companion when I arrived on Auord. We were attacked last night." The Clansman gritted his teeth, remembering. "During the struggle, we were separated."

"Attacked? How?" Morgan sat back down. He supported his chin on steepled fingers, watching Barac intently.

"They hit during the storm." Barac considered Morgan for a moment, then added: "They had mind-deadening devices. Conveniently stolen, I am to believe. Maybe I do."

The Human digested this in silence, then raised one brow. "Your companion?"

"Her name is Sira. I know she escaped in the confusion." Barac hesitated, unsure of how much to say, how much to leave out. "I can't detect her. She could be anywhere—alone, possibly injured. You know people in the city. You could find her, get her offworld without alerting the authorities—"

Morgan's blue eyes flashed. "While you abandon her? I thought the Clan looked after their own."

"I can't stay on Auord a moment longer." Barac tightened his lips, studying the human's face, frustrated he couldn't reach into the mind behind those scornful eyes and make Morgan do what was necessary, know only what was necessary. He hated having to stoop to reason.

Still, there didn't appear to be any alternative. "Whoever ordered the attack last night was after me," Barac began reluctantly.

Morgan held up his hand. "I want nothing to do with Clan squabbles," he said emphatically. "My time is tight—"

"Kurr and I were checking on a Council matter in this quadrant," Barac went on as if he hadn't heard. "Kurr's been killed. Last night's attack was aimed at me. The best thing I can do for Sira is to lead whoever's after me away from her until I can deal with them."

The impatience drained from Morgan's features, replaced by a shock which darkened the blue of his eyes. "Kurr's dead? But how—his power . . ."

Barac held out one slim hand and gazed at the fist he formed. "Power . . ." he repeated, his voice trailing away to silence. He paused so long Morgan shifted in his seat. Then, slowly: "We of the Clan aren't so different from you, Human. We measure our strength by comparison, one against the other. It tells us who is in control—and who is vulnerable. Or does it? Kurr was killed by power, but by whose? Even as Kurr died, he burned my name into the metal of his ship's floor plate. I," Barac opened his fist, holding the empty hand palm upward. "I can't do such a thing whole and well. But Kurr's the one gone."

"Kurr was a brother to be proud of," Morgan offered gently. "I will honor the debt between us," he said more formally, as someone making a vow.

Barac made no effort to hide his pain, letting it add a cold edge to his voice. "Any debts to be settled are mine, Human." Barac forced himself back to the topic at hand with an effort, trying to make his tone persuasive. At least the being was listening. "If you want to help, find Sira and get her safely off Auord. I'll meet you on Camos as soon as possible." Barac drew a small plate from his pocket. "I had this made in the market—it's the best I can do."

Morgan took the plate, sparing only a quick glance at its imprisoned memory of a woman or girl, dressed in the latest insystem fashion, hair elaborately dyed and styled, eyes too large for the face. Barac tensed. Would he refuse?

"The best you could've done was to leave me out of it," Morgan snapped, but not unkindly. He tucked the plate away in a pocket. "Failing that, tell me the rest."

Barac's ribs burned like a ring of fire. The way Morgan persisted in complicating what should have been simple didn't help. "Tell you what?" the Clansman snapped. "They attacked us last night, on Embassy Row. That doesn't matter. Sira will try to reach the shipcity, to look for transport. She knows the way—and she knows to avoid Enforcers or Port Authority."

"Won't she be looking for you?" Morgan probed.

"No!" At once, Barac knew he'd made a bad mistake; he was familiar enough with Humans to see that Morgan was plainly startled by his denial. The Clansman flushed. "No," he repeated at a more reasonable volume. "I'm not her concern. Sira needs to leave Auord."

"Your ways are stranger than I thought, Clansman," Morgan said with a return to his former coolness.

"I was her escort here, nothing more. Sira must go to Camos; Auord was merely a stopover to change transport. At least, that was the plan." Barac went on quickly, feeling himself forced to explain more and more, wondering if it was worth it. "She's alone," he repeated. "With no power or weapon of her own. Any chance she has depends upon my leaving this world and your helping her do the same."

Morgan drummed his fingers on the table thoughtfully. "This favor of yours will create a debt against the *Fox.* I'll have to pay penalties, extra dock fees . . ."

Relieved, Barac quickly pushed a small clear bag of currency gems in front of Morgan. "If you need more, we'll settle it on Camos." He stood.

Morgan stayed where he was. "You said you can't detect her. Could it be because she's dead?"

Barac froze. It was a reasonable question, but answering it was treading into dangerous waters, even with a "friend." Not answering would probably lose Morgan's cooperation. He sighed.

"I can't detect Sira because she travels under a special form of protection—one that hides her from Clan adepts."

Morgan poked at the bag of gems with one finger. "I'm sure you won't tell me why," he commented.

"No," Barac agreed, tight-lipped. He studied Morgan's face, then added with a sudden recklessness. "But there is one more thing I have to tell you. Because of this protection, Sira will not know who or what she is." And with those words, his face and body shimmered and disappeared.

Jason Morgan, captain of the trade ship *Silver Fox,* and native to a system so distant from this one that few recognized its name, calmly cursed in a tongue definitely not learned in his planet-bound youth. Then he picked up the currency gems and, tipping the bag, let their multicolored richness spill over the tabletop.

"Not enough for this one, Clansman," he muttered, walking out, leaving the gems behind.

Chapter 3

WELL, my chances of leaving Auord seemed to be improving. A comfort of sorts, I decided, but one that did nothing to push away the darkness in my closetlike prison. I bit my lip to stop its trembling as my thoughts twisted through the hours just past, hours spent being poked, prodded, and otherwise treated like a slab of meat.

However, and quite unexpectedly, I was alive. Presumably this meant those same tests had satisfied Roraqk. Of course, the Tulis might simply not have bothered to kill me yet. I shuddered, thinking of the drug they had pumped into me. I felt the same, which didn't necessarily mean normal. What had they given me? And why? What Kort had said made no sense to me. What was a mindcrawler? The word made something in my thoughts slide away.

I shook my head to clear it. Maybe the Tulis were killing me, I concluded, tired to the bone and almost more frustrated than afraid—hungry to the point of light-headedness, too, though by fumbling in the dark I'd found a water outlet and a small basin for essentials. A coverless cot took up the back wall. I'd been lying on it most of the time—finding it hazardous to pace given the lock bar fastened across my ankles.

But rest eluded me. Other questions were waiting, rising and whirling through my mind like eddies in a stream: Who was I? What was I? Why was I sure Auord wasn't my world? Where were these ideas in my mind coming from, trying to order my thoughts, telling me I had to leave? And where did they want me to go?

Once in a while I stopped a question, examined it more carefully, then let it drift loose in the current again. I had no answers. Answers were unlikely to help me now anyway. But I might feel better if I understood.

A series of distant thuds broke my concentration; *thunder,* I thought, then wondered if thunder could be heard so far down. Another series, this time closer, vibrating the walls and floor of my cell. I sat up too rapidly and had to fight dizziness.

I took three step-hops to the door, only to bump my nose abruptly and painfully on the edge of the now open panel. The lights were off in the corridor; the darkness pressed like something physical against my skin. I hesitated, weighing the risks. The lack of light, the lock bar—these I could overcome. But what were those new sounds?

I broke into a cold sweat, suddenly no longer here but back in the night and rain, buffeted by an explosion. Bodies flying past into the shadows, propelled by flame, the odor of cooked flesh. Running, fighting to think . . .

I forced myself to the here and now, but the image lingered, clarifying what I could hear. Someone was fighting a battle—probably on an upper level, or I'd have seen its light. I could hear low cries of hope and confusion from my fellow prisoners. The force fields must be down in the hallway. I drew back against the wall, unpleasantly sure of our fate should it look like the recruiters were losing. I carefully hopped back inside my cell, crouching in the space of floor behind the open door.

First and foremost, I had to be free of the lock bar. I tore at its fastening, succeeding only in breaking the remainder of my fingernails in the effort. Then, with an abruptness that boded ill for the defenders of this hole, the sounds stopped. I breathed as lightly as I could in the waiting silence.

Lights appeared in the hall, not the ones I remembered but dancing spears of yellow . . . voices, footsteps . . . it was hard to remember where I was, to keep my mind focused.

The door swung wide, bumping my knees and startling me to alertness. Eye-stabbing light flooded the room. "Where is she?" demanded a voice I did remember—too well.

A Tuli skidded to the floor at my feet, beams from the globe cradled in its hands racing crazily over the walls

and ceiling. It had been shoved by another entering behind with the haste of the pursued.

Roraqk. His snout twisted over his shoulder—angling
downward so those yellow eyes, reflecting cold white disks
of light, could pin me in place. The frills along his head
were flattened and gray. I cringed, curling myself into a
ball, and showed my teeth in as effective a snarl as a primate could manage.

The reptile holstered his pistol, hooking one hand in his
belt. His other hand, streaked with some shiny green liquid,
he held pressed over a wound high on his concave chest.
"s-Sswitch the bar to her wrisssts-ss," he ordered the cower-
ing Tuli. "Put this-ss on her." "This-ss" was a heavy black
cloak, its edges suspiciously charred. I didn't like to think of
how it came to be in the pirate's possession.

The Tuli panted, its trio of eyes wide and focused elsewhere as it obeyed Roraqk's command. Its stained fur
smelled rank, sour with fear. Port Authority, I decided,
stretching my legs as soon as they were freed. A rush of
optimism gave me new strength which I kept hidden, letting the creature pull me to my feet.

Roraqk took no chances. He reached for the bar across
my wrists, winding a thin glossy thread from his belt
around the bar to link us together. The Tuli moaned to itself—the first vocalization I'd heard from its kind. Its
eyes were closed. Both of us knew what to expect next,
yet I flinched when the pirate fired his pistol and the Tuli
shriveled into a smoking darkness. The globe fell and
smashed, extinguishing all light in the room.

I couldn't move—too afraid of what I might touch. A
warning jerk on the thread broke my paralysis. It drew me
after the pirate into the hall, and I stumbled trying to keep
up with his impatient steps. Roraqk had no intention of
waiting for whatever was about to happen here.

Small portlights huddled in an upper corner as if summoned then forgotten, providing a wan illumination.
Groups of slaves hastened out of our way, their eyes hot
with expectation, yet wary. We made it to the lift without
incident, only to find it sealed.

Roraqk struck the door with a clawed fist. There were
new sounds now, regular hammerings punctuated by the
occasional low thud. I thought they were coming closer.
"Port Authority—or Enforcers?" I asked.

The alien hissed instead of answering and, pushing me to the end of my leash, aimed his pistol at the control panel. This time the beam was concentrated into a brilliant line which sliced through the cover with ease. The disk Roraqk outlined dropped to the floor, striking with a metallic clang and roll. Roraqk compressed his clawed hand into an amazing thinness, sliding it within the revealed cavity, ignoring the white-hot edges as he worked. After several false starts, the lift door opened. "Inssside, quickly."

Deep vibrations shook us as we rose, the lift faltering once then restarting just as my heart tried to pound its way out of my chest. Our journey was longer than my trip down with the Tulis. Sure enough, when the doors opened, we were in an office with windows overlooking a rooftop view.

And we were not alone. A large, powerfully built Human worked feverishly at a desk, stuffing the contents of a drawer into a bag. At our appearance, he snatched a deadly-looking rifle from where it lay on piles of scorched plas records, swinging the dark hole of its muzzle to cover us both.

"Is-ss that any way to greet your partner?" Roraqk said smoothly, although his own weapon remained in his hand.

The rifle lowered, though not completely. "Late partner, close-like," the man responded, dark eyes glittering. He went past us, using one blunt-fingered hand to pull down a switch beside the lift door; the lights in the lift died. "Gas below's on auto—you know that." The eyes slid over to me and I shivered. There was something feline, menacing in their depths. He peered closer, as if trying to see more of my face within its heavy shadow of hood. "This belongs below, too. Dead," the man decided. "The roust's by outsystem Enforcers, you fool, not Port Jellies."

Roraqk chuckled. "Let me introduce my pet-creature," he said, at ease though the floor under our feet continued to shake with new explosions. "I call her Kisssue. You've told me I should keep pets-ss."

"Pet? More like dinner." The man shrugged callously. "Better dead, and left here. Another, ten other such pets I'll get you later. Frat, take C-stock from your own cargo—I won't kick about a couple."

My flesh crawled as Roraqk's claws closed posses-
sively on my shoulder. "There are none like my Kisssue,
s-Ssmegard. She is-ss quite unique. Don't worry, I
s-sshall take good care of her."

What could he know about me? What had the Tulis
learned? I ached to ask questions, demand answers.

"Scaly hide of yours needs care, Roraqk." This from
Smegard, his eyes smoldering in a clear threat. "Think
Enex outsmarted me? Think my Tulis keep your secrets?"

Roraqk's claws tightened punishingly. I fought the urge
to evade that grip, knowing I continued to breathe solely
because of the reptile's interest in me. "This-ss dealt with
Morgan of the *ss-Ssilver Fox*." He gave me a light shake
that nonetheless threatened my balance.

A slow smile stretched the man's thick lips. "Morgan,"
he said the name as though tasting it. Then he scowled
again, the expression better suited to his black-browed
face. "Too many teeth for your profit. Not to mention his
frat'n luck."

A vicious snap of jaws. "Morgan's-ss luck, as-ss you
call it, will not keep me from eating his-ss heart!"

Smegard's lips twisted into a sneer. "You keep wasting
time here, Morgan won't need luck. Dispose of your
Kissue; help me with this. The car's waiting below." The
Recruiter turned his broad back to us, returning to his
packing.

Whether this was bravado or stupidity, I would never
know, for the tip of Roraqk's pistol raised ever-so-slightly
and he fired before I could even think a warning.

"This-ss raid was-ss the lasst of your blunders-ss, mammal," the pirate spat as he sheathed his weapon and again
pressed his clawed hand against the wound in his chest. I
trembled, trying to look anywhere but at the beheaded
corpse as it rustled papers and toppled objects on its way
to the floor. As Roraqk laughed at his own humor, spittle
flung from his jaws and splashed on my cheek. I flinched
as his black tongue followed to retrieve it, leaving a burning trail on my skin.

Roraqk knew his way, without hesitation activating a
second hidden lift that plummeted us down. I fought the
inclinations of my abused stomach and endured in numb

silence. The lift settled, its door opening into a large ground-car hangar.

The conflict hadn't reached this far, not yet. Hirelings milled about the groundcars, all armed, some wearing pieces of body armor; their expressions at the sight of us ranged from hopeful defiance to resigned fear. Roraqk called for a driver and guard as he headed toward a mid-sized vehicle already poised near the doors. The pirate's orders were obeyed instantly, without question, certainly with obvious relief on the part of the chosen pair.

Smegard's absence, and Roraqk's flight, was enough for the rest. Some faded out other doors, some began to climb into groundcars. Armor was abandoned; weapons were not.

Roraqk's guardsman dropped in beside the driver, acti-vating a control that moved the opaque dome over our heads and locked it into place, effectively blinding us as well as hiding us from view. Our groundcar rolled through the doors decorously, pausing a moment as if waiting for a break in some traffic outside that I couldn't see, then slipping forward and away.

I didn't need to see out. We were heading for the ship-city—and the starships. I knew by the return of that grow-ing pressure in my thoughts. It wasn't my choice. I could tell that much, even if I couldn't completely separate what was mine from its influence. And that detached, other set of thoughts cared only about the need to reach a ship, whether transported by this murderer or not. I decided glumly the decisions it forced into my mind could become serious risks to my future, assuming I had a future to risk.

* * *

INTERLUDE

"Haven't seen her." Thel Masim's glance at the image plate in Morgan's hand had been brief, but he didn't ques-tion her ability to place faces. The woman's recall abili-ties were legendary, an asset to her job managing traffic into and out of the shipcity, if less valued by those trying to claim improper fees. Many underestimated the intellect behind her small gleaming eyes and confused the kindness she granted so liberally to strangers with gullibility. Morgan did neither.

"Thanks. Call me if she shows up before I lift, okay?" He peered over her ample shoulder at the screens. From this small room, Thel had access to vids at every entrance as well as those attached to each of Auord's fleet of docking tugs. By custom, there was no surveillance equipment set up around the ships themselves. After all, many were homes as well as transport.

"What's going on there?" Morgan pointed at the screen second to the right. Thel pulled the feed into her central viewer, enlarging it until they could both see the developing snarl in traffic.

"Query sent," she muttered. The screens flickered from moment to moment as Thel and her partners along the shipway exchanged viewpoints. Morgan blinked his eyes, fighting a feeling of vertigo. Voices overlapped at the same time, sounding more interested than annoyed. It was the kind of job that appreciated a break in routine. "Lot of Port Jellies out." "Looks like they're setting up a few checkpoints." "Gonna take a while to sort this mess out." "Hey, those are Enforcers! What's going on, Thel?"

"I should know?" that worthy responded, her voice definitely annoyed. "Should my number be on the list of must-calls? Does anyone expect ace behavior from the Jellies on this armpit planet?" Over her shoulder, "Clear Skies, Jason. I've got your tug on A-one priority."

Morgan pocketed the image of the one he sought, resigned to the fact that between the checkpoints and the growing traffic jam, it was unlikely he'd have any luck before lift. And, Barac or no Barac, he had no intention of missing that tug. "Thanks, Thel. If she shows up, put it on my tab. Give my regards to—"

"Got her."

Morgan stopped at the door, "Pardon?"

"There's your Fem." Thel sounded smug as she keyed down the other images, brought up a close scan of a luxurious private groundcar stuck in traffic, and cut off the voice feeds from the other gates. "And not nice company she's keeping. We all know who that ugly snout belongs to—" When there was no answer, she swiveled her chair around. Morgan was gone.

Chapter 4

IT seemed as though only a few moments passed before we halted to await our turn to enter the main shipway. We edged forward then stopped again, the dome rising to allow the driver to confer with a trio of grim-faced Enforcers. Others stood to the side, Port Authority mostly, sending resentful looks at the backs of the three red-and-black uniformed officers beside us. Roraqk scraped one claw lightly along my wrist beneath the cloak.

I didn't need his warning. New compulsions frantically writhed through my thoughts, overlapping into warnings of danger and fear, all aimed at the various law keepers standing so temptingly close. I couldn't have called out to them for help. As a matter of fact, only Roraqk's grip and some small instinct for self-preservation stopped me from trying to jump from the groundcar and run the other way.

The driver offered a handful of plas sheets with an easy smile, seemingly unaffected by the stern aspect of his interrogators. The sheets were passed to a Port Authority official who waved a hand over them dismissively before giving them back. Smegard's preparations were thorough indeed—and undoubtedly costly.

We continued on, the dome remaining half open. Our groundcar was caught in a line of traffic, moving at a slow but steady pace which never quite came to a halt. The panic in my thoughts subsided again, leaving me wondering what other surprises the conspiracy in my head had in store.

Another, more abrupt stop slid me off the seat on to one knee. Metal and leather made whispers of sound as the driver and guardsman readied themselves. My mouth went dry; more enforcers? "Hold," Roraqk ordered, having stood to peer over the driver's shoulder. The resulting tug on the leash binding us together drew me up with him. "They've flusshed a s-ssmuggler and the traffic's-ss waiting for the all clear. We'll be curious-ss yet law-resspecting, jusst like thessse other good citizens-ss."

At his order, the dome folded completely back. Our groundcar was one of about twenty similar vehicles, all stopped nose-to-tail along the shipway. The sky was already darkening, the sun a far-off smudge of red on the horizon. To one side of us, the ground dropped away sharply to the sea, the cliff edge marked by force field posts. I could smell the salt spray.

Ahead on the other side were the ranks of starships, of every size, shape, and color; their twilight shadows seeming to be all that held them to the ground, though I knew if I were closer I'd be able to see the cabling protecting each from Auord's uncontrolled weather. The always changing shipcity they formed bound this fringe system to the rest of the galaxy. Overhead floated atmospheric transports, some already snugged against one or more individual ships to load or unload cargo, others drifting like clouds in the sea breeze, waiting their turn. Beyond reason, compulsions still tugged at me.

Find my starship.

The problem of which one was mine of the hundreds here was, however, not my most pressing concern.

A tight knot of red-and-black aircars flew past overhead, speeding toward a group surrounding the first groundcar in the rapidly elongating line. I withdrew into Roraqk's shadow, for an instant more interested in avoiding their notice than in my current plight. A shout, followed by the menacing crackle of weaponry, brought an approving chuckle from my captors, their attention riveted on the struggle taking place ahead.

I had no thought, no plan in mind. I simply gathered the slack thread in my hands and flipped it up around Roraqk's neck, pulling back on the lock bar with all my weight and the strength of desperation. The bar cut into my wrists, but the thread sank even more deeply into the soft flesh under his chin. The pirate made a most satisfying gurgling sound, his thin tongue whipping frantically from side to side.

I watched the driver and the guardsman turn. The guards-

man reached for his weapon, only to be stopped by the
driver's hand and warning nod to the passing aircars. "I
will kill him," I threatened through gritted teeth.

The option was taken from me. Roraqk's clawed hands
swung back at an impossible, totally inhuman angle, flashing right through the cloak's hood, one claw drawing a
burning score down my cheek. I flung myself away,
falling half out of the groundcar. The thread grew taut,
choking the alien more effectively than before. Roraqk's
hands tore at his throat. Just as trapped, I struggled
to break free. Someone grabbed me, started pulling me
back inside. It was the guardsman. He'd jumped into the
back seat.

Suddenly the man let out a curse. The handle of a knife
had appeared as if by magic, the blade embedded in the
side of his neck. He sank away from me, his eyes going
dazed, all motion seeming to slow to a dream's crawl.
Only Roraqk's flailing about continued at normal speed.

Somehow I twisted my way forward, just able to reach
the handle of the knife with one hand. Pulling it free produced no alarming rush of blood; the wound was sealed
by heat. The deadly little thing vibrated in my hand as
though still hungry. Without hesitation I passed its sear-
ing blade through the thread binding me to Roraqk.

And without wasting a second seeking the source of my
salvation, I stepped on the writhing body of the pirate,
and launched myself out of the car.

*Run, keep moving, listen with ears deafened by the
pounding of blood.* Muscles tight with the expectation of
death—or at least a shout or two—I dodged between the
groundcars. The growing darkness helped. So did the
nasty skirmish centered around the unlucky smuggler. I
wasn't the only one diving behind servo-transports as the
weapons' fire spread.

The uproar was spreading. The red and black of Pact
Enforcers and the green of Port Authority were everywhere. I began to have some hope—surely the pirates
would prefer to withdraw offworld inconspicuously. Roraqk. Well, he'd consider me worth chasing after what I'd
done. Then again, maybe I'd inflicted some truly permanent damage with that last choking. I grinned.

I took a chance and ran across open space to where a

lumbering freight-servo had obligingly stopped to allow a pair of officials to check its cargo. Cleared, the servo moved on, each of its cars powering up as their connections tightened. The second to last car was loosely packed with crates. My bound hands made climbing aboard awkward, but I succeeded, pushing myself as far in as possible. With a lurch oscillating from front to rear, the machine turned off the main shipway into the shipcity itself.

I could easily get lost here, I thought with satisfaction, as the servo passed in and out of the thick shadows cast by each ship—shadows made jagged and mobile by portlights hovering over the temporary loading ramps. Night had arrived, and I welcomed its cover, if not the cool dampness of the breeze drifting in from the sea.

Ship after ship. Gradually, their average size diminished, and fewer servos were in use. I passed a ramp with oddsized humanoids. *Children,* my memory answered, resonating a host of meanings. This was the docking area for independent traders, then, those without permanent bases or contracts to secure them. Generations were born, lived, and died on such ships.

Far enough, something deep within ordered. I obeyed without thinking and rolled off the servo, not stopping the movement until I reached the deepest part of the shadows. Sitting up on the pavement, I watched the machine carry on into the distance. I shook my head. Why had I left it here?

I looked up, tracing the swell of the bulbous, pitted old ship above me, perhaps a servo ore-carrier. Cables drooped from it like vines on an old house. Was this the ship I'd been meant to find? There was no answer from my mind, no push or pull in my thoughts.

It was blissfully dark and quiet under here. I rested my head against a support leg, gathering the warmth of the cloak as tightly as I could. The Tulis' robe wasn't designed to protect its wearer from the elements. I toggled the force blade back on, careful of its deadly edge, and tried to use it on the lock bar, then gave up. My fingers couldn't stretch far enough to safely touch the blade to the mechanism. It didn't even mar the finish on the bar itself. I shut off the blade and looked at it. Such a tiny thing to have killed, for I had no doubt Smegard's guardsman was

dead. No identification marks, not even a manufacturer's
icon or planet-code. No clue as to its owner or its owner's
reasons for interfering, though I could easily believe that
Roraqk had collected a variety of enemies along the way.

Oh, well. I was still better off than this morning. My
most urgent need now was for a bit of rest. I closed my
eyes and leaned back, trying to relax—and slipped into
sleep.

There was no doubt about it—the world was coming to
an end. I startled back to myself at the roar, deep and
rhythmic, beating through my bones and rattling my teeth.
A beam of light swept past, like a predator seeking prey,
scorching away shadows.

I settled back, annoyed. I had enough things to fear without worrying about a docking tug. I watched as the huge
and ungainly machine lumbered by on its way to the landing field. It wouldn't be long before the tug, tenderly
cradling a starship, would crawl its noisy way back to a
preassigned docking pad among the hundreds of Auord's
shipcity. I wondered what it would be like to live in a city
whose buildings came and went in the night.

I had to get moving, too. There was a direction I should
take. Not knowing why, but accepting it, I stood, eyes
closed in concentration. *That way.* I opened my eyes only
to stare straight into another pair at very close range—
glossy compound eyes, reflecting me a thousand times
over. I couldn't see much else past the beam of the thing's
hand lamp.

"Do you require assistance, young Human?" a voice,
higher pitched than I could remember voices being, penetrated my ear. A shiver danced across my skin—this reaction intensified by the flash of a Port Authority insignia held
out in a delicate claw. Something stupid in my thoughts
whispered at me to run. I held still with an effort.

The light played over my face, and I squinted. "No,
thank you, I'm fine."

"Fine?" The reflections in its eyes shifted in unison as it
canted its head to consider me from another perspective.
"It is not fine to lurk under ship fins—this activity will not
be tolerated in Auord Port. Not by this person with legal
ways to protect. You must return to your proper place."

I restrained myself from saying I'd love to do that. I

made sure my bound hands stayed inside the cloak, and somehow produced a smile. "I'm afraid I did too much celebrating. I came out to get some air. Must have fallen asleep." I tried to look guilty. "I'd rather not wake my friends up at this hour just to let me in—I'll wait—"

"You came out for air?"

I refused to speculate on whether the alien was truly confused or being sarcastic. I pointed my chin at the ship over our heads, keeping my wounded cheek away from its light as best I could without being obvious. "Contracted passenger," I insisted, ready to be stubborn. "I'm on way home from school."

How odd. That last bit sounded like the truth.

It turned its head and light completely upward, then both were aimed at me again. "This ship does not take passengers—only items in little packages. Not alive items." A decision had been made within that unfathomable skull; I doubted it was in my favor.

"I happen to know you're wrong. Let me wait here for the captain."

"It is you who are mistaken, Human. All captains in my sector are known to me. This captain does not take passengers. For the final time, I warn you your behavior is totally unacceptable where I am the protector of the legal ways. Astsh! Daylight is coming. You will be seen by everyone soon!" A dry rustling as its fingers drummed the top of its force stick. "Come. Your passage contract will be checked."

"I'd hardly be carrying it," I heard myself say politely but firmly. "It's on the ship, of course." Where I'd like to be, on this or any ship for that matter—so long as it was leaving this world; such a desire was about the only coherent thought I had left. How was I to be rid of this too-attentive creature, already sucking air through several breathing orifices to continue its argument?

A burst of noisy voices, out of sight but close enough to be clearly heard, swung its attention and light from me for an instant. Seizing the opportunity, I backed away, dodging down the nearest open shipway, hoping the Port official would consider the boisterous group a greater threat to public peace.

I stopped running when the cramp in my side grew to a blinding pain, taking shelter under a ramp. A breeze drifted past, carrying the aroma of someone's breakfast with it. As I gasped for air, my mouth watered. Much more of this and I would welcome even Roraqk's ugly face if he brought something to eat.

My head jerked up. I'd heard no sound, yet felt an incredibly strong awareness of someone, someone near. I pulled myself up, easing slowly to where I could see past the ramp to the dimly lit space between this ship and the one behind it. A figure moved there, walking quickly yet soundlessly away. I knew who it had to be—even as the person slowed, head turning as if alerted, but unsure why. It was Morgan. And, whatever else, he was Roraqk's enemy.

Quickly, I tossed the knife, making sure it was off first, wincing at the loudness of the ringing sound as it fell close by his feet. Morgan stooped and picked it up. I pressed back into the shadows, waiting to see what he'd do. A thin ray of light touched me and was quickly doused. He began walking away again, this time leisurely, arms swinging. I could hear him humming to himself in a low voice.

Well enough, I stayed in the shadows, following at the limits of the sound of his hum. My perceptions narrowed to that sense, concentrating my almost exhausted energy on remaining out of sight of the occasional workers busy loading and unloading cargo. Morgan called to a few, waved a comradely arm, kept their attention.

Our precautions were well taken. Morgan stepped toward an unusually slender ship. *My ship,* I thought fuzzily, with a satisfaction too great to be mine alone. The ship's surface was dark with age, but the designation *Silver Fox* was polished and bright. My blood froze at the sight of a red-and-black uniform waiting at the top of its ramp, and I squeezed behind a line of crates.

Morgan didn't hesitate. He climbed the steep ramp, activating the ship's external lights with a spoken code. They flooded the pavement before the ship, forcing me to crouch down where I couldn't see. "What can I do for you, Officer?" I heard him say with commendable coolness. "My ladings are in order and I've certainly paid sufficient fees, even for Auord's Port Authority—"

The official's words and Morgan's reply were lost to me as another ground tug rumbled by, hooks emptied of whichever ship it had just placed in dock. When I dared peek over the crates, the officer was gone and the *Fox*'s lights had been extinguished. A thin sliver of brightness remained to mark what must be an opening in her air lock.

Now I faced a choice. I knew what my compulsions wanted. Here was my ship. But I gripped the edge of the nearest crate, making myself think. Up that ramp, and through that door might lie safety, or worse trouble than I'd already escaped. Morgan had led me here. Why? An act of conscience, or the quick thinking of a practiced scoundrel? I could lose all I'd gained.

Given a lack of alternatives, I thought wryly, it was a risk worth taking. Who or what Morgan was could wait. I rose to my feet, feeling an immediate and unexpected relief, like a pat on my head.

Forcing down my misgivings, I ran across the open space, hesitated, then drove myself up the ramp, stumbling once on its ridges. At the top, I swallowed, then stepped blindly over the sill of the air lock and entered the *Fox*.

The light inside was painfully bright. As the door closed itself behind me, I simply slid down the wall to the floor. The inner portal hissed open a second later and Morgan stepped through. He secured the lock on the outer door with a slap on its control plate, then stood looking down at me. "I thought it might be you," quietly, with no expression to be read on his face, unless it was a touch of irony.

I pulled my bound hands out of the folds of my cloak and held them up, waiting to see just what my choice had gained me.

During the moment he hesitated, I felt chilled. Then Morgan drew the tiny force blade from its concealment in his belt. Before I could do more than tense, he neatly sliced the control from the lock bar. It dropped from my wrists, and I lurched to my feet.

"You've been in bad company, chit. I'm sorry for that. I never meant you any harm—" Morgan said, tucking away the weapon and stepping back with hands wide apart and open. "Unfortunately, there's no time for explanations from either of us." More slowly, and with an underlying grimness: "I've called up a tug, and I'm due to lift. You're welcome to come along."

I still felt cold when I looked at him, met those blue

eyes I couldn't read. The compulsions in my mind were silent, deadened by this sudden success.

Perhaps Morgan read something in my silence. He moved one hand, held it palm out. On his palm lay not one, but a matched set of tiny handles. "You didn't kill Roraqk," Morgan said regretfully. "But it was a good try."

I shrugged, still reluctant to trust my voice. The movement shifted the hood back from my face. Morgan's hand reached toward my wounded cheek, but drew back at my involuntary flinch. His voice roughened. "Come on. The sooner we're offworld, the safer we'll both be."

"The pirates know you," I said around a tongue too thick to move easily. "Roraqk kept me alive—" I paused— "because I said your name."

Morgan spoke with exaggerated care, as if afraid I wasn't able to hear. I didn't blame him, finding it difficult keeping his face in focus. "I'm not one of them. No matter what they said or how it seems."

Fragments of conversations I had overheard floated in my mind. How easy to interpret them in his favor—or not. I closed my eyes for a moment against the pain so much thinking caused. "Captain Morgan," I answered with a voice much steadier than I expected. "It doesn't matter whether I believe you or not. I must get off this planet."

"And go where?"

A nightmare would be simple compared to the maelstrom in my thoughts at that question. I opened my eyes, surprised when icy moisture escaped down my cheeks. "I don't know," I whispered. "I don't know."

His level, matter-of-fact voice probably helped as much as what he said. "You're welcome on the *Fox*. She's not set for passengers, but you can bunk as crew till her next planetfall."

I released some of my tension in a sigh. "Agreed," I said, at last able to smile. "And thank you, Captain."

Morgan frowned, dropping his eyes from mine. I stared at him, startled and uncertain again. "This way," he said, leading the way through the inner portal into a narrow, curved corridor. Silently, I struggled to move my leaden feet, wishing the deck wouldn't persist in moving. I stepped over the sill carefully. My immediate surroundings grew vague, less important than the need to stay upright. Warm, unexpectedly gentle hands offered support. I accepted, losing the battle of pride and consciousness almost gratefully.

* * *

INTERLUDE

"A mess."

Terk kept his expression fixed in what he hoped was a neutral expression, although he winced inwardly at the icy condemnation in his Commander's voice. "They were tipped—"

"A mess," Bowman repeated, choosing to stare out her window at the shipcity rather than look at the two uncomfortable officers standing before her cluttered desk. "Not only did you lose every witness; not only did you lose four good beings from my staff; you lost most of the recruiters as well."

'Whix tried unsuccessfully to control a tendency to pant, a species-specific reaction to distress. Like Terk, his uniform was marred by battle, scorches revealing the gray gleam of body armor under the fabric. "She was there," he insisted. "We were close."

Bowman came back to her desk and sat down. "A bit of good work," she conceded. "But we've more important things to do than clean up Auord. Prepare my cruiser for lift."

Terk brightened. "We have a lead?" he said with obvious hope. It wouldn't be the first time his Commander suddenly improved the odds.

"Less than that," Bowman corrected dryly. "Six ships got off without being searched. Seems the grounders were too busy with some smugglers we flushed for them to watch their port. And you two were busy checking bodies." She passed a noteplas to 'Whix. "Opinion."

He read for a moment. "Two are local ore carriers. But—interesting—the *Torquad*."

Terk scowled. "Port Authority's always suspected Roraqk of transporting *recruits* outsystem as a favor to his buyers. He's mixed up in this to his scaly neck, you can bet on it."

Bowman nodded. "So pirates have our missing celebrity? Or has she given them the slip and taken other transport?"

'Whix chirped thoughtfully. "The remaining ships are a Regillian passenger transport headed to Camos, a trader, and a private yacht with no listing. Do we contact their captains?"

"Not with the Clan involved. Barac has likely headed offworld as well, possibly with her. I don't want him scared off. I'd like to talk to that one." Bowman pursed her lips and half-closed her eyes in thought. Terk and 'Whix traded glances. "How do we find them?" she said finally.

Terk had taken the ship list from his partner. As he read it, his heavy shoulders tensed, straining his already suffering uniform. "That trader is the *Silver Fox,*" Terk announced. "There's our target."

"Why?" 'Whix protested, before Bowman could respond. "The *Fox* is a one-man operation. Captain Morgan's lift was scheduled well in advance; three planetfalls' worth of cargo are registered against his ship. Hardly a profitable time to become involved with an illegal passenger or two."

"Call it a hunch," Terk said, his heavy jaw thrust forward stubbornly. "Commander, I've run against this Morgan and the *Fox* in the past. It's nothing I can prove—his record's clean. But I don't trust him."

'Whix fluttered his vestigial neck feathers in disapproval; his was a methodical mind, and he disliked Terk's mental leaps. "The *Torquad,*" he said firmly.

Bowman, however, raised one eyebrow, considering them both. "Interesting choices," she commented after a moment. A theatrically fatalistic shrug could not conceal the gleam of anticipation in her eyes. "Regardless of our quarry, it means lift from Auord by dawn. Put your business in order. We won't be back for some time."

"Who gets copied on this?" Terk asked, his mind already running through a checklist of what Bowman would justly assume would be done before lift.

The commander sighed. "No one, yet."

'Whix fluttered uneasily. "Commander? Surely there are species whose position within the Trade Pact might be affected by our current actions and findings. It is our duty to send that information simultaneously to all concerned representatives on the Board, is it not?"

"That's what the regs say," Bowman agreed. She began clearing her desk, using her favorite strategy of bringing her travel case up to one side and shoving anything on top into it. "But it's a judgment call, 'Whix. And in this case, I judge it best to let the Board wait a while longer."

"May I ask why, Commander?"

Bowman's voice was very quiet. "Because this time, I think we are on to something that may affect every member species, as well as several that are not. So we'll keep this matter in-ship until I give the word. Any more questions?"

They had none that felt comfortable to ask.

Chapter 5

"WAKE up."

Unfair, I grumbled to myself, burrowing deeper under my warm blankets, hoping to escape that annoying voice.

"Wake up!" This time the voice was sharper and definitely aggravated.

I pulled my covers down so that I could peer over the edge with one eye, cleverly not committing myself to being awake. The room was dim enough to be featureless; I had the impression the walls were unusually close together. But sufficient light came in behind the figure in the doorway to show me who it was. "Is it morning, Captain Morgan?" I asked doubtfully, poking my head farther out.

"Not by shiptime, it isn't," Morgan announced, yawning as if to prove his point. "You were having a nightmare."

"You woke me up because I was having a nightmare?" I repeated rather stupidly. I hadn't been dreaming. Had I?

"I woke you because your yelling woke me up."

"Oh." I was wide awake now, and embarrassed. I sat up, catching the edges of my bed as it swung slightly in response. "This is a hammock," I said with some alarm. An instant later, realizing I was not being immediately dumped to the deck by uncontrolled and erratic movements, I relaxed. Then apologized, "I guess I was dreaming a bit louder than usual. Sorry—"

He waved away my apology almost impatiently. "How's your face?" Morgan asked, a change of subject I thought was quite deliberate.

I touched my cheek and felt a neat patch of medplas. When had he done this? My memories were definitely hazy after arriving in the *Fox.* There was no heat or tightness remaining. "It doesn't hurt," I told him, realizing at the same time that I could no longer feel the burn on my shoulder.

"It'll probably leave a scar, but you can always get that fixed." He paused. "There's a stall with a fresher just off the galley when you need it."

"Thank you, Captain." My gratitude included the too loose comfort of an unfamiliar tunic as well as the bed. My hair tumbled into my eyes as I dipped my head to stare awkwardly at my bandaged wrists, clean-smelling hair freed of fastenings and tangles.

The compulsions that had driven me here must still have been asleep; in their place was a confusing emptiness, with odd useless bits of knowledge rolling around my thoughts like marbles in a bowl. I didn't know what to say or do. I hadn't expected kindness.

Morgan paused; possibly he sensed my discomfort, because he said: "Go back to sleep, chit." He turned to leave, hand ready to close the door.

Chit? It sounded like something you'd call a child, and a not too bright child at that. "My name is—" I started to say.

Morgan stopped politely, looking back at me, his face unreadable in the shadows. "My name is Kissue. I'm Human—a spacer, like you. The Tulis took my clothes before they put me—" I closed my lips tight, sealing in the rest. I found myself shaking.

"Lights." At Morgan's command, a portlight winked on at ceiling height, making me squint. He took a step into the tiny room. "We went outsystem hours ago. You're safe now, Kissue," he said, dropping to one knee beside my hammock, his quiet voice full of concern. "No one's going to hurt you."

Seen this close, Morgan's eyes were very blue, so vivid they might have been lit from within. I stared into them, unable to say why I believed him, or why my cheeks felt suddenly warm. I amazed myself by daring to touch my fingers to the side of Morgan's face.

My hand might have been a force blade from his sudden flinch to avoid it. Confused, I curled up the offending fingers and shoved both hands back under my blankets. Standing, Morgan backed away from me, his face oddly red under his tan. "Get some sleep, Kissue." This time he closed the door.

I ordered out the lights, slipping down under my blanket, curling myself into as much of a ball as the protesting hammock would allow. But not to sleep. I had new thoughts filling my empty mind. Why had Morgan avoided my touch?

And why did it hurt?

I did sleep a bit more, then hunger and other needs became more important. I ordered on the light and found Morgan had left a pair of used but clean coveralls by the door. I dressed slowly, using the time to think over my situation.

I agreed with Morgan. I probably was safe—at least from Roraqk. I'd also left behind whoever had chased me through the dark on Auord.

Unfortunately, despite safety and a decent rest, I hadn't regained any more of what was missing from my mind. Knowledge of what was around me seemed to float up when I needed it, but I was no closer to knowing who I was. Nor was I any closer to understanding what it was that had compelled me to certain actions, such as getting on this ship. Frustrated, I bundled up the hammock and tucked it back in its cupboard along the wall.

Maybe the compulsions were over. I'd achieved their purpose—to find my ship and leave Auord. Maybe I'd be left in peace aboard the *Fox*.

I felt an itch. But it had nothing to do with my skin. It was inside, somehow.

The feeling subsided the instant I began worrying about it.

Then it snuck back, when I deliberately thought about breakfast. I closed my eyes for a moment to concentrate, not sure what I was feeling. The itch disappeared. I opened my eyes again, frustrated, only to find I'd turned without knowing it to face the wall my hammock slid into, instead of the door of my little room.

And I knew Morgan was that way, somewhere beyond that wall. How I knew was beyond me.

I spun away from the wall and banged the door open with unnecessary force. *Great*, I said to myself. *I'm ready*

*to take some control of my life, and a man I don't even
know has become an itch.*

My door opened into a galley. I glanced back, realizing
that I'd been sleeping in a storeroom—the cupboards lining the walls were probably loaded with galley supplies,
not clothing as I'd thought. Well, Morgan had warned me
the *Fox* wasn't a passenger ship.

The galley was a good size, though, with a gleaming
yellow table and four waiting stools. The room itself was
longer than it was wide, one long wall taken up by a
counter with cupboards overhead and the other broken
by two doors, one leading to my cubbyhole and another
opening on a compact fresher stall. I quickly availed myself of that comfort, then stepped back out into the galley,
thinking firmly of breakfast.

An older but quite sophisticated servo-kitchen beckoned. I moved around the table, noticing that it and the
stools could retract into the floor if necessary. The short,
slightly curved wall to my left was open to the hall, its
airtight door withdrawn. The remaining wall was open to
the blackness of space.

A memory conveniently surfaced before I could panic,
telling me that this was not a hole in the ship but simply
a vis-wall, one set to show a very realistic depiction of
vacuum and stars. I let go of my death's grip on the table
and breathed more easily. Breakfast.

"Good morning, Fem Kissue."

So much for breathing easily. "Morning, Captain," I
managed to mumble, every thought driven from my head
by Morgan's arrival and that damnable mental itch. I sat
down hurriedly.

"Have you eaten yet?" Morgan looked rested and cheerful. When I shook my head, he went to the control panel
of the kitchen. His hand hovered over the first row of
keys. "What do you like to have for breakfast?"

I had no idea. My stomach growled impatiently before I
could think of an answer.

Morgan grinned, an expression that made his face years
younger. "Since you're that hungry, let me suggest a spe-
cialty of the house."

This day was not going well.

* * *

Some time later, I swallowed the last crispy bite of a fruit bread and grinned across the table at Morgan. "I feel like a new person," I said truthfully.

"Ready for a tour of the *Fox?*" Morgan asked, picking up both our dishes and tossing them into the kitchen's receiver.

Not if he planned to test my so-called spacer's knowledge, I wasn't. This being a concern I didn't intend to share, I dredged up a smile and nodded.

I needn't have worried. Morgan loved his ship; showing her to anyone was obviously something he deeply enjoyed. All I had to do was look attentive—and try to keep up with his energetic strides.

Morgan told me the *Fox's* history as we went. She was an old, well-used ship, originally a planetary patrol cruiser, at one time carrying seven crew and able to outrun most ships her size. Her subsequent owners had gradually stripped the crew quarters and holds for cargo space. Years of plodding service as an ore carrier followed. Eventually, there was little left of value.

Morgan had recognized the worth of the old ship's abused and neglected engines, and risked his savings to buy her. He spent whatever he earned to refurbish her, in time restoring most of her original speed and maneuverability. He installed bulkheads to divide the ship's interior into a set of four holds. Now, the *Fox* made a tidy profit transporting small, urgent cargoes, often through hazardous space.

There was more; in fact, our tour took the rest of the morning. I think Morgan mistook my eager listening for the natural reaction of a fellow spacer. He went into technical specifications at the least encouragement, dwelling on the improvements he wanted to make, as well as those already accomplished.

Morgan couldn't have known the improvement he was making in his passenger, and I wasn't about to tell him. As he described every detail, part number, and code, each loving explanation rooted itself in my mind, crowding away the emptiness with his knowledge of the *Fox*. I hadn't realized how starved I was for information until he provided it. This was a meal infinitely more satisfying than the one already in my stomach.

By the time we were heading back toward the galley, my intense interest had had an unforeseen consequence. I was making Morgan nervous. His descriptions began to include a rather repetitive, "Don't go there without me." I could understand Morgan not wanting a stranger—especially one who arrived uninvited—roaming through his precious ship.

What I couldn't understand was Morgan's behavior. There is no excess space inside any ship, which meant that I often had to squeeze close to him to see what he would show me. Each time, he separated from that contact very quickly, as though I disturbed him.

"It's not often I get to show off the *Fox,* Kissue. I hope I didn't bore you," Morgan concluded as he waved me into the galley.

"No," I said sincerely. "I enjoyed the tour, Captain." I stood beside the table, trailing my fingers along its smoothness.

"You probably need to rest," he said. "There are rectapes in the left-hand drawer, and the table has a viewslot."

I did feel tired. But there were questions I needed answered. "Where are we going, Captain Morgan?"

Morgan raised one eyebrow. "I was wondering when you'd ask. Ret 7 is my first scheduled stop. We arrive in four days, noon shiptime."

Too soon, whimpered a thought that wasn't wholly mine. I ignored it, taking a seat and motioning Morgan to join me. He sat slowly, taking a plas notebook and pen from a pocket.

"What happens to me at Ret 7?" I asked, careful with my voice and expression.

"That's your choice, Kissue," Morgan replied. "I have to warn you. It's not a good place to make a connection, unless you plan to go farther out. Liners do arrive from time to time, but there's not much routinely scheduled."

"Where do you go next?"

His face became expressionless, his blue eyes slightly hooded. He made a show of consulting his notebook. "I have three more stops planned: the *Fox* has cargo for the orbital station at Theta B798, a pickup at Plexis Supermarket, then Ettler's Planet."

The names meant nothing. I looked around the soft gray walls of the galley, carefully avoiding the black one full of stars. "I'd like to book passage on the *Fox* to Ettler's," I said casually.

Morgan whistled thoughtfully through his teeth, rolling the pen in his strong-looking hands. "Expensive. You don't look to be in a position to pay."

"Then why did you take me from Auord?" I replied.

I surprised him into a short, humorless laugh. "A question I still can't answer to myself, chit." A flicker of something in his eyes. "Put it down to a desire to twist the reptile's tail."

I closed my lips over what I might have asked; there were more immediate matters to settle. "I can work for my passage," I suggested. "I want to go to Ettler's."

"Why Ettler's?"

"That's my business, Captain. Do we have a deal?"

He seemed to find his pen and pad fascinating. "It's a long passage. Do you have any ratings?"

If he meant experience, I didn't dare lie. "No."

"So I'll have to train you before you could even do maintenance," Morgan said, looking me in the eye and not seeming in the least surprised by my confession. "I'll want you out of my way," he warned. "The *Fox* has no room for passengers straying around. I fly her alone, and that's the way I like it."

"I can learn. And I'll stay out of your way."

"It'll be two weeks at least—"

"I could use the peace and quiet, believe me, Captain," I said, hopeful he wasn't seriously objecting.

"To Ettler's, then." He stood, holding out his right hand. I made my hand reach out and accept the quick grasp of his, wondering why the simple gesture felt so full of meaning.

Morgan went to attend to his ship. I sat, busy with my own thoughts. Idly, I picked up the pen he'd left on the table. Its metal was still warm from Morgan's hand.

My fingers wrapped tightly around it, without any orders from me.

* * *

INTERLUDE

Barac locked the door of his rented room behind him, wishing the effort could keep his problems outside as well. The tall, lean Clansman stretched and then winced as the movement pulled his aching ribs. Bureaucrats.

"You're late."

Training locked Barac's muscles to immobility. He used his eyes and deeper sense to seek the source of the soft, low voice without success. "I think you have the wrong room—" he began to thin air, only to close his mouth as a figure slowly materialized before his eyes. The form of a woman grew distinct, then clear; her blue-black hair tumbling in heavy waves to frame a pale and dramatically beautiful face. Her eyes were light gray and stormy with emotion; her generous red lips were thin with anger. The only flaw to the effect was the way her feet floated a hand-breadth above the floor.

"Rael," Barac said with disgust. "I hope you know you scared me out of what wits I'd left—" Keeping a wary eye on the ominously silent Clanswoman, Barac strode past her to the room's servo-panel. He tapped a request for Denebian wine—an expensive Denebian wine. When the panel opened seconds later, Barac took out two glasses. He turned, holding one glass of wine out toward Rael. At her slight nod, he *pushed* the glass with his power out of normal space, into the M'hir.

The glass winked out of existence, reappearing the same instant in Rael's hand. Barac hid a sigh of relief. It would have been most embarrassing if Rael hadn't accepted his offering. Alone, he couldn't pass an object through the M'hir from one hand to another. Barac raised his wine in an appreciative toast. "Thanks for coming so quickly, Rael."

Rael lifted her glass, checking its color, frowning. "No thanks to you for wasting the effort." The Clanswoman—or rather her image, for Rael's physical form was on a planet a considerable distance from Camos by Human measurement—lowered into a chairlounge Barac couldn't see. She adjusted the silken panels of her skirt so her long legs could stretch. Since Barac had last seen her, she'd had the skin of both arms and legs altered to the dappling of a Gentek—probably a current Denebian fad. When she kicked her feet free of her slippers, which promptly disappeared from view, Barac noticed the dappling extended to her toes as well. He was mildly curious as to whether the coloring went to other areas of her body as well. Rael finished settling herself and looked at him.

She smiled, a brilliant smile quite without warmth. "Let's say the fee you proposed was interesting—as a starting point. I presume it'll be for more than repairing your pretty face," the Clanswoman added wickedly, surveying the livid bruises extending from Barac's ear to chin. She cocked an exquisitely shaped eyebrow. "Actually, I was planning to get in touch with you myself, Cousin."

Behind her light words, Barac sensed a disturbance, a troubling of the M'hir he registered as anger. He tilted his glass, watching how the wine effortlessly held its level, thinking how well it matched Rael's usual approach to life. The storm cloud she carried with her today was un-usual, but Barac had little doubt as to its source.

Or that he had better deal with it first. "What's wrong with the family today?" he asked, casually sipping from his wine.

The M'hir, in which Clan power dipped and mingled, through which image and form could be sent at the speed of thought, quivered between them as if charged with static. Barac cursed silently, quickly tightening his shields far past the limits of politeness, withdrawing from the M'hir, limiting his awareness to this room. As a *di* Sarc, Rael's power within the M'hir was several magnitudes greater than his. And *suds* learned early to protect themselves.

Rael graciously ignored his withdrawal—or didn't care. She stretched, a deceptively easy movement of her long arms that rolled muscle under her dappled skin. Her eyes were shadows behind a drift of hair. "When is your Join-ing with Risa?" she asked, instead of answering.

Risa sud Annk. The sound of her name ignited a des-perate longing; it coursed through Barac's body like a disease, upsetting all reason. His Risa.

Only Rael di Sarc had the gall to form spoken words around the central hope of his life—of any unChosen one's life. Barac stood, feeling too vulnerable sitting, then be-gan to pace around the room.

"Have they told you when?" she prodded, aware of his reaction and not hiding her amusement. Those Chosen were often cruel to those still ruled by need. Barac hoped to be amused and cruel himself one day.

He balled his fists, kept desire from his voice. "The

Council hasn't decided—probably soon." It couldn't be soon enough. To meet Risa, his intended . . . Barac forced his mind back to Rael. She had fired that name at him for a reason. "Why?"

Rael brushed back her hair, her eyes leaping into the light, their expression of pity holding him still. "Refuse to be a candidate for her Choice, Barac. Otherwise, I promise you won't survive."

It was like a belly blow, driving out his breath and sending a wave of nausea up through his brain. "Council decides the matches. Risa—" he couldn't help the naked need in his voice this time, "—will be right for me."

"You unChosen think with your guts." Rael's eyes continued to pin him, her full lips curving into a shape of disgust. "Try to use your head instead, Barac, and be grateful you've me to fill it. I happened to meet your Risa ten days ago. Oh, she's ready to Choose, all right—will you listen to me!" Rael's power swelled and rammed against his shielding, quelling his eager questions before they were more than thought. "This Risa is no more *sud* than I am, Barac. Those on Council are mad to think you could Join with her."

"But I must." Barac tried not to tremble, hearing at first only what mattered. Kurr, Sira, all other thoughts melted under surges of passion. Choice. It was his turn. He'd waited so long for his Joining, to have a mate of his own, to be complete. And Risa was ready for him. Rael said so.

Then the rest of what Rael was saying sank in past his excitement. "Council selected me as her candidate," he protested. "They don't make mistakes. You're wrong, Rael—"

The form of the Clanswoman shimmered as though he saw her through waves of heat, the image she was projecting through the M'hir affected by emotion if not by physical distance. Her rage pounded at his mind. "Sometimes I wonder why I bother with any Sarc," Rael said scornfully. Then her image firmed. She leaned forward, put her hands on her knees, and hissed, "Risa *di* Annk has already tried to Join!" The abrupt end to her rage in his mind should have warned him. "And the candidate failed."

Of all his questions, Barac could only form one. "Who?" he demanded, tasting bile in his mouth.

"Faitlen's second son. Osbar di Parth. You knew Osbar, didn't you?"

Yes, he did. Barac closed his eyes, involuntarily remembering a summer night, a night warm with promise, a night full of the unheard voices of a rare Clan gathering. Even rarer, Clan children. He, Kurr, Osbar, and the other unChosen males sneaking away. Tag in the dew-wet grass. 'Port and seek among the dark hedges.

Then, safely out of range of adults, someone starting the game called Chooser-Loser, the child's game that teased instincts deeper than survival. Barac could almost feel the hot sweat of the ritual grip, his right hand locked in another's, his knees wet from the grass. He could almost sense the strain of channeling power into brute force, aiming that force through the M'hir, against another's, struggling to conquer.

It was just a game, but it was for boys only. Without needing to be told, Clan children knew today's girl would be tomorrow's Chooser, driven when adult to test any unChosen male's mastery of the M'hir, to challenge that mastery with her unique power, to kill the weak with a thought.

It was just a game, after all, just children pretending in the dark, giggling with excitement and a touch of delicious fear. There was no risk, no true Joining, no climax. That would come immeasurably later, when, one so-distant day, the struggle would be against the full power of a true Chooser. Young boys talked about it among themselves, intrigued and titillated, sure of their tomorrows.

The ones old enough to be called unChosen didn't talk about it at all. Their tomorrows were much less certain. Win or even hold your own, and a Chooser's Power-of-Choice would turn from weapon to a promise of paradise. Win or tie, and become one in the Joining, the forming of a permanent bond through the M'hir, connected across distance, mated for life, guaranteed a future.

Lose, and die.

In the child's version, the loser got a headache and a fair bit of teasing. Barac had won some matches that long ago night. But of course, as only *sud,* he'd lost to Osbar.

As Osbar had lost the real game to *his* Risa.

His thoughts had been unguarded; Rael followed the

memory to the present and sighed with him. Her power had cooled but her voice remained harsh.

"Make sure you understand, Barac," Rael said. "Your Risa ripped Osbar's mind open like a knife. The witnesses said he didn't last her testing long enough to draw air for a scream. You must refuse her if you intend to live."

Barac felt like a moth offered the brilliance of a flame to die in and struggled to keep his mind focused. "Risa?"

"Disappointed. Eager to try another candidate. She's not getting any older, you know." Rael's fingers traced the ripe swelling of her own breasts with an absent pride.

Barac's eyes followed her movements. Of course he knew. Choosers waited like buds for the stroke of spring, unchanging, unable to flower within the warmth of Joining, as if frozen in time. *As Risa waits for me,* he thought in a horrified daze of longing, then recoiled. "The Council lied to me."

"You're surprised?"

One last burst of need tore through him. "How can I refuse?" he wailed.

Rael raised a brow. "By showing some common sense, Barac. The Prime Law gives the unChosen the right to three refusals. Risa's only your first. Sira and I will back you if there're hackles about it."

Sira. How could he have forgotten? And what of Kurr? The sick realization that his passion had so easily pushed Kurr's murder aside cleared the last clouds from Barac's mind. Like the wine in his glass, he felt a centering calm restore the universe Rael had tipped.

"Risa can wait, Rael," Barac said without so much as a twinge. He returned to his seat, carefully preparing what he had to say. "It's Sira we need to talk about. She's in danger."

Rael raised one elegant brow. "Sira?"

"Yes. Sira. She was on her way back to Camos—"

"Back? What are you babbling about? Sira is studying history or something at the Cloisters." Rael's voice was flat and definite. "Ossirus knows why she loves stuffing her head with the stuff, but she waited long enough for the chance. Of course she hasn't left—"

"I was Sira's escort on Auord," Barac interrupted heavily. "I don't know why Sira left the Cloisters. Or when. Sira couldn't tell me. Rael, she was under a full stasis block." He took a deep breath. "Have you heard anything about a candidate for her?"

"Stasis." Rael's face seemed to close, as if over an unpleasant memory. She shook free of it with an impatient toss of her hair and her look at Barac was purely malicious. "Well, you can't be making that up to annoy me. If Sira had been herself, she'd have made shorter work of you than Risa would, dear Cousin."

"I thought at least Sira was safe from your tongue." Barac glared at Rael, forgetting power and rank in his anger.

Rael flinched, then made an elaborate and graceful gesture with her right hand. "Forgive me," she said, the fire in her eyes fading into puzzlement and concern. "Sira knows I sometimes forget her pain and think only of my pride." Rael paused, then sighed. "No. Of course there's been no news of a candidate. Why do you say she's in danger? Where is she?"

Barac relaxed only slightly, the cool evening breeze being drawn down to the room by the wall vents drying some of the sweat on his forehead. He took a deep breath. "I don't know where she is. I lost her."

"You lost her," Rael repeated as if the words made no sense. Her wine spilled and she *pushed* it away, annoyed at the distraction. "And Sira still in full stasis?"

Misery in his eyes, Barac nodded. "We were attacked on Auord, in Port City itself. Clean, professional job—if I hadn't had an Enforcer on my tail, they'd likely have finished me." Barac rubbed one hand over his eyes. "When I came to, Sira was gone and a Pact Investigator named Bowman was set to ask all the wrong questions." He took a large gulp of his wine, not tasting it. "This Bowman knew about Sira, if not who she was. I wasn't that groggy. I think Sira did the only sensible thing and ran. Somewhere." Barac hesitated. "You know I can't scan for her in stasis."

Rael sat up suddenly, tension in every line of her body. "You're hiding something. Something worse."

"Bowman is investigating a murder—Kurr's murder." Barac felt Rael's shielding break; her shock echoed in his mind as it flooded through her clear, cold thoughts.

Then the sensation vanished as Rael regained her control. "What of Dorsen?" Rael's words were clipped.

Barac shuddered and dropped his head. "Gone." Three lives lost, now. Kurr's Chosen, her link to her mate locked through the tiny mind of their unborn child, had been dragged into the M'hir at the instant of Kurr's death. Even so, she might have been held in reality by her Watcher, but for tragic timing. Kurr had been sleeping, his life signs strong, the customary time to grant the Watcher a short reprieve from what was almost always a routine vigil. Death had surprised them all.

It wasn't thought to be a quick ending, dissolving in the M'hir; the taste of lost power and personality lingered to haunt any who traveled nearby, encouraging nightmares as well as caution.

Barac roughened his voice deliberately, knowing this wasn't the time for grief. "Kurr and I were about to start some scanning along the Acranam Corridor. Harc asked me to help guide Sira through her stopover on Auord. I was kin, after all, and had met her before. Kurr went on, alone." And alone, had been vulnerable. Barac nursed that pain, drew strength from it. He would find Kurr's murderer.

Rael rose, seemed to stand right in front of his eyes. "Let me see," she demanded imperiously. Barac considered for a moment, then nodded slowly. His mental shields thinned and dropped as their surface thoughts merged.

Barac allowed Rael to direct his memories, cringing despite himself at the pain bound inseparably to reliving the blast globe's explosion. She followed his path to the present, experiencing with him the disastrous news that Sira hadn't reach Camos. And the quick excuses he had produced to quell suspicion here that all was not well on Auord.

"Bah!" she spat, severing their linkage so abruptly Barac felt disoriented. "Bad enough you contacted that Human again. But to deliberately lie to the Council about Sira? What were you thinking of?"

"Betrayal."

There was silence as their eyes met, and Barac watched Rael add the word to the facts she had just obtained from his mind. He saw reluctant conviction settle small lines around the edges of her mouth. "Yes. You're right, of course," Rael said slowly. "How else could such attacks be timed? But who? The Council may use pawns like

Kurr or Dorsen, you or I. But not Sira. I can't believe they'd risk her in any way."

"You know what they're capable of, Rael," Barac argued. "What would they do if she was escaping them?"

Rael drew in a startled breath. "What do you see that I don't? What do you think has happened to Sira?"

Barac shook his head. "I don't know. My Talent, as you so often remind me, is not the strongest. Yet since losing Sira, I've had the taste of change in my thoughts. A foreboding." He watched for her reaction. "I think it has to do with the Human, Morgan. He might just be other than he seems—"

"Your Human?" Rael's mouth curved around laughter she restrained with an effort. "You Scouts are obsessed by them. I doubt your Morgan has tried to find Sira."

"You could be right, Rael." Barac was unconvinced. "But we have to find her. I have a ship ready to return to Auord." He paused, then added more to himself than to her: "But I will talk to Jason Morgan again."

Chapter 6

I RAN my fingers along the smoothness of the spoon one last time before tucking it lovingly in its place beside the pen and record tape. I replaced my extra coverall on top of my illicit collection, then closed the drawer with a satisfied pat.

So now I was a thief. When I worried about this, I consoled myself that I couldn't have been a real criminal before losing my memories. I was lousy at it. And soon my victim, who wasn't exactly blind, would notice how things were vanishing whenever I watched him work. I cringed at the thought.

But anything Morgan touched, held in his hands, was completely irresistible. I had to have it, as if second-hand it was Morgan himself.

Which was the other side of my current obsession. Folding my guilty hands together, I sat down slowly, shaking my head. There was something not quite right about how I felt when I thought about Morgan. Despite the pushes and pulls in my mind, I knew there had to be more to life than daydreaming about the warmth of a man's hand.

However, the part of me that could think for itself had little better to offer. And at least I had a home.

I curled up in the chair Morgan had found for me. It, a plas crate for a table, and my hammock now constituted my world for however long I could convince Morgan to let me stay.

And I had no intention of leaving the *Fox* at Ettler's.

I had a plan—if I could overcome my criminal urges before being caught. Morgan had given me a selection of training tapes. He was trying to keep me busy. But I knew the *Fox* was easily big enough for both of us. All I had to do was make myself so useful he'd want me to stay.

I pulled out the tape marked *"Calculating Stowage in a Vacuum,"* and reached for the hand viewer. Two weeks to Ettler's meant no time to waste.

The light in my room dimmed briefly. The signal for shipnight. My second night on the *Fox,* with Morgan. I prepared for bed, planning my dreams carefully. If they revolved around a certain ship's captain, that was my own business.

But dreams rarely obey one's waking fantasies. As I slipped deeper into sleep, it was harder to hold on to thoughts of Morgan, to remember I was safe on his ship, and he was only steps away. I lost control, falling into a dream that had nothing to do with pleasure.

Sounds—babbling, incomprehensible sounds—battered me. I was moving, yet the sounds followed. Moving, no, I was running. I couldn't stop running over the grassless plain, pursued by voices in overlapped confusion, forcing me to run more quickly than was possible, yet never quickly enough.

At first, the dream plain stretched featureless and flat, but wherever I passed, misty forms heaved themselves out of the ground to pace beside me, to pluck at my hands and arms. I could feel my heart pounding, as my gasping breath tried to fill aching lungs. There was no sense to this bizarre race, which was perhaps the most terrifying part of all. I willed myself fiercely to wake up or at least to turn and see my pursuers. Instead, I stumbled in the dream world and went down beneath a moving, whispering mass of shapeless weight. A scream tore from my lips.

And from someone else's. I jerked up in my hammock, thoroughly awake and trembling, to stare at the man once more silhouetted in the doorway. A silence filled the space between us, making me confused by what I thought or dreamed I'd heard.

"Finally," Morgan said, his voice oddly ragged. "I thought you'd never wake up this time." Dropping his hands from the sides of the doorframe, he leaned against one side of it instead, his face tucked in shadow. Gradually, his breathing grew quieter. "Are you all right?" he asked, more calmly.

"Lights," I ordered instead of answering, squinting as

the little portlight anchored to the cubby's ceiling obeyed. Its brightness washed most of the shadow from Morgan's face, revealed his tired-looking eyes and tousled hair.

"Lights out," Morgan countermanded, fading back to a silhouette. "It's late, and we go insystem today. Good night, Kissue. And no more dreams for a while. Please."

After he closed the door, I ordered on the light and searched my room for a com panel or anything that might be a listening device. Morgan's ability to notice my nightmares was becoming more than an embarrassment.

Morgan didn't join me for breakfast, so I couldn't ask him how, if he'd been asleep in his cabin at the aft end of the *Fox,* he'd known I was having a nightmare. What I remembered about dreams didn't suggest anyone could share them.

I tried to make sense of the tapes until my eyes were sore and my thumb red from flipping the view advance. Time for a break, I decided, refusing to admit to myself that the walls of my tiny room were closing in or that I was noticing a slightly metallic taste to the air. If I wanted to become crew, I'd have to learn to prefer this metal-shelled home to open sky.

But there wasn't any reason I shouldn't take a walk. Once out of the galley, I found myself drawn to the aft section of the *Fox.* I stood outside the closed door to the control room.

He was inside.

I turned away, though a compulsion wheedled at me to lurk outside the door until Morgan came out.

I discovered it was possible to walk through the *Fox* without retracing any steps, since there were two possible routes from the engine room to the control room, one that passed the galley and the other one that passed Morgan's quarters. A short corridor connected the two about midway down the ship.

By my second loop, I began making up emergencies in my head, losing all sense of time in fantasies. I would find a problem that threatened Morgan's beloved ship and solve it in the knick of time. Or Morgan would rush to rescue me. Regardless, my fantasies always ended with his deep blue eyes smiling into mine. By the time I passed

Morgan's cabin for the fourth time, I dared imagine the touch of his hand.

I wound up dumped from my daydream by an uncontrollable hammering of my heart. I stopped, leaning against the bulkhead, wondering how much more of this insanity I could take without humiliating myself completely.

Without consciously making a decision or plan, I found myself turning around in the curving corridor, walking slowly back toward Morgan's cabin.

A few more steps, then I stopped. It would be locked, I reassured myself, looking at the unmarked door. My hand trembled slightly as I touched the access pad.

It opened and my heart took up its pounding again, driven by a strangely delicious fear. Still, I hesitated. Why was I here? Surely I'd stolen all I could reasonably hide, I thought cynically, daring my compulsion to make sense. I needn't have bothered. My feet decided to move of their own accord. I found it simpler to agree than to argue.

Lights came on automatically, but something was wrong. I panicked, thinking Morgan had somehow already found me out. Then, as my eyes sorted the odd shadows into hues and colors, I gasped, stepping into the room, my fear and doubt forgotten.

There was barely room to turn, yet turn around and around I did. The small cabin contained the essentials: a pull-out bed, a full-sized fresher stall, desk, storage cupboards. But I noticed these details later.

Every available surface glowed with the colors of exquisitely detailed plant life. Hints of eyes and curious noses peered from beneath multihued leaves at cupboard corners and wall joints. My color-starved eyes could scarcely absorb it all. Painting this must have taken years.

A movement, real—not captured in paint—teased the corner of my eye and I stopped, examining myself critically in the mirrored tile of the fresher. A stranger stared back: not tall, but slim; pale skin beginning to darken in the ship's light—except for an angry red scoring on one cheek; wispy, light-brown hair tending to slide over gray wide-set eyes. The eyes were old, perplexed. The entire image was disjointed, awkward, as if pieces of different people were grafted together.

I turned away from my colorless self. Against my will, I tried the handle of the first set of cupboards, my fingers grasping smooth metal overlaid by a drift of small violet flowers. Fragrance from petals in a bowl fooled the senses, added to my guilt.

"What are you doing?" a very cold voice said from behind me. I started violently, then drew a quick steadying breath before I turned to face him.

"I—" I began to speak, then closed my mouth. What could I say? And Morgan's face was hardly encouraging— thin, white lines ran from his nose to the corners of his grim-set lips. "I meant no harm," I finished rather weakly. I hadn't known eyes could be so hard.

"That remains to be proved," Morgan snapped.

I spread my hands helplessly and let them fall. His nearness overwhelmed me. I wondered if the ship's gravity had somehow shifted. "I wanted to see where you lived."

Morgan drew a slow breath, then perched on one end of his desk, carefully moving the bowl of petals out of his way, that motion sending a delicate freshness of scent between us. His face was only slightly less angry. "Look, chit. It's time we had a talk about something."

"I don't like being called that," I muttered, feeling blood returning to my cheeks.

"That's because you don't understand it," Morgan said disconcertingly. I risked looking up at him. Most of his anger must have faded; he seemed more thoughtful than upset. "Chit is a spacer term—just means youngest on a ship." A pause. "But you wouldn't know that, would you?"

I shifted my weight and glanced longingly at the door. When I remained silent, Morgan's face became impossible to read and his voice was deceptively feather-soft. "Where did you get the spacer gear on Auord?"

"It was mine," I said in a small voice.

"No. It wasn't. And I think you owe me the truth, Kissue," Morgan countered, with a wave to his violated quarters, ablaze with dreams of a planet.

I shrugged. "I found the coveralls the morning I met you." It seemed another lifetime. "They were better than what I was wearing."

"Why?"

"My clothes were wet from the rain," I looked at him steadily, wondering, then added: "and I had to get to a starship. I thought dressing like a spacer would help."

Morgan's mouth thinned. "And how did you figure that?"

"You wouldn't have helped me otherwise."

"Is that what you believe?"

I met his eyes, saw something in them that looked like disappointment. "No," I admitted. "You've been kind, Captain Morgan. I—" I paused, then went on: "I don't think many people would have helped someone who snuck up on them in the dark. I wish I could repay you."

"I'll send you a bill," Morgan replied rather uneasily. "That's enough by trader standards."

"Not by mine." I took a deep breath, but before I could continue, compulsions swelled up and burst. My hand reached itself toward him. "I offer you Choice, Captain Morgan," I heard myself say. "I offer myself."

My skin tingled, as if the air was charged with static. The thing in my mind, having done its worst, vanished, leaving my mind a whirl of remembered fantasies and unknown hopes, colored as flamboyantly as the walls of Morgan's cabin.

And now he knew.

Mortified, I watched as Morgan shut his eyes briefly, as though collecting his wits. He sighed, then opened his eyes again. "I appreciate your gratitude, Kissue," he said, his tone and expression very serious. "And it's very natural for a younger person, like yourself, to develop— feelings—for an older person, like me, who helps a person. A younger person."

This sounded a bit confusing, but I grasped his meaning. He understood! Instantly, my embarrassment faded. Morgan didn't sound upset. Perhaps this hunger was something I should feel; perhaps he felt it too. I slid my foot forward, leaning a bit closer to him. Morgan shifted back instantly. I froze, suddenly and dreadfully unsure.

"What's wrong?" I asked, trying to sound confident. My mouth was dry; perversely, my palms were wet and I wiped them surreptitiously against my coveralls.

"I can't be what you want, Kissue," Morgan said quietly.

What did I want him to be? I studied Morgan's face, dwelling on the curve of his mouth, the place where his throat pulsed with each breath. I imagined how his cheek might feel against mine, and my breath caught. I couldn't help moving forward another step. The smell of him mingled with the fragrance of the petals in the dish.

Morgan's face turned dusky red under its tan. He twisted and stood to put the small table between us. "Kissue, listen to me. You're still a child—"

"I'm no child."

"Well, you're no woman yet either," Morgan countered.

Needs beat through me, wantings, longings so intense I could barely think. I stretched out my right hand, watching it tremble. "Morgan, I need—"

"What?" he asked gently, his blue eyes empty of anything warmer than sympathy, the table still carefully between us. "Do you even know?"

I stared at him. A throbbing pain began in my forehead, intensifying until it was like a drill centered above my left eye. "Yes," I heard myself say. "I need to offer you Choice, Captain Morgan."

"That's more than anyone's given you, isn't it?"

His words meant more than he realized. And did more. Emotions pounded through me, feelings I couldn't name rushed back and forth. Overwhelmed, the compulsions fragmented, their support somehow lost. As they withered and collapsed, they took secrets I'd barely began to sense along with them.

"I've never been offered Choice," I answered at last, blood gone cold. "It wasn't possible for me."

"And you believed that?" Morgan's eyes darkened. "That's wrong, Kissue. People must make their own choices, their own decisions. Their own mistakes, if necessary. That's what freedom is. Hell, that's why I'm out here, instead of sitting behind some insystem desk."

"You make your own choices, Captain?" I sank down in his chair, keeping my eyes on his face. "How?"

After looking at me suspiciously, Morgan sat down on the edge of his desk. "How do I choose? Depends. I learn all I can about a situation. Then I think about my own feelings—at least if there's time to think—"

"You think it's wrong for me to offer you Choice."

He hesitated, then said softly: "If I understand what you mean, and I believe I do, it's not wrong for you to want someone to care for you. I'm flattered you want me as that person. But you can't force such a choice on me or anyone. And I don't think you've given yourself time to think about this."

"All I can think about is you!" I insisted, frustrated and confused. "I need you—"

"No, you don't. Listen to me, Kissue," Morgan's voice grew firm. "Your feelings for me are not real."

How did he know that? I closed my mouth over what I'd planned to say.

Morgan raised one eyebrow and continued: "Do you know me?"

"Know you?"

"What's my favorite drink?" he demanded, ticking each rapid question off on the fingers of one hand. "What kind of life have I had? What scares me? What do I dream about?"

I tilted my head and considered him, suspecting some trick. "I need to know these things about you? Before I can offer you—me?"

Morgan smiled approvingly. "And much more. And I need to know you. People don't make decisions about each other, how they feel, without learning about each other."

"So you know these women on Auord," I said, feeling my face grow hot again.

Losing his smile, Morgan shook his head. "No. Of course not. I have physical needs like anyone else, Kissue. I don't know how to explain—" he paused, then said: "C-cubes are great when you have to eat in a hurry, but nobody would live on them unless they were starving."

"C-cubes?" I repeated, startled more than helped by his analogy.

"Forget the cubes," Morgan said, shaking his head with mild exasperation. "What I'm trying to say is that what sends me to a portside brothel is not what you are feeling for me."

I frowned. "I don't see any difference."

This time, it was Morgan who leaned closer, and I who pulled away. "Trust me," he said, sitting straight and spreading out his hands. "You aren't looking for a partner for sex, Kissue. You're looking for someone to be attached to emotionally, someone who cares for you." Morgan looked somber, his eyes shadowed as if by a memory.

"That's love, Kissue, and it's not something you can just ask for from another person."

Love? The word resonated with meanings, most of them strange, none describing the drive I'd felt, the emptiness still inside me. I looked down, staring at the petals in the bowl in an effort to collect myself.

It didn't matter why or how, I thought. I had exposed my innermost self to the only person whose opinion mattered to me. And he showed me the truth. I was a shallow, selfish thing. He was right to reject me.

"Kissue?"

I couldn't look up. My hand half-traced a gesture between us in the air before I stopped it, confused to find my fingers moving on their own, clenching them into a tight fist. "That's not my name," I heard myself say.

"Oh," Morgan didn't sound surprised. I peered up at him through my hair. "What should I call you then?" he asked with a slow smile.

My name. I'd left it behind in the dark, lost it that night—or had it been stolen? Shivering, I fought the panic that rose with any attempt to remember more. Dangerous. Dangerous. "Kissue will do," I said numbly, standing up and moving to the door.

Morgan moved quickly to block my way. "Wait."

There was a green pen and four small tools sticking up in his chest pocket. "My name is Kissue," I told his pocket firmly.

"You said it wasn't."

"Let me leave," I ordered.

His hands went to my shoulders, resting there like weights. "I thought you wanted to stay," he said very gently.

I dragged my eyes from the pocket to Morgan's face. Moments ago, I'd fantasized about standing like this, gazing up into his vibrant blue eyes. But my fantasy hadn't included this horrid vulnerability, this confusion.

My face must have shown both quite clearly. Morgan carefully lifted his hands away and moved back. "Tell me your name," he said quietly but firmly, still patently intending to guard the doorway.

"I don't know it." I sank back down in the chair, its arms coated with a pattern of winter ice. "I don't know who I am. Or what." I went on, words now flooding out of me as if a dam had burst. "I might even be a spacer. Nothing's as it should be, I—" I waved my hands downward. "I'm not as I should be." Rubbing my forehead helped numb the throbbing there, a pain that intensified the harder I tried to think.

I continued: "All I know of myself begins in darkness—a storm, the rain. The night we met on Auord, to be precise, Captain. I begin then."

"What can you remember?" a gentle prodding, no more. "Can you tell me what happened that night?"

"Sounds—I can't identify most—angry sounds, an explosion. Danger. So wet and cold—" I squeezed my eyes shut, the better to isolate every random recollection. "Running. I knew I had to run, to get away, to find my ship. Someone, someone stayed behind. I don't know if it was to give me time to escape, or if he was the one I ran from," I sighed, frustrated.

"Escape—from what danger?" I realized I'd heard the question more than once, and opened my eyes to look for Morgan. He'd left the doorway and was again perched on the table.

"I don't know," I sighed. "Sometimes I remember fragments of a face; mostly I remember some terrible, formless danger, then running, walking . . . rain." I tilted my head, about to tell him about the compulsions that had kept me on my feet past endurance. The words were pulled away from me before I could form them.

"I knew I wasn't safe on Auord," I said instead. "I found these clothes and, when it seemed you could lead me to a ship, I followed you."

"Out of all the ship owners carousing in Port City that night, you followed me," he echoed, but as if to himself. There was an odd bitterness in the set of his mouth. An old memory, I decided, inclined to be envious. Morgan said more briskly, "What can you remember about your belongings?"

"Nothing useful," I admitted with a shrug. "A dress, soaking wet, shoes definitely not meant for puddle-running."

"You didn't have your keffle-flute with you?"

I looked at Morgan blankly. "My what?"

He took my left hand and turned it over. "These calluses," he rubbed his thumb over a parallel set of ridges on my palm. "I knew a professional keffle player once, a good one. He had the same marks."

Had I been a musician? I looked at my hand suspiciously. "I'll take your word for it," I said after a moment, wondering where my music could have gone.

"What about the name you gave me—Kissue?" Morgan's eyes glinted like those of the hunting cat he'd painted stalking along the tape shelf.

I flushed. "Kissue was the name Roraqk used for me. I didn't know what else to say."

Morgan considered this for a moment, swinging one leg methodically back and forth. "I'm no med-tech, but I've tended a few injuries in my time. You had some bruises and cuts, that nasty burn on your shoulder, when you came on board, but I can't see them doing this. However, there are ways of removing memory, temporarily or permanently, ways that don't leave obvious traces." He ran a hand through his hair. "I don't know what to suggest. Perhaps the Enforcers—"

I was relieved and alarmed at the same time. "No! The Enforcers would take me back to Auord!" And make me leave the *Fox,* I added, but to myself. "I just need time, Captain Morgan. Maybe my memory will return."

"What if it doesn't?" he cut across my plea, almost brutally. "What then?"

"Then I go on from here, Captain Morgan. What else can I do?" I winced at a sickening increase in the throbbing sensation within my skull.

I felt a touch, ghostly light and strange, on my forehead. It was gone so swiftly I might have imagined it, save for a sudden relief from the pain in my head, a momentary scent of homely, safe things. Startled, I stared at Morgan as he withdrew his hand. The throbbing began again, but more softly, as if at a distance.

"What did you do?" I demanded, perplexed and more than a little frightened.

Morgan's eyes were oddly dark. "Don't be afraid," he said, as if sensing my response. "I've a small—gift. I helped your pain a little, that's all."

I did feel better. The strain of searching my meager memory was gone, and the ever-present ache had almost disappeared. I doubted it would help my peace of mind to know how Morgan accomplished that feat with only a touch, or if this "small gift" stretched to eavesdropping on my dreams.

"Well," Morgan said briskly, again as though fully aware of my thoughts. "On to our first order of business."

I eyed him suspiciously. "That being?"

Morgan looked down at me, the corners of his mouth beginning to deepen in a smile. "A proper name for you, chit. I'm sure you don't want to hang on to Roraqk's."

"Then you'll let me stay?" Oh, where had that plea come from? I closed my lips tightly over it, but held his eyes with mine.

His brows rose ever so slightly. "You wanted passage to Ettler's."

I hadn't realized relief could hurt. "I thought you might want me to leave. After what I did."

"Oh, that," Morgan said gruffly, glancing around his cabin. "I trust it won't happen again?" At my nod, he brought himself back to his assigned task with a visible effort. "A name," he said. "We'll need one you can live with for my manifest, anyway. Ret 7 is a stickler for protocol."

I looked at him helplessly. "I don't have any suggestions to offer, Captain."

Morgan considered this, then nodded curtly. "Trader ships usually carry kin as crew. That's our best bet—no one will ask questions about a second Morgan on the *Fox.* And I suppose I could use a bit of help around here."

"Thank you," I said sincerely, keeping to myself the surge of possessiveness his naming gave me. I had some of him after all.

"And as for a first name," Morgan paused. "What do you think of Sira?"

I couldn't account for the expectancy I read in his eyes and dismissed it as my imagination. "It's better than Kissue," I agreed, anxious to finish this odd business of gaining a name. "I only hope it doesn't have an owner likely to object."

"No, Sira Morgan," said Morgan slowly, as if tasting the words. "No, I don't think it does."

Chapter 7

FROM that moment, although I didn't realize it then, the pattern of my days was set. To pay for my passage and food, I learned the tasks of the Hindmost crew of the *Silver Fox*, Karolus Registry. If these included some I suspected Morgan dreamed up just to keep me out of his way, I wasn't about to argue. I healed at the same time, climbing into my hammock each night cycle too exhausted to dream.

Not that Morgan was idle. He divided his time among three occupations: studying journey tapes purchased from other traders (looking for opportunities, or checking for changes in language or culture since his last visit), endlessly fine-tuning the controls and engines of the *Fox,* and patiently (and not-so-patiently) helping me find my way around his ship.

It was the helping part, I decided, which tended to plant that frown between Morgan's brows. This was my third shipday since Auord. We were in the anteroom which led to the main hold. Though completely walled on three sides by lockable storage compartments for less bulky cargo, the tiny room efficiently contained enough space for a desk and viewer table. It was Morgan's office for bookkeeping and other trade-based work, and now my study chamber. Morgan tapped a finger on the stack of tapes next to my hand.

"Correct me if I'm wrong, Hindmost Sira Morgan," his tone making me want to cringe. "Aren't these the ones I gave you yesterday?"

I looked at the offending stack carefully, covering a pair of tapes definitely not on my study program with a casual elbow, hoping the acrid disinfectants in the room wouldn't start my nose running again. "I've been busy, Captain."

The finger tapped again. "Didn't you agree to review these basic procedures?" Maybe I was imagining a growing frustration in his voice. "I don't have the time to teach you what you could pick up from the tapes, even if that were part of our bargain."

I shared Morgan's disappointment in my progress, but couldn't bring myself to explain. Reluctantly, I reached for the first tape in the pile, this one, as the others, gray-stained and worn from years of use. These were likely Morgan's own; no wonder he thought me ungrateful.

Morgan thrust a long arm past my nose and snatched up the tapes I'd hidden. He read the labeling silently. My face grew hot.

The captain of the *Fox* pulled the chair from his desk and sank into it. "You could have told me, chit," he said almost wistfully. "It's nothing to be ashamed of—"

"No?" I glared at him.

"Have these helped?" He held up the language tapes I'd stumbled upon in desperation.

"No," I admitted.

Morgan rose and went over to the tape storage. He selected five tapes and returned to me. "Try these."

I inserted the first one into the machine. Instead of meaningless text sprawled over the tabletop, a ship's cargo bay formed itself, similar to the one behind the massive door at my back. A voice began to recite, in unaccented Comspeak, the procedure for hold decontamination. I halted the presentation and stared at my hands. "Thank you, Captain." I knew my voice lacked enthusiasm.

"Not every spacer reads Trade script, chit," Morgan said matter-of-factly, as he gathered up the other tapes and filed them. "Regulations call for ships to carry visteach tapes as well." He paused and I looked up. "Neither of us know what your life was like before, Kissue. But if you want to learn to crew on a starship, you have to work together with others, which at the moment is me. Crew is closer than kin—it has to be. Don't hesitate to tell when you need help with something again."

Some hard, tight place inside eased ever so slightly as I listened. "I'm sorry, Captain."

His voice became gruff. "Just finish these tapes today.

I've enough to worry about without wondering if you're going to blow an air lock cleaning the vents." As Morgan was leaving, he turned. I halted the tape and waited. "And if you need help?"

"I'll ask," I promised. Blue eyes assessed my sincerity and then he nodded.

"See that you do. Just start simple and you'll be okay."

"Start simple. Fine advice," I muttered to myself, taking my time entering the door codes on the wall pad. What could go wrong with cargo hold maintenance? I'd thought the same about refilling the servo-kitchen—that less than pleasant memory made me glance anxiously back into the main hold.

The door consulted with itself, digesting my instructions with sullen clicks. I peered into the hold again, eyeing the rows of plas crates and bags suspiciously. The unfortunate eruption in the galley had followed a similar feeling of accomplishment. I stared at the door indicators, calculating. There should be enough time.

Dashing back into the hold, I went to the load I had re-arranged, and tugged at the straps securing it to the wall. By jumping up, I could hook my fingers into the overhead straps, breathing clouds of moisture into the chilled, odorless air. They bore my weight without sagging. Satisfied, I let go and turned to leave, only to smack into the closed door panel. A peaceful whirring sound began, signaling the removal of air from the hold—standard procedure to kill vermin. I should know; I'd coded in the instructions.

I didn't want to see Morgan's face when he found out—of course, the odds were I'd get my wish. I rushed to the pad on this side of the door, hesitated with fingers outstretched and shaking. What was the opening code? I forced myself to breathe more slowly, calmly, trying to ignore the sound of the pumps as I concentrated on the number sequence. There. I entered the last number, only to have a second door panel slide into place before my eyes.

No more time for mistakes; I couldn't seem to fill my lungs now no matter how deeply I breathed. I looked around hurriedly, spotting the outlines of a locker to the left of the door. Keeping one steadying hand on the panel, I fought to lift my feet, my legs growing loose and weak. My fingers clutched a proper handle—not another servo-mech to argue with, thank Ossirus. I pulled, half-falling in the process.

Bless Morgan, and his tapes, I added a moment later, drawing huge breaths from the helmet of the evac-suit. I closed my eyes, wanting to savor the simple act of survival. No fresh spring air could smell better than this stale, human-enriched stuff.

With the helmet locked over my head, and the suit sealed as per instructions, I closed up the closet and returned to the puzzle of the door. The index finger of each glove bore a short, blunt nail, sized to fit the keys of the wall pad.

This time, without panic to crowd my mind, I remembered the proper sequence and entered it. The inner door retracted. An indicator showed the reversal of the pumps, returning atmosphere to the hold. I leaned a bulky elbow against the nearest carton to wait, still enjoying the acrid taste of the suit's air supply, content to have survived at least one mistake unnoticed.

Not that Morgan made much of my occasional slips, I thought, honesty overcoming my embarrassment, though he'd been a bit testy about the minor flood in the aft corridor (which hadn't really been my fault, since the plumbing was ship-original). The outer door swished open, and I removed the helmet quickly, half-expecting to see the captain of the *Fox* standing there with brows slightly and eloquently lifted.

This time the only witness to my folly was the portlight hovering with servo idiocy over the wall pad I'd used to lock myself in the hold. I waved it to its shelf, annoyed, then summoned it back again. I didn't need to make another mistake. I made sure I replaced the suit exactly as I'd found it.

The door closed, the indicators read complete vacuum, and I sighed, done at last. Why did everything have to be difficult, no matter how long I hunched over the tape table? None of my nodes of memory held anything about ships or machines. It was equally hard to bear Morgan's patient instruction and tolerance.

I shook myself mentally, tired of self-pity. I was fed, clothed, and beyond the reach of whatever danger had chased me through Auord's dark streets. And, far from being a slave, I was learning a trade, albeit with frustrating slowness. My calluses were well-earned, I decided, examining the palms of my hands with an odd pride. I'd be a spacer yet, qualified to scrub floors and shift cargo with any crew.

After one final look, I sent the portlight to its resting place, done with time to spare. I headed for the galley, inclined to celebrate my success—and survival. When I arrived, I stuck my head around the corner cautiously. Morgan wasn't there. Refusing to acknowledge I was relieved, I went to the console and selected a hearty soup.

I sat at the narrow table and sniffed the aroma drifting from the cup appreciatively, then frowned into the steam. The smell was familiar, tantalizing, echoing a dim memory of another place, a place open to a crisp mauve sky. My empty hand curled as if around a warm round of bread. The memory diffused and vanished.

As I tried in vain to recapture it, I noticed the wall screens were again set for a view of some section of space, stars wheeling in a gently accelerated movement. I put my back to them, definitely not spacer enough to enjoy that view with my meal.

My thoughts turned to the present. I went over my success, feeling a peculiar contentment—a contentment which extended to where I was, and with whom. Morgan. I almost trusted him—certainly I respected his love of this ship. I fished a large piece of something from my soup and popped it between my teeth. The texture was odd, but when I bit down, the taste said meat.

I knew why I was contented. It was my past, whether the image of Roraqk or the hazy blankness of before, that made me unhappy or uncomfortable. Morgan spoke to me only of the operation of the *Fox,* accepting my presence on his ship as my only claim to existence, which, in fact, it was. I was "chit" or "Hindmost," or, rarely, some more emotional appellation. It raised a most comforting wall.

In return, I kept certain questions to myself. Morgan didn't volunteer his past. Several areas of the ship were off-limits to me, including the control room—a wise decision, based on what I'd already accomplished in less critical areas.

I finished and gave my tray back to the servo unit, out of habit nodding politely when it thanked me. Viewed from this side of dinner, things had gone rather well this morning. In fact, I faced the first moment of leisure I'd had since coming on board the *Fox*. I should decide how to enjoy it. Leaning back, I lifted my feet to the tabletop and contemplated my surroundings. A mistake.

The galley was ten paces long and five paces wide, most of that table and seats. Morgan could touch the ceiling with his hand. Behind me, I knew those stars whirled through an empty blackness. Ahead, the oval door showed only the far wall of the corridor, brightly lit and stark. Only an outline beside the servo unit revealed the entrance to my corner of the *Fox,* the galley's storage cubby.

I noticed the taste of the air for the first time: clean enough to smart, metallic on the back of my tongue. I shook my head to dismiss the notion, making an effort to see the walls as protective rather than enclosing, to feel the galley as cozy rather than close. It was so difficult to fight my growing claustrophobia I began to wonder about Morgan. How could anyone willingly live in such a box, especially alone? Yet I knew Morgan usually flew the *Fox* single-handed, and made no provision to carry passengers.

If this was part of a spacer's life, I'd better learn to like it. Planetfall on Ret 7 was close and it, as every one I'd face in the future, would give Morgan an opportunity to leave me behind. And I had to stay here, I knew, alarmed at the mere thought of leaving the *Fox* or her captain. I was safe here; I had to stay with Morgan. But would Morgan let me?

* * *

INTERLUDE

Morgan drummed his fingers lightly on the panel. The com light winked from yellow to green as the connection was accepted.

"Morgan here," he said.

"Bowman," the voice introduced itself, a warning bite to the word even through the com. Morgan settled deeper in his chair, glancing around to be sure the control room door was locked behind him.

"And what can I do for you, Commander?" Morgan kept his voice casual, as between friends.

There was a delay before her answer, as though Bowman was taken aback. More likely, Morgan decided, she was clamping down on her temper. "It appears you left Auord with something I've been looking for, Morgan."

So the helpful Enforcer at the shipcity had been a spy after all, Morgan thought to himself in disgust, or else there had been other eyes watching the *Fox*—and Sira's arrival. "I have quite a wide selection of cargo, this trip, Commander," he said, truthfully. "Anything in particular?"

"Don't play games with me, Morgan," her voice now coldly precise. "I know you have the woman on the *Fox*. You took her from Auord—right under my nose. Why?"

Morgan's lip twisted in a sneer, and he was glad he'd never bothered to install a vis-com. "It wasn't Pact business."

"It damn well was and is my business! Now, Morgan." He grinned at the reasoning tone which suddenly crept into Bowman's voice; she must have remembered their comlink would last only as long as he wished. "You aren't planning to up the tab on this one, are you? I've a budget—"

Morgan's grin faded. He thought of Sira's face when she'd first boarded, the shocking brightness of blood etched against the pale skin of her cheek, the desperate need to trust in her eyes. She worked hard, mistakes or not. He wasn't a fool. He knew she was trying to prove herself to him, to win a place on the *Fox*.

His hand reached for the com panel before he stopped himself, shaking his head. What was he thinking? Instead, he made his fingers into a fist and brought it down by the com slowly enough to keep it soundless. "No," he said, but to what, he wondered.

"Good," Bowman answered with apparent relief. "You've matched orbits with me before, Morgan, and been quiet about it, too. I don't mind telling you that this passenger of yours could be just what I need to open some eyes about Clan meddling. What's your next planetfall?"

Morgan's eyes flickered to where the yellow edge of the current trip tape protruded from the control panel. It would be easy to flip it out, insert another. Easy and pointless. They were deep in Trade Pact space; Bowman would find him. Besides, profit was what he was after, wasn't it? "Ret 7," Morgan said. "This shipday."

"Good." A cat's purr. "You can drop her at Malacan's—"

"Sira's not some cargo to be dumped—" The moment the words left his lips, Morgan wished he could grab them back.

"Sira?" Bowman's voice became guarded, suspicious. "Are you sure you can trust yourself, Morgan? What exactly is your situation?"

Morgan swore silently. "I'm the closest thing you have to an expert on the Clan, Bowman. I haven't been *influenced,* if that's what you're worried about." He hesitated, then went on, knowing it was useless. "She's not what I expected—"

"I'll find out for myself. Thank you, Captain. You know what to do. Bowman out."

Morgan tilted his head back, examining the ceiling. "I promised her freedom," he finished to himself a long moment later, aware of a pain whose power quite astonished him. His only defense was to refuse to name it.

Chapter 8

I STOOD on the *Fox*'s ramp, shivering in the moldy dampness, peering curiously up at the faint disk which was all the clouds revealed of Ret 7's feeble sun. The morning's rush of cargo handlers was already underway. From where I stood, I could see spacers pounding down the ramps of neighboring ships, joining a growing crowd aimed at the shipcity gates, all out to commandeer local transports so they could get to the native city before the rain started again.

Self-conscious, I tugged to straighten my coveralls, glancing over my shoulder to check if Morgan had re-opened the portal for any last minute instruction. He hadn't; the door remained sealed against the ever-present damp-ness. "Miserable little hole," Morgan had said, dismissing Ret 7; I had to agree.

It didn't help that there wasn't a proper shipcity. The docking tugs plunked starships anywhere along this stretch of the road leading into Jershi, the native capital. At least the Retians had the sense to make some pavement—other-wise the starships would be ramp deep in the ooze the na-tives loved so much.

Had I ever been on this world before, tasted its rain on my lips, pulled its heavy air into my lungs? Had I . . . I gave myself a stern mental shake, dismayed to be day-dreaming when Morgan needed my help; I couldn't afford to miss this chance to prove myself, not if I wanted to be-come crew on the *Fox*.

I dodged among larger beings, all jostling for a better position in line. The others seemed to take my darting around them good-naturedly enough; perhaps I looked the part of a spacer well enough to pass. Morgan had advised me to be early—he wanted me to rent one of the few manual craft available. The *Fox*'s cargo profit was not sufficient to be squandered on servocraft.

Lucky again. A stubborn wisp of fog parted on the same cumbersome-looking groundcar we'd rented yesterday, parked close to the ramshackle gate marking the edge of the shipcity. Its owner, a lackluster native of few words and potent odor, grunted with annoyance as I approached.

"Not you again," she complained in excellent Comspeak, eyeing the tokens in my hand but not reaching for them. "What your captain paid barely covered fuel. What about the wear and abuse you put my poor vehicle through, what about—"

"What about its faulty air-treatment system?" I countered very loudly. "Yesterday we had to drive through the Rissh Marshes with the top open!" The town of Jershi and its surrounding wetland smelled high to humanoid noses at the best of times. The sudden lack of interest from the spacers standing behind me brought a scowl to her wizened features. There had, of course, been no such problem. Two protruding brown eyes blinked.

"The system's been repaired, Spacer," she lied equally loudly.

" 'Bout time," I said, straight-faced, but triumphant. "Here's our rental, in advance. The captain will have it back by sixth bell."

"Fourth bell, and without a scratch!" She snatched my currency and waddled away, bare feet slapping the mud, toadlike and gray among the taller, predominantly Human spacers.

"More spare parts for His Lordship's toy, Morgan?" The jeering voice was clear over the sounds of bargaining and motor starts.

"*Fox*'s business, not yours, chit," I said righteously over my shoulder, unsure of who had spoken at first. Then I spotted the somewhat brighter blue of a crewman from *Ryan's Venture* standing by the vehicle lined up next to mine.

Morgan had told me something of the *Venture,* and her captain, Ariva Ivali, after our landing. It pleased him immensely to be docked fin-to-fin with the larger and much newer ship. As Morgan put it, he and Ivali were competitors—a rivalry that was familiar, if not overly friendly.

I didn't expect their encounter on Ret 7 to improve the relationship. Apparently, *Venture* had preceded us here by several weeks, and was struggling to unload enough cargo to pay her costs, let alone make some profit. Morgan, on the other hand, had no sooner settled the *Fox* after docking than a buyer named Malacan Ser called. Hom Ser was the agent for the local ruler, Lord Lispetc. And his Lordship was desperate for Morgan's posted cargo—repair components. Damp rot was not kind to the delicate innards of expensive offworld com systems. That the new components would ultimately fail, and for the same reason, didn't seem to matter at all.

Morgan told me all this with a surprising lack of enthusiasm. He was so glum, in fact, that I hesitated to congratulate him. I put it down to frustration that he hadn't stuffed every hold of the *Fox* with com components.

Putting all this to the back of my mind, I slipped into the groundcar, happy to be outside despite a tendency to distrust anything not of the *Fox*. As I drove back to the ship, contentedly whistling a light little tune whose words I couldn't remember, it was easy to imagine I was already part of her crew, not just an inconvenient passenger lending a hand. The thought had considerable charm; it would be wonderful to stay Sira Morgan, spacer, a real person with a place of her own.

I guided the groundcar to a spot alongside the ramp, slightly surprised to see the larger hemicircle of the hold door was still sealed. The afternoon rain clouds were piling up in the sky, but probably wouldn't spill anything for an hour or so. As a precaution, I left the roof up on the car before calling to the *Fox* to open the inset crew door.

Morgan was waiting for me inside the air lock; he was holding a thin plas pack in one hand. I halted, eyeing it and him suspiciously, before asking: "Do you want me to help you load the cargo?"

"No. Something's come up, and I have to stay on board. But you can do something for me. There's an important package I need delivered." He paused. "It's not far, on the near edge of town. I've drawn you a map."

I considered several less-than-tactful remarks and regretfully shelved them, in light of the unusual tightness around Morgan's mouth. Quietly, I took the plas sheet he handed me and glanced over it. "Malacan's Fine Exports," I read out loud. "Fourth block, Trade Quarter."

"Give this package to Malacan Ser himself, and no one else. Wait for him to open it," Morgan said, then stopped, looking at me. "He'll have some further instructions for you, Sira. I want you to do whatever he says."

My stomach lurched under my heart and I tasted bile at the back of my throat. "What?" I whispered, swallowing hard.

Morgan's voice sharpened. "Wasn't I clear, chit? Now hurry. Hom Ser is waiting."

I found my voice again. "Let him wait! I don't take orders."

Morgan's eyes were as remote as distant stars, his lips a thin, forbidding line. We stared at each other for a long moment. He broke the silence first. "I thought you said you wanted to learn how to be crew. Changed your mind already?"

"No!" I protested quickly. "No. Of course not. I just don't understand," I finished lamely, wishing he wasn't acting so odd.

Morgan didn't soften, as I thought he might. Instead, he handed me the small package for Malacan and an even smaller bag of local currency. "While you're gone, I'll be packing up His Lordship's order," he said, as I tucked these into a pocket and resealed the seam. Morgan paused. "You're sure you can handle the groundcar on the in-town road?"

I nodded. Feeling strangely miserable, I turned to leave, refusing to acknowledge any misgivings by prolonging the conversation. I reached for the door control only to have Morgan's tanned hand arrive first, holding it closed. I twisted to look up at him.

Morgan removed his hand, staring at it, disconcerted. "What is it, Captain?" I asked quietly, after a moment's silence. "What haven't you told me?"

His face was carefully controlled, unreadable, but his eyes betrayed him. I gazed into their blue depths, searching for anything else there but pity. I blinked rapidly, wrenching my own eyes away to focus on the deck. This was it; I knew without words. Morgan was leaving me behind—here, now, with this Malacan Ser, on this repulsive, soggy planet. I should have expected it. I should have—

"Sira—"

"It's all right," I said too quickly, cutting off his now distress-filled voice, not wanting any more lies. "I can follow orders."

Morgan tilted my chin so he could see my face. "I didn't plan this, Sira," he said. "I want you to know—"

I struck away his hand. "Didn't plan what, Captain Morgan? For me to be valuable cargo? Aren't you a trader? And how convenient—I can even deliver myself! That is why you tried to trick me into going, isn't it?"

Morgan leaned one elbow on the bulkhead above his head and sighed. "Maybe I thought it'd be easier. Which doesn't change a thing, Sira—you must go to Malacan. Now."

"You said I should make my own choices."

I might have struck him; his face paled, and red spots appeared on each cheek. "I know what I said."

"Was that a lie?"

"No." Morgan ran one hand through his hair. "No. It was just—optimistic." He shook his head. "Sira, you have to go. If you stay, they'll simply come to the *Fox* and collect you. At least, by going, you've made something of a choice. It might help."

"I'll go," I said flatly, then challenged him. "If you sign me on as crew."

Morgan stood up straight, eyes full of speculation. "Why?"

"Crew," I insisted. "By your own rules, that makes you responsible for me, Captain Morgan, on ship or off."

Morgan smiled very slowly, an unpleasant and humorless stretching of lips that I somehow knew was not aimed at me. "Why not?" he asked himself. "Why not. Ship's recorder on," he ordered more briskly. "Record Sira Morgan as current crew—assigned ashore, Ret 7, under Captain's orders. Recorder pause." He looked at me for a moment. "You have to accept the contract," he said. "Recorder on—"

"Contract accepted by Sira Morgan," I told the air firmly.

"Recorder off," Morgan finished, holding out his hand. "Welcome aboard, Sira."

"Profit and safe journey, Captain," I said, gripping his hand as long as I dared, not saying what I wanted to say, but not having the words ready either. There was a blurriness to my vision which threatened to spill at any time.

My anger was long since faded. It hadn't been deep; under it I fought to contain a horrid dizziness—afraid I was losing myself again. I gripped reality desperately.

"Safe journey," Morgan echoed. "I hope you find your answers, Sira." He opened the door.

I blinked rapidly, trying to ignore the tears that made a prickly trail over each cheek, and stepped backward out onto the ramp. The air lock slid closed in my face, sealing Morgan within the *Fox*—excluding me. Answers? What an empty thing to want.

I drove the groundcar away from the *Fox,* threading it among the cluster of ships, bumping off the pavement that ended at the gates onto the mud slick the Retians optimistically called a road. It was a "convenience" for offworlders. Off the road, as far as the eye could see, which wasn't far given the gloom, were innumerable bobbing shapes moving steadily and occasionally quite rapidly across the flat marshland. The native form of transportation, variously called a multi-terrain vehicle, mudcrawler, or can-of-toads depending on one's preference and company, was a kind of floating tank having both treads and repellers. They worked best on the skin of water which coated the marsh mudflats. Mudcrawlers were not for everyone. The Retian vehicles lacked any shielding; they enjoyed interacting with their environment—whether rain, wave, or mud.

I gritted my teeth at the odd noises coming from my vehicle as I joined the city-bound congestion. The ancient groundcar didn't care much for stop/start traffic, grumbling much like its owner. I fidgeted, tapping my fingers on the control stick, contemplating what lay ahead. I couldn't see the city from here. No loss. Retian architecture ran to lumpy buildings squatting in stagnant water.

Morgan's sheet of directions I had already crumpled and tossed in the back. Now that the *Fox* had me listed as crew, I thought smugly, all I had to do was to order the ship to let me back inside. It shouldn't be too hard to keep out of Morgan's way until lift. I'd worry about convincing him to let me stay later. I began to look for a chance to pull out of traffic and turn around.

A few moments later, my palm slipped on the control stick, suddenly damp with sweat. I stared at it, unsure what was happening. Compulsion? No, this wasn't that familiar sense of someone else's decision pushing on my will. What I felt now was more a vague apprehension, that turning my head fast enough would catch something lurking behind—something with teeth. The hair on the back of my neck rose with the gooseflesh on my skin.

So I didn't like Ret 7. The *Fox* would be lifting off soon. And if Morgan gave me any trouble, there were other ships.

No. I shook my head, automatically slowing to a stop with the traffic, alert for my chance to pull out and turn around. Strange, I was certain this feeling came from outside myself.

It was a warning of some kind. A warning from . . .

Morgan! At the very instant I associated his name with the formless anxiety I was feeling, a sleek aircar roared past overhead. Had they traffic control on Ret 7, which I doubted, its pilot would have permanently lost his or her clearance immediately. What mattered more was my totally irrational conviction that Morgan was in the rapidly departing vehicle—and against his will.

I gunned the old groundcar to its maximum output, pulling out of line in front of a huge transport that careened off the road to avoid me. I slipped off the road myself for a moment, taking a mad swerving course through the mud with a skill that owed much to luck. I bumped back up on the pavement, ignoring the shouting behind me. My first duty was to see to the *Fox*.

Her ports were locked, but the smaller door answered to my hoarse command as I'd hoped. I secured it behind me, heading immediately for the control room. I could tell he was gone; the ship felt deserted.

The forbidden control room door obeyed my voice, too.

Timidly, I stepped inside, looking around me at what was, after all, a simple and ordinary room, familiar from the vistapes I'd studied. Two worn-looking couches waited before duplicate control panels, the left couch with a tray from the galley still hovering alongside one arm. I could smell hot jaffa and noticed steam curling from Morgan's cup.

Shaking my head, I perched myself on the copilot's couch. The seat startled me by curling up on itself to offer a firm support to my back. I pursued my lips, eyeing the complex panels in confusion. There were columns of buttons and toggles whose functions I could only guess. Ah. I recognized the com control with some satisfaction.

But there was nothing to give me a clue about Morgan.

I forced myself to think. I didn't know Morgan's business. But I'd paid close attention to what he'd told me about Ret 7 during our approach. I knew, for instance, that Morgan had visited this world before, and that he had shipped the com parts because of the interest shown by the Retian priesthood during that earlier visit.

I frowned, remembering. Yesterday, Morgan had taken me along when he'd met with the priests, trying to explain why the cargo they'd thought was theirs had already been sold and taking orders for his next passage through their system. At the time, I hadn't thought much of it, beyond deciding Morgan must have a trading strategy I couldn't yet fathom.

The priests had stood watching us leave, their wide lips pressed into wavy blue lines that conveyed frustrated anger by any being's standards.

I suspected there was more to the deal with Malacan Ser and His Lordship than Morgan had told me. I was uncomfortable at the thought that logically followed. Was it me?

A question to ask Morgan—when and if I found him.

The ship was in order, ports locked, security set. Morgan must have gone voluntarily, if quickly. Therefore he had been led to the aircar by someone he knew and at least partially trusted. It was a guess, but a reasonable one, I hoped, that Morgan had been taken from the *Fox* by the priests, who probably had some justification in believing that precious cargo of com parts belonged to them.

Trust. I smiled grimly to myself. I'd learned that lesson. Trust was something I'd grant no one, especially anyone here—including Morgan's Malacan Ser. There was only myself, the *Fox,* and, to some uncertain extent, Morgan.

As plans go, mine possessed the virtues of simplicity and boldness, if little else. Once prepared, I locked the *Fox* and loaded the groundcar, aware of a chill inside which had nothing to do with the damp air of the surrounding marshland.

I set the vehicle's controls to maintain course and sat, chin on fist, staring at the faintly glowing comlink as if to will Morgan to action. If he somehow eluded his captors, he might try to leave a message with the ship. By linking the *Fox*'s main com to this transport's frequency, I hoped to receive any such attempt as well. I tapped the silent com once, for luck, having to trust I'd done it right. It was definitely unsettling to always feel I was doing things for the first time.

The road I chose climbed steadily, its surface becoming firmer and drier as it rose above the wetlands girdling Jershi and the "so-called" shipcity. The vegetation, sparse as it was, changed at the same time, from endless vistas of reed grass, bent by yesterday's winds, to scattered desperate shrubs. There were no settlements here. I suspected the Retians were partly amphibious. Certainly, they preferred to locate their cities and businesses in the center of marshes—the wetter the better. It was a speculation impossible to verify: Questions about life cycle details of other species were impolite at best, and I wasn't sure I wanted to know more about Retians anyway.

These cooler, relatively drier, uplands were more to my taste. They also happened to be the only location where the Retians could employ their imported technology with any reliability. I was heading for the oldest and largest of these installations, one which housed a mammoth data storage unit maintained by the religious caste. Data storage was essential to Retian religion, Morgan had explained, because every ritual required knowing each individual's degree of relatedness to every other living (or dead) Retian. This knowledge determined the right to own land, among other privileges. It was a system rumored to have baffled the computer techs assigned to prepare the installation. Since the priesthood controlled the sale of land, the system neatly precluded immigration, in the unlikely instance that a non-Retian would desire to settle here. Certainly I had no ambitions in that direction.

I turned a corner and the massive building lay below me, its gray-and-brown stone blending at the edges into the native rock walls of the valley. Its relatively dry location was probably unintended by its original builders. There were abundant signs that this hollow had once been as waterlogged as Jershi itself, planet centuries ago. I pulled the groundcar up to a large, unornamented door.

The air was hushed, oppressively humid; the afternoon

rains were close. I stopped where Morgan had parked yesterday, the engine of the groundcar sighing as if relieved.

Yesterday, the instant we had arrived, curious junior priests had thronged around us, bustling and eager to see if we carried the parts needed for their holy machine. I'd found them repulsive, with their loose skin and pawing hands, and kept close to the transport while Morgan was inside, discussing trade with their superiors.

I couldn't see any natives now, and my heart beat faster.

I reached into the carryroll on the passenger seat. By feel, I checked the location of the package sealer, a somewhat unconventional weapon, but the only portable device on the *Fox* not locked under Morgan's seal. Tucked around the sealer were plas-coated computer components, hardly state-of-the-art but advanced enough to impress, I hoped.

The only visible door into the building, a mammoth affair of stone and metal, opened very slowly and silently. Without looking directly at that gap, I lifted up a handful of the glittering components, letting them trickle from one hand to another. My mouth was dry despite the humidity. Guesswork. Hunches. An empty mind shocked into delusion. I could be propelling myself into a situation I couldn't handle, for no reason at all.

But just as I could smell an unfamiliar herb in the breeze, as I could taste the dampness of the storm-laden air, I knew Morgan was near. Perhaps his peculiar "gift" was calling to me. More likely, the compulsion urging me to be near him was at last being useful.

"What are you doing here, Trader?" None of the elaborate courtesy I remembered from my first visit, but at least the priest used Comspeak. I chose my words carefully.

"I wish to trade, Honored Sir. I know of your need for certain supplies—"

The door gaped wider, now revealing a trio of senior priests, robed in red. The leftmost one spoke. "Your captain had traded elsewhere. How can you, an underthing, speak of trade to us?"

I dropped the components into my bag and dared to climb out. "Part of my apprenticeship, Honored Sir, is to use my judgment and share of cargo to make my own deals. If I wish to advance, I have to prove myself. Is it not so with your junior priests?"

"Let us see what you offer." This from the center priest.

"Not out here," I said firmly. "The moisture."

A whispered consultation, then their heads bobbed in unison. Hoping that meant yes, I held the bag tightly and followed them inside.

It was the kind of place where one imagined generations of alterations and additions, done with or without knowledge of earlier plans—all conspiring together into this present-day maze of a structure. I had no doubt that there were different shapes hidden beneath its floors and behind its crisply cornered walls. I followed my guides past dark doorways and empty cubbyholes, through odd tangential junctions. So much for searching for Morgan on my own.

Our destination was a large room with five unequal walls, each lined with plas-protected instruments mounted on sturdy shelves. Several of the instruments were dark and silent. There were no windows; light glowed from imported fixtures of very old design. The floor was beautiful, deliberately uneven, etched in a complex design that wove in and around our feet like ripples on water. It was the nearest thing to an art form I'd seen on Ret 7. I hoped my boots were clean.

"Now we will examine your offerings."

"Trade items, Honored Sir," I corrected cautiously. "With more available." I took out a handful of components and placed them on a five-legged table. Two of the priests hurried forward to pick them up in their limp hands, talking animatedly to each other in their native tongue.

"How much?" said the third priest, not even glancing at the table or his colleagues. I wished I could read some understandable emotion on his wrinkled, wide-mouthed face. His eyes blinked, one at a time.

"These are a gift, Honored Sir." Instantly the table was cleared of its contents. The priests must have tucked them up their sleeves. I took a tighter grip on the bag. "I have many more."

"How much?"

"My captain," I said very quietly, drawing out the package sealer. It looked deadly, with several sharp protrusions and a formidable muzzle. "And safe passage back to our ship."

The Retians conferred again. Then the spokesman asked: "Are you threatening us?"

In answer, I dropped the bag on the table. "No. The *Fox* honors its contracts. Here are the components you need. You don't need my captain. It's a fair trade."

"You are alone." True. The priests were learning fast.

Out the corner of my eye I could see movement in the hallway. I took a quick step back and aimed my improvised weapon at the nearest operational machine. The Retians signaled frantically with their webbed hands to someone behind me, the blue of their lips turning pink with agitation. "I don't want trouble," I said, trying to keep my voice steady and controlled despite a growing fear that they would refuse to bargain—or worse, as a Human might, decide I was bluffing.

Silence, then a brief command from the spokesman sent his companions pushing through the throng of gray-robed junior priests hovering in the doorway. No further movement or sound; they were like statues. What was happening? Were they bringing Morgan—or killing him? I refused to doubt that he was here.

It was only a few minutes, but it seemed an eternity, before I heard a dry rustle of cloth followed by the parting of the crowd in the doorway. I almost sagged with relief at the sight of a figure, head covered in a white hood, towering shoulders above his Retian escort.

"We accept your trade," the priest said, eyes fixed on the bag on the table. 'Take him." Morgan's escorts shoved him toward me. Blind, he stumbled on the uneven flooring before regaining his balance.

"What's going on, Ruptis?" Morgan demanded in a commendably calm voice. "This is no way to conduct—" he stopped in mid-sentence, his hooded head turning until it faced my direction.

How could he—? I spoke quickly before Morgan could say the wrong thing and ruin a plan that was working remarkably well, all things considered. "Our agreement, Honored Sir, includes safe passage for my captain and myself back to our ship."

I needn't have worried. Ruptis and his fellow priests were clustered about the table, chuckling and pawing the

bag's contents as if it were treasure. To them, I supposed
it was. The junior priests had vanished.

Sealer in one hand, I moved quickly to where Morgan
stood abandoned. His hands were stuck together in front
of him with some plasterlike material laced through his
fingers. There was nothing I could do about that now. I
reached up and pulled off the hood. He blinked in the dim
light, then looked down at me with astonishment. I put a
finger in front of my lips and he nodded.

The Retians were already busily at work, one stripping
plas from the new components while two opened their
damaged instruments and rummaged within. Their lips
were almost purple with delight. I decided not to ask for a
guide.

"I can't get this off here, Captain," I whispered to Morgan, indicating his bound hands.

Morgan looked at the Retians, then at the components
on the table, then at me. He began to frown. "Are those—"

"I'll explain later," I interrupted. "I suggest leaving."

Morgan glanced at my weapon and his lips quirked.
"Before we have to use that," he agreed solemnly, well
aware that sealer was about as dangerous as a floor scrub-
ber. "Lead on, chit."

Once in the hall, I paused to remember the route before
choosing to go left. Morgan followed in trusting silence.
This was too simple, something said inside me.

Morgan's low-pitched voice startled me. "The Retians
have a different set of ethics for each caste," he said, as if
reading my thoughts. "Ruptis can climb within his priesthood by repairing the holy machines; his methods won't
be questioned by the other castes, including the civil government. And our paying customer, Lord Lispetc."

Ignoring the last, which was unfair considering the options I had, I remained uneasy. "The priests know they've
committed a crime punishable by non-Retian law. You
could have this world's license lifted."

"Maybe," Morgan answered in a noncommittal voice.
"Though I doubt the Trade Pact has been strained by my
inconvenient detention here. Ruptis knows our politics as
well as his own. Besides," he continued, in a lighter tone,
"we've completed a fair trade, chit."

I didn't bother to answer, since Morgan was speaking
for the benefit of any eavesdroppers. We reached the sec-

tion of the building where the hallway was irregularly broadened by the presence of numerous cubbyholes.

When I had first passed this way, the cubbyholes had been empty. Now, crammed into each like so much package stuffing, were gray-robed junior priests. I stopped, my skin crawling.

"It's all right, Sira," Morgan said quietly, coming to stand behind me. "This is how they wait until needed." Then, I noticed what I hadn't before. Their bulbous eyes were closed by inner, semi-opaque lids. Squeezed together as many as ten to each closet-sized space, the poor creatures couldn't move a muscle until the outermost wriggled and popped free. I began walking again, a trifle more briskly. I found the Retians even less appealing stuffed.

I was ahead, Morgan once more following, when I heard a scuffle behind and his shout: "Run, Sira!" I whirled, fumbling with the package sealer. The last cubby had been vacant, a fact which should have alerted me, but didn't. Now it was a doorway through which two scarlet-robed priests had pounced on Morgan. He heaved them off even as I turned, the material of his coverall ripping from his back in the hands of one of them. Forgetting my weapon was only for show, I ran back, brandishing it and yelling at the top of my lungs. The combination drove them scuttling back through the hidden door.

Like pickled corpses, the hordes of junior priests didn't stir from their positions. Morgan jerked his head toward the now-visible main door. "Hurry," he said, shouldering me ahead, moving rapidly in spite of his awkwardly tied hands. "Let's not give them time to get organized."

As I pushed open the massive outer door, the roar of heavy rain filled my ears. You could set a timer by Retian weather, I thought with disgust, stepping outside and instantly becoming soaked to the skin. Morgan lent the strength of his shoulder to mine to close the door again—as a delaying tactic, it was more moral support than otherwise, but I didn't waste breath arguing. My feet slipped in fresh mud.

"Why aren't they following us?" I demanded, perplexed, as I fastened the groundcar's roof and listened to the muffled pounding of rain on its surface. I'd left it open and the seats were soaking wet. I began powering up the machine, wishing Morgan could drive.

"They don't need to," was Morgan's strange reply. "I hope there's some speed in this pile of junk," he continued, breathing in odd little bursts as though the exertion of climbing into the passenger seat had been too much to bear. I whirled to stare at him.

The dim light in the Retian building had disguised the waxiness of his skin; sweat, not raindrops, beaded his forehead. "I'll live," he snapped, aware of my scrutiny, "provided you get us back to the *Fox*."

Obediently, I sent the groundcar forward through the deepening puddles, keeping one eye on the fuel gauge and the other on the barely distinct borders of the road. My heart was hammering louder than the rain on the roof over our heads. "What's wrong?" I demanded. "What did they do to you?"

Morgan leaned against the side of the transport, bound arms pressed tightly against his flat middle as if to soothe an ache. He looked weary and too pale. "I don't think I mentioned the Retians are poisonous, did I? The older males have a little claw, like a spur, at the base of each thumb."

I accelerated as much as I dared, given the distance we had left to travel. "You mustn't die, Morgan," I told him flatly. Risking a sidelong glance, I saw that his eyes were closing. "Jason!"

Morgan roused enough to look at me, eyes fighting to focus. "Although living doesn't feel like such a bargain at the moment, chit, I don't think I'll die just yet." As a reassurance, it was less than convincing. Morgan went on: "I stocked the *Fox* with antivenom after my last run here. Should have taken some myself yesterday, when things began to get shaky—couldn't give you any—couldn't involve you anyway—" his voice began fading in and out; I strained to catch what he was saying.

Then, with sudden costly clarity: "Sira. Take the *Fox* to Plexis. She's ready; tape's set for auto. If I'm—if you're on your own, find Huido Maarmatoo'kk—he'll help you. Don't go near Malacan. Don't—" With a shudder that told of overtaxed muscles giving up a struggle, Morgan slumped, held upright in his seat only by its harness.

I gripped the steering column tightly, forcing myself to

concentrate on the difficult task of keeping the ancient groundcar on the slick roadway with some degree of speed. For all his talk of antivenom, Morgan was in serious danger or he wouldn't have told me to lift the *Fox*. *Maybe,* I tried to joke to myself, *he's forgotten I'm no spacer.*

My eyes flicked constantly from the road to his unconscious form. I forced down the small panic-stricken voice inside me that kept repeating over and over: Morgan was all I had.

It might have been true. But it wasn't helpful.

I shook my head, peered out through the dense sheets of rain. Morgan die? I wouldn't let him.

* * *

INTERLUDE

Barac sagged after he materialized, his body protesting as the drain on its energy reached near-critical levels. Without greeting Rael, who watched him from the comfort of a lounge he couldn't see, the Clansman staggered clumsily to the servo and dialed for a stimulant. It was dangerous to enter M'hir when weak or tired. Fortunately, over the past hours Rael's image projection had etched a passageway to this room, attracting his power through the M'hir the way a greater magnet attracts a lesser.

"Enough, Barac," Rael said, rising gracefully, hovering above the floor. "This is getting us nowhere."

Barac scowled in her direction, his dark eyes shadowed and unfocused. "What do you want me to do? Sit here? Wait while any memories of Sira fade to nothing under the garbage of their lives? We've gone over this before—"

She shrugged, sending a ripple through the dark mass of her hair, then reached a reluctant decision. "Sit, I can't deal with you in this state." Barac inclined his head with a shade of his former elegance and dropped himself into the nearest chair. Rael relocated her image to stand behind him, her eyes shut as she concentrated. She drew her hands through the air just over his head. The gesture was repeated, lengthened to include Barac's shoulders and arms.

Eyes closed, Barac accepted her gift of strength, feeling his weariness disappear, his body straighten from its exhausted slouch. Rael had mended him once already, repairing his bruises and broken ribs. This giving was more, and Barac was grateful. As Rael worked, he willingly lowered his shields, granting her access to his memory of the preceding hours, wishing for more there than failure.

Finished, Rael moved her image away, noting the alert brightness in Barac's expression with professional satisfaction. "So. You've failed to find so much as a hint of her in any unsealed mind; Sira has not touched the M'hir—I know the taste of her power like my own. Admit that she's left this world," Rael squinted around their surroundings, giving a delicate shudder at the lime-green decor of Barac's rented room. "I don't blame her."

"We can't be sure," Barac said.

Rael arched her brow. "I can. There's no point staying on Auord, unless you're hoping to get yourself killed by the local population before the Council finds out about all this. We can't help Sira by staying here."

Barac longed for an argument to prove her wrong, to keep their search within some attainable boundary. He had none. "There has to be a connection between Kurr's murder and the attack on Sira and myself," he growled. "There has to be," he repeated. Barac went back to the servo, canceled the stimulant, and dialed a meal instead. "Something we can't see," he concluded thoughtfully.

"What we can't see is Sira or your pet Human, Morgan," Rael said, her own tone caustic. "To find one or follow the other, you will need a starship. How do you propose to pay for such a thing? Or are you ready to confess your bungling to the Council?"

Barac frowned down at his plate. "Leave the ship to me."

Rael's head tilted to one side, her eyes narrowing. "You'd better not break any more rules, Barac sud Sarc, not near me. Influencing Humans without authorization will—"

"I'm the First Scout, Cousin," Barac snapped. "It's my business to know where and when to use the Talent. And which Humans can be bent." He took a slow deep breath, trying to calm himself. Pride was a dangerous emotion to show before one's superior in power, even one who was close kin. Temper was likely worse. Unconsciously, his fingers sought the relaxing warmth of the bracelet he wore on one wrist.

"Where did you get that?" Rael peered closer, willing to be distracted. "It's pre-Stratification, isn't it?"

Nodding, Barac held his arm toward her, the designs in the dull metal of the bracelet catching sparks from the room's lights. "It was a gift from Kurr. He liked to collect such things." The reminder thickened his voice. "He cared about our glorious history. He would talk for hours about the day the M'hiray were uplifted from the common clay of the Clan—the day our ancestors became Gods."

"Folktales," Rael said dismissively, then tilted her head, her look suddenly doubtful. "You aren't a zealot, are you? Mother's group turns my stomach."

Barac frowned at the disrespect in Rael's voice. Her mother might be Mirim *sud* Teerac, and no longer the First Chosen of her household, but she was still a formidable presence. Her link to her first offspring, Sira, had remained strong and fruitful for close to two decades, generating power channels through the M'hir that helped bridge the gap for many other M'hiray between Sira's foster home on Camos and Mirim's home on the rich inner planet, Stonerim III. Although Mirim's links with Rael and subsequently to her youngest, Pella, had been a more typical five years each, there was no denying her contribution to the M'hir had benefited all.

Just because Mirim had, since those days of glory, spent her time and the funds of her few followers searching for the lost Homeworld and its so-called M'hir-free life—the location of which all knew the Clan Council had refused to share—she did not deserve scorn. To each their own passion, was Barac's motto, as long as they politely kept it to themselves.

"Of course I'm not a M'hir Denouncer. And Kurr wasn't either," Barac said. Then he couldn't resist. "But there is a Clan Homeworld, Rael. A place where this metal was mined and crafted." His laugh was more bitter than amused. "And I can believe that if this place still exists, the Clan who could not touch the M'hir probably have folktales of their own about us, the M'hiray. The brave and powerful First Families—730 of the new breed of Choosers and their Chosen—who gathered together during the Stratification of our kind and simply left. Do they remember our great-grandparents as children who found one world and its people too small for their new abilities? Or as uncontrollable despots told good riddance and thrown out?"

"And is there any point to any of this musty debate, Cousin?" Rael pantomimed a yawn. "Doubtless the Council knows your answers, and by the Prime Law the rest of us will be informed if the past ever matters again. I'm satisfied with our ways. As your brother should have been, *sud*."

Barac trembled, striving to control his tongue and temper, aware that Rael was within her rights to remind him of his place. But Kurr's loss was too new, and her easy dismissal of Kurr's beliefs cut too deeply to ignore. "Kurr was *di* Sarc, Rael. I shouldn't have to ask for courtesy in his name. And if you're so concerned about the Prime Laws, I suggest we turn our attention back to your sister's problems."

Rael gestured appeasement, but her hands traced the ritual with detectable reluctance. Barac spared a moment to wonder if she'd leave him, allowing this concern to float to the surface of his thoughts. The Clanswoman shook her head immediately. "Sira needs more than *your* help—however well-meant," she added graciously. "But before you stretch the Prime Law beyond recognition by tampering with more Human minds, Cousin, there may be another way." She took Barac's silence as encouragement. "Let's do the Human thing. Call in the Enforcers to help us find our lost relation. If this Bowman already knows of us, where's the harm? And she may well have information about Sira we don't."

"Bowman wears a mind-deadener," Barac's lips twisted. "We can't sense what she's thinking, feeling—"

"So what? There are always some Humans we can't influence, but they can be handled. We're far from helpless, Barac, just because we can't control this one. Let her trust her machines; let her underestimate us. We can use that attitude to our advantage."

Without answering, Barac finished his meal. Rael waited with unusual patience. Finally, he shoved the remains into the disposal and wiped his hands. "I don't know, Rael," the Clansman said doubtfully. "It's risky. Bowman's met Jarad; she knows about the Clan."

Rael's face might have been a work of finely sculptured stone. "She knows one di Sarc. You'll present her with another. What could be simpler?"

"You'll come yourself?" Despite his misgivings, Barac had to smile, his dark eyes beginning to gleam. Then he shook his head. "It's one thing for me to be with Humans—Scouts do it all the time. You can't risk leaving a trail connecting you to that Human through the M'hir."

Rael's eyes took on a dangerous luster. "I am Chosen. I go where I will."

Barac sighed. "Rael, if you leave a trail that links us both with the Enforcers, whoever is Watching the M'hir will taste it and alarm Jarad. You know that." He thought a moment. "I'll bring Bowman within Deneb's system. No one would question your movements there."

"Inconvenient," Rael complained, then lifted her shoulders in a philosophical shrug. "But perhaps wise."

Barac nodded. His smile faded beneath another thought. "But Bowman mustn't learn about Sira."

"I'm not a fool, Cousin!" Rael hissed, her power flaring in an emphasis that burned across Barac's mind. "Bowman will learn what we need her to learn—and live to remember it only as long as it suits us."

Chapter 9

"CLEAR me, you slimy toads, or I'll tell the ship it's an emergency and you can watch us blast-dry your road!"

The com was safely off. It was a satisfying, if impossible, notion. The *Fox* obeyed Morgan first and, in a limited way, local Port Authority second—I was at the bottom of her list. Morgan lay in a coma, sealed in gel by the ship's med unit.

And Ret 7's Port Authority kept us locked to the ground, refusing a tug and clearance to the *Fox* with a professional courtesy bordering on insolence. It didn't matter to me whether the priests, or His Lordship, or both, were behind it. I wanted off this mudball.

The crew of any other trader would have called in the Enforcers by now. Such blatant local interference could potentially cost Ret 7 its listing for trade, let alone its license as a spaceport, were I to speak into the right ears. Spacers, especially those in trade, placed a high value on their freedom to come and go. But I couldn't call on that kind of help. My compulsions wouldn't even let my mind hold the idea without a struggle. Some time ago, a decision had been reached without my participation.

I glared at the com panel. Making a decision of my own, and praying it was the right one, I terminated my link to Port Authority and punched in the call numbers of my neighbor: *Ryan's Venture*.

The captain herself answered. I cleared my throat. "Captain Ivali, this is Sira Morgan—"

"How is he?" she interrupted, with an urgency that suggested a sincere concern. Our arrival had been observed after all. I enjoyed a vision of *Venture*'s crew lurking about in the torrential rain, and likely ankle-deep in mud, to watch for me.

"We have a medical emergency on Board, *Venture*. My captain had a disagreement with a Retian adult," I hoped she knew enough Retian anatomy; I didn't dare be specific. "I need to lift—"

"Do you need additional crew, *Fox*?" No hiding the concern this time. Whatever lay between Jason Morgan and Ivali was now being ignored in the face of an outside threat. *Spacers do stick to their own,* I thought, *given high enough stakes.*

"No, thank you, *Venture*," I said with genuine warmth. "Captain Morgan was able to prepare the *Fox* for auto lift. But Port Authority won't give us clearance."

"Outstanding contracts?"

"None, *Venture*."

There was a startled pause. Apparently, Ivali knew something of Morgan's business on Ret 7. "Are you certain, chit?'' she said in a suddenly hostile tone. "You know the penalties incurred by breaking a recorded contract. You leave, and they'll fall on us all."

"We have no valid outstanding contracts, *Venture*," I repeated firmly. "Our merchandise turned out to be substandard." *Or will be shortly,* I revised to myself, estimating the time it would take before the priests finished their changeover to the components I had sabotaged. "Clients contracted to that merchandise won't be held to payment."

A brief pause. "May I ask, young Morgan, how you managed that?" Before I could answer, Ivali continued, her voice sounding as though she struggled not to laugh. "On second thought, save the explanation for your captain." More formally: "Without outstanding contracts to protect, Port Authority can assume no control over off-world shipping. The other insystem captains and I will intercede on your behalf. Make your preparations."

"Thank—"

She cut off my gratitude. "Take care of Morgan, chit. Tell him I expect some profit out of this next time we meet. *Venture* out."

Preparations? Beyond studying and restudying a vistape on lift procedures, what was I supposed to do? The course and servo pilot were set, capable of handling the ship completely on their own—which left the living component of the *Fox*.

I went down to Morgan's cabin to check on him, irrationally stepping as quietly as possible though I knew he couldn't hear me. The room was bathed in a gentle mauve light, washing its brilliant colors to a monotone of shadows. A slightly too-clean smell filled the air. Only minutes might have passed since I had half-dragged Morgan here, shouting for the med unit, only to find it activating the moment Morgan's unconscious form touched his bed. Sensors and handling arms had extended from their concealment in the wall to touch and assess, delicately cutting free his clothing as well as the plaster about his hands. Unable to help, and queasily unwilling to watch, I'd left the room. When I returned, Morgan was already encased in a healing cocoon of med-gel.

The gel covered his face, smooth, gray, and opaque. I hated the look of it. For all I could decipher of the med-servo's few indicators, Morgan could be dead and the stupid machine merely preserving his body. I hesitated beside him, feeling useless and unwanted. Questions without answers crowded my mind. Why had I rescued him? Why was I still on the *Fox,* when it was so clear Morgan had arranged to leave me behind? Where were we going now, and why?

Why was my hand moving lightly, restlessly over the hard surface of the cocoon, for all the world as if I could do something more than the machine? As if caught by my attention, the fingers of my right hand curled into a loose fist, quiet once more. Morgan had eased my discomfort with a touch, I recalled. Had I once had such a talent? I wondered.

Pain seared along my every nerve. I pressed my hands to my head, crying out at the burning there. Simultaneously, the sensors on the panel of the med-servo went wild. The cocoon, immobile itself, pulsed with varying colors as if the body buried within writhed in echoing pain. Or was I the echo? Hunched over waves of my own agony, I watched the machine whir and click, administering a concoction from its depths through tube openings along the cocoon. My pain eased in perfect harmony with the quieting monitor.

I ran from it—not the machine, but from its unconscious occupant and the connection I knew was somehow being forged between us. Anyone who thinks there isn't room for terror-stricken flight shipboard, hasn't tried. I was able to run until I crumpled into an exhausted, horror-ridden tangle of arms and legs, muscles shaking, mind mercifully empty of thought.

The dependable *Fox* accepted the clearance code and docking tug on her own, obedient to the medical emergency lying in his cabin. She lifted from Ret 7 with neither her Captain nor crew in any shape to notice. With an unheard deepening in her engine's roar, the *Silver Fox* headed outsystem, bound for the Plexis Supermarket.

* * *

INTERLUDE

Bowman had a philosophy: Shipside, she took her time eating, and woe to any crew member who interrupted her pleasure. This was a prerogative viewed by old-timers on board in much the same light as the need to clean ventilators, or monitor scans. It occasionally inspired amused contempt among recruits. Bowman was aware of both attitudes and valued them equally—which was not at all. Shipside, she ruled.

Bowman sucked the juicy flesh from each of the pickled nicnics on her plate slowly, with full attention to their flavor, rolling the ovals over her tongue deliberately before swallowing. Barac sud Sarc watched with something approaching awe. "There's more," Bowman offered with contented confidence. 'Whix supervised the provisioning personally.

"Another time, Commander." Barac eased his back surreptitiously. "We really must discuss my cousin."

Commander Bowman couldn't stop a small frown from drawing her eyebrows together. Then, recalling her feelings when Barac had made his reappearance on Auord, she wiped her lips delicately. "There are certain fundamental constraints in the way *we* travel about, Clansman.

This stopover you propose near Deneb will take time, divert this ship from her intended course, and—"

"How can you have a course," Barac interrupted, "if you don't know where you are going?"

Bowman's frown deepened. "I always know where I am going, Clansman. I simply don't see any need to inform you."

"You're following a ship that lifted from Auord the day after I was attacked."

"Possibly." She tilted her head. "And you look better than when I last saw you. Care to explain that?"

Barac counted slowly, to himself, collecting his patience, before he spoke. "You want to find Kurr's murderer. So do I—"

"Now." She paused, sipping from her cup. "I thought you had other obligations to take care of first."

Barac abhorred the deadness which encompassed the dangerous mind across the table. It was maddening to have to rely on her voice and face for clues. "It seems my other obligation may be linked to this matter after all, Commander."

"All right, Clansman sud Sarc," Bowman said, surprising him with an enigmatic smile. She tapped the rim of her cup with a sturdy forefinger. Barac was momentarily distracted by a scar which crisscrossed the finger and wormed across the back of her hand; how typically Human, to retain such a blemish. "We're currently on course to Ret 7. Seems a ship recently out of Auord left abruptly and failed to register a true course with Port Authority."

"To evade you?"

"Terk thinks so."

Barac didn't bother turning to look at the taciturn enforcer whose mental deadness was combined with an unblinking stare hard enough to bore holes. The commander was not quite trusting. Pleased to see him, definitely—for what she could gain. Barac clung to the hope that Rael was right—that they would gain more in return. Bowman was formidable for a Human. And all her people wore implants, making Barac feel alone on the ship, even when face-to-face with others. The conflict in sensation tended to make him queasy.

"When I first mentioned this other obligation, Commander Bowman," Barac said, "I wasn't free to explain it to you."

"And now?"

He hated the clearness of her eyes. They missed nothing, tested everything, and veiled her thoughts as well as the implant did. "I was escorting Jarad di Sarc's daughter, Sira di Sarc," Barac began, finding it repugnant to name names, but knowing he had to offer Bowman something. "The attack on Auord might have been aimed at Sira. We have our internal rivalries, of course." Barac spoke the lie with confidence; a Human should believe it. How could any of them imagine the simplicity of Clan politics, a system based solely on personal power, measurable instantly and without error?

"Fem di Sarc didn't come to us or any agency on Auord."

"She wouldn't," Barac said. "But I've reason to believe she's left Auord."

"Does Hom di Sarc know his daughter's missing?"

Barac felt his control slipping and drew within himself to master it. Bowman covered his silence with a moment's satisfied attention to her dessert.

"I appreciate that you find it distasteful to deal with me, Clansman," Bowman said at last. "But you are here, so I assume you've decided you need me. Let's try to put our mutual suspicions to one side for a moment. Now. Would you know if di Sarc's daughter were dead?" Barac looked away.

"So," Bowman said, obviously intrigued. "I can tell you this much—she was taken in a sweep by recruiters and either escaped or was taken offworld. We narrowed down the possibilities to a handful of ships."

"Recruiters. Slavers, you mean!" Barac half-rose from his seat, bile rising into his throat, almost blinded by power which surged and seethed without target.

"My people are good, Barac sud Sarc," Bowman went on, unaffected. "But the vermin had their bolt-hole ready. Personally, I think di Sarc's daughter escaped in the confusion of the raid. Would you consider her capable of this?"

"No," he said, without thinking, then flushed and sat back down. "I don't know. Sira has led a very sheltered life, Commander. She's not used to strangers."

"Until now."

"Do you know where she is?"

Bowman scowled at the remains of her supper. "I did. Now I'm not so sure."

Barac put all the persuasiveness he knew into his voice. "Then we do need my cousin, Commander. Rael can help locate Sira for us."

"How?"

Barac smiled to himself. Bowman hunted secrets. In this case, what good would a gift of the truth do her? "Rael is a M'hir taster," he explained willingly. "She is able to sense changes in the M'hir due to individual power, much as you tell the difference between the foods on your plate by taste alone. She can also trace the path of the power through the M'hir to find a location in space. Rael can lead us to Sira, no matter where Sira is."

Bowman rose slowly, trying in vain to recapture her contented feeling of moments before. It never paid to conduct business over a meal; already her stomach rumbled ominously. She gazed thoughtfully at Barac's elegant, handsome face, assessing the odds. He smiled at her, a smile with a shade too much charm to be Human. Obviously, the Clansman was using her.

Bowman smiled back. She'd wanted to find Sira before the Clan did, but there was nothing wrong with being flexible. After all, what she really needed was proof of Clan trespassing in Trade Pact affairs. If she offered the Clansman a target, maybe he'd provide her with just that.

At any rate, it suited her aggravated stomach. "Terk. Adjust course for Deneb. Make sure you request priority clearance and dock. I don't want any delays." Terk left. "Now, Clansman," Bowman said silkily. "Do you know a Human named Jason Morgan?"

Chapter 10

"APPROACH control for Plexis is on the com." I stayed in the doorway, safely distant, my muscles so rigid I felt them tremble. But my voice sounded normal enough to me. "They're asking for you."

The figure on the hammock gave a small cough, dry and ragged. I winced with Morgan, then, despite my misgivings, I moved forward, passing the cup from the tray beside the hammock to Morgan's outstretched hand.

Our eyes met and held. His face was paler than before his stay within the healing gel cocoon, pale and with bones closer to the skin. In this changed face, Morgan's unusual eyes were like pools of some dangerous liquid. They were puzzling at me now; I could feel it.

I let go of the cup too soon. It dropped to the floor before either of us could catch it. Without speaking, my face hot, I poured another and gave it to Morgan more carefully, quickly wiping up the mess and stepping back as he drank. It seemed his eyes were trying to dig into my soul.

"You're afraid of me," he decided finally, as if amazed. "Why? What's happened?" Then another thought flickered behind his eyes. "Is it because of Malacan?"

Maybe I should have gone. Certainly I needed more distance from Morgan—his mere presence disturbed me in a way that I couldn't ignore. "Ret 7's long gone," I said. "And I'm not afraid of you." It hung in the air like an ultimatum.

To whom, I wondered. I'd hoped everything would return to normal once Morgan woke up and was free of the cocoon. Normal? An ironic way to feel about the compulsions stuck in my head in place of memory. But what I'd experienced hadn't been a dream, I realized, controlling a shudder; no one could wake me from it. No more fantasies.

"I have things to do—" I said, turning to leave. A hand, more bone than flesh, dropped lightly and warmly on my wrist.

"Sira, wait. Let me explain—"

I jerked free, the panic beginning again, the insidious sense of him magnified a thousandfold by his touch—that touch I'd dreamed of once. I fought to control my breathing; it helped control the fear. "Save your explanations for Plexis," I said roughly. "I've stalled them long enough. The *Fox* needs you." My hasty exit was more of a rout.

I'd found the control room fascinated me as much as it frustrated—it made an oddly comforting second home. Now, I curled up in the copilot's couch, warily eyeing the machinery humming and winking to itself on all sides. A small, green light flashed wearily on the com panel. Plexis again, wanting details I couldn't provide or invent.

I didn't turn at the sound of Morgan's slow but steady steps, preferring to watch him out the corner of my eye. He checked the panels with a series of darting, intelligent looks, then settled into his own seat with a contented air. Controls raised themselves to his hands, a deepening burr and clatter marking the response of the ship to its captain. I sighed with relief, thinking the *Fox* would probably echo me if she could.

"There," Morgan said after a moment. "Plexis has accepted our ident and released a spot on the ring for us." One hand stroked the panel idly. "I've put my life into the care of this ship before now."

I shivered. "Is that the best choice? Learn to trust a machine?" I rose to my feet, feeling clumsy. Morgan was with his ship; I wasn't necessary.

Morgan stopped me with his voice. "There's nowhere to run on a starship."

I didn't move, keeping my back to him. "I know," I said almost lightly.

"Please sit down, Sira."

It was easier to obey than to resist. It was the same on every level of my thoughts: Parts of me were starting to slip away and it was simpler to watch them go than to fight for them.

But Morgan's voice was like an anchor: "Tell me what you're feeling."

"What I'm feeling?" I echoed. "I wish it were so simple, Captain."

"I can't help unless you let me!"

Undecided, I turned without grace and faced his searching blue eyes. How could I explain the connection continuing to forge itself between us, when it mystified me? "I'm changing," I gave him my greatest fear, without any hope he'd understand it. I didn't.

"How? Has more of your memory come back to you?" Did I imagine caution sliding behind his blue eyes? "Or is it something between us?" The color returned to his pale cheeks. "I haven't explained, or thanked—"

"You won't tell me the truth, anyway, Morgan," I interrupted sharply and saw that bolt strike home in the tightening of his lips. "Nor am I sure I want to know. Anyway, keep your thanks until you find out what happened while you were unconscious. The *Fox* and I needed some help to leave Ret 7. I'm reasonably sure you'll find a debt recorded by *Venture*—a substantial one."

Instead of the dismay I had expected, Morgan actually grinned. "An account firmly in my favor, Sira, though I'm sure Ariva wouldn't have bothered you with that small detail. Well done. And I do want to thank you." Then his smile faded. "You look worse than I feel. I don't think you've slept or eaten since lift. You're no good to the *Fox* or yourself in such a state. What's wrong?"

"I haven't felt hungry, or tired," I admitted, startled to realize his observation was the truth. I looked at my hands, only now seeing the bones prominent on my knuckles. How had I existed for the two days since Ret 7? I had been in a cocoon of my own, perhaps, until roused by the approach alarms. That wasn't what mattered. "I'm changing, Captain Morgan," I repeated. "Inside. In some ways, I feel as though I'm waking up. My mind is sharper, clearer—healing, perhaps."

Morgan raised a brow. "That can't be what's burning your jets."

I sighed again and shifted, dredging up a smile from somewhere. "To be honest, Captain, I don't want to talk about it at all." Yet his expectant look forced me to continue. "I feel myself changing in other ways, too; I don't know how, or why, or where it will end." I leaned forward, eyes intent on his, willing him to understand. "All this changing scares me. Whoever I was before is a stranger now. How can I miss what I don't know? But what if I'm about to lose Sira Morgan, too? How can I accept that?

"This must all sound mad to you," I finished. Or was I mad already? my thoughts churned.

"Come here," Morgan ordered gently, patting the end of the pilot's couch. "Come," more firmly, when I didn't move. "I'm doing well to sit here at all, chit," this reminder delivered with a more familiar snap of exasperation. I obeyed, unhappy at his proximity but drawn from my own concerns by the grayness under Morgan's skin.

"If the *Fox* is ready, you should—" I began.

Morgan shook his head emphatically. "Docking at a supermarket isn't something you do on auto. You never know when some fool will try to cut ahead on your approach. I plan to stay right here." He'd drawn his knees up to his chest so that we could share the pilot couch. Now he rested his chin on his arms where they crossed atop his knees and considered me thoughtfully. "You said you weren't afraid of me, Sira," Morgan said at last, eyes shadowed. "Why can't I believe you?"

I flushed. But I remained as far away from him as physically possible—a defense that was also betrayal. "Is there a reason I have to sit here?" I asked tightly.

"Yes." Morgan's voice was stern and kept me still. Raising his head, he brought one hand to rest lightly upon my shoulder. I shuddered, instantly aware of a strange reverberation as my rapidly beating heart acquired an echo that was at once more powerful and distant. I tried to smother the sensation, to control the urge to gasp with panic.

I wasn't the only one afflicted. With a curse, Morgan snatched back his hand. I dropped my head, suddenly weak. "When did this start?" he asked, his voice very odd.

I found strength somewhere and looked up at him. "So you felt it, too?"

"I don't know what I felt."

The shock on Morgan's face was vastly reassuring.

"When you were taken by the priests, I knew it," I said flatly. "When you were in the cocoon, I felt your pain. My nightmares disturbed you across half the ship. I think you'd better explain what's happening between us—explain it and make it stop."

Morgan's face took on a keenness, a sharpening, as though curiosity could burn the last weakness from his body and mind. "I confess to wondering how you were able to arrive in time to save my neck from the ceremonial claw. Hmmm."

Before I could avoid it, Morgan's hand pressed warm and firm against my forehead. A force, a *power,* flowed along that bridging, suspending me in an unnatural lassitude that permitted not the slightest movement or sound.

Release came when Morgan chose to remove his touch. I scrambled away, backing until I felt the copilot's couch against my legs. "It's been you!" I burst out furiously, accusingly, my breath coming in tearing gasps. "All this time, all the things I've been feeling were your meddling! What are you? What have you done to me?" The pirate's term, *mindcrawler,* trembled on my lips.

Morgan looked drained, tired. I was reminded again of how recently the cocoon had released him. "I haven't been meddling, as you call it," he said heavily. "What I can do—well, I can't do the kind of thing you've begun feeling. I don't know anyone who can." He hesitated a long moment. "Maybe I do."

"Sira," Morgan continued in a oddly thickened voice, "I was paid to take you with me from Auord."

"What are you talking about? I didn't have any currency," I said impatiently. "That's why I've been cleaning the holds."

Morgan thumbed the latch from a cupboard under his seat. He reached down and pulled up a clear bag of currency gems. "I was paid by a Clansman named Barac."

I'd have been less astonished had Morgan sprouted antennae from his forehead. "So I should thank this Barac person for rescuing me from Auord," I said, not sure why I felt bitter. "Whoever he is."

Morgan's smile was unpleasant. "I wouldn't thank him too soon, Sira. I can smell trouble, believe me. And the deal stank of it. The Clansman had a holo of you, told me your name was Sira. He played on how you were alone, without memory or protection—he sounded sincere.

"Yet Barac couldn't or wouldn't stay himself to help you. Oh, no. He had to have *me* find you. To take you from Auord and deliver you to Camos." His lips twisted, changing the smile into something frankly stubborn. "I've done a lot of things in my time, Sira, some of them less than legal. But I don't transport slaves."

"I find that hard to believe," I retorted. "Since instead of taking me to this Barac, you decided to sell me on Ret 7."

Morgan leaned back on the couch, then rolled his head so he could look at me. "That wasn't my decision."

I swallowed hard, reduced to staring at him. Whatever expression was on my face made him swing his legs around abruptly and sit up. Before he could speak, I said: "Roraqk," thinking I finally understood.

"God, no!" Morgan lunged to his feet, swayed a moment, then sank back down. His voice and expression were appalled. "Sira, I wouldn't give air to that creature!"

I gripped the fabric of the couch behind me for support. I badly wanted to believe Morgan wasn't in league with the reptile, but could I trust the source of that desire? "I hear piracy pays well," I heard my voice say. "Profit is what a trader lives for, isn't it? Mind telling me why I'm so valuable a commodity?"

Morgan gritted his teeth, making a muscle jump along his jaw. We locked eyes for a long moment. "I found myself in a situation, years ago," he said finally, his voice rough at the edges. "As a result, I had to choose whether to lose the *Fox* or to supply someone with information from time to time. Lately I've wondered if I made the wrong decision."

"Roraqk," I said again, deliberately throwing that name between us.

His lips twitched. "On the contrary. I've been helping an Enforcer named Bowman gather information on the Clan. She's the one so interested in this Barac—and now you. You'd have to ask her why."

I gasped, feeling the blood draining from my face, shivering as if cold. Morgan kept still, watching me, a brooding cast to his eyes as if he'd expected my reaction. I stared into his steady blue gaze, my mind exploding.

Avoid the Enforcers, stay hidden, stay safe; the compulsions I'd naively thought gone for good burst through me, tumbling on themselves, engulfing Morgan's face with images of fear: *avoid, stay, hide, run.* I screamed, without sound, *Don't take him. He's all I have.* I fought for control on some level part of me almost recognized.

And won.

Something snapped. Dizzy, I sat down on the copilot's couch. Like probing with a tongue for a sore tooth, I probed my thoughts for any sign of the intruder's will. None. I was more bruised than triumphant. *If all I have is Morgan,* I admitted to myself, *then all I have is a self-confessed spy who for reasons of his own has put himself between me and at least two different pursuers.*

"It all comes down to you, Morgan, doesn't it," I said, trying not to sound resentful. "All I know is what you've told me. I don't know any Bowman or Barac. I don't know anything about the Clan or a world called Camos." I paused, then realized I had no choice but to go on. "I want to believe you mean to help me. I don't want to think about being on this ship, going who knows where, with someone I can't trust. A little proof would be nice."

Morgan's face had regained its mask of careful neutrality. He spread his hands. "I can't prove anything I've said."

"Can't or won't?"

"Think what you choose, Sira."

I absorbed that in silence. Still, our presence here, on the *Fox* instead of on Ret 7, had to be proof of a sort. "And you can't explain what's happening between us, why I can feel what you feel."

He shook his head very slowly. "Perhaps the Clan knows, but they tend to keep their secrets."

"Are you Human?" I asked with sudden deep suspicion.

Morgan laughed, a hollow sound, then sank back on his couch as if suddenly exhausted. "Yes, chit," the words half muffled by the arm he threw over his face. "I'm pure stock, too. I can recite twenty generations of ancestors, right back to First Ship. Before then, things do become muddled. But, yes, I'm Human."

"You're more," I said finally, when it seemed he was finished.

"Or less."

The pause that followed his cryptic suggestion was too long. I walked over to his side and gazed down at him. He was breathing deeply and evenly. His eyes were closed, his exhausted face guarded even in sleep. I touched his arm with my fingertips.

It was rapidly becoming a familiar shock, this extension of my senses to include the movements of Morgan's blood, the rhythm of his breath. At least Morgan was much less alarming while asleep. I resisted the urge to immediately draw away. What was Morgan? I tried not to listen to the small voice within that asked: What was I?

I sensed my body learning to isolate the incoming information in some strange new way, making it easier by the second to keep my own breathing steady, to ignore the rhythms of his. Part of me accepted this ability as quite normal. Part of me was nauseated by the duplication of sensation.

"I'm becoming part of you, whatever you are, Jason Morgan, whether I want to or not," I said, very softly.

A resonance of memory coursed into my empty thoughts and softly coalesced into form—memory, no, much less than that—sensation. This link between us was only beginning, the first of other unknown changes.

For the first time, I worried about its effect on Morgan. Was there some danger in it to him? Or to me?

Morgan tossed uneasily in his sleep, perhaps reacting somehow to my disturbing turn of thought. I moved away. As I went to the other couch and slowly settled myself, I continued to watch him.

Ignoring for the moment the likelihood that Morgan had some scheme afoot to make a profit from my continued presence on his ship, I had to think about the future. The Enforcer, Bowman, wasn't likely to be pleased with Morgan; neither was this Clansman, Barac. And in the back of my mind, I hadn't shaken the feeling that Roraqk was still after me. Three sets of enemies for Morgan, courtesy of his newest crew member—who might even be an enemy herself, I added reluctantly, troubled by the strange link growing between us and where it might lead.

Yet whether I could trust Morgan or not didn't really

matter. Somehow, he was important to me in a way that now had nothing at all to do with fantasy or compulsion.

On Plexis, I decided, I would leave the *Fox* and Morgan.

A shame Morgan hadn't warned me that freedom could be so unpleasant. I looked around at the panels and lights, already homesick.

Chapter 11

"WELCOME to Plexis Supermarket, Sira."

I stepped out of the air lock behind Morgan, trying not to trip over the cables snaked across in front. I had no trouble remembering what a supermarket was, but the reality was daunting, especially here. After all, this was *the* one—the first of its kind.

I'd read a vistape about Plexis. The story was popular, especially on fringe worlds where instant successes were as hoped for as they were rare. Decades ago, an enterprising industrialist named Raj Plexis had risked everything to build a refinery to process ores within asteroid belts. Her plan had been appealing in scale. Plexis designed a mobile station that would literally engulf a metal-rich asteroid, processing its ore on route to the nearest market. With a talent for fund-raising that would have shamed a loan shark, Plexis targeted wealthy backers interested in doing without the then-current system of orbital refineries and the independent fleets of ore carriers that supplied them.

Unfortunately, Plexis couldn't have anticipated the arrival of new technology to selectively harvest asteroid fragments and dust. Suddenly, anyone with a ship could scoop a profit out of the void. Mining claims quickly carved up every fringe asteroid belt with detectable metals. There was literally no room left for Plexis' giant refinery to operate.

Her backers abandoned the project with comic haste, leaving Plexis with a space-worthy and useless refinery of immense proportions, partially completed, and a reputation well on its way to becoming the joke of the known galaxy. For most, the combination of financial ruin and ridicule would have been enough for one lifetime. Plexis had other plans.

Within a year, her refinery appeared in shipping lanes, sporting the glittering sign that would become common-place along the entire outer system fringe: "Plexis Super-market. If You Want It, It's Here!" Plexis had stuffed the refinery's cavernous interior with shops carrying luxury goods normally confined to long-settled inner systems. The outer hull had been studded with a maze of ship con-nections, a parking lot for traders and spacers, buyers and sellers. Plexis Supermarket was exactly what customers had been waiting for—a gigantic peddler's wagon. Within ten years, every sector of the Trade Pact had its own super-market cruising its sparsely settled fringe. And Plexis her-self was an extremely wealthy legend.

Here I was, setting foot in the most famous shopping concourse in explored space.

"Are you planning to gawk all day, or can we get go-ing?" Morgan adjusted my helmet as he spoke.

"Do I have to wear this?" I mumbled, trying not to in-hale the wet laundry tang of the suit too deeply. Morgan had rigged the hookups to allow me to breathe the station air and hear what went on around me without the comlink. But it was already hot and stuffy.

"We don't know who could recognize you," Morgan repeated his earlier argument. He picked up the leash of the grav cart. "I'd rather not take chances on Plexis."

I tossed my small bag of belongings on top of his cases. "I might have friends here."

"And maybe enemies." Morgan frowned at my bag. "You won't need that. Leave it stowed."

I compressed my lips. "You said these were mine."

Morgan eyed me for a moment, then shrugged his shoul-ders. "Okay, but don't say I didn't warn you. It's risky car-rying anything around below the upper concourse. Your things would be safer inside the ship."

Morgan worked the little cart past some low hanging wires. I followed, tilting my helmet-covered head so I could see as much as possible. But what I could see of the much-vaunted supermarket looked more like a dingy re-pair shop.

"This is Plexis?" I blurted out, disappointed.

I caught the corner of his lips twitching in a smile. "Just

the backside, Sira," he said. "Parking's cheaper. And we're less conspicuous."

Then, before I could ask another question, Morgan continued: "What matters is that Plexis should be safe."

His choice of words silenced me as I was sure Morgan had intended. Safe? Safe from what or who in particular, I wanted to ask, but Morgan seemed preoccupied and I decided to wait in case my questions jarred him from some full-scale plotting.

I strode behind him down the narrow corridor, lifting my feet over bulkheads every so often. Our corridor opened at last into a much larger area. I could hear voices, but I couldn't see past the shoulders of the group of spacers standing in front of us.

"Damn. A tag point."

"What's that?" I asked Morgan, trying to peer around him.

"I forgot about the air tax. We didn't post a shopper's bond. If you're not a customer, you have to pay for the air you breathe. Keep the helmet on; I'll think of something."

Morgan went up and stood in line behind two other Humans. The bored-looking official, an Ordnex by his multi-jointed fingers and lack of nose, was reading out some monologue. I watched as we moved closer. He was using a tool shaped like a hammer to apply a waxy-looking patch to the right side of each being's face.

It was Morgan's turn. "DoyouacceptresponsbilityfortheairyoushareonPlexis?" the Ordnex droned rapidly. Morgan nodded and bent his head so the tag could be applied. When it touched his skin, the patch glowed for an instant, then went a pale blue.

Morgan pulled me in front of him, so I was helmet-to-nasal opening with the Ordnex. This unwelcome intimacy blocked the view of beings who had come up behind us in line so I saved my objections for later.

"We have a bad case of ysa-smoke addiction here, sir," Morgan said in a low-pitched voice, rapping my helmet with his knuckles. "Makes her useless for days. About all I can do is lock her in the suit; if I don't, she'll find a dealer and be puffed in minutes."

Where should I kick him? I noticed Morgan's hand slipping past my arm to grip that of the Ordnex. A very familiar-looking bag of currency gems sparkled for a moment

before disappearing somewhere in the official's loose
robes.

"Igivehertagintoyourkeeping,Captain," the Ordnex announced. "Mysympathies.Isuggestyoutrythepostingboardfor-
anewcrewmember." Morgan gave a half bow and pushed me
ahead.

"Ysa-smoker?" I snarled, when we were out of range.

Morgan chuckled, tucking my tag into his pocket. "Terrible habit, Sira."

After the tag point, we had to wait our turn to jump on
the ramp to the first shopping level. I found it first alarming, and then exhilarating to be surrounded by beings of
every size, smell, and shape. Morgan let a couple of openings go past, both near clusters of Humans. Then he spotted
an opportunity to his liking, yanking the cart and me after
him into the midst of a crowd of Turned Missionaries.

The Turrned gazed up at us with their great disk-shaped
eyes. No wonder they were so good at converting the un-
godly—those oversized brown eyes could melt stone. I
was busy examining my own soul for flaws, when we
reached the end of our trip and the crowd on the ramp
surged out into the shopping concourse.

It spread out as far as I could see. The heads of shoppers made a seething knobby carpet, broken only by the
occasional stilt-legged servo festooned with purchases.
The thousands of voices blended together into an indeci-
pherable roaring noise that quickly became a background.

I couldn't make out much directly across the expanse
from us. The side closest to me was a solid wall of storefronts, goods spilling out of each so that as we walked, we
were weaving our way in and out of furniture to suit any
body form, used engines, clothing (I think), old books in
good shape, new books in terrible shape, painted vases,
and stuffed women.

I stopped suddenly, my helmet almost buried in a truly
awe-inspiring pair of artificial mammary organs. Morgan
grabbed my arm and pulled me into the main flow of
pedestrians. A hopeful salesbeing halted his charge in our
direction with a look of disgust.

"This is the wholesalers' floor, chit," Morgan yelled in
my ear. "Don't look interested in anything, or the access
to the *Fox* will be jammed full of junk before we get
back."

"Well, so much for sightseeing," I growled, but to myself.

I followed Morgan's lead for what seemed a very long while—considering we were in a station—and soon had had enough of the press of bodies on every side. Not only did they block my view of anything more interesting than elbows bending in assorted angles, but the warm air inside my helmet was inclined to treasure the less pleasant living aromas of which sweat was the mildest. For all I knew, some of the odder-shaped beings I rubbed shoulders with could well be using the air we shared on Plexis for more than respiration.

My nose itched. The reflex to scratch came about a millisecond before my self-control. I quickly switched the movement of my hand into a wipe over the visplate of my helmet, hoping none of the spacers around me noticed. Behind that cover, I stuck my tongue out at Morgan.

At last, the crowd began thinning. I could tell because I could see floor again. Maybe it was time to make my move. Habits, all that remained of the powerful compulsions that guided me before, tugged at my decision to leave Morgan with alarmed little jerks and twists. I had grown quite good at ignoring them.

Morgan glanced at me, mistaking my expression, which was likely bleak, for something else. "Plexis isn't what you expected, is it?" There might have been a twinkle in his eye. "Wait till you see the upper levels. They're all the vistapes say and more."

We entered an area where the current of the crowd was broken into eddies and streams that had to pass around clusters of tables. The lighting here was set for shipnight. Overhead, hundreds of tiny portlights hovered, obedient stars against a distant metal sky. Along the walls, broad beams of garish light cut clean-edged slices across the shadowed floor, as various entertainment facilities enticed their space-weary guests. An appalling noise throbbed in my ears and rumbled under the foot plates of my suit. Music—lots of it, played loudly and badly.

I slipped my bag from the grav cart, watching Morgan take a couple of steps into the night zone before missing my echo. He halted in mid-stride, turning. My hand was tight upon the handle of the little knife in my belt, for what reason or purpose I couldn't have said. I felt the tension flaring between us as something physical as his piercing blue eyes narrowed in comprehension.

"If you're opting off the *Fox,* Sira" Morgan said, ignoring my defensiveness, striding back to stand before me, "I won't try to stop you. Just listen to me first."

"I'm listening," I responded tightly, my eyes fixed on his face though movement and sound from passersby made me shiver. Or was it something I sensed from Morgan this close which raised gooseflesh on my arms, something less easily deciphered than the rhythm of his heart?

"Plexis runs an open port, Sira," Morgan's low-pitched voice was rough. "Anyone can dock; all they have to do is pay for air. The next ship in could be Roraqk's—or the Clan."

"I'm not planning to stay here," I said.

"What do you plan to do?" Morgan asked more quietly, reassured, I supposed, that he had my attention and I wasn't about to bolt.

"There are lots of ships here," I said, trying not to be obvious as I backed a bit away from him. "Ships need crew."

"And you think a week Hindmost on the *Fox* makes you qualified?"

I felt myself redden and welcomed the anger. "I'll find a ship. You don't need to worry about me," I said. *And if I stayed on the* Fox, *maybe you would,* I added to myself, feeling a return of that foreboding.

Morgan nodded slowly. "All right. But let me ask around," he said reasonably. "I could find you a good berth, a chance at an apprenticeship. There'll be captains I know here; they say everyone shows up at Plexis eventually." He paused, waiting as a group of Human spacers, definitely the worse for wear, sang their unsteady way by us. When Morgan spoke again, his voice was low-pitched and urgent, his blue eyes burning with intensity. "Sira, you saved my life on Ret 7. That's a debt I intend to repay. This isn't the time to leave me. Not here. Not on your own."

I scuffed my feet, sorely tempted. After all, what Morgan was saying made sense, more sense than an odd warning rattling around in my admittedly busy head. But being near him made me nervous. The link I felt between us made me very nervous. And what was to come might be worse.

Before I could decide, a man in the crowd hesitated as he was about to pass us, then stopped, turning to face me.

Human, I thought, *and rich.* He was well-dressed in what looked to be organic fur and silk. Instead of a blue cheek patch, he wore the gold patch of a customer. Morgan's face smoothed into a polite smile, but I could see his eyes appraising the stranger warily.

"Anything we can do for you, Hom?" Morgan asked.

The man's face swung to Morgan, his expression one of confused impatience. "No." He turned once more to me, his dark eyes squinting as though that would help him see through the anti-glare coating on my helmet. I was grateful for its protection when he whispered: "Who *are* you?"

"No one you'd know, Hom," Morgan said firmly. He stepped in front of me, this motion ominously smooth.

The stranger frowned at Morgan. Morgan's body immediately lifted into the air and flew into a table, scattering both chairs and their occupants.

Nifty trick, I thought, not sure whether to worry about Morgan or myself.

"Who are you?" the magical stranger whispered again. He stretched out his hand as though to touch me. I blinked as the helmet disappeared and I could see him clearly.

Two things happened in rapid succession. The man's face drained completely of color. Then he vanished.

A tiny whoosh of air filled the space where the man had once stood. I staggered, felt someone's grip steady me. I met Morgan's eyes.

"Was that Barac?" I asked incredulously.

"Clan," he said, his face grim. "But no one I know. Let's go," he urged, pulling both the cart and me into a pool of shadow between two doorways. Then he quickly slapped my cheek, once, hard enough to bring tears to my eyes.

"Before you complain," Morgan suggested, holding up his blue-stained fingers to silence me, "remember who took the helmet." I reached up to my stinging cheek and explored the waxy patch now immovably fixed to my skin.

Our leisurely pace now changed into something closer to a run. Morgan dodged through any gap in the surrounding mass of people and tables, once electing to push through a decorative clump of bushes rather than slow down. I pulled at a leaf as I followed him, but it was firmly glued to its stem.

At this pace, we soon reached our destination, which turned out to be a restaurant with a lurid sign over its double doors proclaiming: *Claws and Jaws—Complete Interspecies Cuisine.*

I didn't bother to argue, being too busy watching for people able to appear and disappear at will, not to mention fling bodies into furniture with a frown. I breathed easier when Morgan closed the restaurant doors behind us.

The exterior of the restaurant had been misleading. Inside, there was a subdued hum of voices, barely louder than the soft chimes that rang as we passed them. A bowing attendant appeared out of nowhere. Morgan handed her the lead to the grav cart. We were waved ahead of others waiting to be seated—or whatever eating position suited their body forms. As we entered the dining area proper, I tilted my head, entranced by a delicious, seductive aroma.

Morgan smiled at my reaction. "Welcome to Huido's, Sira, the best eating on Plexis."

"Liar! The best eating in the quadrant!" This bellow was from an approaching mass I'd assumed was a servo, given its metallic luster and two pairs of assymetrical arms. The being, moving on pillarlike legs that ending in preposterously balloon-like pads rather than feet, used its larger, lower pair of arms to sweep Morgan off the floor in an embrace I devoutly hoped wouldn't aggravate the man's recently healed injury. Morgan hammered his fists on the shining armor plates that served the ungainly creature for shoulders. Fortunately for my peace of mind, he was also laughing.

"Put me down, Huido, you big oaf. You make me forget what manners I've got." The being gave him one last bruising squeeze before setting Morgan back on his feet with a tenderness totally belied by his appearance. "Huido Maarmatoo'kk, I'd like you to meet Sira Morgan."

It took all of my courage to accept the claw, the tip of one of the smaller more flexible-looking arms, that was gently offered for my touch. I restrained a shudder at its chill hardness; Huido's ancestry was certainly other than

mammal. Black and glistening, the creature stood as tall
as Morgan, yet its shoulders and bulbous back blocked
most of the space in the lobby entrance. Its head looked as
though a pair of saucepans decided to take up life as the
top and bottom of a helmet. As they pulsed vertically,
ever-so-slightly, the black shadow between them danced
with the gleam of dozens of independently mobile eyes,
each on its own short stalk. I tried to imagine a reassuring
softness to the set of four, no, six, clustered at the moment
to examine me.

"So, Brother, you finally bring a shell-mate to my home.
You honor us with your presence, Fem Morgan." His
voice originated from somewhere within that hood, and,
though perfectly understandable, was deep, rasping, and
regrettably loud. I opened my mouth to correct his interpretation of my name only to meet Morgan's blue eyes.
He shook his head, once, very slightly. I closed my lips
into a firm line and glared at him.

Supper, served after a tantalizing delay that made me
wonder if any servos were involved in its preparation,
was all the aroma had promised and more. Huido kept us
company by drinking warm beer, the only Human food—
as he put it—worthy of his refined palate. I had a feeling
it was more likely the only Human food his nonhumanoid
system could tolerate, but was too polite to ask. Drinking
was how I thought of it, not having the word to describe a
process consisting of pouring large amounts of liquid into
the orifice at the tip of his top right-hand claw, then tucking the claw tip into that dark boundary that served for a
face. The following satisfied slurp crossed any species'
boundary.

Eventually I burrowed deeper within the friendly arms
of my chair, reveling in the drowsy pleasure of pleas-
ing my own palate and appetite. I listened to Morgan's
and Huido's ongoing conversation about people and
places with only half an ear, just as happy to not have to
take part.

We were sharing Huido's private table, perched to
overlook the packed restaurant. Privacy from the common
area was provided by a shimmering webbing which looked
like the work of a deranged and overlarge spider, but,
judging by the crisped brown leaves of a plant which had

dared grow close to the strands, was likely a force field of some kind. I wondered if it could keep out Clan as well.

A living waiter, not a servo, collected my plate and offered me a delicate glass filled with pale gold liquid. I thanked him, accepting the drink. My thoughtful silence spread to my companions and they both looked at me.

"Was it not the best food you have ever consumed?" Huido boomed at me.

Morgan leaned back, admiring the prisms of light within his own glass. "Best agree with him, Sira. He's likely to serve the poor chef as the next course if you don't."

"Bah," the alien dismissed Morgan's advice with a click of his upper two handling claws. "There's no market for Human flesh on Plexis. On Ormagal 17, though—"

Although expression was impossible to read from a face consisting of shell shadow and glistening, stalked eyes—his mouth being nestled somewhere deep within their cluster—I decided I was being teased. "Your food is superb, Hom—" I hesitated over the pronunciation of his name.

"Huido. To the mate of my blood brother, I give my name, tanks, and yes, my soul!" I blushed at this, then was mortified to be embarrassed. Huido, obviously well-acquainted with Humans, roared his approval. "You see, Brother? For how many years have I told you to begin a Hatch of your own?"

"Since you learned what one was," Morgan answered readily.

"Well, it's taken you long enough," Huido retorted, not the least deterred. "While I have twenty mates in my home to cheer me—" He sounded smug. "And two more arrive within this planet year. The delights of the pool—" he stopped and several eyes swiveled to look at me. "Do you swim, Sira?"

I choked on my wine. Morgan took a look at my face and said quickly: "What we need, Huido, is a quiet, restful place. A place where we won't be disturbed for a couple of days."

Huido didn't answer immediately. Instead his eyes, usually divided in their attention between the restaurant, ourselves, and his enormous mug of beer, riveted together on Morgan's face. It was an unnerving focus, as was the now-brooding silence from the huge, glistening creature.

Morgan merely raised a brow, and his glass. He smiled, I thought a shade too deliberately. "Docked after a long run—Sira and I have been working very hard, old friend. Is a bit of peace and solitude too much to ask?"

Huido lifted one arm and snapped his claw, making a cymbal-like sound that brought the waiter scurrying to our table to gather the last dishes and bowls. Huido rose ponderously. "From the look of you both," he said stiffly, "you'd best refrain from the pool and sleep for a month. I will make the arrangements."

When we were alone, I turned to Morgan. "What are you up to?" I hissed.

Morgan reached out and grasped my hand. I allowed it, looking at him with concern as I sensed the laboring of his body through the touch. His skin was tinged with gray. "You're not safe, Sira. I doubt anyone on Ret 7 will forget you. And now you've been spotted here by the Clan. Let me help," Morgan paused, tired eyes fixed on mine, an almost pleading note to his voice. "Believe in me a while longer. Stay. Once you're safe, I promise to help you leave when and how you choose."

Without thought, my hand turned until my fingers could wrap around his. There was a warmth inside me able to move of itself, without conscious effort, down my arm, across that physical link. I felt it reach Morgan, sensed him grow stronger. His face lost some of its pallor. At first wide with surprise, Morgan's eyes softened until I thought I could drown in them.

"I can take you there now," Huido announced, snapping the binding between Morgan and me. I took a deep, shuddering breath, as if shaking free of a spell, releasing the grip of my own fingers and pulling free of the gentle resistance his offered.

Huido's promised refuge turned out to be a suite of rooms behind his restaurant, reached by a passage through the kitchens. At the door, Morgan hesitated, then stretched his hand toward the shadow beneath the edge of Huido's hood carapace. The sparkling eyes parted and long, deadly-looking jaws sprang from the darkness, their twin needle-like tips closing to lightly indent the skin of Morgan's hand, then disappearing. "Guard our backs," Morgan said so quietly I almost didn't hear the words.

Fuel lamps, not antiques but looking newly-made and functional—a costly luxury on a station—hung from metal hooks at intervals around the walls of the room we entered. After locking the door, Morgan chose to light three of these instead of ordering on the interior portlights, thus bathing the center of the room and the entrance to an adjacent hallway in a warm, yellow glow. Shadows pooling in the corners added to the effect, offering rest for the eyes. The furnishings were colorful, with rounded corners that encouraged curling up with a good vistape and reader.

"Let me take your cloak, Fem Morgan," my companion offered with a sweeping bow.

Frowning, I pulled the evac-suit from my shoulders and arms, letting it fall to my ankles so I could step free of it. Underneath I wore my faded blue spacer coveralls. "What are we doing here, Morgan?"

He grew still, as if put on guard by my question—or by my refusal of his aid. "Getting some well-earned rest."

"Are there viewports?" I asked, ignoring this last as I searched the walls with my eyes. They were covered with thick, multitextured hangings of cloth—hand-made blankets, I decided.

"No," Morgan said, heading toward the hallway with his belongings. "Plexis doesn't encourage visitors to see who's coming and going from her docks." He left me standing there.

I examined some curios on a shelf, not sure what to do with myself, not sure whether I was trapped or safe. A sudden heavy thud made me jump. I ran toward the sound, fearing anything and everything.

Down the hall, the light was brighter, revealing a central kitchen area with doors on two walls. Morgan lay crumpled on the floor in the center of the kitchen, one hand clutching the side of a counter, the other pressed to his ribs.

I dropped to my knees beside him. His eyes were half-closed, his breathing labored. "You fool," I scolded angrily, helping him up to a kitchen chair. "You should be back in med-gel. I'll take you back to the *Fox*—we can leave—"

His hand fastened on my arm, its grip stronger than it should have been. "No!" Morgan's voice was a whisper, but his tone was fierce. "Stay away from the *Fox!*"

I sank into the other chair, staring at him. "Why?" When his lips stayed closed in a stubborn line, I leaned forward and kept his eyes on mine. "Malacan Ser," I said, abruptly certain of several things, including Morgan.

There was no outward sign of reaction, even weak from his convalescence Morgan had more self-control than that, but through his hand on my arm I felt the effort that control required. "So," I said quietly. "There was a price for me, after all."

Morgan's eyes flickered, then held steady. He shook his head very slowly. "Some things are not for sale. Not by me."

"Can you ever go back to the *Fox*?"

His fingers relaxed, releasing their tight grip on my arm. Perhaps he realized how the contact had betrayed him. "The *Silver Fox* will shortly disappear," Morgan said lightly, as if it didn't matter. "I expect Morgan of Karolus will also fade from the lanes for a while. Such things are easy enough to arrange in the belly of Plexis."

I rubbed my thumb in little circles over the smooth cool surface of the tabletop, concentrating on the simple motion in order to gather my thoughts. So much he was leaving unsaid. So much I didn't understand. Morgan heaved a sigh and gently brushed the back of my hand with the tips of his fingers. I looked up at him.

"Sira," he said soberly, eyes unnaturally bright in his wan face. "I made some bad deals; promised things I shouldn't have. It happens. I didn't know you—couldn't have known—" he stopped, drawing a breath. "Well, let's just say a lot of things about you are different than I expected. All I can say is, we're together in this." His lips quirked upward as if he sought to lighten the moment. "Until, of course, such time as you decide you've had enough of this excuse for a trader."

"You're babbling," I said, but as gently as I could. "We're both tired and overfed, Captain. I, for one, could use a night's sleep." Without asking his permission, I caught his arm as he rose unsteadily, sliding my shoulder underneath. "We can talk in the morning."

Morgan accepted my help, nodding in the direction of his room. Once there, I eased him down onto the bed and stood back. He sank down with a sigh of relief, eyes closing. "Will you be all right?" I asked, hesitating. What words could I use to offer help, when I didn't know what I could do?

Morgan understood, however. "A blanket, Sira, and a night's rest. Save your gift," he paused and opened one eye. "We might need it."

Chapter 12

MORGAN may have been exhausted, but I found myself more inclined to twitch than to relax. Perhaps it was the change from the *Fox*. The station's sounds and vibrations were similar to the ship's, but lower-pitched and distant. They made me uneasy, as if something was wrong. The air tasted peculiar, too, which could have been the thought of sharing it with thousands of strangers.

So, instead of trying to sleep, I tucked myself under a blanket and listened to music. The tape I'd found was unmarked—a personal recording perhaps, made by the person whose apartment Huido had casually loaned us. The music's soft sound matched the desert colors decorating this bedroom, an eerie crooning reminiscent of wind as it curled sand and carved rock.

I let my mind drift with the melody, and found myself pondering the disappearing stranger, the Clansman. Was he buried in some reluctant memory? Why had he ignored Morgan until forced to use some kind of power to push Morgan out of his way? The Clansman had known me the instant he'd seen my face. Yet the obviously powerful being's reaction had been fear. Of me? I shook my head. That hardly seemed likely. But then, what did I know of my former self?

Now, I had a name, Sira Morgan. And a friend—perhaps two, if I counted the gallant Huido. I smiled to myself. I'd come a long way from the emptiness of that first night, when my mind was hollow and ridden by compulsions.

I'd accepted their guidance, I realized abruptly, accepted it the way I would a hand offered to help me stand after a fall. Yet now I was almost certain that whoever stole my memories was responsible for the controls planted in my mind. The hand offered to help was the same one that had pushed me down.

Why hadn't I wondered before about the compulsions and their source? I'd probably given more thought to the pattern of freckles on the backs of my hands. That lack of curiosity was suspicious in itself.

What else was in my head waiting to take charge, to twist me its way without explanation? The uncomfortable thought tried to sneak away, to lose itself somewhere. I held the slippery thing fiercely, determined not to forget. Sira Morgan would be in charge of her own thoughts from now on, I swore to myself, knowing that promise was the most important of my short life.

The music began scaling up into an anguished crescendo too close to my own feelings for comfort. I hit the button to turn it off.

I stretched and had to yawn. My eyes were gritty when I blinked. Time to splash some water on my face.

As I dried my hands, still undecided whether to sleep or find breakfast, my reflection in the mirror caught my eye. I leaned forward, pressing my hands flat on either side of that face to hold it still. Gray eyes with a hint of black stared back just as intently. "I know you," I said. "You're Sira Morgan, crew on the *Silver Fox*. Didn't we meet on Auord?"

I tilted my head and the image tilted in mocking synchrony. "Do you know who I am?" I asked Sira Morgan, watching her lips shape the question but not the answer.

"Sira?"

I knocked over a bottle of soap as I whirled around, half expecting to see the Clansman forming from air behind me. "Don't do that!" I scolded Morgan.

He smiled apologetically. "Thought you heard me knock."

Morgan had changed clothes and looked to have used the fresher in his room. His blue eyes were bright again. Too bright. They held the same odd glow I'd last seen on the bridge of the *Fox,* when Morgan had used his own unusual power to lock me in place.

"I'm getting ready to sleep," I said warily.

He backed out of my way, but didn't leave. "We don't have much time, Sira," Morgan said, watching me closely. "I need to talk to you."

"Fine," I said with another yawn. I guessed his appearance meant morning had arrived. So much for sleep. "Let's go in the kitchen and have some—"

"Here is better."

The bedroom? I raised my eyebrow at him. Morgan looked distinctly uncomfortable. "I don't recall repeating my offer, Captain," I said. *And I won't,* I thought to myself, all too aware of the link between us, holding together the rags of my dignity like a defense against the ache in my right hand, the emptiness he alone could fill. "I choose for myself."

"I'm sorry, Sira," Morgan said in a tight, strange voice. "This time, I don't see any choice for either of us. The Clan are on Plexis. I have to find out why you can't remember your past."

I was startled by his quick move to take hold of my arm. Before the protest left my lips, his other hand pressed hard on my forehead. His impossible eyes reached deep into mine. I felt dizzy, disconnected, drowned in blue.

Then I blinked. I was lying on the bed. Immediately, I tried to get up; my right arm was asleep and my fingers prickled as I flexed them. "Morgan!" I shouted, then wasn't sure why.

"I'm here." A soft voice from the dark. He must have dimmed the lights.

I swung my legs over the edge of the bed, but didn't get to my feet. My thoughts churned in slow motion. "Is it morning?" I ventured, rubbing my eyes with my left hand.

"Have a drink. There's sombay on the table." His voice still soft.

There was just enough light to find the carafe and cups. All I could see of Morgan were two glints that marked his eyes in the shadows. I cradled the warm cup in my hand, took a sip of the spiced liquid. Then I remembered.

I lunged to my feet, the cup and contents flying from my hand in his general direction. "What have you done to me?" I demanded, ordering up the lights with a snarl.

Morgan squinted at me. He was slouched deep in a bowl-shaped chair, a chair he'd moved beside the closed bedroom door. My cup had missed, but dark brown sombay trailed like bloodstains between us on the creamy carpet. "I've done nothing."

I hesitated at the tone of his voice. It was angry, a deep

hurt kind of anger such as I'd never heard from Morgan before. I sank back down on the bed. "What did you do?" I asked again, this time very quietly.

"What I vowed I'd never do—to anyone," Morgan said, his lips twisted and sour. "And I did it to you. My trusting friend." He took a deep drink from the glass in his hand. It didn't look like sombay. "And the real joke of it all, Sira," Morgan continued, his voice dripping with bitterness, "is that I'm not the first to rip my way through your thoughts without asking. Oh, no. And that person did a much more thorough rape than I."

My legs and arms hung limp. They belonged to someone else; by some unfathomable coincidence, they remained attached to me. "I don't understand—"

"I know." Morgan drank again, deeply. "I know how you feel. I know what you hope for. Damn it, Sira, I saw myself through your eyes!"

"Why did you do it?" I asked, as icily calm as he was distraught, refusing to admit to myself how it felt to be so utterly exposed.

"Your thoughts were clear, you know, like crystal," Morgan said, all at once meeting my glare, his blue eyes dull. "Beautiful, clear thoughts. Gods, that you trusted me so much. Cared for me. And I was so sure I knew what was best. Now—"

"What are you drinking?" I asked when he stopped.

"Water."

"Then, tell me what you did before I throw something else," I said firmly.

He sighed, a deep shuddering breath more like a sob. His feet thumped to the floor as Morgan straightened. He put his drink down. "I invaded your mind," he said very slowly, as if determined to spare himself nothing. "I couldn't warn you—or ask."

"Why?"

"You might have fought. I don't have the skill to overcome resistance without hurting you."

Which made his actions more reasonable, if not exactly pleasant to contemplate. I held my head stiffly, imprisoning his gaze with mine. My hands were fists, but I tucked them behind my back. "Did you discover any worthwhile secrets to sell to Malacan Ser? Or are you trading with the pirate now?"

"No," Morgan denied my accusations passionately. "I was trying to help you! The Clan knows you're on Plexis— you saw how well I can hold just one of them off. The only defense we have is to find out why they're after you."

I shivered and drew my legs up, hugging them to my chest with both arms. "Did you?"

Morgan lifted his shoulders and let them drop. "No."

"Someone erased my memories, didn't they," I said with I thought commendable self-possession under the circumstances. "Someone used a machine or drugs—"

"No. Your memories aren't gone. They're smothered." His voice quickened, grew harsh. "Whoever did it didn't have the time or maybe the skill to be very subtle. Massive areas are blocked; parts of your active mind are disconnected. I couldn't begin to assess the extent of the interference." Morgan stood up with a curse and jerked the chair away from the door. His back was to me. "As I said, I'm not the first to assault you. Just the latest."

Beyond any doubt, I believed him. A whisper of knowledge, partial, clouded, spoke to me of such obscene skill, just as I knew there were those who practiced it at whim. Morgan wasn't one of them. I walked up to him and felt his shudder at the touch of my hand on his shoulder. "Is there anything you can do?" I asked him.

"Haven't I done enough!" Morgan exclaimed, head turning so his eyes could blaze down at me. He subsided. "I'm out of my orbit here, Sira," he said in a more normal voice. "I've some talent as a telepath, but no real training. I've scrounged bits and pieces from anyone who'd talk to me without asking questions. What's been done to you— I'm not sure I can touch it, let alone clear any of the blockage."

I kept my voice level but firm. "You owe it to me to try." This time, I took Morgan's arm and pulled him around to face me. "You must try," I repeated. "I'm not afraid."

Morgan shook his head, but cupped my face in his warm hands. His thumbs stroked my cheeks once, soft as air. "Then why these tears, Sira?"

"Sira . . ."

"Sira . . ." I twisted about at the absurd echo, dimly conscious of Morgan's gasp. What I saw evoked an uncomfortably dualized reaction—part of me accepted quite calmly the barely visible female figure hovering just above the carpet. Another, probably saner, part was aware of the clamminess of my palms.

"Sira . . ." Again that ghostly naming, the voice even fainter than the just discernible figure.

Another very quiet voice, but this breathed into my ear. "Don't answer," Morgan whispered. His tanned hands moved in an odd throwaway gesture toward the figure. As suddenly as it had appeared, the apparition vanished.

The bedroom was implausibly normal again, as if nothing untoward had occurred. I could almost believe that myself, if it weren't for the pounding of my heart.

"The Clan," I whispered. "They've found us."

Morgan walked over to where she had been, the vision definitely female if hard to see otherwise. He scuffed the carpet with his foot. "They're close," he half-agreed. He looked at me, blue eyes glowing. "If you're sure . . . we have to hurry."

Without a word, I went to the bed, lay down, and closed my eyes, waiting for Morgan to impose unconsciousness upon my mind once again. But he didn't.

How can I describe what followed? There was no sensation beyond the by-now familiar light touch of his warm hands; no sight, no sound. I could have been dreaming save that I was definitely awake. Yet something was happening as I lay under Morgan's power, something gathering slowly at first, then more rapidly—gaining momentum every second.

Images began to swim up behind my closed eyelids. I saw the interior of the *Fox*. Flashes of malignant yellow and threatening heavy-browed scowls were all that I glimpsed of Roraqk and the Recruiter—their memory whisked past.

There was a sudden swelling, a pressure that grew until it burst within my mind. From it floated a face, a stern face, lined but vital, with fierce eyes overlooking a hawk's beak of a nose. *My father,* I acknowledged with a casual certainty which astonished the pastless part of me. I scrutinized this face, searching for any hint or expression, watching his lips mouth soundless words.

That image was abruptly gone, replaced by a view of a luxurious cabin. On a private yacht: I knew without being told that here was one clue—how I had come to Auord. But from where? I strove to direct this search for the first time, no longer content to view at random.

I saw it—or was in it, for the sensation of being in this place was so strong and immediate I expected to be able to reach out and feel the objects around me. A room—no, a series of rooms. No particular luxury here, as on the yacht, but, rather, comfort and what I recognized as the oddments and personal effects of a lifetime. I seemed to drift to a window only to find it barred as I had somehow known it would be. Just as I knew there were other barriers, some unseen and some obvious; all serving the same purpose. To keep me there? Or was it to keep out—to keep out—

Something shoved back at me, a muscular push against my will, like the compulsions that had ridden me before but this time incredibly stronger, concentrated into pain. It was a trap, I knew it, set for anyone who touched my deeper thoughts. It licked like flame along the link to Morgan, burning as it went.

I called on a part of me I hadn't known existed, seizing the pain, holding it. I felt as though I was being consumed, then made myself refuse the image. I somehow pushed the pain farther and farther away. After an eternity, the burning stopped.

I fought my way to the here and now, struggling, frantic with fear that I hadn't been quick enough.

Morgan lay crumpled on the floor beside the bed, his head between his arms as though he'd tried to save himself. Trembling, I touched his face, his hands, trying to use the sense I had of him to make sure he lived. I could feel his heart, laboring but strong.

"Sira . . ."

She was back. Enraged, I *pushed* the vision away with my mind, just as I'd pushed the pain away from Morgan. Her form became wind-torn at the edges, then was gone.

Working in frantic haste, I put a pillow under Morgan's head and a blanket over his body. My mind felt fuzzy, unfamiliar, a bit like wearing new shoes. What had Morgan done to me? I touched his hand, once ever so gently. Then I grabbed my small carryroll and ran.

Knowing the vision would follow.

* * *

INTERLUDE

"Damn the excuses, Barac! I was close, I know it!" Rael's rage flared against his shields. He could see the strain the past hours had etched onto her face. "How dare they interrupt me!"

Barac noticed the discomfort of the Humans present but had little time to spare for them. Unless calmed, Rael was more than capable of refusing to help him any further. "The Enforcer thought—"

"I doubt there was any thought involved." Rael threw up her arms in a gesture of disgust. "Explain to them again, Barac. I am not to be disturbed while I scan the M'hir—I don't care if there's a sun going nova in our path! Now I've lost it. Argh . . ." The cabin door refused to slam, but no other element of Rael's ire was missed by the three in the corridor.

"Who was it Fem di Sarc lost? Did she sense your Sira?" Bowman asked, eyes bright.

"She didn't say. Stay on your current heading," Barac added, relaying the message Rael had scorched into his mind during her dramatic exit. "We're very close. One more contact, and Rael will have a precise location for you."

Bowman smiled. "In this case, close is good enough, Hom sud Sarc. Plexis. I knew—"

Barac heard a sudden scream, more mental than sound and left Bowman standing openmouthed outside the locked door.

Rael was hunched over, tears filling her eyes. She looked up at him. "The M'hir," Rael managed to gasp. "She threw me out of it."

"Who?" Barac demanded, going down on his knees in front of his suffering cousin, careful not to crowd her. "Who did this?"

"It was Sira," Rael answered, her voice a whisper.

"That's impossible. Sira—she's in stasis, Rael!"

Rael looked sick. "Not any more, Barac. I don't know how it's possible." She hesitated. "Your Human, Morgan. He's a telepath."

Barac found himself standing and stumbling backward before he thought. "No!" Yet how many things that detail explained, he realized, his doubt already dissolving.

"Yes! The stink of him contaminated her power in the M'hir." Rael wiped her eyes, impatient with her weakness. "What has he done?"

"We'll find out," Barac vowed. "And Morgan will pay."

Chapter 13

RAW nicnic was incredibly awkward to peel, but a handful of the fruit was all I'd been able to grab during my discreet exit through the kitchen of the *Claw and Jaw*. Huido's cook had ignored me, busy with a masterpiece insistent on crawling out of the pot, and I tried not to examine his work too closely. I'd found the inconspicuous back door I'd expected. After all, no one really wants to see where the scraps go after dinner.

I found myself in a service corridor. It snaked off into station distance, a machine world lined with waste canisters chewing their contents and servo-controlled delivery carts muttering past on business of their own. The occasional courier drone screeched by overhead.

I trotted behind one of the carts, having picked it at random after tossing my handful of nicnic peels into a happily belching canister. I'd made a good choice; the delivery cart soon paused before a wide door, moving inside as the door folded itself into the ceiling.

I followed the cart into a receiving area of some kind, alert for any signs of a guard or security. A metallic clang gave me just enough warning to avoid the set of handling arms that swung into place beside the cart and started offloading its cargo. The plas eyes on the arm nearest me swiveled my way, gleamed orange as if assessing my stature as a package, then swiveled back to focus on its task.

By turning sideways, and leaving some skin behind, I was able to squeeze past the other side of the cart. A door meant for someone considerably shorter than I beckoned, and I tried the handle impatiently. It opened with a smooth click, letting me through.

I blinked. The twenty or so beings in the room blinked at the same time—and much more effectively, since each was a Turrned with eyes the size of my hand. I was standing on what was definitely an altar, complete with fragrant smoking candles and dishes of what might have been wine.

"Servo's working fine," I said, somewhat breathless, waving vaguely behind me as I negotiated the tiny stairs leading down from the altar with some difficulty. "Don't need to thank me. Always glad to help."

The Turrned purred to each other with rather alarming loudness. I kept smiling and nodding, moving firmly toward the exit. The Turrned tilted their heads to watch me, limpid brown eyes brimming with sincerity. One spoke to me, I couldn't tell which. The voice was high-pitched with an underlying vibration as though the speaker purred at the same time. "You are troubled. Stay. We will pray for you."

Such kind beings, I thought with a rush of warmth, stopping in the doorway to the concourse.

A burly Human entered through the door as I hesitated, shoving me out of his way with one sweep of his thick arm. "This the Mission?" he demanded, scowling down at the tiny Turrneds who all blinked up at him. "Heard you gave out food." He looked to be a spacer, but his overalls were shabby and without any rank insignia.

This time I spotted the one who spoke. Its throat swelled with each word, even though the pursed lips stayed closed. "You are troubled," went the purr. "Stay. We will pray for you."

"I want something to eat," the man said, but less roughly, already under the spell of those beautiful brown eyes.

"You are troubled. Stay. We will—"

I smiled to myself, bowed to the missionaries, and went out into the concourse.

The crowds were as I remembered, location not seeming to make a difference. Everyone was in a hurry, making me wonder what merchants had to do to get anyone to stop and buy. I inserted myself into a lane of foot traffic moving at a comfortable pace and immediately felt much less conspicuous.

I put my hand in my left pocket, checking on my ident card. Morgan had given it to me before we left the *Fox,* in case the station authorities demanded some proof that I was registered crew. Now, I hoped it could be my ticket off Plexis.

I hadn't counted on Plexis itself being a problem. Hours later, with sore feet and an empty stomach, I entered the lineup for yet another automated ramp and wondered, not for the first time, just how big this place was. At least I'd managed not to circle back into the area where Morgan might be. But I was no closer to finding a ship of my own.

Being sandwiched between a pair of servos gave me a chance to lean on something as the ramp pulled its mostly living cargo to the next level. So far, all I'd found was more wholesalers, the seven levels I'd tried so far identical, if progressively richer in their offerings, to the one where I'd first entered the station. My spacer garb was becoming more conspicuous. I resisted the impulse to check over my shoulder.

The servo in front of me disembarked and I hurried to follow before the one behind rumbled its impatience. The machines wouldn't trample anyone, but they would summon their operators if kept from their work long enough.

Something was different here. I drew out of the crowd—that moving, aimless mass of machines and shoppers hadn't changed—and found a quiet spot from which to survey my surroundings.

The air had a fragrance suggesting growing things nearby. The walls were lined with storefronts, but no goods spilled out into the main passageway. Instead, broad doors stood invitingly ajar, each one that I could see from this vantage point manned by a servo that greeted any who entered.

Wait. The crowd here was different. Everyone I could see sported a gold shopper's tag on a cheek, or the appropriately corresponding body part. My blue tag was going to stand out for sure. There were spacers here, but the ones passing by had an air of prosperity that signaled credits to burn.

If I'd been with Morgan, I might have had the confidence to enter one of those stores and see for myself what was so tantalizingly hidden inside. As it was, I felt dangerously conspicuous and looked frantically for a rampway down.

"Can I help you, Fem?"

The voice was courteous, no more, but I jumped. The security guard, as typical on Plexis, was both friendly and well-armed. I couldn't place his species, but it was humanoid standard except for the delicate furring that covered his head and seemed to go down the sides of his neck. He smiled warmly, likely on the reasonable premise that today's loiterer could be tomorrow's big spender, and repeated his question. "Can I help?"

"Yes," I said quickly, relieved that I had no automatic aversion to his uniform to deal with—evidently that compulsion was also gone for good. "I've gotten off on the wrong level. I wanted to find," my stomach growled on cue, "a good place to grab some breakfast."

"New on-station?"

I nodded. "First time. It's bigger than I thought."

His smile grew wider, revealing purple caps on the tips of what on a human would be first molars. "There are twenty-three more levels above this one, Fem. But you want Level 3, spinward $^3/_4$. There's a food and relax center there as well as the main posting office for outbound ships. A must stop for every spacer on Plexis. You'll see."

The guard's directions were, of course, easy to follow. I quickly found myself back among other beings with blue tags and less-than-new clothing. And just in time to suit me. I no longer dismissed my urge to look over my shoulder as mere nerves. I was being followed.

There were two of them, both spacers by their apparel, both passably Human. The clothes reassured me that they weren't Clan. Humans were quite common on Plexis. So, however, were what Morgan referred to as scum. After all, credits being spent attracted those who sought easier ways of earning them than work.

The only problem with that theory, I decided, working my way with what I hoped was a nonchalant air through a snarl of offspring orbiting a sweet-vendor, was that there was nothing about me to make such experts see me as a likely target. I was surrounded by beings festooned with purchases and obvious wealth. Why pick on me?

The answer, that they knew who I was, sent a cold shiver down my spine.

So far I'd been able to stay in public places, but my shadows were gradually moving closer. If I turned and stopped abruptly, not a wise move in the midst of the shopping traffic, I could have touched one of them.

There. The relax center the guard had recommended. I abandoned politeness and pushed my way forward, not bothering to look behind. It was a public place and, hopefully, a place that would help me get off Plexis.

An hour or so later, I chewed thoughtfully on the pastry I'd purchased with the few credits in my pocket, eyeing the posting board. It was an immense screen, long enough to exhibit some of Plexis' curve as it stretched off in the distance. The ship listings that paraded along it must have had some meaningful organization. There were plenty of others in this vast room who glanced up at the screen, nodded wisely, and made comments to their companions about cargoes, risks, and opportunities. I couldn't make any sense of it.

My shadows had followed me in, but seemed content to sit in the food area where they could watch the entrance. There was another way out, however. And I was ready to try it, having filled my empty stomach at last.

There were tables loosely arranged in a quiet back corner of the room, far enough from the doors to the various entertainments to be away from the noise, but easily seen. I'd overheard enough conversations to know that the tables displaying yellow placards were staffed by representatives from ships looking for permanent crew. There were six of these at the moment. The green placards were for temps only, a commitment much more suited to my needs and abilities.

I approached the nearest of the two green tables, only to have the placard removed as the beings stood up and shook hand to tentacle in agreement. One chance lost. I couldn't resist glancing over my shoulder. My shadows had spotted what I was doing and were moving this way. I hurried to the next table and quickly dropped into the empty seat, pulling my bag up on my lap.

There was a woman already seated at this table. She

dressed like a spacer, of course, though so did everyone else in this part of Plexis. Her air patch was blue—here just on business, then. Although fit and lean, her skin was wrinkled under its tan, her dark brown hair peppered with gray. I was sure I'd never seen her craggy features before. Or was I?

"Name?" she waved a hand missing two fingers.

"Sira. Sira Morgan." I said, having made the decision to stick with what was on the ident card in case I had to produce it. Morgan. He might look for me. Or he might not. Both options made me unhappy.

"Sira Morgan." The woman recorded something on a hand pad. "Name's familiar," she added casually. "I'm Gistries San."

I resisted the temptation to look around and see where my shadows were now. "Morgans get around," I said, noncommittally.

She looked up. "Last ship and posting?"

"Hindmost on the *Silver Fox,* out of Karolus." I'd placed my bet now, I thought. Morgan hadn't told me what story he'd concocted to hide the *Fox* on Plexis. I could only hope it wasn't the sort of thing to spread.

Apparently it was a safe bet. Gistries made a couple of entries, then grunted with satisfaction. "Nice to have someone admit to being Hindmost for a change," was all she said. She curled a lip disdainfully and pointed a booted toe at the posting board. "You've no idea how many claim to be grade A pilots instead!" She looked me up and down once more. "I see you have your duffel. Ready to go now?"

No questions about why I'd left the *Fox* or why I wanted only temp assignment. I was suddenly unsure, in spite of this Gistries' businesslike demeanor.

Her dark eyes grew speculative. "Sorry to sound in a rush, but I'm due onboard for final prep. You can come with me if you'd like to check out the ship, maybe meet the captain before signing. He likes to take on a couple of new maintenance hands when there's a good cargo on board. I've already found two, but I'd like another. Turnover's pretty high on midrange traders, you know. Up to you." She began packing up her things.

There were footsteps behind me. Without looking, I knew my shadows were lurking as if waiting their turn. "I can go now," I assured her. If I didn't like the ship or its captain, I'd come back. For now, what mattered was eluding my pursuers, whoever they were.

Gistries, who had waited with unexpected patience, smiled when I stood up. She tipped over the green card. "Great. Let's go. You won't be sorry, Sira. My captain has a history of very profitable voyages."

* * *

INTERLUDE

"How's your head?" Huido asked, easing himself with a contented sigh into a chair expressly designed for his massive bulk, the claw tips of his lower, and larger, two arms resting comfortably on the floor.

Morgan ignored the question. The blinding headache he'd awakened with was the least of his worries. "Any word?"

The Carasian's multiple eyes examined Morgan warily, years of practice letting him recognize an unusual grimness to the human's pale features, a dangerous set to Morgan's eyes and mouth. "Nothing yet. Plexis is a big place. Be patient."

Morgan wasn't inclined to patience, especially not since waking up on the floor of the room with a pounding head and the sick realization that Sira was gone. "Did you get anything from the Plexis security?"

"They were reluctant; it took two cases of Brillian Brandy to loosen the record strings. The *Torquad* docked after you. But so have twenty other ships, including two Enforcers."

"Bowman's lot I expected. I can deal with her. But Roraqk." Morgan cursed. "Sira's out roaming the decks of this damned station, and you know he has half the station staff on his payroll."

A small click as the Carasian signified his agreement. "Still, an outright kidnapping on Plexis would be risky, even for Roraqk," puzzled the alien.

"Not if he smells profit sufficient to buy him a nest site anywhere he chooses, with no questions asked."

Too restless to remain still, Morgan stood and paced,

grimacing as the motion jarred his sore head. It was a pain he'd earned for himself, all right, just what he deserved for tampering with a mind whose complexity was only now becoming clear to him. He hoped Sira knew it hadn't been her fault.

"Ransom from kidnapping your mate?" Had Huido eyebrows, they would have shot skyward. "Forgive me, dear friend, but—"

"Roraqk expects nothing from me." More briskly. "You're certain he's still in dock?"

"Yes." Huido shifted uncomfortably, the overlapping plates on his abdomen sliding over each other with a soft hiss. "But are you certain Sira is on Plexis? There have been departures. I have a partial list—" he broke off as Morgan tapped his forehead suggestively.

"Sira's still here. Somewhere. I know."

Armor glistened wetly as Huido rotated his head to bring all of his eyes to bear on the smaller Human. "So. Sira shares your gift. What else haven't you told me?" He paused. "Why do I suddenly find it difficult to believe this romantic tale of another Morgan on the *Fox*?"

Morgan's mouth twisted wryly. "I haven't lied, just let you believe what you wished. Face it, you've pestered me on the topic of partnering for so many years I owed you! Sira's important to me. And she's saved my life. Twice," Morgan's voice trailed away pensively as he rubbed the ache behind his forehead. Huido clicked his upper claws impatiently.

"If she is not a Morgan," he complained, "then who is she—and why does your Sira tempt a master pirate?"

"A pawn in a game much bigger than I thought, Brother." Morgan roused from his contemplations. "And someone who shouldn't be used that way."

Accepting Morgan's unwillingness to explain further, the Carasian switched to practicalities, standing noisily. "So we're going to search Plexis with Roraqk and his crew on our backs. Your visits are never dull," As Huido spoke, his dexterous claws pried open a cabinet, revealing an assortment of hand weapons highly illegal on several planets, but then, almost nothing was illegal on Plexis. He carelessly tossed a biodisrupter to Morgan, who caught it from the air with practiced ease. "We hunt?"

"We hunt," Morgan confirmed grimly. "As long as it takes." Almost to himself.

Huido shrugged philosophically, selecting some lethal weaponry of his own to hang from clips embedded in the chitin of his chest. "As I recall, my chef has an acceptable recipe for lizard." A chuckle of amusement echoed hollowly within his huge body.

The muted sound of a door chime interrupted further speech. Huido clicked his annoyance and looked apologetically at Morgan. The Human merely shrugged, taking a seat on the couch which faced the doorway, slipping his weapon beneath a cushion as he did so. The Carasian paused to snap a fitted vest over his own armament before bellowing an irritated: "Enter!"

"What is the meaning of this intrusion, bottom crawler?" Claws snapping menacingly, Huido heaved toward the door as he saw the two figures behind his anxious servant. "You bring no one up here unannounced!" With admirable restraint, Morgan nodded a noncommittal welcome.

"Don't terrify poor Ansel, Huido. I doubt it was his idea." As one of the shadowed figures ventured closer, eyeing Huido cautiously, Morgan added: "Meet Barac—I'm sure you remember him from one of my wilder tales. And. . . ?"

"My cousin, Rael," Barac showed his relief to be past Huido's ominously silent figure. The Clanswoman didn't spare the giant a glance. Morgan felt a warning raise the hairs of his neck.

"Friends of yours, little Brother?" Huido easily inspected both visitors simultaneously.

"We have been," Barac said hastily, as if daring Morgan to challenge this. Morgan kept any response from his features and, more importantly, from his thoughts. Huido waved his apologetic and confused servant away, closing the door and stationing his own bulk before it with deliberate intent. *Against any opponents but these, old friend,* thought Morgan. Barac was trouble, but Morgan found himself feeling more uneasy about the woman, Rael. Though most of her beauty had been obscured, there was no mistaking the original model for the projection that had called to Sira. And had she been the one to attack him through their link?

"She's not here." Rael's voice was like silk, but her

tone was bored and imperious. Huido's head tilted. Morgan signaled him to remain silent. There was no need for any other warning; Huido's species used mental channels of a totally different order from Human or Clan.

"You really shouldn't have taken Sira away from Auord without contacting me, Jason," Barac said quickly. He seemed conciliatory—an attitude Morgan had hardly expected and one he distrusted thoroughly.

"And how was I to do that, Clansman?" Mildly.

"Where is Sira?" snapped the Clanswoman.

"It's never wise to be impatient, Cousin." Without being invited, Barac took a seat opposite Morgan. "Rael doesn't fully appreciate our situation, Morgan. You can understand that we, as Clan, are rarely limited in our dealings with other species. Rael hasn't come across Carasians before," a gracious nod to Huido, "nor has she noticed your weapon, which I'm sure has us both in its sights."

Rael's large green eyes narrowed speculatively at this, then shifted, becoming strangely unfocused as Morgan turned slightly to meet her gaze. Their eyes locked for a long moment. Rael shuddered abruptly, looking away with a startled curse before staring at the Human with quite a different look in her eyes—one of shock. Morgan merely continued to smile pleasantly, lifting the protecting cushion from the weapon held loosely but competently in one lean hand.

"Now why doesn't it surprise me that you can't be *pinned,* old friend?" Barac asked softly, menacingly. Huido shifted ominously. "Rael is quite accomplished, you know. Much more powerful than I. And what does that make you, Morgan?"

"It makes you both fools," Rael hissed furiously, wheeling on her cousin. "This Human knows nothing beyond tricks we teach children! I could destroy him—"

"But you won't." Morgan tossed his weapon aside, his pose deceptively relaxed, a flash of his eyes quelling the uneasy Carasian. "We know each other well enough, Barac."

Rael was far from silenced. "I know you, all right. You can't hide the stench of your power from me!"

"Where is Sira, Morgan?" Barac made an effort to

ignore his cousin, to concentrate again on the imperturbable Human. "I know you can be reasonable when it suits you." An honest puzzlement filled his voice. "What can you hope to gain by obstructing us? Don't you realize how I've protected you all these years?"

Morgan's smile didn't reach his icy blue eyes. "I don't recall asking for your protection, Barac."

"Barac—" Rael growled.

"Not now, Rael!" Barac lost control momentarily as he harshly cut across her speech. Huido shuffled, alert to the tension in the room if not sure of the reason. "I don't know what Sira has said to you, what may have happened to cause you to distrust me—"

Morgan's smile was mocking. "When did the word trust enter into it, Clansman? As I said, we know each other well enough."

Barac swallowed his planned retort to this, obviously thinking hard and fast. "We had a bargain—"

"Bargain? You asked me to find Sira. I did. You asked me to help her off Auord and out of danger. I did. Perhaps I've done more to help Sira than you expected."

"I expected some truth!" Barac accused hotly. "Now I find my old friend is a telepath of no minor strength as well as a smuggler and a liar. And probably a kidnapper as well. Did you sell her to those planetside filth?" He halted, stricken in mid-thought, then went on hoarsely, as if against his own will: "Or was there something about her you had to keep for yourself—"

"Stop this!" The rebuttal came from an unexpected source. "Don't persist, Cousin," Rael continued, eyes flashing. "You're close to wearing out my patience."

Barac refused to look at her, his angry gaze riveted on Morgan. "I asked for your help in finding Sira, Morgan. Now I find she's been on your ship, recorded as crew, and now appears to have vanished once more. Tell us what you've done with her!"

"Believe what you choose, Clansman." Morgan was tired and more than aware of the passage of time—not to mention his aching head. "I don't know where your Sira is now, nor do I care. She left my company once we docked. I expect she's gone outsystem on one of the hundred or so ships that were ready to lift when we arrived. Is that helpful enough? Now. What about some compensation for my time, my effort? I've docking fees to pay, in case you hadn't noticed—"

"Name your price." Rael's voice was low.

"My price?" Morgan studied her for a moment, abruptly more puzzled than offended. The Clanswoman returned his look with a suspicious scowl. Her long, vibrant black hair framed a delicate, yet strong face. Her body was superb, shown to advantage by her dress as well as the tension of her anger. Rael's dislike of Morgan was whole-hearted and tangible—yet at that moment, the Human would have sworn that he'd never seen true beauty in a woman before.

Rael shuddered. "Stop staring at me, Human, before I forget you may still be of use to us." Morgan started, uncomfortably aware in the ensuing silence that he had been gawking at her as if he were at a glamour show.

'He's drawn to your Power, Cousin," Barac clarified for her. He arched a sardonic brow at her wide-eyed stare. "I told you I know Humans—"

"Impossible," Rael said unsteadily, her eyes unaccountably frightened. Morgan realized with shock that her fear was of himself. "I refuse to believe this, Barac. You are no—"

"Mind yourself, Rael. Don't you feel his interest in everything we say?" Barac glared accusingly at Morgan. "You may scorn my protection, Human, but your life will be a great deal shorter without it."

Morgan rose to his feet. "I should think our business over, anyway, Barac. Forgive me if I don't wish you luck."

Barac remained seated. "The spoken word easily hides the true nature of things, doesn't it, Captain? Yet say I believe you. Isn't it odd Sira would leave you for another ship, if she had a position as crew and you were taking such good care of her? I'd have thought she would prefer to stay, to remain close to her benefactor. Or were you more?"

"Enough!" Rael exclaimed in a voice grown deadly. "You forget yourself, *sud*. Do not force me to remind you. This Human may be slightly more than we thought at first," she ignored Morgan's mocking bow, "but our time is wasted pursuing this folly of yours. We've our own means of verifying his information."

Barac scowled and stood. "As you wish," he gave in grudgingly. "We'll be back if we don't find her; count on it, Human." All pretense of friendship was gone from Barac's harsh voice. Morgan's smile was amused.

"I'll send you my bill, Clansman."

Chapter 14

THE simplest thing could change a person's perception of reality, I decided. In my case, I could blame the pink spot on my cheek where an air tag had so recently clung.

My companion, Gistries San, had worn a blue tag, like mine. But it wasn't exactly like mine. My tag had been obtained under, shall I say, irregular circumstances? But it was real. Gistries' tag had been just plain counterfeit.

It would have worked, and I would have stayed a happy enough fool a while longer, had there not been a line at the tag point on the way to Gistries' ship.

There were three operators manning the tag point on this level. When we'd arrived, the operator nearest us was dealing with some complaint or other, a disgruntled line of those waiting their turn growing longer immediately. The next operator waved some of these over to her counter, and Gistries followed this group with myself in tow. We ended up five back.

I'd looked over my shoulder uneasily, trying not to be obvious about it. My shadows had followed us; hopefully we'd finally lose them on the other side of this checkpoint. The two lined up peacefully, despite not moving quickly enough to beat the trio of Denebian spacers who good-naturedly bumped into me and cheerfully apologized. Shore leave.

The next operator suddenly had no one left in his line, and waved at us. I tapped Gistries on the shoulder to get her attention and started hurrying to the other counter.

A hand took hold of my arm just above the elbow and jerked me to a stop. Startled, I looked down at Gistries' hand and then up to her face. Her eyes were cold and hard. "This line will do, chit," she said firmly. She didn't release her grip.

The Denebians swayed and chuckled their way into what should have been our place at the empty counter. I didn't bother to turn and see my followers move up to stand at my back. "Who sent you?" I asked, glaring at her.

"Just keep calm and there'll be no trouble. Got it?" Something pricked through the fabric at the base of my spine. I felt the sharpness, but it didn't penetrate the skin.

"Got it," I whispered. The sharpness disappeared, but I knew I was trapped.

When it was finally our turn at the counter, we were faced by a sharp-eyed Human, one who looked quite capable of noticing a hair out of place. I leaned forward so the Human could remove my tag, forming a vague plan to complain about the charge, or create some kind of disturbance that would stir the interest of the plentiful security personnel scattered around the tag point.

Instead of peeling off my tag, the man touched it with a rod. The tag dropped into his hand and he laid it on the counter next to the device that would read it. The tiny blue thing humped itself into the maw of the reader and I realized with wonder that it was alive, a tattle-tale rather than a recording device.

The operator peered into the top of the reader. "15.35 hours of breathing," he snapped, the lights from the readout reflecting on his prominent cheekbones. "Automatic transfer to the account of the *Claw and Jaw*. Rich place for a spacer to run up a tab," he commented, raising his head and cocking a curious brow at me.

I opened my mouth to speak, but Gistries had already pushed me ahead, keeping her hand on my back as though we were friends.

" 'lo, Malcolm," she greeted the operator in a casual tone. "How's the family?"

I closed my mouth.

The tag operator winked at her as he removed her tag. He smiled as he saw the readout, then said in a low voice, "Amazingly enough, you've been here 27 hours and I'm going to have to charge you for, lessee, 300 hours of air, Gis."

"Fine with me, Malcolm. Always a pleasure doing business with you. Just make sure the *Torquad*'s docking ring stays unlocked."

"A pleasure doing business with you, too, Gis."

The *Torquad*. Roraqk's ship. I couldn't believe how gullible I'd been. I turned desperately toward the tag operator. He met my eyes, then carefully looked away, saying "Next?" The two behind us were processed without a word.

Gistries kept her hand flat against the small of my back, propelling me ahead, her firm touch a warning not to struggle. She'd taken my bag in her other hand. We moved quickly, passing two cross-corridors leading to other docks, until we reached the *Torquad*'s air lock. A guard, this time not station security, but a nondescript Auordian with green beads sewn through his hair, stirred from his post beside the air lock, weapon swinging up to cover me, then lowering as Gistries grunted something incomprehensible, the language guttural and unlike any I'd heard.

The air lock was larger than that of the *Fox*. Gistries and I waited while the outer door cycled closed and the inner one began opening. My two followers had remained outside. Gistries hummed to herself cheerfully.

"And what does he want with you?" she said out loud, surveying me with a shake of her head. "Usually I can tell the value of a deal, but you? You puzzle me, Sira di Sarc."

Another guard, this one silent, fell in behind us in the ship's corridor. "Sira di Sarc?" I asked, licking my lips after saying the name, as if its taste would make it familiar. "You have me mixed up with someone else. My name is Sira Morgan."

"Huh," she grunted. "Not likely."

We entered a lift. I tried to keep my mind off who was waiting.

Roraqk dipped his snout toward me as we entered the long curving control room of the *Torquad*. He didn't seem the least surprised. "My Kisssue, at lass-sst."

There was nothing to be gained by showing how much he scared me, so I raised my chin and said firmly: "My name is Sira Morgan. Not Kissue."

"Not ss-sso. Your true name is-ss one well known to

me, ss-Sira di ss-Sarc. I've been looking for you for ss-so long, I'd begun to think you were some drug dream of my dear friend's-ss. It is-ss not eassy to hide from my connections-ss. Yet, you came to me on Auord—a gift of fortune. And you come back to me now. I'd have been ss-so disspleassed to have losst you." I felt Gistries' shiver through the hand she'd locked around mine.

"You're mistaking me for someone else, Captain Roraqk," I insisted, though small warnings raised the hairs on my arms.

"Don't look ss-so worried, Fem di ss-Sarc. I've no dessire for merchandisse as-ss ss-specialized as-ss yoursself." Gistries chuckled at this. Roraqk continued to regard me fondly—or was his look more one of appetite? "You ss-should be glad my friend on Acranam wants-ss you as-ss you are, without drugs-ss or any damage. You certainly couldn't go to anyone elsse intact."

I sensed, almost touched, a web enclosing me, woven from threads I couldn't see or understand, pulling at everyone who came near me—even Roraqk. A surge of fury shook me. An odd emotion, considering I was helpless. Helpless? *Only for now,* I promised myself grimly, peering at the lizard through carefully lowered eyelids, *only for now.*

The pupils of Roraqk's eyes shrank to dangerous predatory slits, as though he read my determination. "I've been ass-sured you are pathetically harmless-ss, Kissssue. I find thiss-ss eass-y to believe. But I warn you, Giss is-ss very ssensssitive to mindcrawlers-ss. Aren't you?"

Gistries' hand locked over the handle of the weapon in her belt, the knuckles white. There was something not quite sane in the look she threw me.

Roraqk walked over to his command bench, sat down, and pulled a thin tube of some dark substance from a compartment. "Do you know what a marvelous-ss opportunity you are, Kissssue?" He dipped his tongue deep within it, that member whipping back between his jaws with a cargo of foam. "I like to pay my debts-ss promptly." Another dip. "Ah, from you, little Kisssue, I ss-should gain a resss-spectable profit."

"I don't know what you're talking about," I spat. "I haven't done anything to harm you."

"Indeed not. You amuse me, Kisssue. Forgive me. S-sSira Morgan iss-ss what you prefer. And why did I not know thiss-ss before?" the words savored rather than spoken. "I try to learn everything about my friendss-ss: who they hate, who they love." His frills were extended and pulsing with blood and color. Roraqk was definitely enjoying himself. "Which bindsss you to Morgan of Karolusss?"

I met his glistening yellow eyes with an effort of pure will. "Morgan's nothing to me."

"Ssso."

"Yes. Anyway, he made me work without pay, and tried to stop me getting a better post. Why do you think Gistries found me at the crew board? I wouldn't give this," I snapped my fingers, "for Morgan of the *Fox*."

"Well, well," he chuckled. "Morgan means-ss nothing to you? Why do I find this-ss hard to believe, little Kisssue? Are you trying to tell me you do not know your name was-ss regisstered on Ret 7 as-ss part owner of the *Fox*? That, in the quaint way of traders-ss, Morgan hass-ss assigned you Master's-ss rights-ss upon his-ss death?" He began one of his dreadful drooling laughs. "How wonderful—ss-shall I kill him and help you gain this-ss prize?"

Stunned, my face must have revealed everything I needed to hide for there was a menacing triumph in Roraqk's eyes. Throwing caution aside, I said furiously: "Harm him and we'll see how long you survive. Spacers stick by their own, Pirate. There'll be a hundred ships after you."

Roraqk laughed so hard I felt my heart grow still and cold within me. "But Morgan has-ss lossst the right to ss-such aid—and ss-so have you. Plexisss lissstss your *Fox* as-ss misss-sing. Do you think s-some nassty pirates-ss have attacked her? Delicious-ss!" he chattered, threads of hot, wet spittle lashing across my face. "I couldn't have done better myssssssself!"

I hated the sound of his voice, hated it with an intensity I hadn't dreamed I was capable of feeling. My hands shook, and I clenched them together.

"Captain."

The interruption came from Roraqk's henchman, Kort.

"We have a problem," he began, then stopped, looking at me.

"Don't worry about my Kisssue, Kort," Roraqk said. "We have no ss-secrets-s."

Kort's pale eyebrows met in a scowl, but he went on obediently. "I put out the call to get the crew back as you ordered, including the ones sent to look for her. They've been detained. Some frat about air tags."

Beside me, Gistries cursed under her breath, but not quietly enough. Roraqk angled his head to stare at her. "What do you know of this-ss?"

"There were lineups at the tag point coming in just now," she answered promptly, but cautiously. "Didn't seem anything unusual."

"Gsssst," Roraqk hissed in fury. The pirate's yellow eyes dilated, their center a dark, speckled orange. His twin frills rose, pulsing with purple and red. "Not as-ss uss-ssual, fool! We have Enforcers-ss on ss-station. One is-ss docked only four racks ss-spinward. Thiss-ss trouble is-ss meant to delay me." He whipped around, grabbing Kort with one clawed hand as he moved. "Get me Plexis-ss on the com."

Gistries put some of her tension into a push that sent me flying onto a bench. "Stay there." She leaned against the bulkhead, dividing her attention between me and the backs of Roraqk and Kort as they worked over the com system.

I sat, outwardly calm, inwardly anything but. There had to be something I could do. Was there some way to make them understand that this wasn't Sira di Sarc sitting here? That I was Sira Morgan, a person without a past, or enemies? Well, with the exception of a couple of toads on Ret 7.

I agreed with Gistries. I wasn't worth all this. Unfortunately, Roraqk wasn't about to let me walk off his ship based on that argument.

The bench was hard, and not quite proportioned to suit humanoids. I eased my hip and Gistries narrowed her eyes at me in warning.

I felt a sudden, desperate longing for the *Fox*, to go home. I wanted Morgan.

Morgan. In a way, I became deaf, overcome by the power

of the thought of him. Abruptly, something tore away from me. I was suddenly light-headed, freed of the litany by some means which part of me almost understood.

What had Morgan's tampering done to me?

Into the exhausted quiet of my mind, a single word intruded, so gently that at first I didn't recognize its foreign origin. *Here.* I choked down a startled cry, glancing at Gistries to be sure it hadn't been noticed. She was looking over at Roraqk, who was hissing something furiously into the com, claws waving as if seeking a target.

Had I actually heard something in my thoughts?

Once more I thought of Morgan, of how I needed him, dropping my head down to better concentrate. Again his name seem to snap away from me. *Morgan.*

Sira? more than a name: an identification at once richer and more complete. My doubts vanished—if not my bewilderment. This time my *Morgan!* was a joyful peal of triumph.

Softly! My head's sore enough . . . but how? The slightly annoyed taste to Morgan's puzzlement was so clear and familiar I sagged with relief. This wasn't my imagination, then, though what it was would undoubtedly worry me when I'd time for such concerns. *Sira?* fainter—I had to strain to sift it from the background noise of my own thoughts. There was an undercurrent of pain.

Morgan! In this strange medium, there was no masking my alarmed concern.

Here. A pause. *Where are you? Hurry . . .*

The first image that came into my mind was this bridge. Useless, useless. What else did I have? Yes. I had no difficulty visualizing the protruding jaw, the gray scales and colored frill, the malicious eyes set beneath a hairless knobby brow.

There was an answering surge of black rage—a hate so deep I winced to receive even a fraction of it. And under it all was dread that Morgan couldn't keep from me. The name formed through the blackness: *Roraqk.* A pause in which I felt nothing and forced myself to wait. Then: *We're coming. Be no more than they think.*

And what am I, Morgan? I asked silently, suddenly frightened by this incredible conversation.

A rush of warmth, like spring sun on bare skin. It faded,

became a wisp, then was gone. Hugging the remnants of that strange comfort, I tried to relax. It was important to have reached Morgan—an admission I made freely to myself without attempting to probe any deeper. As to our nonverbal communication, Morgan would have to explain that one next time we met.

If we met, I forced myself to correct grimly. This was no story tape, with a timely rescue and justice for all.

Chapter 15

I SQUIRMED on the bench; it had been at least an hour since Roraqk had left the control room of the *Torquad,* and even Gistries' sour stare had lost some of its ability to stop my fidgeting. Boredom could really take the edge off fear.

"I can be worse than him," Gistries said with an almost conversational lightness. "Don't think to give me trouble." She hefted my bag with one hand, keeping the other on her weapon.

Trouble? I looked into her rock-hard eyes and forced a smile out of my dry lips, cracking the bottom one and tasting blood. "I'd rather have something to drink," I said, careful to keep my voice polite. "And eat."

Gistries turned and barked out a sentence in their mutual language to Kort. He grunted something over his shoulder, most of his attention on the control panels. Gistries shrugged, then nodded at the open door. "Let's go."

I led the way back down the oddly deserted corridor, the taste of ship air enough like the *Fox* to make me melancholy. The *Torquad* must have been considerably larger, however, since we took a center lift to another level. The silence was oppressive—all I could hear was the sound of steady breathing from behind my ear, and the rattle of small buckles being handled by an impatient hand.

Our destination was a door Gistries opened with a slap against the access pad, revealing a good-sized cabin. She entered with me, locking the door before taking a seat with the obvious intention of staying, one leg comfortably draped over an arm of her chair. Her cold, hard eyes remained fixed on me as I walked around.

It was nice enough, if you liked your luxury obvious.

My feet sank into lush, deep red carpet, patterned with hints of gold. The walls were paneled in what looked like real wood—though I found that extravagance hard to believe even on a pirate ship. The furnishings, chairs, lounges, desk, and oversized bed, were lavish, too, with carving or inlays on every surface. One door led into a fresher stall the size of the *Fox*'s galley. The other door was beside Gistries, and locked. Since Roraqk was on the other side, that was fine with me.

As a prisoner, I was advancing. The only sour note sat in an overstuffed blue chair, watching every breath I took.

A knock on the door. Gistries snaked to her feet, her hand wrapped around the grip of her holstered weapon in spite of being on her own ship. What was she expecting?

What arrived, guided by the same sullen Auordian that had admitted us to the air lock, was a servo cart covered with dishes which steamed and bubbled.

He left it in the middle of the room. Gistries waited until the door closed, the lock snicking in place, then went to the cart. She poked at the dishes, finally choosing a bread stick and a slice of some meat before returning to her seat.

I pulled a small chair up to the cart and sat, determined to ignore both my watcher and my fear. At least long enough to eat.

There was a stew in one of the small pots. I lifted the lid and sniffed at its spicy aroma. A memory curled around the edges of the steam. Enora had used this same spice in her tea, the one she brewed for sore throats which didn't really work but tasted delicious.

Enora? I sniffed again, wanting to remember anything more. There was a sense of protection, of wishing Enora were here with me now. Then the chill as I realized I had no idea if this Enora was a friend, servant, or mother.

Gistries shifted. I felt her eyes on me. "You're an odd one," she said at last, her voice slightly less harsh.

Memories faded. I began eating the stew, soaking bread sticks in the broth to make it a more substantial feast. I'd already learned not to count on my next meal arriving with any regularity. Gistries swung her legs around, sitting so we faced each other across the cart. I could hardly object, but my appetite faded significantly. I made myself eat anyway. She chose a piece of fruit.

"He won't hurt you, you know," Gistries said a moment later. I looked up and met her eyes, surprised.

"I find that hard to believe," I said. "Especially when Roraqk looks at me as though I'm next on the menu."

Gistries' tight face broke into a myriad of fine wrinkles that was almost a grin. "Just between us—he doesn't like Human. Says it's salty."

I swallowed hard, having really lost my appetite now, trying not to think about how Roraqk might have made that particular culinary discovery.

"Besides," she went on, mouth full of fruit, "you're a guaranteed sale, Sira di Sarc."

"Guaranteed sale to whom?" I asked, concentrating on pouring myself a cup of sombay without spilling the hot liquid.

She looked uneasy, then glanced at me assessingly and shrugged. "There's this grandee on Acranam—" Gistries stopped at my blank look and said impatiently, "Even Roraqk jumps to someone's call, you know." A darkness came and went in her eyes. "Roraqk's not the only one in the business who jumps to Yihtor's. This Yihtor's had a call out for you in particular for years now. You should've seen Ror—"

Yihtor. Whatever else she said was no more than mumblings. I almost shuddered under the impact of that name and the whirling, chaotic thoughts it triggered in my mind. I felt dread, instant and powerful, but totally unfocused.

Then, a tiny fragment of memory cracked open upon a face, a driven, desperate face.

I fought to hold that merest wisp of a thought. Others . . . I remembered others, faceless, standing with me. Enora had been there, had been angry. The memory whirled away. All that was left was that recollection of a man's face, pale with fury.

And a name. "Yihtor di Caraat," I said flatly.

Gistries hadn't noticed my reaction, being well into the remains of a fluffy sweetpie. "Old stuff, huh," she said around a mouthful, as if we talked about a mutual friend. "Kind of thing always circles back. I had a—"

A strident alarm shattered our strange truce. Gistries booted the cart away with one foot. It righted itself with a machine complaint, but not before several plates toppled to the carpet. She banged an urgent fist on the door. It opened. She turned to look at me over her shoulder, her weapon already out and ready.

"Be smart, Sira. Pleck will be on guard outside. And there's vids inside. I'll be back."

* * *

INTERLUDE

There was an armed guard posted outside the air lock: a hard-eyed man who scrutinized every passerby in the corridor, living or machine. This was not unusual on Plexis, and none who passed appeared to notice.

Where the corridor ran spinward of the air lock, a set of portlights had failed, throwing a convenient pattern of shadows over the two figures waiting there.

"Well? Is Sira there?" Huido rumbled, having kept silent longer than usual.

Morgan was apparently resting, leaning comfortably against the corridor wall, eyes thoughtful. "I don't know. And with the Clan around, it's not worth the risk of using mental touch to find out. But Roraqk's on board."

"Bold as a sandbat." Huido clicked his claws, a small and irritated sound. "You'd think he owned the station." The alien's sponge-toed feet tended to stick to the metal floor plates, making him shift to free them every few minutes. "If we're going to stand out here the rest of the day, I'll need a drink."

"Here's some water." Morgan passed Huido a canteen. "I don't plan to be out here much longer."

"I want another ss-shift ss-started," Roraqk hissed to his lieutenant. "I leave this-ss pessthole tonight! Bowman is-ss breathing down our necks-ss—"

Kort, the only indispensable member of Roraqk's crew and so the only one impervious to his leader's rages, looked up from under the panel he was repairing. "The Enforcers are making our contacts here very nervous."

"Then go and reass-ssure them that angering me sssshould make them even more nervous-ssss." The pirate ignored Kort's departing salute, turning to pace the now-empty control room, claws making tiny pricks of sound as they pulled free of the deck mats. He paused to stare out at the darkness beyond the prow of his ship.

"Nothing like crew trouble," commented a dry voice from behind. Roraqk's whirl was inhumanly swift, but his drawn pistol remained pointed at the deck when he saw the twin weapons already aimed at his midsection.

Confidently. "How convenient, Morgan of Karolus-ss."

Morgan's face was expressionless, but the blue of his eyes shone cold and deadly. "You seem shorthanded, Pirate. And I assure you one of us will fry you before you touch any of those controls." The almost imperceptible backward movement of Roraqk's thin hand ceased.

"What are you after?" he hissed. "The female?" A blink of yellow eyes. "Or ss-some payment?"

Huido clicked a threat. "Your tongue could shorten your life span, lizard. Where's Fem Morgan?"

A fanged grimace. "Fool. You ss-should know better—"

"You should," countered Morgan very softly, moving close enough to gather up Roraqk's weapon, then stepping back. "I can take the answers I need, Roraqk. But I'd prefer to stay clear of the cesspool in your skull." Morgan allowed a thread of his power to invade the surface thoughts of the scaled creature.

"Mindcrawler!" accused the lizard, visibly shaken.

"I'll know if you lie to me," Morgan promised evenly, keeping the effort he expended from his face, keeping his emotions equally well-concealed. "And I see no reason to let you live if you do."

"Then take her," Roraqk hissed. "And ss-see how long you can keep her!" With that, he gave a deep, visceral cough, spitting out a thin spray, catching both Huido and Morgan by surprise. They ducked, Morgan throwing up one arm to protect his eyes. Huido lunged forward, claws snapping. Too late.

"Where did he go?" Huido bellowed, spinning around. Two eyestalks stretched out and down to examine the smoking holes in the chitin of his chest. "Look what he did—those will stay till I molt!" he complained.

Morgan had torn off his jacket and stood looking at the ruin of it. "Nasty little creature, isn't he? We'd better find—" A klaxon sounded, deafeningly loud in the narrow control room. The floor began to vibrate. "The lift warn-

ing! Help me here, Huido, quickly!" Morgan ran to the
control panel, began laying in overrides, trying everything
he knew to interrupt the launch sequence, snapping commands to Huido. The klaxon died away, its place taken
by shrill voices on the com as Plexis station protested
desperately.

"Hang on to something," Morgan ordered, tight-lipped.
"I can't stop her."

The *Torquad* shivered once, delicately, as she pulled
free, shaking off the scaffolds and lines tying her to the station, in the process cracking the seals that protected Plexis
the way the tap of a spoon cracks an eggshell and spills its
contents. Emergency bulkheads slammed into place, locking in the precious air, locking out vacuum as well as the
unlucky station personnel, passersby, and spacers in the
corridor when the *Torquad* made her departure.

Morgan looked at the viewscreen for a moment longer,
sick but unable to turn away, watching bodies drift and
bump their way out the gaping hole that had been a docking ring.

"Who's going to shoot at us first?" Huido asked without
expecting an answer, claws still locked around a pillar in
the center of the control room. "Plexis or the Enforcers?"

Chapter 16

WHAT was going on? The alarm continued to shrill, making it hard to think. I fought panic, knowing there was nothing I could do locked in here anyway. And if the *Torquad* blew apart, I'd probably never notice.

The door burst open. Roraqk himself, not a crewman, stood there. Streams of spittle hung between his teeth, spittle that smoked and gave off a sulfurous odor. I stepped back.

"Come." He motioned me into the corridor impatiently. Swallowing, I moved past him, careful to stay away from his dripping jaws. I thought suddenly of Auord and the Enforcer raid on the recruiters. There was the same air of pursuit and purpose about him.

We hurried down those almost familiar corridors, passing two sealed doors before Roraqk stopped, pointing down a spiraling ladderway. I climbed as quickly as I could, his needle-clawed feet threatening to step on my hands. After only one level, the ship heaved. I flung my arms around the nearest rung, hanging on with all my strength. Above me, Roraqk did the same, hissing what sounded like his laugh. A sudden, heavy vibration thrilled from the wall into my bones. This was no gentle release and acceleration from the station. The *Torquad* was powering up for an emergency lift.

A giant's hand crushed my neck into my shoulders as the ship threw herself from the station and its gravity field with a total disregard for normal procedures or for the lives of those aboard. I gasped, close to blacking out.

The world steadied. "Get out at the next level," Roraqk ordered.

Another identical corridor. This time, Roraqk went ahead

of me, stopping to open a storeroom door. He pushed me in, then followed, sealing the door behind him. I pressed against the far wall, trying to keep from touching any part of him.

I sneezed. The air was dusty and full of an acrid odor. A tiny rustle and squeak made me turn to look at what I leaned against. The wall, and the one opposite, were lined with small crates, no, cages, stacked one upon the other. I could see hundreds of tiny eyes peering at us. They made no sound beyond a restless patter and shifting of cage litter.

With an absent air, Roraqk flipped a door open on a cage near him, reaching inside to capture a bit of struggling pink fur. He tossed the animal between his teeth, the crunching sound almost as loud as the squealing.

Next, Roraqk flung open a locker, tossing evac-suits from it onto the floor. "Get into one, quickly," he hissed.

What was he up to? As I obeyed, I watched him pull on his own suit. Roraqk spared a moment to clean his jaws with a twist of cloth before putting on his helmet. I sealed the last clasp on mine, automatically activating the air and comlink. Through the com, Roraqk's breathing filled my ears, out of sequence and shallow.

We went back into the corridor, this time Roraqk leading me by one arm and swinging his heavy head in a constant search. I tried briefly to struggle free of his grasp. He cuffed my helmet hard enough to make my ears ring. For the moment, I marched along without further argument.

Then I saw the air lock ahead. I began to struggle again, this time with everything I had. The Enforcers must be attacking; he was going to dump me into space!

"If you do not cooperate, you will die," Roraqk hissed over the link, grip firm on my arm, my struggles useless. "I'm voiding the ss-ship."

"Your crew—" The foolish question died on my lips. I watched Roraqk punch in a complex number sequence, overriding the safety on the air lock. Why? What did he hope to gain by killing everyone else on board?

Then, I knew. Morgan was here. And Roraqk was going to kill him.

I threw myself on the pirate, his surprise allowing me to knock him away from the panel. He twisted, incredibly supple despite the suit. I clenched my gloved fingers into fists and pounded on any part of him I could reach. His arm swept up in a swing that cracked the seal of my helmet. I could see his jaws snapping, frustrated by the clear plas between us.

I pulled back, then butted my helmet down on his chest with all my strength. Roraqk's gasp sounded through the comlink with satisfying clarity. Again I struck, hard enough to make my ears ring again. Then hands from behind yanked me away.

Roraqk's slender lieutenant shoved me to one side. "What's going on?" Kort demanded, his gaze flashing from the winking panel to where Roraqk was rising to his feet.

Roraqk snatched the weapon from Kort's hand. He turned and flipped a final control on the air lock panel. Kort screamed and launched himself forward, dying instantly in the attempt. The still glowing muzzle of Roraqk's weapon swung to point at me. I stood there trembling with rage and the aftermath of our struggle. "Always-ss you surprissse me, Kisssue," he said, his voice tinny through the helmet.

I pulled off what was left of my helmet, defiant. "I'm no good to you dead. Reset the air lock. I'll tell Morgan to leave you alone."

Roraqk's teeth chattered in one of his laughs. His meaning was unmistakable.

"You should have listened, Roraqk," said a very cold, deliberate voice from behind me. I closed my eyes for an instant, shaking. I suppose I hadn't truly believed until now.

The pirate didn't hesitate. He moved rapidly, jerking me around until I was hard against his chest. I was looking directly at Morgan at last, and met his eyes with a totally unwarranted sense of security. He was unarmed, standing loose-limbed and relaxed before a small hatchway. His eyes didn't leave Roraqk after that one quick reassurance to me.

"We wait. How amussing." Roraqk's voice boomed through the helmet. His arm pressed against mine, lifted to aim his weapon directly at Morgan. I was afraid to move in case he fired in reaction. "I will ss-so enjoy ss-seeing you die, Morgan of Karolus-ss. And this-ss annoying little pet of mine."

Morgan's eyes became slits. There was a sudden un-natural calm all around us. We three could have been alone in the universe. I stared at Morgan, watched his face begin to gleam with sweat, saw the artery along his throat pulse.

Roraqk's arm fell away from me. I dropped, rolling away. Neither he nor Morgan moved; somehow they were locked together. I didn't try to understand. I hurried to the panel, hitting the emergency seal button, sagging back with relief as the lights went a reassuring green.

Roraqk's jaws were agape within his helmet, his thin black tongue flailing. I stood, awed and a bit afraid, glancing from Morgan to the pirate. Slowly, Roraqk folded at the knees, crumpling down to the deck. He stared up at Morgan, one hand keeping him from complete collapse, the other falling loose and releasing its weapon. I grabbed it as it rolled.

Morgan's hands clenched spasmodically. Roraqk's head drooped forward until it rested by its snout on the floor.

Morgan staggered and I went to him, offering my shoulder. He leaned on me, without a word. With the touch, the sense of him flooded me, his pulse wildly fluctuating, strength almost sapped.

"You could've waited for me," rumbled a new arrival. Huido stooped through the smaller doorway, training a nasty-looking rifle on Roraqk, then gave the pirate's body an appraising push with one huge round foot. "I've settled what crew were left."

"Help me with him," I demanded.

"I'm supposed to be helping you, remember?" I twisted to meet Morgan's eyes, seeing what I was astonished to recognize as uncertainty.

"Are you all right?" Morgan asked finally.

I could only nod. There was something unfamiliar between us, something tense and strained. As I sensed it, it was gone. Morgan drew his other arm around me, enfolding me with a comforting tightness that also supported most of his weight. I burrowed my face against his chest, willing to stay for a moment, unwilling to allow my mind any questions. Not now. Not yet.

* * *

INTERLUDE

Commander Lydis Bowman squeezed her eyes closed, then opened them deliberately, determined not to lose her temper. After all, she worked with beings of every shape and talent, bending and flowing around their customs until her own humanity was, frankly, a bit rusty. This business with the Clan required only an extension of that attitude, an accommodation or two.

But, Bowman thought bitterly, 'Whix and all her subs knew she expected eye contact during a report—it was the one cultural need Bowman refused to give up. Holding 'Whix's shifting emerald gaze was aggravating enough at the best of times; his eyes were fitted to the sides of his feathered head so that light from behind sent distracting prisms through their bulging lenses. 'Whix usually did his best to keep an attentive, forward focus for his commander, but in recent days the Tolian had developed a habit of keeping one huge eye on whichever of the Clan were present. Bowman was left to hold the gaze of his other eye with both of hers.

"A female answering Fem di Sarc's description was seen in a Turrned Mission, sublevel 384, spinward third," P'tr wit 'Whix reported, rounded beak open to pant slightly in the, to him, overly warm ship's air. A veteran spacer, he normally wouldn't have shown distress, but the expression on Bowman's face was enough to throw off his equilibrium. His inner lids irised half-closed, then opened. When he stopped speaking, the feathers flattened over the tiny speaker embedded in his throat.

"If Sira is here, why haven't you found her yet?" Rael demanded.

Bowman glared at the Enforcer, at least at the one eye obediently bent in her direction. "What about Roraqk?"

"Unclear, Commander." If sighing were part of the Tolian's repertoire, he would have sighed. "I am encountering the usual lack of cooperation from Plexis. Their security insists Roraqk's a regular, reputable customer. The first story was that the *Torquad* blew dock by accident. Now they are suggesting that Roraqk's ship was taken over by pirates." 'Whix ignored Terk's derisive snort. "According to air tag records, Roraqk was aboard when the *Torquad* blew dock, but, in support of their claim, most of his crew was on station, heading for the *Torquad*."

"And died for their efforts," Bowman said, "Along with twenty-five others, a number likely to increase when Plexis restores the seal and can do a proper count. Not to mention the damage to the station." Bowman added, more to herself than to anyone present: "Why?"

"More to the point, why are you wasting our time with local matters, Commander?" Rael's voice was dangerously sweet. "Why aren't your people out trying to find Sira?"

"Piracy's a Trade Pact violation, Fem di Sarc," Bowman said, wondering how many more times she'd have to repeat it. "Roraqk may have paid for a clean slate here, but I've enough on him to warrant a sweep. And I won't let him throw this in my face and lift clear away. I'm sorry you're going to be inconvenienced." Her mouth tightened, a signal that straightened Terk from his casual stance. "My cruiser will be going hunting. We'll be back to pick you up when we're done."

"So now what?" Rael asked. "How do we find her? Who do we go to now? Where's your Morgan?" Her lips thinned over the Human's name.

Barac tilted his cup to drain the last of its contents into his mouth. He swallowed, grimacing at the bitter taste. "If I knew the answers, we wouldn't be sitting here."

Still, the Clansman regarded their new surroundings with a certain satisfaction, treasuring this one small victory. Morgan had used both bribery and a touch of mental persuasion worthy of the Clan to muddy the records of his arrival and ship. His efforts to disguise the *Fox* as the *Wayfayer,* Omacron registry, might have worked.

Except that Barac had been desperate. He shuddered inwardly at the risk he had taken. Passage through the M'hir sidestepped normal space. But there were limits. It took power to keep the focus, to hold the visual image that was all that would pull one safely out of the M'hir again.

Though no one had ever measured real time elapsing in the M'hir, subjective time increased with the distance of real space traveled. And the longer one's mind had to dwell in the M'hir, the more power it took to keep focused.

If the distance outmatched the power needed, well, the Clan called it *dissolving,* that instant when thought and form fragmented within the M'hir. What was left was a faint disturbance to haunt other Clan minds, a chill signal of the consequence of overreaching one's ability. A ghost. Barac's first teacher had ended that way, providing a far more effective warning to her class than she'd likely intended. Aspard di Sawnda'at, convinced that mental disciplines she'd learned from the Omacrons had enhanced her power, had tried to set a personal endurance record in the M'hir.

And, as anyone traveling through the M'hir near Omacron found out, quite a bit of Aspard was still there.

Yet Barac had taken his own version of that same risk, visualizing the familiar galley of the *Fox* and *pushing* himself through the M'hir at that vision without knowing for sure if the *Fox* was remotely within his range.

You could have luck like that once in a lifetime, Barac decided, determined never to take that chance again. The Clan expression for something irrevocably lost, *dropped in the M'hir,* was too close to reality.

The only flaw in Barac's victory had been the almost immediate arrival, by quite ordinary means, of Constable Russell Terk.

"It's an old trick," Terk had explained brusquely, passing through the air lock with innocent presumption. "I checked station records for ships posting a bond against their docking fees." Seeing their lack of understanding, Terk had grinned, an expression that did nothing to brighten his heavy features. "Plexis won't unhook a bonded ship and send it spinning when a payment's late. And what popped up but a bond supplied by Morgan's friend, the Carasian."

Now they sat together, in the galley of the *Fox,* outwardly civil, but Barac, for one, ready to strangle the smug Enforcer.

"All this doesn't explain why you are here," Rael asked. "To spy on us?"

Terk's eyes simmered with some emotion Barac couldn't read. "Hardly. How am I supposed to watch you when you pop in and out whenever you choose?"

"Why are you here?" Barac insisted.

Terk looked from Barac to Rael suspiciously. While he knew they couldn't affect his thoughts through his mind-shield, his awareness of their capabilities put him on edge, made him unconsciously hunch his thick shoulders. Finding the Clan on the ship ahead of him had badly shaken him. He couldn't understand why the Clan had so far tolerated his presence. Diplomacy. Well, it wasn't one of his faults.

"I tried warning Commander Bowman about Morgan before, but she doesn't believe me," he replied. "She's got some idea I have it in for him. But I know what I'm talking about. I convinced her to let me sniff after Morgan. I decided to check out the *Fox*—"

Rael glanced at Barac. She had rebuffed his thought that Terk could be useful, but this sounded unexpectedly promising. "Where do you think Morgan is now?"

"He's not here."

Rael scowled at this, suspecting humor, but Barac raised a brow. "Meaning?"

"Meaning he wouldn't have stayed on Plexis. People know him here. The Carasian's vanished, too, and he's as close to Morgan as skin. I say they've lifted."

"No ship has been cleared by Plexis since the *Torquad*. Surely you're not suggesting—"

Terk's scowl looked permanent. "Bowman wouldn't listen to me. Probably you won't either. But I never trusted Morgan—not a bit. He's too frat'n lucky. I've lost count of the times I've chased him down for a cargo check only to have him dump before I so much as order him to stop."

"You think Morgan is working with the pirate." Rael's face had grown very pale. "You think he's on the *Torquad*."

"I can't prove it," Terk said, taken aback by the passion in her voice.

"No need," Barac said bitterly. "It all fits. Morgan's on the *Torquad*— he's gotten away from us."

"What about Sira?" Rael's power throbbed forcefully beneath the distress in her voice. "Has he taken Sira with him?"

Wincing, Barac raised one hand. Rael damped her power, but he could still sense it, swelling like a wave in midocean, awaiting only a shoreline to crash against—or Morgan. "What if Morgan's been working for Roraqk all along?" he said to them both. "The Human might have taken Sira from Auord to throw us off the track, planning to meet Roraqk here." He paused.

"Roraqk's fond of kidnapping," Terk supplied.

"Yes," Rael said quickly. "He and Morgan must be planning to ask a ransom from Jarad. It would be easy enough to learn he's rich, influential."

Barac looked as though he would disagree, then glanced at Terk and thought better of it. "Your father wouldn't pay a ransom," he said.

Terk shook his big head grimly. "Wouldn't matter to your Sira if he did. Roraqk doesn't return hostages in one piece."

Rael shuddered. "If we convince your commander about this, Terk, would she take us back on her ship?"

He shrugged. "If Commander Bowman expects action, not a chance. Nothing personal, but she doesn't trust you."

"What kind of care would she take, even if she believed Sira was on the *Torquad?*" Barac started to pace. "This is impossible. We were so close. And now to be stuck here while you Enforcers bungle—"

Terk's gaze was remarkably clear and guileless for a Human. He waved a hand at their surroundings. "Who says we have to stay on Plexis?"

Barac's smile held a clear threat. "Are you suggesting we give up?"

Terk leaned back, folding his hands behind his head. "I was thinking more along the lines of some private hunting, Clansman. Seeing as how you have a nice fast little ship here, ready to go, and I'm not a bad pilot. My orders were to check out Morgan . . ." he let his voice trail away.

Barac and Rael traded glances. There was no need to merge thoughts. "We agree, Human," Barac said, "but what do you get out of this?"

Terk actually smiled. "Me? I get a chance to practice my diplomacy."

Chapter 17

ALL I needed to restore my outlook on life was an unbroken rest, a change into clean clothes, and a meal eaten with friends instead of enemies. I could even laugh at Huido's urging that I tan a piece of Roraqk's hide as, if I understood him, a form of counting coup.

For himself, the Carasian now sported an assortment of new weaponry, collected during his half of the fight on the *Torquad*. Only three crew members were left alive: two currently locked away in a very secure holding pen belowdecks, not the first so carried, judging by the names scratched on its walls. The third, Gistries, had come closest to stopping Huido's sweep through her ship, and he was quite proud of the scar she'd carved into his chest armor. Unfortunately, her misplaced loyalty had landed her in a med-cocoon. At least her injuries were not life-threatening.

The *Torquad* herself, damaged in her escape from Plexis, was limping toward the nearest discreet insystem facility. Her initial burst of speed had put us well ahead of any pursuit.

I sat at one end of the galley's main table, turning over and over in my hand a plate holding an image Morgan had found. He'd wasted no time checking the *Torquad*'s data storage for the name Roraqk used for me. There was nothing in the accessible records listed for Sira di Sarc, but there had been a file on a man named Jarad di Sarc, a wealthy politician native to the predominantly Human world of Camos. According to Roraqk's cryptic notes, this Jarad was either someone to avoid or a potential, if dangerous, target.

I'd stared at Jarad's image on the screen, recognizing it from visions yet unable to recall any feelings of connectedness to the stern, harsh face. My father. There had been no reference to a family at all within the records.

Then Morgan found a second image, the one I was currently holding in my hands, hidden beneath a simple security overlay. I looked at it again, still seeing nothing more in it than Jarad and a young girl standing in a line outside an ordinary enough restaurant, obviously unaware their image was being recorded. I requested the date for the tenth time. It still came up as 13,456.22 GS, 110 standard years ago.

It was quite reasonable that Jarad was a young man in the image. Humans, and indeed most humanoid races, usually lived into a second century. Morgan had sensibly concluded that the girl in the image was my mother.

I hadn't argued. But the girl was me. I hardly needed the stray memory of that day, that place, the excitement of a rare excursion out, to tell me; I could look in a mirror and see the same face right now. So either the image was falsely dated or retouched for some reason, or I was at least seventy years older than I appeared today. This seemed a conclusion better not shared with my friends. I turned off the viewer as Huido snapped his lower handling claw for our attention.

Morgan looked up from his dessert, a gleam in his eyes, and pushed aside his plate. "Wondered how long you'd stay quiet."

"Quiet? Who wants quiet? Nobody!" Huido announced noisily. "Everything is settled, until we get to Ormagal Prime, that is, and try to get this bucket repaired by those bandits, so all we need now is beer. And whatever intoxicants you two prefer, of course. A nice Chardonnay perhaps?"

Morgan raised a lazy brow at his friend. "On this ship?"

"There were Humans in his crew," I pointed out.

"Don't encourage him, Sira. We'll all pay tomorrow." Huido clicked something incomprehensible and left on his mission. "I hope you're up to a Carasian's idea of a celebration," Morgan warned.

I stretched, free, at peace. "Let's hope he's up to mine!" I hesitated. There were things I wanted to say. I looked at Morgan, and realized there was no need.

A smile that warmed. One lean, brown hand reached

over the table to hold mine, another heartbeat synchronized with my own.

I regarded him, thinking sadly of what he'd left behind. "You paid a stiff price, Morgan."

He gave a wry grin and toasted me with his cup. "What's gone, is gone." Then quickly, as he saw the flinch I couldn't help: "There's time now, Sira. Time and a new ship. What more could we ask for—ah, here's our scrounger with the answer!"

Huido maneuvered his way to the table, his claws and chest clips festooned with an incredible variety of bottles. I, for one, welcomed the interruption. Morgan had every right to be proud of his accomplishments and if he could bear to leave the *Fox,* so could I. I let the moment pass, resolutely plunging into our celebration. Sometime into the second bottle of wine, neither of us tapping into Huido's precious beer, I succeeded in subduing the strange turmoil produced by Morgan's gentle words and touch.

So I blamed the wine for my nightmare; coupled with the strain of the past few days, it was no wonder I tossed and moaned instead of sleeping.

In my dream, I sat in a thronelike chair, unable to move. Figures were clustered at my feet, empty-faced, blurring into one another; only their hands were distinct, hands that groped for me. I tried to avoid them, but couldn't. Every soft touch shuddered through my thoughts, clamoring for attention. I closed my eyes and mind to them.

True silence. I opened my eyes. The figures were gone. I was alone in darkness, only a glow from my skin anchoring me to myself. This was hardly better than the hands. I tried to wake up.

As I struggled to free myself from dreaming, I felt a thought, not mine but a stranger's, sticking to the dream like lint. I tried to brush off its whisper, only to feel it begin again somewhere else. I was afraid and helpless to name my fear. I was . . .

Awake. I relaxed my hands from their death's grip on the blankets, blinking the sleep from my eyes, the details of my dream fading. I cared more about the throbbing headache centered over one eye. I fumbled for the lights, thinking glumly that I had no head for wine.

On the top of a pile of clothing compiled from the lockers

of the crew's quarters, again by the talented Huido, I found a robe and shrugged it on with a sigh that stretched into a yawn. Once I found something to ease my headache, I'd be able to go back to sleep.

The galley was the logical place to look. I started rummaging through the cabinets at the far end, the twin rows of tables and benches stretching empty behind me. Some of the people who sat here once, talking, passing dishes, had likely been among those who died at Plexis. I rubbed my eyes, wishing I could pick and choose which memories to keep.

"Can't sleep?" Morgan asked softly. I turned, not surprised, and watched him pad gracefully toward me. He looked disgustingly cheerful.

"Let's just say you warned me about trying to match Huido's capacity," I looked at him out the corner of my eye as I spotted the object of my search and brought the bottle down to the counter. "Why are you up, if not to nurse a well-deserved hangover?"

"I sensed something wrong," Morgan answered with unexpected seriousness. I faced him, puzzled. "I thought you might need me," he explained. "What woke you?"

I shrugged away his concern and swallowed the mild painkiller I found. "I had another nightmare." I was mildly surprised Morgan hadn't shared the dream. "I've already forgotten it. I'm not used to so much wine."

Morgan frowned, eyes searching my face. "I felt more than that. I felt you call me."

I grew uneasy, abruptly aware of where he was leading the conversation. "I didn't—"

"And you haven't tried," a gentle accusation.

I didn't need the warning upheaval in my confused thoughts to know I wanted to avoid this of all topics, especially now when I felt far from up to a contest of wits.

Even more gently, he said, "Sira, I understand why you want to forget what happened."

Something gave way, and I was fiercely angry, though I wasn't sure at whom. "Do you, Captain Morgan?" I demanded bitterly. "Do you understand how I feel when each day I'm being turned into someone I don't know? Someone who's bought and sold by pirates; someone with a past known only to the dead? And now you want me to accept hearing voices in my head?"

"Voices?" Morgan repeated, quick alarm creasing his forehead, sharpening intent blue eyes. "Who else have you heard?"

I stopped on the brink of an answer, unable to form words. Mutely, I made a helpless gesture. "I don't know why I said that. It was just a nightmare."

Morgan approached, reached out swiftly to capture my hands. I felt myself being drawn into clear blue depths as our gazes met and held. There was no sensation beyond a feeling of lassitude, of relaxation. Then he released me. His eyes returned to normal, no longer engulfing pools, in a face showing considerable strain. Released from the spell, I recoiled from him. "How dare you—"

"Sit," a harsh command. Startled, I obeyed, watching wide-eyed as Morgan strode over to a wall-com and called Huido to meet us in the control room.

"What is it?" There was something dreadful in Morgan's face, and he didn't answer me, merely beckoned me to follow. I glared at his back, then hurried down the hall after him, on second thought shoving the bottle of painkiller into a pocket of my robe.

We rounded the last bend and Morgan stopped short of the control room door, putting out a hand to hold me back. I'd seen what alarmed him. The floor ahead was marked with a line of even dark red spots, each slightly rounded. The spots led through the open door.

Just then, Huido pounded up from the opposite direction, mumbling and rattling for all the world like a badly-tuned servo. So much for the element of surprise, though who or what we were to surprise I couldn't tell. Huido clattered to a stop when he saw Morgan and me. "What?"

Without bothering to answer, Morgan leaped forward, rushing into the control room. I couldn't have said why I was right on his heels. Huido rumbled behind me.

Our grand entrance was wasted on the person busy at work on the control panel—or what was left of it. Morgan cursed and grabbed a seemingly deaf Gistries away from the wreckage. She didn't struggle, just stood peacefully in his hold. Blood dripped from cuts on her hands, from her wounds, and from the ruined ends of the med-connectors she must have ripped loose to escape the cocoon. Med-gel coated her skin and hair, turning her into a statue of blood-marbled gray.

Leaving Morgan to deal with the pirate, Huido found an extinguisher and sprayed its foam over the flames where broken wiring and insulation had ignited small fires. The alarms were silent, but the ventilation system had already begun scrubbing the smoke from the air.

"We should get her back to bed," I said, shaking off my paralysis. Laying my fingers on Morgan's arm, I was shocked by its rigidity—it was like steel. The pounding of his heart hammered against mine. Yet Gistries wasn't trying to break free.

No, Gistries wasn't. I met her eyes and my breath caught in my throat. Gistries' eyes? No. Someone else was there, staring at me, *knowing* me. Yihtor. Behind her eyes, what was Gistries threw herself against bars, a captive, pitiful thing.

And Morgan fought for her. I felt his struggle coursing through my hands on his arm. He fought, and his efforts were scorned by the stranger in Gistries' face.

Immediately, without knowing how or what I did, I gave Morgan strength, sent energy surging through our contact. Gistries' body slumped suddenly in Morgan's arms.

He eased her to the deck, propping her against his shoulder. I bent down beside her, smoothing the gel-streaked hair from her face. Under the gray, her skin was deathly pale. Most of her blood must be on the floor. There was some on my hands. I braced myself when her eyelids rose again. But this time, the eyes looking at me were Human and full of pain.

"Thanks," Gistries said. Her head rolled on Morgan's arm to face him. "Time, Captain. Space clean." A tremor ran through her body that I felt through Morgan.

Morgan laid her down on the deck, careful not to jar the tubes protruding like darts from her neck. I looked at him in surprise. Morgan deftly twisted free a handweapon from those hanging on Huido. The Carasian stood stoically, looking down meaningfully at Gistries.

"What are you doing?" I said, unwilling to understand. "She needs to go back to bed—"

Gistries looked up at me, her face wrinkling in an attempt to smile. "Captain knows what I need, little one." Her voice faltered, then firmed. "No need to leave parts to claim, Captain. I've no kin. Don't let that mindcrawling Yihtor use me again . . . never again. . . ." This last was a plea so infused with fear that I shivered even as Morgan nodded and fired.

Chapter 18

I KNEW Morgan was back before the murmurs of his voice and Huido's came indistinctly through my closed door. In my distress, the sense of a wider awareness, of the opening of another type of eye, was so pronounced I merely accepted the knowledge without question. I was dressed in a dead person's clothes and sitting on a dead person's chair when he entered.

Morgan stopped just inside the doorway. "Sira—"

"Why did you have to kill her?"

Morgan passed his hand over his face, exhaustion written there. I stood, one hand on the desk for support. "Tell me," I insisted. "Tell me what happened to Gistries. I don't know. And I must."

Morgan took the chair and sat heavily. He looked the way I felt. "How much could you sense?"

I didn't like remembering. "Someone else. Which meant it wasn't Gistries' fault!"

"No." Morgan's lips twisted into a bitter line. "It was mine." His gaze burned into mine, almost as tormented as Gistries had been. "Gistries knew. She'd been used as a gate by him before. Sooner or later, Yihtor would have crawled back inside her. Even with your help, I was barely able to thrust him away. I couldn't keep him out. I couldn't protect her."

"Yihtor." As I said the name, Gistries' face filled my mind: the pain in her eyes, her smile of release as Morgan fired. Sometime in the remembering, I found myself cradling Morgan's head and shoulders against me. I wasn't sure which of us cried first.

* * *

Morgan brought a tight fist down slowly, resting it on the ruined panel. "I've checked the two in the hold. One's from Goth and the other pirate's half-Tidik; neither are susceptible to mental invasion. Huido's doubled the locks anyway."

I hated being in the control room. The blood was gone, but Gistries' pain wasn't. I paced; it was more useful than screaming. "What happens now? Can you fix this?"

Huido poked a clawtip into a still-soft runnel of melted plas. "You haven't lost your sense of humor," he rumbled.

"Yihtor didn't leave us stranded. We're going somewhere," Morgan said. "The *Torquad* has a course set and engines at maximum. A course we can't change."

I walked over to the controls, my feet moving slowly, and gazed down at the congealed metal. 'We're going to Acranam. Yihtor is using the *Torquad* to bring me to him." I whirled on Morgan. "Will Yihtor crawl behind my eyes next? Or is he there already, hiding in my dreams, reading my thoughts, controlling what I do?" My voice rose to a shout that echoed in the now-useless control room. I shook my head as Morgan moved nearer. "I'm not hysterical." As a reassurance, it rang hollow in my own ears, yet eased some of the tension from his face.

"I'll know if he tries to attack you." Morgan appeared to recognize this was less than helpful. "You said you knew his name. What else do you remember?"

I made the effort to reply calmly, aware that Huido's eyes were gathering like a storm cloud aimed in my direction. I knew he was less convinced I wasn't about to act the puppet.

"Yihtor's name was familiar when Gistries mentioned him before we left Plexis, that's all. No, wait," I caught an errant thought. "When I heard his name, I saw a face, his face. It was angry." I added slowly, "A face I hoped never to see again."

"This is too much for her, Morgan," Huido broke in, the implied pity bringing heat to my cheeks. "If we must continue, let's do it where we can sit and have a drink. We're not needed here." A click at the destroyed panels said it all.

"Go ahead, we'll be with you in a moment," Morgan agreed almost absently. After Huido left, the control room seemed much larger. I could feel Morgan's thoughtful gaze resting on me.

"That's all I know," I told him after a heavy pause, thinking that was the next question, looking up at his face.

"I know a bit more."

Sensing his reluctance to continue, I stepped forward impatiently. "Tell me."

"Rumors, mostly. Rumors of a powerful Clan outcast who sells his abilities to whoever can afford him. A base on Acranam would fit. That space is full of runners and pirates."

"And he wants me." Time stood still. Morgan's compassionate yet grim face swam before my eyes. The Clan again. "Why? What does Sira Morgan mean to Yihtor, to Barac, to any of them?"

"It's Sira di Sarc they're after," he reminded me.

I was silent. The name was strange yet familiar. I wasn't fond of it.

Morgan went on softly: "You're related to a wealthy, prominent politician. That meant something to Roraqk, at least. I don't know about Yihtor."

"Jarad is my father." I hesitated; Morgan deserved more. "He brought me to Auord."

"Yes, I know."

I stared at Morgan, oddly comforted by the thought of my experience safely stored behind those now gentle blue eyes. It was as if he'd been with me, had shared my past instead of just remembering it. "Why did he leave me?" I wondered out loud.

"Maybe Jarad was injured in the attack," he paused. "Or, I'm sorry to say, killed. We have only Barac's version of what happened."

I contemplated that night on Auord—explosions, compulsions, fear. My father's face didn't belong in it. "He wasn't there," I concluded. "But why would he leave me if there was something wrong?" *With me,* I added to myself.

Morgan sighed wearily, running one hand through his hair. "Sira, your father has managed to carve out a commercial and political empire in Camos Cluster without acknowledging your existence in any way that Roraqk could find. To hide you so successfully took currency and purpose. To keep you hidden meant that prison you remember."

"Why?"

His mouth tightened. "Why? People hide or imprison what they want to protect. Or what they fear."

The Clansman on Plexis had feared me. "I was some-one else," I said carefully, sinking down onto the same bench where I'd been made to wait for Roraqk's next move. "When her memories were blocked, Sira di Sarc was gone, flushed down an Auordian sewer with the rain. Why do they still care about her?"

"We're going at this backward," Morgan said abruptly, as if fired by an idea. I had a feeling I wasn't going to like it. He sat beside me, face intent. "Maybe it wasn't *who* you were that mattered, but *what* you knew. If you knew some secret, something important about the Clan. . . ."

I tapped my head suggestively. "The body's buried here? Great. So whoever blocked my memories wanted Sira di Sarc to die. And let me guess: Yihtor and the rest want Sira *Morgan* to die so Sira di Sarc can come back to life and answer their questions. Any guesses as to who else wants something?"

"I know what I want." Morgan tweaked a loose lock of my hair. "I want you to be happy."

"Which me?" I arched one eyebrow at him.

"You won't stay two people forever, Sira. The block isn't permanent."

I twisted around to look right at Morgan. Despite his light tone of voice, his mouth was set and tight. "I'm go-ing to start remembering everything?" I asked, and won-dered at the lack of enthusiasm in my voice.

"I didn't say that," he corrected quickly. "What I found in your mind was a series of blocks, imposed one after an-other—all carefully linked. It would have been much easier to erase your memories altogether. Why bother with something so complicated and fragile? I'd say the blocks are meant to be removed."

"Can you?"

"No." His disappointment in himself was plain.

"Jason," I said very softly, putting my hand on his. "What will happen to me if these blocks are removed?"

"You'll remember your past."

I searched his face. "No. What happens to this me?

What happens to—" I tightened my grip, allowing my sense of him to expand until his heart was all I could hear. Then I drew back.

Morgan sighed. His eyes were dark and troubled. "You've been Sira Morgan so short a time." He lifted my fingers to his lips before releasing them. Then his mouth worked itself into a smile. "And look at the effect you've had on people. Sira di Sarc can't be that different."

I found an answering smile somewhere. It was probably as transparent as his. "We'll face that when and if it comes." Knowing it was futile, I couldn't help wishing I'd found another ship on Plexis, left Morgan as I'd planned. Gistries and all those lost would be alive. We wouldn't be imprisoned in this ship. And Morgan would have his *Fox*.

I shook off the what ifs. Time to worry about the now. "Can you teach me how to protect myself from Yihtor?"

"Maybe." Morgan spread his hands wide. "I won't lie to you, Sira. It may not be possible. We don't know how strong you are—or were."

So. My mouth dried, but my heart beat steadily. I held Morgan's gaze with my own, reaching one hand to tap the weapon in his belt. "Then I expect as much kindness as you gave Gistries," I said. "Your word, Captain."

Morgan's blue eyes met mine directly and calmly, though his face lost all color. "I will never let Yihtor or anyone else control you, Sira. I swear it."

* * *

INTERLUDE

"Power!" Rael's voice was sharp as she ran into the galley, startling Barac. He'd been trying without success to adjust the setting on the viswall; he didn't care for wheeling stars with his lunch. He looked up hopefully.

"Morgan?"

His cousin placed both hands on the table and leaned forward, her black hair curling behind her arms to form a cloak. Her nod was brusque, but her dark eyes shone with triumph. "That Human, yes. And some other—an unfamiliar taste. Clan." Her lips thinned. "They twined around each other like snakes. But through both I sensed Sira!"

Instead of relief, Barac felt a sudden numbness. "Could you give Terk a location?"

"Yes. I've told him."

Barac slid to his feet and walked over to the com panel by the door. He called up the pilot, asked a question, feeling a foreboding that only intensified with the answer Terk supplied.

Rael had made herself a cup of sombay; she watched Barac return to his seat. "What's wrong?"

"According to Terk, this course you've given him is taking us to where Kurr was killed."

"Kurr?" From the blankness on Rael's face, she'd forgotten. Barac didn't bother feeling hurt. He pushed back the image of his brother's limp body, saving it.

"Kurr was strong, Rael, a Second Level Adept, probably closer to First. Whoever overpowered him could take either of us. Sira is in danger, too."

Rael tapped her fingernails once firmly on the tabletop. "Not Sira. No one could overpower her."

Barac shook his head. "If Sira's still in stasis, even partially, she can't protect herself." He paused. "But you say you felt her use her power."

"Yes, I did," Rael admitted reluctantly. "It was unmistakable."

"What has happened?" Barac asked.

"I don't know." Rael sipped her drink, once, then again. "Perhaps Sira was never blocked."

"I was with Sira on Auord," Barac countered. "She was blocked then. If her power's free now, it has to be because of Morgan. Something he's done. Something about him."

As Rael began to shake her head, he went on, his words tumbling over each other in his haste. "Listen to me, Rael. Stasis can be broken. And there's been no one else close to her with enough power, Human or Clan."

Her eyes lowered, then snapped up. "You're speculating. The Council wouldn't believe you for an instant."

Barac gained hope from the note of indecision in her voice. "But you do."

"Morgan is *Human*. His bastard power can't affect one of us." Her teeth were clenched as if the words she spoke had to be forced past an urge to retch.

"That's what we've been told. Think, Rael," he urged. "What if that's not true? What if Morgan's power is able to truly touch Sira's? What if he can draw her from stasis, reach into the M'hir and call forth—"

"Stop it! This is obscene!" Rael lashed out, eyes sparked with anger. "I should take you to Cenabar for total reconstruction. This obession with Humans—it's warped your mind, Barac. They are nothing! Morgan is nothing!"

The galley walls flickered. Barac spared a moment to be grateful Rael hadn't inherited her grandfather's telekinetic abilities, or he'd probably be wearing the table around his neck by now. As it was, he gasped for breath, fought to stay conscious against the pounding of her rage through the M'hir. "Stop!" he pleaded. "Just listen, Rael. Please."

"Not to more of your wild ideas about Humans," she warned, drawing so far back into herself she became invisible to his other sense. "They are nothing. Their excuse for power is locked here and now, just like this," she waved her hand at the galley. "Can any Human send a thought through the weave of space, like a needle through cloth? No. Can any Human summon the strength to pull physical form after their thoughts, like thread? No. Do Human dreams trouble the peace of the M'hir? No."

Barac said quietly: "Don't make the mistake of underestimating them, Rael. There are Humans with respectable abilities. And never forget that their technology lets them accomplish what we do by thought alone."

Rael snorted. "Tricks. Humans have no true power."

"Kurr believed if they were left to evolve without our interference, some might develop it."

"Honor to your brother, but I'd expect Denebians to swim before that!"

"Think about it, Rael. Is it really impossible? Or have we seen no talent like ours among them because the Council keeps its fingers spread to detect any troubling of the M'hir—and is ready to "alter" any Human mind that approaches it? We've been taught that the Stratification took place because the Talent appeared in a few Choosers, then spread to more each generation, until our ancestors no longer had a common goal with the unTalented. What if that development had been stopped? What would we be now?"

"You're trying to convince me your Human . . . that

Morgan can . . . No. It's *not* possible." Rael's face was pale, but Barac sensed she was listening more openly now.

"We're all uncomfortable with Humans, Rael," he said. "They look like us, more than any other species we've encountered. But to our deeper sense, Humans are so wildly different, so strange, consumed by needs that are almost incomprehensible to most M'hiray. Their obession with tools. Their compulsion to crowd together, to coat planets with their kind until the pressure of being together has them erupting outward again. Let's face it—a species that can love and hate itself at the same time is not easy to live with."

"True." Rael didn't quite smile. "A sense of humor helps."

Barac chose his next words with care. "Let's find Sira. You can talk to her," he said quickly, before Rael hardened again.

"Why can't we just stop interfering?" Rael said almost to herself. "If Sira's able to function, it doesn't matter how or why she can, Barac. What matters is that she doesn't need us anymore. We could be back within range of Plexis in two days. I could get transport to Deneb; you could come back, pick up your hunt for Kurr's murderer."

Barac reached for her hand. At the same time, he dropped his shields at every level. Rael drew back, made as if to twist her hand free, to refuse the contact. He held on, sending his fear through the M'hir, across their link.

Sira may not need you, but I do, Rael, he sent, the truth of it filling his thoughts and flooding hers. *It doesn't matter if you believe my ideas about Morgan. You know I'm not strong enough to defend myself from Kurr's murderer. And I'm not strong enough to escape Sira if her power as a Chooser has been released. I'm asking for your help.*

Barac pulled back into himself, restoring his shields and freeing Rael from the unwanted intimacy of his thoughts, hoping her silence meant she was considering all he'd said. He knew he wasn't the heroic type.

But then, what sane person was?

Chapter 19

MORGAN had insisted on certain precautions before my lesson in self-defense. While I couldn't argue with his concern, I wasn't happy about being locked in the galley, with Huido stationed outside with orders to shoot whichever of us acted odd.

"Tell me again how Huido is supposed to check us out," I said to Morgan, eyeing the closed door with considerable doubt. "I thought you said Carasians aren't telepathic."

Morgan grinned. "True. But Huido assures me he'll know if one or both of us is being influenced. He said our *grist* would smell off."

I allowed myself a deep sigh. My chances of surviving to ripe old age now depended on the olfactory ability of a being whose nose I couldn't begin to find. "Then this had better work."

Morgan nodded, then touched my cheek with the fingertips of one hand. Words, crisp and clear as if spoken aloud, appeared in my head. *The idea's simple enough. You will form a mental shield, a covering that hides and protects your thoughts.* His grin bubbled through our mental link. *We'll start with an exercise I learned from an Omacron trader.*

Close your eyes. Good. Now imagine building a wall of stone, a wall which exists solely within your thoughts. Small blocks rest on their neighbors, fitting tightly together; the whole feels stronger than any part. Try to sense the construction as it grows, small piece upon small piece. Good. Now, I'll show you—

Show me? A resonance flooded my mind and the process Morgan described formed in its completeness.

Had I already known, but forgotten? Or was Morgan supplying me with unobtrusive help? *Not so,* the voice in my thoughts answered, amusement and pleased surprise coloring it with warmth. *It seems I'm merely reminding you. You're doing marvel—*

I opened my eyes at the total silencing of Morgan's mental presence. He was smiling down at me, hands spread wide in triumph. "I pronounce you invisible, Sira Morgan! Now if you wish to open your shield—"

Wait. I closed my eyes again. It was ridiculously easy. A child knew how to alter the protective structure, creating windows for safe communication, forming doorways through which more massive amounts of power could be sent at need. In an instant, the structure in my mind was set in all its complexity. It was as if the pattern had lain dormant, waiting to be recalled to function. If only I had known before Yihtor's attack. A worried voice called me back to myself.

"Sira?"

I laughed. "Try to read me now, Captain Morgan!" I challenged with a toss of my head. I stood motionless as his supple fingers hovered on my brow, sensing the effort which brought sweat to Morgan's brow, yet feeling no more than an awareness of his mental presence as it groped along my invisible wall for some crack or entrance. I closed my eyes again, seeking with growing confidence an area seemingly solid but in truth a hidden door. Through it I sent his name soaring. *Morgan!*

Skill, indeed. I could sense the flow of deeper thoughts, but instinctively knew not to reach for them. *Perhaps Yihtor should worry about us! If only we'd time to release more of what you know.* His pride washed over me. Pride mixed with something barely discernible. I looked into Morgan's smiling face, close to my own, and wondered at the strange softness with which he sent my name back into my thoughts.

Something dark began to stir. I felt a surging, a dangerous and repugnant gathering which became an onrushing tide sliding up through my deepest thoughts. It snatched at the link to Morgan, then began to *pull*. . . .

I was nowhere. And it was beautiful beyond words. I was a planet—no, a sun around which all power revolved.

Power flowed like life around and through me, humming in seductive voices, enticing me to stay. . . .

Another was here. No. This was my domain. I collected strands of force, ready for battle, ready to kill . . . Morgan?

Somehow I *pushed* us out of that nothingness. Then I severed my contact with Morgan violently—tearing away to lean gasping against a table, fingers tight on its reality.

Dimly, I was aware of Morgan's anxious questioning, of gentle hands supporting me that I pushed away desperately—almost sick with the aftermath of that alienness. I shuddered at the thought of arousing those foul depths again. "Leave me alone, won't you!" I heard myself snap and was ashamed enough to wave a mute apology.

"What happened?" Morgan's voice was tight and strained. "Have I hurt you? Sira, please! I must know if you're all right!"

Hadn't he felt it?

I couldn't look at him. Not yet. "I don't know," I answered harshly. "There was something inside me. A wrongness." I clamped teeth together and gathered my shredded dignity. "It took us there. To that—place."

A chair pressed against my legs, and I sank into it gratefully, lowering my head onto my arms, weak with reaction. Morgan took a seat across from me. "Place?" he repeated, his voice trailing oddly. "I thought I blacked out for a second."

I shook my head without raising it.

Nothing for a moment. Then I heard Morgan say slowly, "I don't understand. You brought us back, somehow. But from where?"

"I don't know." I shivered harder.

"I pushed you too far," Morgan said. "We can't know what the effect of the blockage might be on your Talent. There could be disorientation, confusion."

Shaken as I felt, I knew the blame shouldn't rest on Morgan. He had only tried to help me. And on some level I knew that place was a part of me, and so was the darkness that forced us there, no matter how dreadful it seemed.

"You couldn't know about this thing in my head, Morgan," I said, raising my gaze to his troubled eyes. "But we have to face another possibility." Morgan cocked a brow as I paused in distress. I made an effort and continued, "What I, what we, sensed is somehow part of me. Could I be insane? Could what was done to my mind have been an attempt to help me?

Morgan leaned back in his chair, taking a moment to consider his steepled fingers before answering. "I can't believe that," he said at last. "It's obvious you knew and used your Talent, probably to a far greater extent than I could teach you. Trust me." His hands reached to comfort mine, but I drew back with an involuntary shudder. Morgan sighed. "What's been done to you wasn't to help you. And what was blocked is much worse than losing your past. If you were once so powerful, so gifted—Sira, they've blinded and crippled you."

"I don't feel blind or crippled," I said, wishing he could understand. "I feel sick. And I'm scared."

Morgan's eyes were haunted. "I won't try anything else. Not when we are in such a dangerous situation."

"No more," I agreed with almost desperate relief. "At least I don't need to fear my dreams anymore. Thank you."

He shook his head, giving me an unreadable flash from his blue eyes. "I showed you where to look, Sira; the rest you did on your own."

I rose from my seat, having vaguely decided to rest in my cabin; I needed time alone. I hoped Huido's sniffer was accurate.

"Sira?"

"Yes?"

"I've been deeper into your mind than I've ever tried with anyone else. I won't say I know what the consequences might be—I don't. But I do know your mind is the sanest place I've been. If that helps."

My hands swept up in a gesture I could no more prevent than I could understand. I clasped the offending members together tightly, avoiding Morgan's eyes. "I wish I knew why I do that," I said with deep-felt bitterness.

"It won't be long before we both do, Sira," Morgan reassured me as he stood in turn. "Go and rest for a while. Put all this out of your mind. I'll finish up here."

I nodded gratefully and made my way around the tables to leave the galley. Morgan's thoughtful gaze followed me. He spoke just as I reached the doorway and raised my hand to knock. "You aren't facing this alone, Sira."

A real smile eased the tightness of my face. I stopped and looked back at his still form. "Wasn't it last night you promised me a night at Sas'qaat's tables after all this, Captain?"

"We'll bankrupt the old fish. Rest. I'll call you when we're ready." With that promise, I went to my cabin, totally unable to explain to myself why I was humming.

Chapter 20

MORGAN'S plan was simple enough. The *Torquad* would go on its programmed journey to Yihtor; we wouldn't. When the insystem approach alarm sounded—causing me to jump half out of my skin—we made our way to the *Torquad*'s escape pods. The two pirates were left locked up below.

The pods were designed to seek a safe landing spot. Huido had disabled their distress beacons; on Acranam, they were unlikely to attract true rescue. A great deal was left to chance, but at least we weren't walking directly into Yihtor's hands. We were buying time.

"Do you have room for all that?" I was admonishing Huido when Morgan came up to us.

"Must you?" Morgan said dryly, a brow raised at the bottles being stowed carefully in the Carasian's pod.

Huido was unrepentant. "You get your nutrients your way. I prefer mine. Besides, you'll have Sira for company. If I get stuck atop some mountain with only this pea-sized ship brain to talk to, I'll die of boredom." The last bottle of the pirates' beer aboard, the Carasian turned to his friend. "Time to go."

Morgan nodded silently. Then he stretched his hand up so Huido could grasp it in his jaws. They maintained this position for a long moment, Huido's eyes intent on the serious face of his friend. I glanced down at the deck.

A huge arm swept me against what felt like the side of a groundcar in a bruising hug. "Take care of him, Sira. He blunders into trouble every time I leave him on his own!" After this farewell, Huido somehow managed to maneuver his bulk through a portal meant for smaller creatures.

It was fortunate his arms were jointed in several locations. Morgan sealed the door and turned to me.

"Our turn. I want to launch simultaneously." He paused and grinned. "Be a shame if Huido took all that beer to the top of a mountain without us!"

I refrained from comment. My recent experience with Huido's drinking habits was not one I planned to repeat soon. I followed Morgan into our pod. There was little room to move among the supplies Morgan had insisted on taking, but room wasn't necessary. Nor was a pilot, for the tiny ship had no accessible controls. Passengers awaited their fate bundled in tight, protective bags. I tried to hide my sudden claustrophobia from Morgan. It was a useless exercise. He tightened my straps and stood looking down at me. "Nervous?"

I surveyed my imprisoned body with acute distaste. "More like gift-wrapped."

"May I?" Morgan asked softly, fingers feather-light on my forehead. A moment of frozen indecision, then I threw away my false pride and lowered all barriers. A whisper of my name. A reassuring warmth. Then I was led into a deep sleep.

"Sira. Wake up, Sira." I could ignore the gentle call, but not the hand trying to shake my arm free of my shoulder. Muttering various dark things to myself, I opened my eyes sluggishly to peer at Morgan. He grinned, and tugged at my fastenings again. "Welcome to Acranam, sleepyhead. I'll admit you didn't miss much as far as our landing was concerned."

I fought my way out of the bag with his help. It was difficult to stand and our carefully stowed gear had shifted to dangle overhead. Morgan began to tap the clips from the portal one at a time. "We're upside-down," I noticed. "Does this happen often?"

"Wouldn't know," Morgan grunted over his shoulder, muscles straining the fabric of his coveralls as he fought the stubborn door. "I've never had to use one of these things before. Hand me that, please."

"Is Huido down safely?" I passed Morgan the tool he indicated, trying to keep out of his way, a difficult process in the tiny space.

"Don't know. Ah," a satisfied sound as the door fell

open. "With any luck, he should be outside—" Morgan's voice became muffled as his head and shoulders disappeared through the hole. A scrambling and the rest of him followed. *Stay inside.* I scowled at the message in my head. Surely a peek wasn't risky. Handholds had conveniently been placed around the total circumference of the door. I pulled myself up until I could see outside.

"You might as well come, then," Morgan reached down and hauled me up with one easy motion to stand beside him. The tiny pod was half-buried in soft earth, a dark scar in the green leaf litter marking an earlier bounce that had just missed a massive tree.

Tree? It was more like a mountain. The trunk was formed of huge buttresses that writhed and joined together at a point far above our heads. No sky could be seen through the dense canopy of its branches, although enough light filtered through to dapple the forest floor. I turned slowly, drinking in the sight, admiring the clusters of pale flower buds hanging on every bare section of branch. Other giant trees formed widely spaced pillars, bearing their living roof over the silent mossy turf. The air was warm, soil-scented, and still.

I slipped down from the pod and took a step. The ground was springy and colored in dull browns and greens by the moss and fallen leaves. "It's lovely!" I exclaimed whirling around. Somehow I had never thought of our destination as a real place in its own right.

"No sign of the other pod." Morgan climbed down from his vantage point atop the little ship. "Not that Huido mightn't be just around the corner. With all this vegetation, we could easily miss each other."

"Can we contact him?"

Morgan didn't answer immediately. He picked a tendril of moss from the ground near his feet and twirled it slowly. "Carasians can't be read by humanoid telepaths. Or so I've been told."

I eyed him quizzically. "You don't sound convinced. Why? Have you tried to reach Huido mentally before?"

Morgan shook his head. "It's not something you try—not unless asked." A quick look at me. "Or if there's great need. The occasion never arose before. But Huido and I are very close." A shrug. "Sometimes I've felt I sensed his presence.

If this thing was less automated, I could rig a usable com-link." Morgan glared at the innocent escape pod.

I'd felt oddly free once we were out of the ship. The forest was peaceful and welcoming. I wasn't surprised by the memory that now floated easily into mind. "Think of him," I heard myself say with unaccustomed confidence. I moved to stand behind Morgan, reaching my hands to almost touch the back of his head.

"Think of the special caress he gives you. I will augment your heart-search." The words were so much gibber-ish to me, although I was already somehow gathering strength. I closed my eyes, opened my awareness of Morgan, then poured something, some power into his memory of Huido—strengthening it with my own remembrance of their silent farewell.

Immediately I was carried helplessly along as the in-credibly strong beam of thought widened, coursing farther and farther until it struck a heaving crackle of a mind. I experienced a disorientation, a skewing of perception that flashed spasms of pain behind my eyes. A reflex clamped down, breaking the connection. I opened my eyes cautiously.

"Whew," Morgan's gasp was pained.

"Huido made it," I commented.

Morgan rubbed his forehead, canting his head around to look at me. "Not nearby, though." A wry smile. "And I don't particularly wish to use my—our power to find him. What did you call it? Heart-search?"

I frowned, not at him. "The idea came from the Sira-I-was." A small, winged creature, jewel-blue, caught my eye as it fluttered cautiously nearby. "It makes me very nervous to do such things." The tiny creature whirled upward to a large group of pink flowers overhead and disappeared.

Morgan had climbed back into the pod. But he heard me. "I do understand, Sira." I heard an unexpected bleak-ness in his voice. "It's not a—comfortable ability."

"Yet you told me that to lose it was like being blinded," I said.

"Sometimes you see too much."

I mulled that over for a moment, watching the peaceful forest settle back to life after our explosive intrusion. "How can you see too much?" I asked at last.

Morgan backed out of the pod and looked down at me. He made as if to speak then closed his lips. Then he asked: "What did you think when you first felt this link between us? Before you understood it or could control it?"

"I was scared to death." I thought about it. "And I was angry. I wanted to stop feeling what was happening inside you and couldn't. I had no privacy, no self, left. I blamed you." I shrugged and smiled at him. "After all, you're the only one it happens with."

Morgan dropped lightly to the ground beside me and held out one hand. Uncertainly, I placed mine palm down over it. The sensation of his life was as real as the warmth of the air, and as harmlessly normal. "It doesn't bother me anymore," I said calmly, meeting his blue gaze. "You don't sense me in this way, do you."

"At the moment, I feel nothing more than touch."

"But," I began and stopped with a frown. What was he trying to tell me?

A wry smile deep in Morgan's eyes. "I learned years ago to quiet my perception of other minds, to turn it off and on at will. It takes concentration and effort, but otherwise I'd have gone mad. If I touch someone with my shields open, as I've done with you, I'm invaded by thoughts and emotions. Layers upon layers of conflicting reactions and responses—to events past and present, to others, and to me." He drew away his hand. "It's a sense I use and value. But there's always a price."

This time, it wasn't a memory that clarified my world, but understanding. Morgan's loneliness was self-imposed. Huido was probably his only friend, his alien mind never a threat or imposition, his emotions offered from a safe distance.

I dug my toes gently into the moss, watching the green strands bend and straighten. "Why haven't you found another telepath?" I was careful not to sound too interested. "Wouldn't someone like that understand, be able to control their thoughts and emotions?"

"I imagine it could be worse," Morgan said with a dash of impatience, as though my question made him uncomfortable. "One slip, one burst of emotion could rip away both shields. No thanks. I don't feel like being that exposed.

"Anyway," he added more briskly, "those telepaths I

know make a living either for or against the Trade Pact, both of which makes them less than friends of mine right now." He paused. "I know a few non-Human telepaths. The Clan. Barac, and now his cousin Rael."

"Rael?" I frowned at the name. "You didn't tell me about her. Who is she?"

"Someone you've met. Here." Morgan's fingers brushed my forehead. A face formed. I examined the image carefully, aware of no answering memory, yet knowing something wasn't quite right with Morgan's sending. The full lips should curve with warmth; the brilliant eyes sparkle with inner gaiety. The hair should fall freely over a brow with no lines of ill-temper marring it. I surveyed the new picture with pleasure. Now she looked as I thought she should. But how did I know? I slammed my barriers down, erasing the smiling face and shutting Morgan out. He was looking at me in a puzzled manner.

"It appears you know a Rael I don't." There was a hint of suspicion in his voice that I instantly resented.

"You know what's in my mind as well or better than I do, Jason Morgan. Isn't it a bit late to suspect me of hiding something from you?" I didn't try to keep back my frustration. "Am I supposed to fear what little comes out of my head?" I stopped, listening to what I'd said.

I breathed hard, staring at Morgan's face without really seeing it, torn by the chaos in my mind. The comfortable but barred room. The signs of a long stay. The certainty of belonging there, of recognizing the right of those who had chosen that fate for me to rule my movements, to isolate me. The key was not the time I had spent there, but why I was now free. If only I could remember!

"You must try to remove the rest of the blockage, Morgan," I said, fighting the turmoil in my mind. "You were right all the time. Everything we do is a pretense unless we know who and what I am. Maybe Sira di Sarc isn't worth the effort and risk you and Huido went through."

Morgan's smile was warm. "You're hardly the one to judge that, Sira." He looked skyward pensively. "Right now, we better be thinking about some sort of shelter—sunset can't be far off. I don't know about you, but I don't feel like sleeping in there." A wave at the tiny, lop-sided ship.

I couldn't agree more. The small door to the escape

pod's cramped interior was anything but inviting. I forced myself to concentrate on the matter at hand, perfectly aware that Morgan was trying to distract me. I looked after him thoughtfully as he climbed into the pod to retrieve our gear. Morgan had also deflected the conversation away from his own life. His loneliness was an echo of mine.

"Don't forget lunch!" I called up, brought to earth by the rumbling of my stomach. An accurately pitched package of ration tubes landed in the moss at my feet. I poked it with my toe and made no move to pick it up. "You'll have to do better than that, Captain, or you'll have a mutiny on your hands. Look at nature's bounty surrounding us and tell me you intend to eat this recycled goo!"

Morgan stuck out his head, removing the tube he was sucking on to say derisively: "Not so much as a drop of water until it's tested. And we don't have time before nightfall to look for edible delicacies. Besides," there was a gleam in his eyes, "this 'recycled goo' only takes one hand, so you can keep working, chit." The grinning face disappeared.

I straightened up, package in hand, only to be buried by a virtual shower of blankets. I could hear Morgan laughing through the pile. Struggling free, I pulled loose a clod of moist moss and cocked my arm, waiting for him to stick out his head.

Chapter 21

ACRANAM'S nightfall had startled me. I hadn't been prepared for darkness that arrived almost as quickly as if I'd ordered the lights off in my cabin, though the heavy shadowing of vegetation above our heads should have warned me.

I smiled to myself, gazing upward. True darkness hadn't lasted long. Almost immediately, it had been broken by the opening of large, glowing white flowers suspended throughout the canopy overhead. The soft light of their petals attracted hapless flying things; once close, they were captured by tendrils dangling almost invisibly below. Although the thought of feasting plants bothered me at first, I admired the flowers.

The fire tumbled to embers; the outermost of these blackened at the edges as they cooled. I hurried to put on more wood, afraid the fire might die on me.

I'd never imagined I'd enjoy watching a fire, yet I found myself staring into its complex, fickle color until I had to rest my hot and dry eyes by gazing up into the cool darkness. A magical night, lit by a galaxy of flowers and centered around this fragrant campfire.

"Going to sit there until morning?" Morgan said as he reentered the firelight, bedrolls in one hand, blankets over the other shoulder. A tiny portlight hovered over his head like an anxious mother bird.

The end of daylight had put an end to Morgan's sketching. He'd packed away his pad after showing me, not without some coaxing, the drawings he'd done. Most were quick, light reminders; I knew he already pictured where they would belong in his cabin on the *Fox*, should he ever have her again. The exception had been a sprig of moss whose dainty capped stalks had kept him hovering in cramped frustration for an hour or more, before straightening with a pleased groan and stretch.

I smiled again. That picture now resided in my pack, unknown to Morgan. It was a theft I could live with, given either of us had a future after tonight.

I accepted my share of the bedding, but refused to stir from my comfortable mossy seat. "I can't possibly sleep and miss all this," I told Morgan firmly. "How often in our level of civilization can life return to the primeval—fire against night demons—brain and brawn against the predators lurking in the dark?" I rubbed my hands together with delight.

Morgan shook out his bedroll at the side of the fire farthest from the pod. He was barely visible, having sent the light back to recharge, his smile betrayed only by a glint of white teeth. "Let's not forget the distort field and life-form monitors so thoughtfully provided by yours truly. I'd hate to slip too far back."

I made a rude noise. "Take the fun out of it if you must. I'm going to take first watch."

Morgan was, by this time, only a lump in a pile of blankets. "Watch all night, if you like, Sira. I, for one, plan to get some well-deserved sleep. Good night. Just don't forget that we've a fair amount of walking to do tomorrow if we're going to find Huido before dark." In the following silence, the crackle of new flames was loud when I added another dry branch.

Though it was an effort to fight the tendency of my head to nod heavily, I was still spellbound by the flames much later when the first whisper of my name brushed my consciousness as a gentle breeze would lift and turn a leaf. *Sira.* I glanced at Morgan's unmoving, featureless form, expecting to see him open his eyes and look at me. Then I realized the voice wasn't his and closed my mind tightly.

I was so terrified that I produced only a faint bleat when I tried to call Morgan. And then even that impulse faded as the projection formed—the image of the Clanswoman named Rael so lifelike I almost warned her about the embers glowing beneath her feet.

This time the projection grew more substantial, almost solid. Her hands were outstretched in welcome. I could easily make out every detail of her face, and its glad expression. And hear her voice. "Sira. At last I've found you. Greetings, dear Sister."

"No!" I shouted that with enough force to scorch my throat. Why didn't Morgan stir? "I'm no kin to Clan."

She seemed stunned. "What are you saying? What's happened, Sira, to make you—"

I shook, suddenly gloriously angry. At last I had a target. "What's happened? Wouldn't a better question be what's been done to me? Oh, I know it all, Clanswoman. I know how the Clan has tried to manipulate and control me. You've failed. I don't fear you."

I did, of course. The sight of her hovering in the fire was enough to raise the hairs on my neck. It was even harder to ignore my worry for Morgan. Couldn't he hear us?

"Fear—me?" Rael's cheeks looked pale. They weren't lit by the firelight, I noticed, distracted. But then, she was really somewhere else. Where, I wondered.

Her words spilled out as if I'd released some floodgate. "Why would you fear me, Sira? You know I'd never send you back. Haven't I always taken your side? Why do you look at me that way—with such loathing?" her voice broke. "My dearest sister—"

"Stop calling me that!" I stood, bristling impotently since the object of my rage was no more within striking range than the flowers over my head. Yet, the Clanswoman's distress would have wrenched sympathy from a rock. Great jewel-like tears overflowed her eyes. Her full lower lip trembled. Confused, I didn't know what to say or think.

"Have you grown to hate us all, then?" her voice was faint. The image flickered as if its motivating force was weakening.

"Why shouldn't I?" I said slowly. It hurt to see her unhappy. I sent a pleading look toward the lump of blankets that hid my erstwhile partner, not daring to lower my own mental barriers.

Her head shook sadly. Rael was now more misty ghost than vivid presence. "Sira, we were heart-kin as well as blood-kin. If those ties are not enough, what more can I say?"

And abruptly, devastatingly, as her image faded completely, I realized the truth of what she had said. Every muscle in my body stiffened and locked. The distance between what I'd thought myself to be and this new Sira was an unbridgeable infinity. Nothing was left for me to believe. I hadn't even known my own species. I was a stranger to myself.

Sira. I knew that mind voice better than any other; it treaded the frozen waste of my thoughts delicately, warily. The wariness betrayed him; it told me he'd been watching, listening, deliberately silent. I couldn't make the effort to care.

I raised my eyes from the dying fire. Morgan, still wrapped in his blankets, shifted to within its dim circle of light and sat stirring up the blaze. Somehow the mental exchange was less taxing. *You heard all of it?* I asked.

Yes, a touch of guilt quickly dispelled by concern. *Are you all right?*

I ordered my body to sit. It obeyed in a strangely disjointed fashion. My hands folded in my lap of their own accord. *Rael called me her sister.*

Very cautiously, but with a familiar resolute honesty: *She named you Clan.*

I nodded unnecessarily. *I suppose she did.* I spent a moment in a slow, inner searching. *Shouldn't something show? Shouldn't I at least feel different?* I threw my confusion and pain across our mental link at him. *I'm not* Human *anymore!*

The intensity of the sending hurt him. I saw Morgan wince, though he poked the fire as if to cover the movement. He chose to speak out loud. "Human or Clan. Both sapient, both civilized, both standard humanoid. So how could you know?"

"But you knew, didn't you," I said, clamping down my own barriers, horrified to discover I was becoming suspicious of him too, of everything. "All this time, I believed I was Human. You were in my head. You knew what I believed! Why—" I stopped.

Morgan's face was difficult to read in the fire-thrown shadows. "Why didn't I tell you?"

"Yes."

"At first, I thought you were trying to fool me. When I knew better, I discovered I was afraid to tamper with Sira Morgan." He was quiet for a moment. I could hear small rustlings beyond the firelight. "You're different from any

Clan I've met, Sira. It's not the blockage—it's something else. I can't describe it." He shrugged. "For a while, I wondered if Barac had lied and you were Human. But then, you began to do things no Human telepath can."

My palms began to sweat. "Why am I different? Rael is my sister. She claims to care for me. I don't know what to think, Morgan. What am I?"

Morgan scowled into the fire. "A pawn."

I jabbed with a stick, ending the glow of a spark that had landed by my feet. "Like that."

He'd watched me. "Once, maybe. But we've managed to throw a few changes into things, don't you think?"

"What do they want, Morgan? Why did they destroy what I was?" I said furiously. "I don't care what Rael said. The Clan are my enemies, not my kind." The words left a taste in my mouth, bitter and unpleasant, like the truth.

Then I sighed, my fury and its heat gone. "Where would I be now if I hadn't met you and joined the *Fox?* You're more my kin than they'll ever be."

Morgan didn't answer. I knew I was Clan and that meant something was different, I realized, a sinking feeling in my stomach. I could read him well enough by now. His face was hidden, but there was disappointment— or was it defeat?—in the set of his shoulders under the blanket.

I switched to inner speech, hoping to feel something more from him. *So I'm not Human. It doesn't change things between us. Does it?*

As he looked up, his eyes took on a glow, but Morgan replied out loud, his mind closed tighter than a drum. "If the non-Human caused me sleepless nights, I wouldn't have lasted one trip outsystem."

"Then what's wrong? Why are you disappointed?" After the words were out, my cheeks began to throb with heat. I leaned away from the fire and its light.

"Disappointed?" Morgan laughed. The sound was hollow. "It's nothing to me what you are, Sira. I knew all along it was unlikely you were Human. Why should I be disappointed?"

I pulled my blankets up with me as I stood with what I hoped was a dignified flourish. "I don't know. But I do know you're lying, Captain Morgan."

I threw down my bedroll at the edge of the firelight farthest from where he sat brooding over the crackling wood. I was huddled under several covers, with one pulled over a nose grown cold away from the fire's warmth, when Morgan's thoughts touched mine.

Forgive me.

For what? I sent to him, pulling my blankets tighter.

A shading of remorse. *For lying to both of us.*

More than remorse, I decided, tasting the emotion Morgan was letting through the light barrier between our minds. Regret. *I'll live,* I answered. What was the matter with him?

I pulled the blanket off my nose so I could look over it to where he sat, still and shadowed. *But my being Clan does make a difference to you. Why? You're not afraid of me, are you?*

His thoughts were flooded by an odd mixture of embarrassment, confusion, and reticence. I withdrew from the contact, rather amused to have for once disturbed the usually imperturbable Morgan.

So much time had passed, I'd settled back to sleep, when a rustling of leaves startled me awake. Morgan sat down a short distance away, a darker shadow among those cast by the last of the flames. "I'd hoped," he said, aloud yet almost as quietly as mind speech, "you'd stay . . . after this business was settled." He hesitated, seemingly at a loss for words, without the confidence I was used to and suddenly missed. "With me."

"What I said on Plexis still holds," I warned him. "I haven't decided to return to the *Fox,* or whatever she's called now." I smiled to myself in the dark. "But it's nice to know I'm welcome."

"It's not that simple!" Morgan's shout surprised us both into an uncomfortable pause. I listened to rustlings in the forest that subsided slowly. Morgan went on more quietly: "What I want doesn't count anymore, Sira. You're Clan, not Human. And I know the Clan better than most, believe me. They're xenophobes. They can barely tolerate alien species. They especially despise Humans."

"You're being ridiculous," I said, and meant it. "I don't—"

"Not now. But what happens when that block in your mind dissolves? What about Sira di Sarc? How does *she* feel about Humans? Why shouldn't that Sira react to me as a typical Clan?"

"After what's happened to me," I paused to curl more comfortably under my blankets. "I doubt I'll ever be a typical *Clan* again anyway, Morgan. Aren't you looking a bit too far ahead?"

There was a strangled kind of sound, then, as if frustrated to exasperation, Morgan pulled me out of my nest with a rough grip on my shoulders. "Just how much of this must I explain to you, Sira? I wanted you to stay with me. Not as crew. With me, always. For a while I dared to think it was possible—but now I know you won't—you couldn't even if you wanted to."

"Oh," I said, my heart pounding in my ears, echoing the thick passion of his voice. How could I have been so blind? He'd been alone for so long. I'd missed Morgan's need, too intent on my own.

Maybe it was less than flattering to be chosen out of no selection at all; maybe that didn't matter. I didn't move from the now-light hold of his hands, aglow with a deep pleasure that was so much more than all my hidden fantasies had promised.

"Sira?" Morgan was peering at me in the dim light.

I raised a hand to stop him. "It's all right, Jason." I blushed as I used his first name, feeling foolish and wonderful at the same time. "I understand now. What you tried to tell me on the *Fox*." That seemed so long ago.

"About what?"

"Love," I said, then closed my lips, unsure what to do or say next.

There was a pause, then Morgan said quite desperately: "Don't, Sira. Don't promise what might not be possible for you to give."

The firelight was now less intense than the glow from the carnivorous flowers above our heads. Morgan was a shadow. Even the miscellaneous sounds of the forest had subsided to occasional whining hums from small, flying things.

"I don't know how to be Clan," I began slowly. "Do I need to learn?" Unprompted, my hand reached out to him. His hand dropped from my shoulder to wrap my fingers in a firm clasp.

The horrible wrongness flared with sickening speed,

dragging at us both. A scream tore from my throat as I fought to contain it, to keep it from Morgan. He spoke. Then agony of agonies, he tried to contact my mind. Away! I had to get away before it overwhelmed him. A wrenching pain. Disorientation . . .

I was nowhere.

And it was beautiful.

I could stay forever, suspended, not breathing, not moving, not truly alive.

Out! I ordered, but where? There was no mark, no distinction in this nothing place.

Wait. There was a passage nearby, etched in bright remembered power.

I *pushed* myself along it . . .

And found my body again. I dropped into the soft grass, hugging my knees, taking deep breaths for the joy of feeling the life returning to me.

Grass?

I drew a shaky breath, relieved to be free of that place, but totally amazed to be lying under a sunny, azure blue sky. I stood up and turned slowly, surveying my surroundings. Dried, yellow turf coated the undulating landscape—and there was no other vegetation or life as far as I could see.

"Oh, my," I said weakly, sitting back down quickly. What had I done?

Chapter 22

HAD I kept a record of my recent past, I was glumly sure it would have been a distressingly regular cycle of having, then not having, the basic comforts of life. Necessities might be the better word. I was taking Morgan's advice concerning native water and food quite seriously—but only because I hadn't had any chance to do otherwise. I squinted up at the blazing sun, passing my tongue over dry lips, longing for the cool night I'd left. However I had brought myself to this monotonous plain, I had to find my way off again soon or die.

The worst of it was, I knew what I had done, if not how to do it again. Under stress, more concealed memory had broken through the blockage smothering most of my past. I had a name for that terrible nothingness that had almost claimed me twice and Morgan once. It was the M'hir.

I had no idea what the M'hir was, but I had somehow traveled through it, bypassing normal space. Which meant I could be anywhere, though I refused to believe I wasn't still on Acranam.

I'd gained other fragments of memory, each tantalizing and useless. I had journeyed like this before—routinely, in fact. More proof, if I needed any, of my heritage. But how? I'd been miraculously lucky to find someone else's passageway through the M'hir. I couldn't try again blind.

There was another, not-so-minor, problem. Although I wasn't more than moderately thirsty yet, I soon would be. Along with thirst would come hunger, and then, growing weakness. How much strength would I need to travel back to the escape pod?

No. Not to the pod. I had to stop thinking of the pod—and Morgan. The darkness deep in my thoughts constantly urged me toward him. I refused to listen. Somehow, I knew this evil within me, this new compulsion, meant to drag Morgan into that nothingness, to destroy him. The pod was the one place I mustn't go, not until I was sure I wasn't a threat.

I sat down on the dry grass, poking small holes in the turf with my fingers, trying not to feel thirsty. It helped to think I was protecting Morgan by my absence. There was no effort, no dispute in my thoughts as to the rightness of my concern for him. For the first time in my foreshortened memory, I was calm and determined. I would not rejoin Morgan, even if I could figure out how.

However, I had no intention of becoming a set of bones bleached by Acranam's sun. So what was left? Not Yihtor. I shuddered as the thought of him crossed my mind. And I couldn't contact Huido. My options were becoming rather limited.

I sighed. Better to act while I was conceivably strong enough to protect myself.

The image of the Clanswoman, Rael, was easy to form. I made myself comfortable, aware that the process might be a long one. I'd no idea how far away she was, or whether she'd help me after I'd scorned her. Careful to maintain every possible safeguard, I made myself into as inconspicuous a mental presence as possible, preparing the questing thought with a skill that came more easily each time I practiced my still uncomfortable power.

The act of sending the thought opened a kind of inner door in my mind, admitting the nothingness of the M'hir. I recoiled, then relaxed slightly as I recognized I was not being drawn in, but simply using some odd new sense. Perhaps the Clan existed partly in that place.

The sun, which I took on faith to be the same one I'd seen the day before, had chased my shadow to my back before I felt the trace of an answer. Instantly, I poured all my remaining strength into the tenuous contact, ignoring the clamminess of my palms. *Rael!*

A flash of surprise, then a reassuring warmth accompanied her recognition, filling my perception. I could feel a path forming between us through the M'hir, becoming wider and more distinct with each input of power. *Sira. But—*

Holding my half of the path open was draining me as

though I'd cut a wrist and was watching my blood pour out on the soil. I tried to hurry my thought. *You called me sister, Clanswoman. Promise you won't betray me.*

Linked to mine through the M'hir, her thoughts were like a mountain pool, so exquisitely transparent that not even the depths were hidden, if I had the strength to search them. *Sister- and heart-kin, Sira. Whatever your trouble, you know you can depend on me.* Concern. *You are fading.*

I've noticed that, I agreed wryly.

Locate for me.

Locate?

I sensed her puzzlement echo my own, but she didn't waste time. *Open your thoughts to me. I'll come to you.* My distrust and suspicion were immediate and impossible to conceal. *You must trust, if I'm to help you, Sister,* Rael's thought tone was blunt.

I don't know you, I said, wavering. *You're a stranger to me.*

Rael's reply was tinged with impatience. *There must be a thousand words for stranger in the explored galaxy. Let one of them be sister—I don't care. All I know is to help you, I must be able to find you exactly and without error.*

I think my own rapidly growing fatigue was more convincing than her persuasion. I closed my eyes and opened the doors to my surface thoughts. Before I could drop more defenses, she said quickly: *Enough, dear Sister. I have your location. Stay where you are. I must make ready.*

I need supplies, water, I sent through the fog suddenly muffling my thoughts. The contact was gone.

With the warm sun beating down on me, I curled into a ball. Barriers restored, tucked down into the dry soft grass like a bird in a nest, I succumbed to the needs of my weary body and slept. What I could do for myself I had done. The next move was up to the stranger who called herself my kin.

Chapter 23

"I SHOULD have brought the galley's servo unit." Rael watched me eat with something approaching awe on her beautiful face. "I've had fosterlings who didn't eat this much at a meal, and you know the calories children need when they are still holding that link to their parents."

Actually, I had no idea, so I grunted something apologetic, though I didn't put down my cup of stew. Over its rim, I eyed her warily, a bit suspicious that Rael and her welcome provisions would disappear again as magically as they'd arrived. The tent fluttering gently in the cool evening breeze was another of her gifts.

"I've learned to stock up while I can," I said when I was at last as full as possible. "Thank you, Clanswoman."

Rael's eyes darkened. "I have a name."

"I'm sorry, Rael," and I meant it. She'd shown me nothing but kindness—demanding nothing, not even an explanation for my behavior, which I could see was a constant source of distress to her. "I've told you I can't remember my past," I said slowly, searchingly. "I'd like to remember you."

Although Rael offered no mental contact, there was a sense of leashed strength about her, an aliveness I could feel even without the visual impact of her vivid beauty.

As much to break the binding growing between us as anything else, I said sharply: "But it's hard for me to believe you and I are sisters. Look at you—and at me." I waved a hand down over my curveless, lean body, still clad in oversized space coveralls from the *Torquad*.

Her angry reaction surprised me. "You've learned to be cruel among the Humans."

The hurt in her voice and face made me uncomfortable.

It was like kicking a Turrned. "Why do you say that?" I said, steeling myself against guilt. "It's obvious we're very different."

After a moment, Rael nodded graciously. Her long, white hand sketched a gesture I recognized, with a small shock, as one I had offered to Morgan unknowingly. "You should forgive me, dear Sira. I must constantly remind myself that you don't understand what you're saying." It was Rael's turn to look uneasy. "Which means I have a lot to explain. I wish we knew what happened to you. Are you certain you won't let me examine your mind? I may not have Cenebar's healing touch, but—"

"No." I shook my head for emphasis. "Oh, I believe you mean well enough, Rael. But what about others of your kind? I can't take the risk." I thought of Gistries and shivered. Never would I expose myself to that.

Rael accepted my reply with a slow nod. "I might feel the same in your position. But don't say my kind, Sira. Regardless of how you've been treated, you are still one of the M'hiray, the Clan. You're not Human." The last word seemed deliberately stressed. I bristled.

"What's wrong with Humans? If you hate them so much, why live among them?" I glared at her. "And why hate them at all?"

"We live among Humans because we must. There aren't enough of us to fill a world, let alone run its economy." She paused. "Even if there were, it's not the Clan way to live piled on top of one another. Power must travel to enhance the M'hir for all." This last sounded like a rote lesson, but I thought I understood it. Had I not used pathways created by someone else's power to arrive here? I tucked away the notion to consider later, not ready to leave the Human issue alone.

"You haven't answered my question."

Rael licked her lips and dropped her gaze from mine. "I don't *hate* Humans. It's much better to just ignore them, you know. Unfortunately, because of your—situation—I can't do that. There's Morgan."

"So?" If she were as adept at reading voices as minds, Rael should have heard the warning in mine. But she didn't.

"Because of Morgan, we must discuss certain delicate matters. Which I am not finding easy, Sira. There are things polite adults don't discuss." She muttered something under her breath that sounded like, "Pella better not hear about this."

Then louder: "To begin with, you must understand that Human and Clan are distinct, regardless of how similar we appear to each other. And we must remain so."

If the tent had been taller, I'd have stood. I had to settle for an annoyed snort. "You're as bad as Morgan for riddles. Say what you mean."

"Words are useless."

"Words must do." I made this an ultimatum.

"Your refusal to open to me is wasting time," Rael sounded exasperated. "I can't sense your feelings, Sira. I don't know you!"

"That makes things nicely even, then." My smile probably contained every bit of the cruelty she'd accused me of earlier. "You've helped me. I'd like to understand your place in this, Rael. But I won't let you near my thoughts."

Eyes that were dark, liquid pools regarded me with a strange sadness. "Then I will do what I can with words." Her lip curled. "However inadequate."

I realized my advantage over the Clanswoman. She'd never needed to read expression; perhaps she couldn't. Better still, I thought, she'd probably never needed to control her own. "Do your best, Rael," I suggested.

"This is such a dangerous time in your life, Sira," she began, each sentence following an obvious effort. "You remain a Chooser. Because, for you, there isn't to be Choice." A flush rose into her cheeks, staining them a faint pink. "The Council examined every possible candidate; there's none—not in the coming generation either. That was their so-called reason behind the decree to keep you from all but family." She smiled, then sobered almost immediately. "In places, you're somewhat of a legend."

Aggravated, I rubbed at the familiar ache between my eyes. Matters were rapidly becoming more, rather than less, confusing. I didn't try to keep the edge from my voice. "No wonder I preferred to be Human. It was certainly simpler," I commented bitterly. "What's a Chooser? What's Choice? How can I be a legend? And by what right does this Council of yours order my life?"

She waved her hands to slow my angry questioning.

"This is impossible! I can't communicate this way." Rael was now distinctly red-faced. There was simply no guile in her. Emotions came and went across her expressive features with an openness I found comforting. At the moment, concern warred with confusion.

She was the one needing reassurance, I realized, amazed. "I'm sorry, Rael," I said, quite honestly. "Take your time. Tell me what you can. I'll try to save my questions."

Rael let out a deep shuddering breath that had something of a sob to it. "I don't know where I should start, Sira. You taught me, remember? No, I suppose you don't. I've depended on you all my life—it hurts to see you like this, to have you distrust me, close your thoughts to me.

"And all that time, plus years before I was born, you've been a Chooser. Now, you seem so young." When I merely stared at her blankly, a smile twitched her lips. "Choosers don't age until Choice is made, although no one's remained unJoined as long as you have. Small compensation for being less than whole."

I thought of the image Morgan had found in Roraqk's records, the image of a young Jarad and myself taken over a hundred years ago, and caught at the edge of an understanding that slipped away from me again. "How old am I?"

Rael's smile faded. "In what sense?"

How could she make a simple question complex? "How long have I lived? How old am I?"

"Well," she said with an absentminded toss of her hair, "you've *lived* for," she paused and thought about it, "110 standard years or so. As for how *old* a M'hiray is, that depends on how much of that time you've spent in the physiological lock of Choice. In your case, as I've said, you've been a Chooser for around seventy-five years. As humans calculate such things, I suppose you are somewhere around thirty years old. You will start from there and live out a normal life span once Chosen. Why do you want to know?"

"Never mind," I mumbled, unsure myself, my thoughts churning with half-understandings and obscure emotions. "If I was, am, this Chooser, then what was I waiting to choose? Why was I a prisoner?"

"Your mind is too empty!" She wrung her hands together. "I don't understand. Stasis doesn't block so much.

What have they done to you?" There were tears in her
eyes again. "My poor sister. If you can't remember
the most basic facts of life, it's no wonder you've forgotten me!"

"Basic to you," I reminded her grimly, "but not to me.
"What am I to Choose?" Somehow, I knew this was important. Without meaning to, I gripped her hands tightly,
squeezing until my fingers bit into her softer skin. When I
realized what I was doing, I let her go, ashamed.

"Your power seeks its life-partner." Rael looked at the
marks my fingers left. Her face was anguished. "You used
to be a gentle person."

"I've changed." Morgan would have heard the pain in
my voice—and understood. Rael took it another way.

"The Human." She said it like a curse.

"Survival," I countered just as harshly. "And if I was so
gentle, why was I imprisoned? Why was I dropped on
Auord with nothing but compulsions in my head?"

From the shifting of her eyes, I knew she picked the
easier question to answer. "You were never·a prisoner. No
matter what you think you remember. You agreed to be
isolated."

"I agreed! Why?"

"To protect the honor of our family. Yihtor's shameless
behavior brought enough disaster—"

My face must have been as transparent as her own in
that moment, for Rael's voice trailed away, a startled look
widening her eyes.

"It always circles back to him," I said bitterly. "What
does he want from me, Rael? I've been kidnapped—and
now marooned on this forsaken world—all by the mysterious Yihtor. Is it any wonder I distrust the very word
Clan?"

Rael's eyes were like black holes in a white mask. "Yihtor is dead."

"Not this one." I remembered Gistries and swallowed
my sarcasm. "Yihtor is alive. Believe me, Rael."

"There's some mistake, Sira. There was a terrible accident, not long after Council refused him. Yihtor was
killed—so were others."

I raised a brow, for once feeling superior. "Believe
what you choose, Rael. The Yihtor who inhabits this planet

is far from dead and has caused me a great deal of grief already."

Her shoulders hunched as if expecting a blow. "What world is this?" A whisper.

"Well, I hope it's Acranam," I replied, surprised she didn't know. "I used the M'hir once since landing, but I—"

"Acranam. It had to be." Her voice rose. "Don't you see—first Kurr, and now this dead name, both tied to this cursed place! Barac is coming here without realizing his danger!"

Barac. The Clansman who paid Morgan to take me from Auord. And who was this Kurr? "You gave me your word," I spat at her, furious and afraid at the same time. "Why would the Clansman come here unless you told him?"

"I didn't betray you, Sira," Rael protested, her eyes darting around the tent as if expecting some loathsome creature to scuttle from under the blankets. She went on quickly: "Before I came to you, I left Barac a message to tell him I was taking responsibility for your safety, as is my right as closer kin. Barac's brother Kurr was murdered as he passed through the Acranam system. Without you to search for, I know Barac will retrace Kurr's journey in order to find his killer. He will bring the *Fox* here. And Barac will be killed, just like Kurr, if you're right about Yihtor."

"Morgan's *Fox*?" I repeated stupidly. "Next, I suppose you'll tell me you brought Enforcers."

Rael leaned forward, her face pale, her voice low and intense. "What use would they be? If Yihtor faked his own death to turn renegade, we'll need the Council itself to save us." I'd thought her face expressive. Now, the ashen look of horror filling it was enough to make me shiver. "Sira! How could I be such a fool?"

The Clanswoman started to pack up gear at a furious pace. In her frenzy, most missed the mouth of the bag. I intervened, pushing her out of the way. Rael said something incoherent, then: "We must leave here at once. Don't you see? I used power to come here. I didn't think there was any risk disturbing the M'hir." Defensively, though I'd offered no reproof: "Barac's good in his way, but he can't follow M'hir trails. And you already knew I was coming."

"Was I better at things like that than Barac?" I asked absently, more concerned with a sack that wouldn't swallow.

Rael looked up. "How terrible to lose so much, Sira. To remember nothing of what you were or did." I restrained the obvious reply and tugged the fastening closed. Rael shook her head sadly, hair tumbling over a shoulder. "You were better." That was all she'd say.

We worked together in silent haste, striking the tent and watching it fold into a tiny compactness. When done, we had all our gear in two packs carried by shoulder straps. I took both, finding their weight vastly reassuring. I was becoming satisfied by less and less each day. The darkness was broken only by the glimmer of unfamiliar stars. A light wind rustled the grass.

"Where, or should I say what, now, Rael?" I asked.

I'd startled her. "The *Fox,* Sira. Where else could we be safe? And I must warn Barac."

There was a way to chain her power, to stop her before she drew us into the M'hir. Knowledge erupted from within my mind and I acted swiftly. "No. I won't."

Rael stood quiescent, though I sensed her probing at the unseen bonds I had formed around her mind. She sighed, a sound softer than the night breeze chilling my arms. "You asked me to compare your power to Barac's. You should have asked me to compare you to yourself."

"What do you mean?" I whispered back, apprehensive of what she would say, though I wasn't sure why.

"You aren't merely stronger than Barac—or me. You are, or were, the most powerful individual ever born to our species, the crowning achievement of generations of deliberate and careful selection for power. As such, and a Chooser, you are the prize beyond hope for Yihtor, should he truly live.

"Sister, let me take us from this world before he knows you're here!"

"He knows," I told her, with utter certainty, identifying the whisper-thin mental presence nosing at the edge of my mind with sickening familiarity. "Remind me how to find my way through the M'hir and quickly, Rael, or neither of us will survive to warn anyone."

Chapter 24

I'D lost Rael, or she'd lost me. It depended on your point of view, I decided. The taste of Yihtor's probe had been enough to panic her completely; not that I'd been immune to fear myself, forced to see Gistries' dying face at the merest hint of Yihtor's presence. In our mutual desperation, I'd lowered my barriers to Rael in order to receive the information on passing form through the M'hir.

And she'd managed to use the moment to break my control and leave me. To be charitable, I was sure Rael thought I'd have to follow her to the *Fox* and Barac. It was a very simple way to suicide, entering the M'hir without the clear visual image of a locate. I'd survived my first attempt only because power in the M'hir tended to follow existing paths, like water collecting into channels. My directionless power had slipped into the path Yihtor must have forged through his trips around his world.

However, with its owner now alerted, I didn't plan to tap that particular route again.

With enough power, it was also possible to travel by targeting oneself at the dimpling of the M'hir surrounding an unshielded mind. Rael's particular talent took that further, since she could send her image or form to where someone's power had recently touched the M'hir.

But for most Clan it was easier and safer to go to a re-membered place. Which meant I'd had a locate to use, one Rael should not be able to find if I were careful. So as she *pushed* herself to the *Fox,* I went somewhere else.

My mind shielded to the best of my ability, I edged my way over a massive curl of root until I glimpsed the campsite. The pod, the dead fire, the bundled blankets were easy to see in the filtered sunlight. Night where I'd been, but day here. If I'd always been on Acranam, I must have slipped past half the planet on each trip through the M'hir. Instead of exhausted, I felt exhilarated.

Where was Morgan? My plan was simple, provided that I could avoid him. I needed more supplies, clothing, possibly even a weapon, in order to seek the shelter offered by the seemingly endless forest behind me.

I needed time—time to think for myself and to discover how to return to Morgan without endangering him. But where was he? I couldn't risk a mental search. I was afraid of the force within me, not to mention who might eavesdrop. After a long moment, I took a cautious step toward the pod, keeping a link to the M'hir ready in case I was discovered.

My stealth and care were wasted; Morgan was gone. I chewed a lip thoughtfully as I packed the goods I thought I might need. There was no indication that the supplies had been touched; no carrying sacks were missing from their hooks. I opened another small cupboard and drew out its contents with my hand, watching it start to tremble. Morgan's blaster.

I ignored my small pile of essentials, turning the lethal weapon over and over in my hands. Morgan wouldn't leave it, not on this world. There was only one means I knew of which could remove a person without a trace. It added up to something I didn't care for in the least. Yihtor had found easier prey.

The blaster made an unfamiliar weight in my belt. Ruthlessly, I dumped out my pack in order to refill it with smaller, lighter items: ration tubes, lights, a medi-kit I regarded soberly before stuffing it on top and cinching the pack shut. In the back of my mind a voice I tried to ignore was producing a virtually endless list of reasons why I should leave well enough alone.

Just as I was about to leave the pod for the last time, I took a final glance around. I tugged open a half-ajar cupboard door. There were two unmarked green bottles inside and the sight of them gave me a wild idea. Perhaps I couldn't contact Huido mind-to-mind, but what was there to prevent me using him as a locate?

Quite a bit, the more rational, less impulsive, portion of my mind replied. Depending on where the alien was, I might end up in worse straits. And although it was theoretically impossible to exit from the M'hir into a solid object, there was no comparable safeguard against Huido's reaction to my unannounced entrance. Despite these and other drawbacks, the notion stayed with me as I closed and locked the pod's air lock. Huido would be a comforting ally.

Once outside, I looked around the campsite, trying not to think of the peaceful enchantment of the night before. I tried not to think too much about Morgan either. The distorts would function for days yet on the pod's powerpak, keeping any native wildlife at bay. Preparing to slip past that barrier, I stopped, shrugging away my doubts. With a whispered prayer, and a firm, if uncomfortable, recollection of the feel of the Carasian's mind, I prepared the locate, concentrated, and *pushed* . . .

. . . only to bump my head soundly on the rough edge of a stone overhang. "Huido?" I called softly, rubbing my head with one hand while the other gained support from a damp rock wall. Once my eyes adjusted to the darkness, I saw I was within the entrance of a large cave.

Outside the cave, a slope covered with a talus of small, round stones flowed steeply downward, vanishing under the forest canopy. There was no sign of the second escape pod. I paused for a moment, awed by the tremendous crowns of the trees I'd so admired from beneath. Huido had come precariously close to his own prediction of perching on a mountainside.

"Huido?" I called again, turning back to the cave mouth, peering unsuccessfully inside. "It's Sira." Still no reply.

My movement to bring the light from my pack was frozen by a cold pressure against the base of my neck. "Oh. There you are," I said hopefully, a cold sweat on my brow.

"Where is Morgan?" I sagged with relief at Huido's bellow, only to be jabbed by the Carasian's weapon. "What have you done to him?" I tried turning my head, but couldn't see him.

"Morgan's in trouble, Huido. He needs our help."

This was ridiculous. I turned around, pushing the weapon aside. "And why do I deserve this?" my voice close to quivering with indignation.

Multiple eyes milled as if in consultation as Huido regarded me for a long moment. Then he rumbled: "Perhaps you don't. I lack my brother's ability to read the truth from a mind. You smell all right." He rumbled to himself a minute. "But I don't like it. You arrive out of the air, with Morgan's weapon in your belt. You wouldn't be the first of the Clan to try to harm him."

The Clan, I repeated to myself, staring up in a vain effort to read something of an expression in his face of shell-shadow and gleaming restless eyes. "You know—"

"You pop out of nowhere. You're Clan or a hallucination." Huido clicked a claw impatiently on the side of his armored head. "Besides, there's always been something tangy in your grist. Where is Morgan?"

I left the topic of my *grist* alone for the moment. "Yihtor has him."

Huido fastened his hand weapon to its chest-clip, making a hollow thrum of distress. A gesture into the cave. "Let's get out of sight. You can tell me what's happened and what must be done."

Huido's pod had indeed come to rest on a precipice, he informed me as we talked over a fragrant boiling pot. I accepted a mug of its contents somewhat warily. "Was this in your supplies?" I asked cautiously, not eager to taste the dark liquid.

A rustle and click. All I could really see of him in the inadequate light from the boxed heat-source were glints of reflection from his shiny eyes and polished shell. "Supplies! Most of those slid over the cliff with that scrap heap of a lifeboat. Besides, who needs processed pap when nature herself is so bountiful. I plan to offer this on my menu as soon as we get back."

I put down the mug carefully, trying not to be envious of his audible delight as Huido serenely enjoyed his own portion. I could only hope his clients had a digestive system as sturdy as his. "We must get to Morgan before Yihtor harms him," I said impatiently.

Huido's eyes formed a rosette of reflecting points. "I

think you are worrying too much, Sira. Morgan has handled the Clan before."

"Yihtor scares *them*, Huido," I reminded the big alien. "He's probably ripped through Jason's mind already. We may be too late." I closed my eyes very briefly.

"Don't mourn him until we see a corpse." Huido's voice drew small echoing rumbles from the cave depths. Then he added, with a perception I hadn't expected: "And don't you believe you'd know?"

More briskly. "At least you can overcome what I'd expected to be the main problem—you can get me down from here, can't you?"

I was surprised into a laugh at the plaintiveness of his question. Obviously, the Carasian had minded his exile a great deal more than it seemed. Perhaps his experimentation with the local cuisine had been triggered by as desperate a need as I had felt before being saved by Rael.

"I won't know until I try, Huido," I cautioned. I wasn't about to let the Carasian know my greatest concern was not how to physically reach Morgan but what might happen when I used Morgan's mind for the locate. I ignored the twisting discomfort deep in my stomach paired with any thought of Yihtor himself.

Huido finished my portion with a smack of approval. "Then there's no reason to delay, little one," he pointed out, tossing the empty cup into the dark to tumble against several others. "We have surprise on our side if we act quickly enough."

He'd been the one delaying. Now that the Carasian was ready for battle, I hesitated. "The only surprise may be ours. Yihtor may well be expecting us. We could materialize into a trap. It could be day or night there—let alone whatever else awaits us."

The Carasian was silent for a moment, then said heavily: "Morgan will try to buy us time. A story concocted to aid our escape will cover an attack even better. So we go now, before he tires."

Or dies, I added to myself, looking dubiously at the giant shadowy figure who was my only ally. My ability to travel through the M'hir was regrettably new. There was nothing in my memory or in the flash of information from Rael to guide me in an attempt to take along another person. But it was impossible to fault Huido's logic or his courage. "This may not work," I warned him. "I could lose one or both of us."

Huido was as unshakable as the rock enclosing us. "It has to be better than walking."

My hand delicately grasped between the tips of a shiny black claw, I closed my eyes and began to search the M'hir for our destination: a trace, any type of mental pattern that would read as Jason Morgan to that mysterious portion of my mind.

Slowly, carefully, I reconstructed Morgan within my thoughts. It was easier than the search I had conducted to contact my sister. I knew the feel of Morgan's mind so well; the rhythms of his body were like my own. It was like searching the M'hir for the other half of myself. As I checked my image for flaws, I found myself dwelling on the sound of his laughter, pausing to remember the strange clarity of his eyes. A longing of intense power filled me and I *pushed* without thinking . . .

. . . Huido drew me hastily into the shadow of a small stone building. As we looked about in astonishment, I felt his light pat of approval on my shoulder. There was no time for conversation. We scrambled farther back as a personal land cruiser sped past, kicking up a light dust.

We had arrived in the midst of a spacious, thriving town. I was astounded by the permanence around me. Acranam was supposedly a recent listing, a newly discovered and empty world. Was that, too, a lie, fabricated to hide this unexpectedly elaborate stronghold of the renegade's? The building we sheltered behind was crude, as were the others lining the wide street, but there were plentiful signs of long settlement.

Thoughtfully, I poked the toe of my boot at the beaten earth. There was more here than a criminal making himself comfortable. There was a scent of empire building.

"Well, where is he?" Huido rumbled as quietly as he could.

With great daring, I flicked out a questing thought and withdrew it quickly, restoring every barrier. The stone wall was warm under my hand. "Here," I whispered with confidence, then, anticipating his next question, I continued: "This must be as close as I can take us. I don't know why."

A nod followed by a careful surveillance. We were nestled in the only shadow within reach. Voices raised in animated speech grew louder, then faded as their unseen owners passed. "Can you use your power to scout inside?" Huido asked once all was quiet for a few moments.

The blood left my face and I almost shuddered. Risk mental contact with Morgan—or worse yet, Yihtor himself? "No," I answered as vehemently as I could in a whisper.

If Huido didn't believe me, he kept his opinion to himself. "Keep watch up front, then. There are other ways to enter unseen." I moved up to the corner of the squat building, ears and eyes straining. From that vantage point, I peered cautiously up and down the street.

To my left, the pavement disappeared quickly into a tunnel of jungle, almost immediately forced into an abrupt turn by the massive trees. To my right, the street was broad and straight, intersecting with other smaller thoroughfares until it also vanished into the green wall of the forest. The settlement thus lay nestled within a circle of towering vegetation.

Admirable cover against an aerial search, I thought cynically. To be fair, the closeness of the luxuriant foliage softened the harsh lines of the one- and two-story buildings, lending them a warmth and color they would otherwise totally lack.

There was no further sign of the local populace—for which I was grateful as I winced at the sound of Huido's assault on the thick wall. The sun beat down with inescapable directness and the oppressive humidity soon clamped my clothing tightly against my skin. The combination would be enough to keep most creatures indoors.

Indoors, I repeated to myself somewhat numbly. I spared an instant to wonder how I'd missed it. There were no doors. The structures across the street overlooked the pavement only by means of small, paired windows. Daringly, I craned around to check the front of Morgan's prison. It was the same. I crept back to where Huido had paused in his fight with the stonework. He was changing the powerpak of a stubby rifle with deliberate care.

"Hurry," I urged him, resisting the impulse to glance over my shoulder. Huido spared two eyes to examine my face.

"You look as though you've seen a ghost," the Carasian commented, snapping the cover back into place.

"This hole of yours may be the only door in this town. Do you realize what that means?" Holding my voice down helped disguise a certain shrillness.

Huido shrugged, lining up his improvised cutting tool. "One Clan, or all Clan. We still need to get inside." Chunks of stone reddened and vanished as the huge being calmly resumed his noisy labors.

All very well for the mentally invulnerable alien, busily directing his beam. My own inner warnings were screaming, and I stayed where I was by will alone. I pulled Morgan's blaster from my belt, then angrily shoved it back. Bluffing with a package sealer was one thing. Could I use a real weapon? Could I harm my own kind? I hoped I wouldn't have to make that choice.

"We're in," Huido's announcement was loud in the sudden silence as he switched off his tool. The jagged hole, large enough for a small cruiser and not to be missed from any distance, I thought with dismay, still glowed along its edges. It opened on an unlit room, apparently used for storage, to judge by the singed crates lining one wall. We stepped inside cautiously; I, for one, thoroughly distrusting the ease of our entry.

Huido might have read my mind as easily as Morgan. "No doors—so no guards."

"No guards we can see," I hissed over my shoulder, having moved to the one door. Something struggled in my memory, some thread of caution stayed my reaching fingers short of the knob. Ignoring Huido's impatient grumble, I crouched before the portal and examined the handle—for what, I wasn't sure.

A wisp of thought, let out carefully through my shielding, floated outward and tested. This was perhaps the strangest use of my power I'd yet attempted. I forced myself to relax and accept the improbable. My probing thought reached farther.

Instantly, I was paralyzed, having unwittingly set off the very trap I'd so cleverly suspected. *Idiot,* I shouted to myself, unable to so much as turn my head to warn Huido. An eternity passed.

An arch of blinding light passed close enough to warm my face. The spell vanished—along with most of the door and its frame. Huido drew me to my feet. "Are you all right?" he inquired absently, peering out into the deserted hallway.

I gaped at him. "Yes. But how did—?"

Eyestalks fluttered with what looked to be amusement. "Morgan has shown me such a trap before. Unless you know the proper mental code, a residual force pins the unwary and holds them for later capture. The machinery used is delicate." A satisfied shake of his blaster. "It was fortunate only you could be so caught." I didn't bother to reply.

Our luck could hardly hold much longer—if luck it was. We searched the building with reckless haste, flaming down two more closed doors. I began to believe Huido. Perhaps Yihtor hadn't expected a rescue attempt, or thought himself strong enough not to fear one. In that case, Morgan's chances were even slimmer. Yet we had been led here, to this place, by the most specific manner of identification imaginable. Morgan was here and had to be alive.

And he was. Huido led the way through a third doorway into a small room, bare save for a single, low cot and its apparently slumbering occupant. I went forward slowly as Huido stopped, both of us mindful of blundering into any more invisible traps.

"Jason?" I called softly. There was no answering movement, no opening of blue eyes in a face more still than mere sleep. Gripped by sudden dread, I reached out and touched his hand. It was warm but strangely flaccid. His heart beat slowly, heavily, echoing the sense I had of his body's waning strength. Huido, peering over my shoulder, gave a menacing growl. I looked up questioningly.

"He has been forced into retreat."

Even this nontelepath knew more than I. I felt a surge of hope. "Then he hasn't been hurt?"

All eyes fixed on Morgan, the Carasian rattled his body armor with frustrated rage. "This is a dangerous state, used only as a last resort. Morgan almost died learning the technique, and then he had expert help to draw him back." With touching gentleness, the alien lifted the unconscious man into his massive arms.

That action set off the alarm I'd feared. I was assailed by a blast of red-hot mental rage. As my mind burned with pain, I saw Huido using all four arms to try and hold a now-writhing Morgan. Before I could recognize the source of the attack, something deep in me responded, creating a barrier around the three of us. The pain stopped. Morgan settled into stillness.

Morgan had been right. This was how I was meant to be.

A decision had to be made quickly, and I realized without surprise that it was mine alone to make. There was only one way to help Morgan any further. I borrowed strength unobtrusively from my shielding and *pushed*. Huido and his helpless burden vanished. Relieved of the extra responsibility, my shield resumed its more customary configuration, strengthening until the attack wavered and finally ceased.

Perhaps I should have mistrusted the impulse to stay, to await Yihtor's next move. Perhaps my swelling confidence in my unseen strength and the increasing ease with which I could summon it was another sort of trap, luring me into a dangerous lack of caution.

And just perhaps there was a trace left of the Sira Rael remembered—a Sira willing to at least find out why she had been hauled across space to this meeting.

But the Sira who stood poised and alert, barriers firmly in place, eyes searching the gloom was a Sira who intended to take control of her own fate. I was no longer a piece to be moved at whim over some inexplicable game board. If the mysterious Yihtor thought otherwise, he would be the first to be surprised.

* * *

INTERLUDE

Frozen by astonishment, the figures in the control room of the *Fox* formed a strange tableau. Huido recovered first, shifting Morgan's limp body so one handling claw was free to menace the gaping Clansman and the pilot with a disrupter. A swift gesture with the weapon, and the latter moved away from the control panels.

"A weapon isn't necessary," Rael snapped as she strode into the room, taking in the situation at a glance. She uttered a small cry at the sight of Morgan. "What has she done?"

"Come no closer, Clanswoman," Huido warned, moving back warily, armor grating against the metal bulkhead, leaving dark streaks in the paint. "Where is Sira?" Eyestalks were bending in every direction as the Carasian attempted to find out for himself.

Barac found his tongue. "We should be asking you. Why do you expect to see her here? And what's wrong with the Human?"

Huido shifted Morgan's weight absently, but didn't lower his weapon. "Sira must have sent us here by her power and remained behind to cover our escape. We were in Yihtor's stronghold."

Rael's face grew ashen. The look she traded with her cousin was full of meaning. "Then Yihtor has her now?"

"I will go back," Huido fixed all his eyes on Rael. "Send me while you care for Morgan. My blood brother retreated into himself to protect us."

"How can we send you," Rael said flatly, "when we don't know where you've been? The locate is buried in that scrambled brain of yours. You must know we can't read your thoughts."

Huido clipped his weapon to a ring in his upper plate, then tenderly laid Morgan on the pilot's couch. He used a shiny clawtip to push back a lock of hair from the Human's pale face. "Then what you need is here, Clanswoman. Sira must have expected you to help him—if only in order to gain a chance to capture her yourselves."

"We've never intended harm to her, you big fool," Barac's voice was tight. Faint stains of red tinged his high cheekbones. "Yihtor isn't one of us. We're here to bring him to justice—and to help Sira if we can."

Huido removed Terk from the other seat with a multi-eyed glare, then made himself comfortable. "Help Morgan."

"We indeed have no other choice," Rael agreed, regarding the motionless Human with a remote compassion. "And perhaps Sira is only forcing us to do our rightful duty. This Human is as much a victim of Yihtor as any of our kin."

"I don't care about your kin," the Carasian stated with a low growling note. "Nor do I care about justice. Aid my brother, and we will rescue Sira. But for the sake of my debt and his—not for you."

"Understood," Barac waved the confused Terk from the control room. "And the sooner we begin, the better."

Chapter 25

THE tall, lean figure stood framed by the shattered door, frozen at first, staring at me. I remained equally still as the present merged with memory. "You've gotten older, Yihtor," I said finally, in a conversational tone which quite impressed part of myself.

Yihtor bowed, his bright gray-green eyes never leaving my face. "You have not, Chooser," a heavy satisfaction in his voice.

"No," I said without discomfort.

Yihtor's head tilted as he considered me with a closeness I knew couldn't penetrate my shielding, yet which had a chilling effect. I had the sudden feeling that he was nonplussed by something about me—whether some oddness in my behavior or strangeness in my appearance, I couldn't tell.

I studied him, too, disturbed to find him attractive. There was the same vivid life in his features I'd found so remarkable in Rael. His blond hair was thick, framing a high, broad forehead, accenting a dark tan. There was a tautness to his build which suggested fitness and strength. He was a handsome one, all right. But he still reminded me of a toad.

One long hand sketched an unfamiliar gesture, part salute, part beckoning. "Come with me, Chooser," Yihtor said. "Acranam boasts far more beautiful and comfortable surroundings than these."

I raised a brow and didn't move. "You kept Morgan here."

This time Yihtor's discomfiture was obvious. "Why do you care about a Human?" His eyes darted around the room as if my presence had clouded his senses until now. "You've taken him. Why?"

"Why did you?" I countered. "Morgan had nothing to do with you—"

"Nothing? He interfered with me—stole my property—my ship!"

"Your property?" I picked up the word, challenged him with it. "Your ship? So you're merely a pirate."

I'd angered him, a frown smudged the handsome brow, but the Clansman's voice was controlled and level. "My interests are far wider than you could imagine, Chooser. And they are none of your concern. Nor is a Human." A slow step forward. "What occurs from this moment on is all that need interest you."

I rechecked my mental barriers. There was danger in the Clansman's deliberate advance; belatedly I remembered Gistries, and Rael's fear. "Stay away from me," I warned him, ready to launch myself through the M'hir. Yihtor stopped immediately.

"Just allow me your hand, daughter of Jarad. It is your purpose here. It is our destiny." His eyes had taken on a luster, a glow. An awesome power throbbed against my shielding—a potential more than a threat.

"The Choice is mine," I said, the words rising from nowhere, as I retreated a step without knowing why.

"The Choice is yours, Chooser," Yihtor agreed instantly, bright eyes hooded and hard to read. He remained motionless for a moment, then slowly reached his right hand out to me. "Once, we were interrupted by fools. Since that day, I have learned other ways to control and use power, ways that increase my strength within the M'hir a thousandfold, ways our deluded Council thought to hide. Join with me, power to power. I, Yihtor di Caraat, offer you Choice, Sira di Sarc."

Things were not going as I'd expected. I glanced from Yihtor's compelling face to his outstretched hand and back again, my mind sundered into fragments, my thoughts in chaos. Gistries' torment, Roraqk's death, Morgan—all faded as if part of a dream. I needed . . . what? I was only part of what I was intended to be. I must find and Choose . . . I looked at Yihtor with a sudden understanding—knowing beyond doubt he was empty, too.

Yihtor, my completion? "No!" My rejection welled up, deep and utter.

Yihtor lunged forward, taking me completely by surprise, and grabbed my hand in a tight hold. "How dare you!" I hissed; at the same time bewildered that the simple touch of his hand offended me so deeply. The roiling darkness I'd felt twice before surged up, overwhelming my consciousness. This time I welcomed it. The heaving force struck outward, seeking my defiler, knocking Yihtor back against the wall. He leaned there for a moment—eyes wide with shock, pain, and something else.

"Who has touched you?" Yihtor demanded, breathing heavily. "You're no Chooser!"

I seriously considered making an exit, but hesitated, curious despite my caution. "What do you mean?"

Yihtor sucked in a deep breath and held it, eyes narrowed in speculation. He raised his hand, fingers outstretched, and drew the outline of my face and shoulders in midair. Done, his hand clenched into a tight fist which he let fall to his side. There was disbelief on his face, quickly replaced by satisfaction.

"Sira, forgive me." Yihtor smiled with incredible charm, stirring a traitorous warmth within me. "I don't pretend to understand what's happened to you. Somehow you're still a Chooser—at least partly so. Forgive my impetuousness, please. The thought you might Commence for someone else—well, it drove me a little crazy."

Impetuousness? Although I was cloudy on the details, one fact was clear. What Yihtor had attempted was against any code of behavior. He deserved nothing but my contempt.

Unfortunately, Yihtor must have been more experienced than Rael at reading expressions. Before I so much as sensed his intention, the Clansman vanished and, where he'd stood, another figure crouched. As I concentrated with desperate speed, my body shuddered under the impact of a bolt of stun and I crumpled.

I stared at the floor, fighting unconsciousness, refusing to give in to panic, continuing to strain mentally even as I saw the toe of a boot out the corner of my eye. With a sensation of bursting a barrier, I *pushed* and the floor beneath my cheek . . .

. . . roughened into hard, packed earth. I held back a

sob, more than content to lie motionless in the safety of Huido's hillside cave.

* * *

INTERLUDE

Morgan's eyelids twitched, then opened slowly. He held himself still, acknowledging the anxious gaze of all of Huido's black and shiny eyes with a glance. His blue eyes widened briefly as he recognized the *Fox*'s control room.

Rael's hand hovered close to Morgan's forehead for a second. She smiled with satisfaction. "A full recovery, Human. Retreat's not a foolproof technique."

Huido helped Morgan sit up. Morgan hesitated before trying his voice. When he spoke, the sound was reed-thin and husky. "Sira?"

Barac and Rael exchanged glances. Huido answered slowly: "Sira found me. She used her power to transport us to where you'd been imprisoned, in the renegade Clansman's city." A pause during which Huido twisted several of his eyes in order to watch the pair standing across from him. "There was some kind of mental attack—something which affected you and Sira. She stayed behind and sent us here."

Barac glared down at Morgan as if the Human were the source of all his troubles. "Leaving me to wonder if Sira wanted us to help you or get rid of you. If she's chosen to stay with a ghost—"

"Yihtor's neither dead nor a ghost, Barac," Rael snapped. "And Sira wouldn't stay with him willingly." Her eyes fastened upon Morgan's. "Sira wanted us to help you."

Morgan raised a brow. "Which bothers you," he said.

"My opinion is irrelevant. I don't question my sister, whether I understand her or not," Rael said firmly, before Barac could speak, a warning flash of anger tightening her lips. "I've helped you, as she wished. Now we need something from you—a trade, let's say, for your life, Human."

"Sira."

"You dare—" Rael stopped, gathered herself, and

damped the swelling of her power. Her eyes were bright and hard. "My sister is not something to be traded by you or anyone else, Human. I'll save her. And I'll look after her until she's healed. Away from you."

"But you've admitted you need me," Morgan said coolly. Huido's eyes clumped to focus on his friend's face. Lights winked to themselves in greens, yellows, and blues on the control panels, oblivious to the tension in the room. "Why? To help you find Sira? How do you expect me to accomplish that? I tried searching for her with my power on Acranam. I couldn't find her."

Barac seemed to shrink into himself at Morgan's words. Rael spared him a quelling glance before answering. "We have no need for your pitiful abilities, Human."

"Then what do you want?"

Barac answered. "We need a reference to lead us into Yihtor's base. With that, we can travel there and rescue Sira, hopefully before Yihtor detects us."

"We do not choose to reveal ourselves to Yihtor by scanning the M'hir," Rael said as if this should be obvious even to a Human.

"In other words, you can't search for Sira without exposing yourselves," Morgan said, easing back onto his elbow. "What makes you think I'll help you?"

"You'll help because Yihtor may have Sira. You can't ignore Yihtor di Caraat, Morgan," Rael said, leaning closer. "We are asking for your help. Much as I'd like to rip your thoughts apart to get what I want, I won't. There are *ethics* involved." She licked her lips. "And penalties for violating them. Yihtor chose to fake his own death, to disappear. This put him outside of our laws. He has rejected the self-control that protects our species," Rael's lips thinned. "A self-destructive trait. He must know too many Humans."

Morgan's face was smooth, calm; they might have discussed some technical aspect of his ship. His voice was perhaps too steady. "I promised Sira I'd never let Yihtor control her."

"A promise you haven't the power to keep," Rael said. "Lower your shields, so I can read the locate. I'll open my thoughts to you, if you don't trust me."

"It has nothing to do with trust, Clanswoman. If you need some remembered experience of the place, I've none to offer." Morgan's lips stretched in what was more snarl than smile. "Yihtor attacked me at our campsite. I'd been searching for Sira, trying to sense any thought or trace of her. Protecting myself happened to be rather far from my mind. He overwhelmed me before I realized I was being attacked. All I could do was retreat, hide my will, my memories." A brief pause. "Until now, I didn't know he'd moved me from the camp."

"So much for helping you," Barac began unwisely. "We'd be further ahead if we'd left you a vegetable." Huido snapped his claws in quick, vicious motions as he advanced menacingly toward the Clansman. Morgan waved a weary hand to stop him.

"Barac's right, Brother; Sira made a poor bargain." The Carasian reluctantly subsided, contenting himself with rocking back and forth, eyes fixed on Barac. Barac was silent, but his fury was obvious. Rael's gaze never left Morgan's face.

"Part of Sira's power has returned to her," Rael said at last. "Perhaps enough to let her deal with Yihtor herself. I just hope—what?" This was addressed to Morgan as she noticed the brightening of his face.

"I've always maintained," Morgan answered with a return of his former cool tone, "you Clan are blinded by your prejudice against machines."

Barac tilted his head to one side, anger forgotten. "I recall a few lengthy discussions—or were they monologues—on that subject. I was a captive audience, if you remember."

"Oh, I remember." Morgan stood carefully, keeping one hand on the slick blackness of Huido's arm, and moved over to examine the controls. "Who's been flying her?"

"Me," said a new voice. Morgan turned and actually beamed at the sight of Terk.

"Russ, my old friend! So Bowman has you chauffeuring civilians, eh?" As the out-of-uniform Enforcer turned dusky red, Morgan chuckled with a touch of malice. "Never mind. I'm actually glad to see you."

Terk scowled. The events of the past few days had done nothing to improve his opinion of Morgan. "Your brains totally addled?"

"Come now, Russ. Don't be modest. Aren't you the

best scan-tech in the quadrant?" The others had begun to show a glimmering of hope, although Rael, for one, was also looking perplexed.

Terk, on the other hand, looked decidedly surly. "I don't know what you're talking about. Bowman wants your hide. The word's out on you at last, Morgan—"

"You agreed to follow our orders, Enforcer," Barac said mildly enough. Terk scowled but subsided.

"How can he help us find Sira and Yihtor?" Rael's brow was raised in inquiry. "He has no power."

Morgan laid one hand affectionately on the control panel before the pilot's couch. "Ah, but our good Enforcer's an expert with scanning equipment—"

"Of which I've seen none on this scow of yours."

Morgan cheerfully ignored Terk's interruption, and shook his head at Huido's growl. "We do have Terk. And we have a pilot—a much better pilot, I add with all modesty. We each have our gifts, Russ. And we have the *Fox*—a much better name than *Wayfarer*, don't you agree. So if Yihtor has built himself a city, we should be able to find it." During this little speech, Morgan moved over to the panel before the copilot's couch. He touched a series of buttons seemingly at random, then stood motionless, eyes shut, hands steepled in a gesture that drew surprised approbation from Barac.

"Mind-locked. When did you—" Then he, too, was silent as the panel slowly flipped itself until an entirely new array of levers, buttons, and screens were revealed. Terk exclaimed incoherently, rushing forward to peer greedily at the exposed instruments. Barac opened his mouth, then closed it over a question he doubted would be answered.

Morgan stood back, watching quietly. Rael turned and looked at him. "See? I can be useful, Clanswoman," he said in a low voice, pitched for her ears only.

"Very useful, Human," she agreed in a similar tone. "Good. I dislike wasting my time or strength." Then Rael shrugged. "We're reasonable people. We would have delayed restoring you had we known you couldn't provide the locate. We wouldn't have harmed you."

"And if I come between Sira and the Clan?" A mere whisper of sound. Morgan's pale face was impossible to read. He might have been asking the time.

"An unwise position," Rael narrowed her eyes in speculation as she looked at Morgan. "Unwise and dangerous." Suddenly, her mouth twitched into a tiny, conspiratorial smile. "You begin to interest me, Human."

Morgan bowed slightly. "I'm honored, Clanswoman."

Rael's voice remained light, but there was no mistaking the warning in her eyes. "Just don't get in my way."

Chapter 26

THE boredom of waiting out the paralysis of the stunner had blurred into a long, unexpectedly peaceful sleep. I woke easily, lying in the silent darkness, letting the bits and pieces of days before drift past and sort themselves into order. Events had worked in my favor after all; Morgan and Huido should be safe with Rael. Yihtor? Yihtor was a distant problem.

And I was safe—safe and hidden where no one could find me. Locating through the M'hir to another person took intimate knowledge: the kind I'd gained of Huido from Morgan's mind during our heart-search for the Carasian; the kind which had settled around the edges of my link to Morgan. Who would know me? Only Morgan knew *this* Sira, and he wouldn't help my enemies; one of the very few things of which I was sure.

Later, after a carefully rationed meal from Rael's supplies, I sat looking out over the mist-hung treetops, admiring the myriad stars of Acranam's night sky. The occasional grunt and rustle from the forest below echoed into a deep peace. This momentary freedom, this solitude, slipped around my thoughts like a cooling ointment. I stretched back against the rock, relaxed enough to want to think. Was I any wiser concerning the Sira-that-had-been? Or her business here?

I itemized what I knew, marking each recollection with a poke into the moss by my feet. Rael called me a Chooser—as had Yihtor. The term meant nothing to me, I thought, then frowned; it had been important enough to them. Yihtor had been furious when he thought I wasn't one, then placated when his probing reassured him I remained at least partially as he expected.

I paused to drink slowly from my canteen. Okay. So what was a Chooser? Someone who selected or chose something. What? Oh, yes. I felt my cheeks warm as I remembered what Rael said: a life-partner. That was clear enough. Yet Rael referred to this business of Choice as if it had nothing to do with me, but rather was decided by some ruling Council and, more puzzling, by this power in my mind.

I watched a shooting star trail across the night sky as the answers slid into place with a neatness that signified the truth, or at least a good part of it. What I thought of as an evil force, that darkness which menaced Morgan yet saved me from Yihtor—I couldn't control it, not to any extent.

So I'd been right, in a way, to wonder if a mental disorder had led to my imprisonment among the Clan. Something inside, something a part of me, was capable of acting on its own. Those actions, not mine, were the source of the Clan's concern.

Nice to have a clear goal, I decided, satisfied by my reasoning if not its result. I'd have to learn to control this force within me before I went back to my friends. Friends? Kin? I stabbed a finger into the moss, reaching the grit and rock beneath. How could I claim any connection to people I didn't know?

A dark cloud drifted by and a face formed where the light of the rising moons brightened it to soft gray. I almost whispered his name, then stopped, overcome by a sudden agony of self-consciousness. A ridiculous reaction, considering how alone I was.

I hated being alone. Hated being away from *him,* the correction coming from some uncontrolled place in my mind. I ignored the words and almost the thought. I was used to fighting myself by now. And to winning.

So much for the romantic jungle hermitage—given that I was equal to the task of surviving away from civilization anyway. At least my ability on that score needn't be tested for a while, I mused, one hand resting on the plump pack I'd stocked, was it only yesterday?

My shoulders were beginning to ache; the rock wall I was leaning against had grown cold. Reluctantly, I decided to withdraw inside to the warmth of Huido's heating box for the night. I took one last look at the now cloudless sky, feeling just as empty and cold. I bit my lip until it hurt. I would not be controlled by some mindless force of instinct. I quivered with the effort to remain rational, calm, in command of myself. My hair stirred.

Stirred? I reached my hand cautiously upward only to snatch it back as a lock lifted softly to meet my fingers. Suddenly I was blinded by clouds of hair growing longer, lusher, vitalized by some life of its own.

I tried to contain the stuff into some kind of order, then ceased, helpless as hair wove itself about my fingers. Moments later, I found myself cautiously moving aside long strands which flowed with unfamiliar weight over and past my shoulders. By moons' light, it was beautiful, glowing, with glints of deep gold.

Eventually, the stuff hung quiescent down to my waist, no longer crackling with life, at last behaving more like hair. But such hair! I stroked the heaviness of it with an almost guilty delight, distrustful of its origin.

When I finally settled beside Huido's box for a hopefully uneventful sleep, I took some of my new hair in one hand and rubbed it slowly against my cheek, breathing its brand-new scent. My blocked memory seemed closer somehow. I almost caught hold of something vital, then hissed with frustration as the thought swirled out of reach and was gone again. *Patience,* I told myself sternly. The present was becoming more complicated than my past. Tomorrow would be soon enough to begin exploring the source of my problems.

Awake, I'd been careful not to let my thoughts stray toward dangerous territory. Asleep, and dreaming, though my mental barriers remained in place, the rest of my mind began to drift. I dreamed a face, imagined it smiling in welcome, and greeted it like a fool. *Jason.*

Only a dream, yet the face lost expression—hiding behind that mask of protective stillness Morgan could assume so easily. The eyes searched, but didn't see me. *Rael? Is that you?* His lips were moving, but I couldn't hear sound, only feel the words. Rael?

It's Sira, I corrected him, strangely loath to be so mistaken, even in a dream. What was wrong with him? *Are you all right?*

Rael, come quickly—I was shocked when my sister's

face came into view alongside Morgan's. She was looking
at him with a question in her dark eyes, one hand lazily
sweeping heavy black hair back over her shoulder. I
stared at the picture formed by the two of them, tormented
beyond reason yet unable to look away—to wake up—to
refuse the vision or the pain it brought. Somehow I fought
the blackness rising inside me. Somehow I kept still. Until at last, exhausted, I was able to open my eyes and erase
the final dreadful image of Rael's slender fingers on Morgan's brow.

The sun was already up, sending fingers of dust-filled
light into the back corners of Huido's cave. I took a carelessly generous drink, then compounded my folly by
pouring more of the canteen's contents over my hot face.

It had been more than a dream, I told myself grimly. Less
than real, perhaps, but with sufficient truth in it to make me
think. My sister was everything I wasn't—beautiful, mature, whole. Why shouldn't Morgan be with her? Maybe
even want her?

I shook my head to clear it, but couldn't. The rational
part of my brain was aghast at the depth of my jealousy.
Who was I to presume I knew Morgan's mind? And what
about my sister? Surely Rael should be able to choose for
herself.

Why had I used that word? The canteen dropped to the
floor where the last of its contents poured out unheeded,
darkening the sand of the cave floor. Choose. Chooser.
The darkness buried deep within me had indeed made its
Choice. I felt short of air as the inevitable reared up to
confront me. Of course I was jealous of Rael. Or rather
my power's dark aspect knew jealousy. I remembered the
compulsions I felt on the *Fox,* how I had been drawn to
Morgan before I'd ever developed any true feelings for
him. Jason Morgan, though he was mercifully unaware of
it, had been chosen by that obscenity within me.

I spotted the now-empty canteen and picked it up absently—far more concerned with the implications of this
latest revelation. What was I now, if this meant I'd made a
choice? A Chooser—or some other Clan thing I didn't
know? Yihtor sensed something different about me,
something he didn't understand. What did it all mean to
Morgan, who was, after all, Human and not Clan? Could I
go to him safely or not?

My instant desire to go to Morgan was almost over-
powering; the thought made my heart pound wildly and
the blackness in me rise again.

No.

I gripped the strap of the canteen tightly, made myself
think about another need. I was thirsty. I built up the
thought of thirst until I could almost imagine my lips
were dry. It was a relief to have my mind and body agree
on something.

I could see the small stream from the cave, threading its
glistening path along the base of the rocks and vanishing
quickly under the forest canopy. The sun was bright, forcing me to narrow my eyes to slits, but it wasn't high
enough to produce the punishing heat so apparent in Yihtor's stronghold.

It took all my attention to slide down the talus slope under some sort of control. With each step, my foot sank
into pebbles and I slipped more than walked. Huido could
never have made it without falling.

As I scrabbled at loose stone to slow my headlong rush
downward, something struck me from behind. The shock
of the blow sent me flying all the way to the narrow
streambed, scraping elbows and knees. I had time for a
too-close glimpse of formidable claws and a drooling,
fanged mouth before concentrating with frantic speed. I
pushed . . .

. . . and sprawled on the cool earthen floor of the cave. I
didn't dare look outside. Such was the power of suggestion, my mouth was already feeling thick and dry. Once
my nerves settled, I would have to try to reach the stream
again. But next time I would step through the M'hir, Morgan's blaster ready in my hand.

*   *   *

INTERLUDE

"Rael, come quickly!" Morgan's voice was low-
pitched, but with an underlying urgency that drew the
Clanswoman to his side immediately.

"What's wrong?"

"There's something—someone—here. No," a disgusted shake of his head, "whatever it was is gone now."

Rael glanced around the small galley. They were alone, Barac taking his turn resting in Morgan's cabin while Huido and Terk manned the controls. The ship was in low orbit around Acranam, sweeping from pole to pole. Rael returned her gaze to the Human, one brow raised curiously. "What did you feel?" Her fingers hovered over his forehead.

"My name—an unclear image. I thought at first it was you trying to contact me."

Rael looked faintly insulted. "Why would I do that, Human?"

"Forgive me, Clanswoman." Morgan chose to be amused, but on another level he was impatient. "Who else or what else could it have been?"

"You'd know Yihtor's touch?"

"I'll never forget it. It wasn't him. And my shields are tight. How would he have found me?"

Rael chewed on a thought for a moment, her expression showing distaste. "Could it have been Sira?" she asked with obvious reluctance.

"It was very strange, faint. No, I don't think so. I'd know Sira."

"Do you really think you know my sister?" Rael's smile was condescending.

"Do you?"

Rael bristled. "Of course. I'm her sister, and heart-kin as well."

"And what does that matter? Sira barely remembers your face." Morgan shrugged slightly. "I don't mean any insult, Gentle Fem. The reality is that you and I know different Siras." He pointed to the servo-kitchen. "Care for a drink? The selection's fair, as I'm sure Barac's discovered."

The Clanswoman accepted graciously, but her dark eyes continued to smolder as she took a seat opposite Morgan. "One thing I want you to remember, Captain. Sira is Clan—not Human. All your dealings with her must be based on that fact."

Morgan raised his mug in acknowledgment, but said firmly: "An accident of birth, Rael, one *my* Sira isn't very pleased about."

"And neither are you?"

Morgan examined his drink. Then he looked directly at her, his expression full of some emotion Rael couldn't interpret. "What do you want me to say?"

"Nothing," she answered, too quickly. "I shouldn't have asked. No matter what else you are or have done, Captain Morgan, you've risked a great deal to help my sister. I want no reason to wish you harm."

There was a quiet buzz from the com panel. Morgan rose, then turned to glance back down at Rael. "The scanners have found something worth looking at—if you'll notify your cousin? I'll be in the control room."

With a troubled frown, Rael watched him go.

Chapter 27

I FOUGHT my hands, frustrated by the way they trembled and cramped instead of obeying me. This time I won, forcing them to tilt the canteen to my lips. I took a small sip, then made my fingers replace the cap and tighten it. I let the canteen fall on my chest and held it there, comforted by its weight.

My mind drifted more now, no matter how hard I tried to hold a thought. Most often, I forgot where I was, imagined myself on another world, dreamed of storm-driven sand. Afterward, I would wake to find my fingers bloodlessly tight on the canteen.

Shafts of weak sunlight peered into the cave: the afternoon of another day. *Two days,* I remembered, my thoughts tired and slow. Two? Or had it been more since I'd last looked outside, been able to stand and walk. The canteen was lighter and I was weaker. The fever was gone, for now.

Somehow, I'd held my mental shielding in place as tightly as I gripped my canteen. He was waiting, I knew, lurking outside the edges of my delirium, the worst nightmare of all. I used my dread of Yihtor for strength, having drained every other source long ago. Once or twice, I'd weakened and tried to go to Morgan, to call for help. But the fever had robbed me of that ability as well.

The tiny drink cleared my mind, a gift I didn't appreciate. The trouble with thinking clearly was the icy certainty that I was going to die soon, here and alone. A tear I couldn't afford chilled my cheek.

A sliver of sunlight flickered across the palm of my hand, quickly disappearing. I tried to quiet my breathing, groping for the blaster at my side. Whatever shadowed the cave entrance made no sound. When the ray of light returned an instant later, I let go of the heavy weapon with a small sigh. My eyelids drooped. I was so tired.

It started like a dream, but was more, I knew, even in my sleep. I was in a darkly paneled room, lit by floating portlights, their globes confined at varying heights by rope tethers. Artifacts were displayed on wooden pedestals placed near each light. The floor wasn't even, rising in steplike layers, irregular in shape.

I wasn't alone. A tall man part of me knew as my father was walking around the collection, examining each piece in turn, the only other life in this place of dead things. The jewelery here was no longer to be worn against warm skin but only looked at; the toys and treasured games no longer to be played with but merely dusted as necessary and observed.

There was another level of remembrance. I somehow knew that the objects' order and arrangement in this place mattered. Some objects were given more prominent display than others, regardless of their apparent value.

There were family names with each object. I realized abruptly that I was looking at a genealogy, exhibited as belongings and organized to display each individual's power in the M'hir. This was the Hall of Ancestors, my father's most private sanctuary.

The intensity of light on each object varied. None were unlit, but some were illuminated more intensely, to capture the attention of a visitor. The brightest light shone on a small, ragged piece of fabric, embedded in a crystal that reflected a brilliant pattern over the entire room, claiming its supremacy over all.

Again a node of knowledge quietly coalesced. This scrap, so carefully preserved, was all that remained of the personal effects of my great-grandmother, First Chosen of the House of S'udlaat, the leader of the M'hiray during the Stratification. The words were hollow, someone else's history, no longer mine. Yet I knew the brilliant illumination was the more accurate remembrance of her, the scrap of cloth only its anchor. Sira Morgan, that part of me, felt warmed by the thought of being able to name an ancestor, could imagine the gentle touch of a grandmother's hand. Another part of me knew simply a fierce and possessive pride in her power.

This was a place I had come to often, though I hadn't particularly cared about old things. But why?

I think I slipped from memory into delirium again, deeper than before, losing any answers that might have escaped the blockage in my mind. In my delirium, I heard voices, an incomprehensible chatter. Motion followed: at first jarring so that I muttered in protest, later smooth and almost lulling. There was a coolness, a spreading relief from the fever's burn.

I woke to find my latest fever-ridden dreams had been the truth. The cave was gone. I was curled between smooth sheets in a room which looked depressingly familiar. Two highly placed windows filtered sunlight, softly illuminating a bedroom better furnished than Morgan's prison, but I'd little doubt its function was the same. Yihtor had found me after all.

"How do you feel?" asked a female voice.

I turned my head on the pillows, frowning as I tried without success to identify the woman standing beside my bed. Spiderwebs of age lurked in the corners of her eyes and mouth. Her hair was piled above her head in a complex structure, as if trying to add some height. She was still short. I disliked her instantly. "Where am I?" I asked.

A small, wise smile appeared, giving her face a faintly crafty look. "Caraat Town, Fem di Sarc. Capital of Acranam. The Lord Yihtor has graciously extended his hospitality to you."

I sat up, pleased to discover no lingering dizziness, feeling better every second. "Tell Yihtor I've no intention of accepting anything of his, offered graciously or otherwise."

The old woman chuckled. "What do your intentions matter, child of Jarad? My son and I have waited far too long for you." She scowled. There was something disturbing about the look in her eyes as they swept over me. "I hope we've not waited in vain. For whom have you Commenced, girl? It had best be for my son."

"Commenced?" The word meant something, something vastly important. Ignoring her, I flung myself from the bed, rather surprised at my strength, and hurried to the mirror on one wall. Yihtor's mother came and stood at my shoulder, an unwelcome witness to my first look at the change which had taken place.

My body was gone.

At least, the thin, angular one I used to wash and dress was gone. In its place was a figure that rounded the plain white shift I wore into unfamiliar curves. My face—I moved my fingers incredulously over soft skin which was no longer sallow or scarred but which glowed with life. I touched my lips, tracing their fullness. Only my outrageous hair was unimpressed by the changeling I faced, tumbling in heavy red-gold to frame a face transformed from gaunt to radiant health. "I was sick—" I began, more to myself than to the leering figure at my side.

"Nonsense," Fem Caraat said. "Though it's as well for you the aircar pilot spotted your escape pod. Choosers aren't expected to huddle alone in caves during Commencement, Sira di Sarc. It was a foolish thing to do. What if you'd been attacked by some animal?"

I didn't bother to answer; her concern was for her own plans, not for me. Instead, I surveyed my image more critically, looking at another stranger, though with features hauntingly like those I remembered. The gray eyes were still my own and held the confused puzzling in their depths I was certainly used to feeling. This change was something I should have expected, one part of my mind said matter-of-factly. But there was something very odd about the timing.

"How do you feel?"

Her self-centered solicitude was becoming annoying. I turned away from the mirror. "How should I feel?" I snapped. "First I almost die of fever, and now I'm a prisoner here."

A chuckle. "Well, you should feel marvelous, if memory serves me."

I stared at the old Clanswoman, unwilling to acknowledge she was right. Strength surged from my head to my toes; I felt alive in every part of my body. I had probably never felt as well in my entire life.

But what truly mattered was inside. I concentrated, reaching for the M'hir.

It was like pushing against a wall, a wall of some thick sticky substance that gave a bit then held firm. My shields worked, but my questing thought was effectively imprisoned within my head. I was ordinary again, I realized, and didn't like it at all.

I looked at Fem Caraat.

She smiled cruelly. Her finger pointed to the bedside table. The small bottle with its accompanying syringe told the story all too well. "Roraqk's drug," I said. I'd have strangled her cheerfully if I thought it would do any good.

"Actually, we supplied the pirate. The forests here provide us with many of our needs. So elegant, don't you think? And much easier on all of us, my dear. You really wouldn't want us to use other methods. Now tell me." Her hand gripped my shoulder. "For whom have you Commenced?"

I shook free. "You've no right to question me, old woman," I answered coldly, while my thoughts were busy calculating chances, my eyes searching the doorless room for any possible aid. Of course, life would have been simpler had I known what she was talking about, but Yihtor's mother was the last person to whom I'd admit any ignorance.

Then, we were no longer alone. Yihtor stood beside his mother, his face tight and beaded with sweat. Fem Caraat whirled on him, hissing: "This is no place for you!"

"Who tampered with her?" he demanded in a hoarse voice.

My back stiffened. "Who hasn't, Clansman?" I snapped.

Fem Caraat waved her thin hand at me furiously. "Be quiet, girl." Then to her son, "Go!"

"How can she refuse me?" he said almost plaintively, looking down at the Clanswoman. "The Power-of-Choice burns in her—I can feel it. It calls me."

My own power was smothered by their drug, but I could feel a surging pressure I knew was Yihtor's. His mother moved to stand directly between us, why, I wasn't sure. Not that I wanted to refuse her surprising protection.

"Be patient. The Joining will take place tonight before our guests—as planned." She stressed the last word.

This seemed to calm Yihtor. His green eyes lost some of their fire. "I can wait," he said. "But no longer than tonight." He disappeared.

Immediately, the room seemed larger. Fem Caraat scowled at me and shook her head. "You are driving my poor son mad." Then she grinned, the expression deepening the lines around her eyes. "As a Chooser should."

"I don't know what you think you're planning—"

"Of course you do. And you should be honored that your magnificent power will be linked to that of the House of Caraat, as it always should have been." She stepped toward me and I backed up involuntarily. "Did you think we wouldn't find out what they planned for you? Did you think Yihtor wouldn't have a watch on the Cloister, waiting, spying, knowing eventually you'd come within his reach? Did you think we'd let them dump you on Auord, to be used for their plans, when you belong to my son?"

Her breath was hot on my face as she moved nearer, crowding me. "Power," she said in a grating whisper, talking more to herself than to me. "Power is everything, daughter of Jarad. Names, lives, the future—all that matters is to gather power and use it. We left the Clan because the Council refused to grant my son the power he desired and deserved. Now he will have it.

"Once we were a passionate people. Pairs sought each other because it was their destiny, not the dictates of a Council. They lived or died by their own natures. Tonight Caraat Town will see the return of passion as we celebrate the Joining of Caraat and Sarc. You will fulfill your destiny. You will Choose and Join with my son."

"You can't impose Choice," I said, sure of that much.

"No, we can't," her agreement surprised me. "But my son hasn't wasted his time, Chooser, waiting for you to come. He has prepared himself. He hunted out secrets, stripped the knowledge he needed from the best minds in the Pact. If you do not or cannot Choose him in the natural way of our kind," she gave a little shrug, "that will be your end. But not ours."

"What are you saying?"

Her next words rang against my ears like blows. "If necessary, Chooser, we will simply strip your mind to an empty and harmless husk. A waste, but don't worry, your body and its potential will be well cared for.

"After tonight, there will be a fruitful Joining between the House of Sarc and that of Caraat—whether you have a mind to notice it or not."

She chuckled again. "There are clothes in the cupboard in your size, Fem di Sarc. We've had a great deal of time, you know, to prepare for you."

Fem Caraat picked up her skirt and vanished, leaving an unpleasant feel to the air.

* * *

INTERLUDE

"There it is again. You'll have to look close—it's quick, all right." Terk's voice held none of its usual antagonism as he and Morgan crouched over the tiny screen. The copilot's couch had given up trying to mold itself to accommodate Terk's unusually broad shoulders. "There! Did you catch it?"

Morgan looked at the Enforcer with respect. "How you found it, Russ, I'll never know. Perhaps you've got some of the Talent yourself."

"It was just a case of scanning for flux using the C-978 meter, rather than steady—" Terk's pleased explanation was cut off by the arrival of Barac and Rael.

"Have you found Yihtor?" Barac's hair was tousled from sleep. His resemblance to Sira was noticeable. "Well, did your gadgets work or not?" Barac demanded somewhat impatiently.

Terk grew businesslike. "We've detected a large power source, Hom sud Sarc. Easily sixty quarats. Enough to supply a good-sized city."

"And well-disguised. I'd say we have him," Morgan added.

"Or he has us," Huido mumbled darkly. "What's to keep the *Fox* off Acranam's screens?"

Morgan's smile was dangerous. "And what would Yihtor see? One small ship, most likely another smuggler or pirate seeking to sell or buy. If we know a code, we land, if we don't, he blows us up on approach."

"Or destroys any unprotected telepathic mind he touches," Barac's face was equally grim. "As he did to Kurr before his ship penetrated the system." The last was bitter and low.

"Kurr was killed here?" Morgan repeated slowly, eyes darkening.

Rael and Barac traded glances.

"So you aren't here looking for Sira," Morgan accused

coldly. "You've set her up as bait to lead you and the Trade Pact to this Clan renegade. You've been using her—"

"No!" Barac denied fiercely. "I don't know how Sira came into this—but it wasn't anything I planned, believe me. I was coming to Acranam before I knew Sira was here; I was following Kurr's last journey." He paused and drew a steadying breath. "I didn't know Yihtor lived. Neither of us did until Rael learned of it from Sira, and felt him for herself. That crasnig has power enough to swat Kurr like an insect, and good reason to want to keep from the Council's notice."

"However, our concern at this moment, Cousin, is Sira," Rael interjected very quietly, her voice deliberate and calm. She raised her hand behind Barac's head. Her fingers spread slowly. "What matters is ensuring her safety and well-being. She is your kin as well."

Morgan saw Barac close his eyes and wince, almost as if he fought to reject the soothing calm emanating from the Clanswoman. After a moment, he shuddered and relaxed, the emotion draining from his features, leaving them set and numb. "The renegade will concentrate his defenses at his own base," he said. "His foremost defense will be himself."

Morgan's thoughtful gaze touched each face. They waited, no one sure when or how Morgan had assumed leadership, but all aware of it. "Well, our weaponry is somewhat limited," he said at last. "I suggest we pool our abilities, Barac. We'll take Huido along, and leave Terk to mind the ship—"

"I can't go if Sira's there!" Barac said, looking startled.

"Barac!" hissed Rael. The Clansman subsided. There was a pregnant silence during which Morgan waited patiently, one brow slightly raised. "Our arrival will have the virtue of surprise," Rael continued smoothly. "I think you overestimate Yihtor, Barac. Yihtor is, after all, one to our—three." Her lovely features were hard. "And our combined power must be directed by me once we are ready to attack. If that's acceptable to you, Captain?"

Morgan bowed a silent acknowledgment, but his eyes were fixed on Barac. "It's fine with me." He stressed the last word.

"Barac will come with us," Rael countered quickly. Her

look at her cousin was almost pleading. "He worries about old business. He makes too much of the matter." The last was plainly a warning.

Morgan's face had assumed its inscrutable cast. His voice held a silken menace. "This old business wouldn't have anything to do with a rather nasty job of blockage, would it, Barac?"

The Clansman's surprise was obvious. "Blockage? What are you accusing me of now, Human?"

"Barac had nothing to do with Sira's condition, Captain," Rael said, suddenly wary. "He has neither the skill nor the power."

"Then what is he afraid of?"

"What he fears is impossible."

"It's not impossible," Barac countered almost wildly. "You told me yourself that Sira—"

"There's nothing to tell." Rael's eyes flashed a warning. "Our time is being wasted with this."

"That's for me to decide," Morgan snapped. "Especially if I'm risking my neck with the pair of you. Barac?"

Rael made an unladylike noise and vanished into air. Barac sighed and turned his dark eyes to Morgan's relentless blue ones. "Leave us!" This to Huido and Terk. Neither moved until Morgan gave a terse nod. Once they left, Barac sat in the copilot's couch and regarded Morgan with an unusual intentness.

"So, Barac?" Morgan prompted.

"As you've noticed, Morgan," Barac said ruefully. "My cousin and I have a difference of opinion concerning Sira. It has to do with very private matters."

"Secrets become liabilities, Barac."

"I suppose." The Clansman lifted his slim shoulders and let them drop. "When Sira arrived on Auord, she was in a state we refer to as stasis. Certain of us voluntarily submit to the process in order to travel in safety."

"Voluntarily?" Morgan's eyes never left Barac's. "Sira's memories are almost totally suppressed—including most of her power. For God's sake, she believed herself Human! And you're telling me she submitted to this of her own free will?"

"Yes." Barac stopped, chewed his lip for a moment. "Perhaps," he temporized. "It should have been her decision, but I can't say for sure." He gathered himself visibly. "Stasis isn't meant to harm. Sira would never have been left alone. Choosers must be protected. That's why I was with her on Auord."

"Choosers?" Morgan pounced on the unexpected word.

Barac sighed and went on with a defeated shake of his head. "Our ways aren't like yours, Morgan. The constraints of our lives differ probably as much as yours do from your shelled friend's. For one thing, we of the M'hiray, the Clan, choose our life-partners in order to increase the power."

"Telepathy?" Morgan asked incredulously when Barac hesitated. "The Clan's been selecting for power?"

Barac frowned. "It is not something we decided, Morgan. You have touched the M'hir. Part of our unconscious selves is always there, mingling on some level with all other living Clan, as the air on your ship moves in and out of all our bodies. The M'hir is inseparable from the Clan; it gives us abilities and strengths your species needs machines to accomplish. But the M'hir has also been a curse to some."

"Sira."

Barac's nod was heavy. "When our females are ready to mature, they are driven to search the M'hir for a mate—we call them Choosers." A moment's longing filled Barac's voice. "Choosers assess the power of any unChosen male who comes near. But Joining, the life-pairing through the M'hir, is only possible with a mate of equal or superior strength. Lesser males—lose." Another brief hesitation as Barac searched for the right words. "In my great-great-grandfather's time, losing meant, at worst, loneliness. In the last few generations, as our Choosers have grown more powerful, losing has meant death."

"And you accept this."

"We've adjusted," Barac said quickly. "We're not barbarians, Morgan. The Council carefully selects candidates for the more powerful—the more deadly—Choosers. UnChosen males, myself included, are protected. I've no intention of dying at the mind of a stronger Chooser." He scowled. "What other option did we have? Accept that to be weak and male was to die?"

When Barac paused again, Morgan said with disbelief: "By finding equal or stronger partners for the Choosers, your Council just pushes the whole process further and faster. Is power all that matters to the Clan?"

"It is status, wealth, and survival," Barac's voice was resigned. "Would you give yours up?"

"The thought's had appeal," Morgan ran his fingers through his hair. "And more. But it's part of what I am."

"Then imagine what it would be like to live among those who value it, practice it. Imagine growing up with the minds of friends in yours. Imagine a culture where every contact is based upon instant and mutual knowledge of power."

"And Sira? What was her place in that culture?"

Barac's dark eyes sparkled. "Many believe the peak of our evolution arrived with her. Sira is the jewel of our race, Morgan: the most powerful Chooser ever born. Powerful, desirable, and quite fatal. Fatal, because there hasn't been a male born to match her. She's an irresistible trap, both bait and poison to any unChosen male. Now do you understand why I don't dare come near her?"

Morgan tried to reconcile this image of Sira with the woman he knew and failed totally. "She was with you on Auord."

"Stasis temporarily dampens a Chooser's mind. It's only used if the Chooser must travel during the time of Choice." Barac sighed. "I was shocked and flattered to learn Sira was coming to Auord and I was to be her escort. She's quite famous among us, you realize, more like one of your entertainment vids than a person. So many years hidden, isolated—my mother would tell me about her." Something in Morgan's face prompted Barac to add quickly: "It wasn't against her will."

Morgan seemed to be on the verge of an outburst, then closed his mouth and finally spoke in a slow, measured tone. "If the blockage, this stasis, of Sira's mind protects you, I don't understand why you're afraid to meet her now. And why did Rael want to keep all this from me?"

Barac shook his head. "Rael's uncomfortable with you, Morgan. You're Human, and, well, it's just not customary to talk about Choice and Joining."

"You're doing it."

"I'm a First Scout. It's my job to communicate with aliens." He watched Morgan closely, almost smiling as the Human accepted the label without taking offense. "I can accept our similarities. Clan like Rael can't. She needs to believe we're different. But I think you're the key to what's happened to Sira."

"Me?" Had Morgan been less startled, he might have prevented the rising note to his voice. "Because I removed a bit of the blockage?"

"Did you?" Barac shuddered. "Better you than me. No. You see, stasis is flexible, changeable. By its nature, stasis is an imposition—an artificial chain around the Chooser's true nature. It can't hold if the Chooser is kept near an unChosen male of suitable strength. Her power will strive to respond—and will, if the male can be touched. What I fear—and Rael won't accept—is that Sira's blocked power is responding to yours."

Barac waited for Morgan's comment, then continued when none appeared forthcoming. "If I'm right, Sira's stasis could already be seriously weakened or lost entirely. And if she's now functioning as a Chooser, we may both need to fear her."

"What about Yihtor?" Barac could read nothing from Morgan's expression. The Human had himself tightly back under control. "Why does he want Sira?"

"Yihtor was tested by Council as a candidate for Sira, but was refused during final testing. The unChosen feel the need for Choice, too," Barac's voice went softer for a moment, caught by his own feelings. "You've seen insects fly to a flame? The power of a Chooser within the M'hir is like that to us. And the stronger the Chooser, the brighter the flame." Barac blushed and continued. "Yihtor persisted. He tried to see Sira in person, despite the refusal, a breach of custom and law which disgraced his entire family."

Barac sighed heavily. "If Yihtor confronts Sira, and she's now free of the stasis, we won't have long to worry about him, anyway."

Morgan went over to the controls and checked them absently. His mind was elsewhere. "You're assuming Yihtor will begin to play by the rules. Why?"

"Choice can only be offered, Human, from Chooser to unChosen. The risk is the male's. We cannot force our females—as your species is known to do."

Morgan turned to Barac with a cold, piercing light in his eyes. "Your opinion of Humans aside, for the moment,

I hope you're right, Clansman. My impression of this renegade and those he deals with doesn't allow me your touching faith. And what of Kurr? Think, Barac—Sira's mind has already been tampered with; Yihtor's had her drugged and kidnapped in order to bring her to Acranam.

"Rael was correct in at least one respect. I don't think we, or Sira, have any time left to waste."

Barac's lips tightened. "Just you remember what I've told you, Morgan. Sira won't be happy if she finds out she's killed you."

"I won't be too happy about that either," Morgan replied steadily.

Chapter 28

CLEARLY, Yihtor had spared no expense in order to turn this frontier world into a home. The glittering scene I surveyed from my vantage point at the head table could have come intact from any of the better insystem banquet rooms. There were a hundred or so people gathered around small tables; these were set with attractive randomness within the domed hall. Fountains whispered in the distant corners. It was a far cry from the wilderness surrounding us and a potent statement of Yihtor's determination to rule here.

The crowd, many of whom I caught staring at me, was remarkably uniform. Everyone I could see was young, well-groomed, and animated. Regardless of whatever expression darkened my face as the unwilling guest of honor here, the majority of the celebrants were enjoying their leader's success.

Another course came and went. The food was probably excellent, but I couldn't taste it, though I was hungry enough. It wasn't a particularly cheering thought that my body and mind didn't always share the same opinions. If Yihtor had his way, that split could soon be permanent.

I scanned the faces below, struck by the oddness of watching excitement. Few individuals spoke aloud. Hand gestures were plentiful and often interfered with the process of enjoying the feast. It was easy to hear the bubbling of the distant fountains and the soft background music supplied by a lone musician. Indisputable evidence that everyone present was indeed Clan. Even the serving staff carried themselves with that unconscious arrogance.

Yihtor had noticed my inspection. "I—we have many faithful supporters on Acranam, my dear Chooser."

"Bought by pirate leavings?" I asked bitterly, ignoring the jab of Fem Caraat's fingers in my ribs.

"Actually, no," Yihtor replied politely, courteously offering to refill my glass, nodding slightly when I refused. "Most of my wealth and influence comes from a service I provide. It is an ability of my own, one which I believe may be a first among the Clan."

He wrapped his fingers around a bowl of fruit and raised it to the level of his eyes. "Imagine, Sira, that this is the mind of a Pact scientist, say a Human whose research might uncover some secret about the M'hir. When I served the Council, I learned how to enter such a mind, to erase key thoughts so that the research would fail. Very subtle work."

There was a chuckle beside me as Fem Caraat found something in this funny.

Yihtor turned in his seat so the bowl was between us, suspended over the floor. "Since then, I've learned how to pluck out what I—or a customer—wants from a mind," he reached into the bowl with one hand and removed a cluster of nicnics.

Then, Yihtor released the bowl and its remaining contents. The delicate crystal shattered on the floor. "Not subtle," he said with mock regret, "but very profitable."

Knife-edged shards of crystal glinted among the pieces of fruit. I looked up at Yihtor. "You can do this from here?" I asked in horror.

"Not yet," the Clansman admitted readily. "Physical contact is required. And there are beings whose thoughts I can't touch. Still, it's quite a good living for me—and so for my followers."

He waved his long hand, drawing my attention back to the crowd. "Most you see here came with me long ago. Not all of us were as obedient as you when the Council tried to dictate our lives for us. And others came later."

"And all were converted to your view of how things should be? Why do I find that difficult to believe, Renegade?"

Fem Caraat glowered. "How dare you speak to my son like that! He—"

"Silence, old woman," Yihtor's voice was low and chilling. "Leave us." Their eyes met briefly, then hers dropped and she stood.

"I'm First Chosen here," she said uncertainly, her look toward me full of sudden fear.

Yihtor deliberately turned back to his food, dismissing his mother. A good pair, I decided.

We were now alone at the elevated head table. Ironic. Those watching us, between bites of their sweet course, probably thought Yihtor and I were deep in some mental conversation, closer inside than out. How important was appearance to Yihtor's control over his followers? Was all this to make them believe I was here willingly? I felt the tentative stirrings of hope.

I should have guarded the whimsy: Yihtor's long hand closed upon my arm just above my elbow. An affectionate gesture to those watching; a painful crushing of flesh over bone in reality. I met his gray-green eyes with deliberate intensity. "You're damaging the goods, Renegade," I said tightly. "That's not part of the script tonight. This is all for their benefit, isn't it?" I waved and several returned the salute.

He released me, smiling a rather nasty smile. "We'd make a formidable pair, daughter of Jarad. Your strength and intelligence added to my own—we could dominate the Council itself!"

"I'm sure you know the answer to that. Shall I tell your *faithful* of your kind offer—and its catch?"

Yihtor leaned back and chuckled softly, for all the world as if I'd amused him with a flirtatious story. "Tell them. Tell them and see for yourself the extent of their loyalty to me, and to me alone. Those who've been with me since the beginning would give their lives for me without question. Those who came later can no longer oppose my will.

"So tell them, Chooser. Amuse me as is your pleasure during our Joining Feast."

"I may be your prisoner," I said through my teeth, wishing I had something to throw. "But I'm crew on the *Silver Fox.* Spacers protect their own."

Yihtor wrinkled his nose in disgust, then gave a short laugh. "Invoking Humans, Chooser? What do they have to do with us? I'd expected threats from the illustrious di Sarcs—"

"My name is Sira Morgan. I'm crew on the *Silver*—"

"Stop." Yihtor's face turned stormy. "I know what was

done to you, and why. That obscene experiment came all too close to ruining you forever. You should be grateful I've intervened."

"What experiment? What possible reason could anyone have for taking my memory?"

"It is over. That is all you need to know." Yihtor's frown faded. "And tonight is the beginning of your new life."

Unfortunately, I knew what he meant. "I can't Choose you," I said evenly. "You must know that by now."

Yihtor's expression didn't change, but his hand trembled as it reached for his cup. "Don't worry, Chooser. I will make it possible."

"By taking away my mind? What use can I be to you then?" I protested.

"To rule here is nothing," Yihtor said, taking sips from his steaming cup. The aroma was nut-sweet and almost gagged me. "My plans don't include permanent exile here for myself and my followers." A sidelong look at me. "Nor do they include allowing my power to be lost from the gene pool of the Clan. I intend to father a dynasty of supremely powerful beings—a new ruling class of Clan, whose power in the M'hir will be tasted by all. Perhaps even, in time, the Homeworld itself!

"And you, Sira di Sarc—daughter of Jarad and Mirim, granddaughter of the Houses of Mendolar and Teerac, Serona and S'udlaat, descendant of the most ancient and powerful lineages recorded by our historians—you will bear those sons and daughters for me. Since you have conveniently Commenced, I really don't care if you remain able to enjoy your destiny."

I came close to losing my few scraps of supper. I stared down, fighting for control, hating my new, so-useful body. Better to be mindless. *No,* I said to myself, reaching a new dark calm. I welcomed a ripple of memory, floated with it to what I needed. The control center of life was vulnerable here, and there. I could do it. I would do it. Once the drug was gone, I'd take my own life before Yihtor could steal my awareness of his defeat.

At such a moment, I was jarred by the feel, or was it a taste, of some change about me. With Yihtor's attention momentarily claimed by some entertainers beginning to set up their props before our table, I looked around the huge room, frowning as I found myself searching the shadowed corners near the ceremonial doors. What was it I sensed? And how could I sense anything through the mind-numbing drug? For the sensation was strong enough now to recognize as a mental stirring—too faint to be identifiable, yet definitely there. Could the drug's dosage have been weaker than Roraqk's? Could Yihtor have been so sure I'd prefer to Choose him when the time came that he ensured my mind would be free? I fought to keep my reaction from him.

The nagging feeling continued. I lowered my gaze to my plate, feigning an interest in the latest offering. Something was about to change. I'd be ready. It was less than hope, but more than I'd had.

* * *

INTERLUDE

"I tell you there's no one here." Rael stood in the middle of the roadway, her frustration with their cautious exploration of the deserted town obvious and shared by her companions.

"We could be watched," Huido warned, his own impatience schooled by experience. Eyes swiveled to examine the dark, paired windows overlooking the street. "Can you be sure these are empty?"

"We're quite alone," Rael repeated acidly. When neither Barac nor Morgan showed any disagreement with her claim, Huido's eyes settled into a more relaxed pattern.

"Suggestions, Clanswoman?" Morgan asked. "I didn't think our major problem would be getting Yihtor's attention."

A small frown showed Rael's puzzlement. "I agree, Captain. Where could they have gone? And why?"

Barac had stepped away from the group, looking up and down the empty thoroughfare. Now he came back, head lowered ever so slightly, as if he waited for an attack. "Why no doors?" His tone was tense. "Is this a town or some kind of prison?"

Morgan seemed at ease, but his eyes and other sense continuously surveyed their surroundings. "No. Not a prison. Yet hardly a convenient place to live, unless—"

"Unless Yihtor's people were all Clan," Rael finished with reluctant conviction. "It makes sense, Barac. Living this way would mean having to move through the M'hir constantly; they could build up their own paths on this world much more quickly than usual."

Huido shuffled his broad feet.

"What does it matter? They're not here anyway."

"It matters a great deal," Barac disagreed instantly. "The three of us together may not be enough against Yihtor. We can't manage so much as one more Clan as an enemy—and how many might live here?" A look meant for Rael. "Yihtor faked his own death—how many others might have done the same?"

"The *Destarian* exploded with twenty of our people on board," Rael answered thoughtfully. "It wasn't long after Yihtor's supposed accident. There could have been others."

She fell silent, her eyelids half-closed. Then they snapped open. "The M'hir here burns with pathways. There are almost as many as on Camos itself."

"We have to notify the Council," Barac said urgently. "Before it's too late—"

"I'm not leaving Sira here," Rael said firmly, not needing to glance at Morgan.

Barac sighed fatalistically. "Then let's find her. And then can we run? We can't afford to die without warning the Council about this place."

Rael gestured to the rows of buildings. "Do you suggest searching for them through the M'hir? That should get Yihtor's attention for us."

Morgan was smiling gently at a memory. "Do either of you know how to augment a heart-search?"

Barac and Rael traded startled glances. "What do you know of the heart-search, Human?" the Clansman almost snarled.

"Sira helped me check on this big lummox, here," an affectionate rap of knuckles on armor. Morgan didn't appear worried by the pair's surprise or Barac's tone. "It seems an eavesdropper-proof method."

"It is," Rael concurred after a long moment during which she and her cousin communicated silently. "I shall—"

"No," objected Barac aloud. "It must be Morgan."

Rael's beautiful face lost all color. "This isn't the time

or the place to debate your outrageous theories, Barac. I'm the one best suited to imaging Sira."

"Rael." Morgan's voice was quiet but firm. "Barac told me what he thinks may be happening between Sira and me. I know you're reluctant to accept his idea—it's strange to me, as well." His eyes had darkened, exerting force unconsciously. "But while Sira may remember you one day, Rael, right now I'm closer to her than anyone else. If that matters at all to this technique, and I think it must, then I'm the only possible choice."

Rael looked unhappy, but there really was no logical argument. They all were aware of the truth in Morgan's words, but, as they hunted for some sheltered place in which to attempt the search, Barac drew close to Morgan's side. "The word *choice* was an unfortunate one, Human," he muttered. "The heart-search could have the effect of triggering Sira's power. You might not be able to withdraw in time to save yourself."

Morgan let Rael and Huido go ahead, before turning to look directly at Barac. The Clansman's face showed concern. Morgan was oddly touched. "Why are you so sure Sira would harm me? I've been in mental contact with her before."

"Harm you?" Barac said. "Haven't you listened to me? She'll kill you. She'll drag you into the void and leave you to die. And it wouldn't be Sira—your destroyer would be a mindlessness, an instinct, less under her control than the orbit of this planet." He stamped one foot on the packed earth of the roadway for emphasis. "Rael doesn't believe me, but you must, for both our sakes. I think your power is alike enough to ours to trigger Choice. And you couldn't survive Sira and the M'hir, Morgan, even if you were Clan and not merely Human." Barac shook his head sadly. "No. There's no hope for either of us if Sira has been completely freed from her stasis. Unless Yihtor were present . . ." His voice trailed away behind a sudden thought.

"What about Yihtor?" Morgan asked impatiently, noticing Rael and Huido had stopped in the shadow of a building to wait for them.

Barac ran one hand through his hair. "I don't know. Council rejected him for some reason. But the nature of the Power-of-Choice is to find and select superior power.

Yihtor's should be more attractive to Sira's than ours. He might distract her from us." His lean, elegant features took on a ruddy hue. "This is very distressing for me, Human. What should be kept private is becoming our usual topic!"

"Not as distressing as it is for Sira," Morgan reminded him grimly.

"From your point of view, perhaps," Barac's reply was slow. "Maybe from hers—I don't know this new Sira as you do. I find it difficult to ignore my fear. And I suggest you learn to share it, Morgan. For your own good."

Chapter 29

I SQUIRMED again in my padded chair. A servant noticed my wiggling and stepped up to my elbow.

"More wine, Fem di Sarc?"

I grunted something negative, curling my hands around each other in an effort to hold them still. My bones itched. I found it harder as the hours dragged past to keep my twitching to myself and look dignified.

Looking dignified helped. What else could I do with all eyes turned my way, knowing all the unheard conversations were about Yihtor's Chosen? I looked down at the other guests, envying their privilege of walking among the tables or over to admire the fountains, not to mention their ability to leave.

If I glanced right—but I refused to acknowledge his presence by so much as that. I could feel Yihtor, anyway, like some cold draft sliding down my spine. He constantly and contentedly stayed by my side, acting the emperor he planned to become—with or without my consent. His confidence had beaten the wisp of *something* I'd experienced earlier into fantasy.

"Ah," my host gave a long sound of satisfaction at the approach of a pair of Clansmen, each wearing robes of ornately paneled white. One carried a pair of roughly carved wooden goblets; the other held a matching pitcher.

Spectators in the hall were quick to notice the new arrivals. They hurried excitedly back to their seats. My boredom vanished with a cold thud in my stomach. It was time. There was no doubt in my mind that here was the heart of the ceremony of Joining to which Yihtor had referred.

"Your ignorance of the ceremony is unimportant, daughter of Jarad," Yihtor said, voice pitched for my ears only. "Do as I say and do." The bearers, both older than the majority of those here, placed their burdens on the table in front of me.

I concentrated on their faces, my attention caught by something strange. It wasn't their expressions; it was a lack of awareness. They were like sleepers moving through a dream. No, I decided; it was something worse, something I'd seen before. They were hands and face, skin and flesh, moved only by Yihtor's will.

Gistries, I thought, swallowing bile, forcing myself to look straight at the fate she'd died to avoid. I hadn't understood, never truly believed she'd been right.

As I studied the mindless Clansmen, I felt a draining beginning at my head, moving down to chill my shoulders, arms, and upper body. It was as though my lifeblood was melting away, leaving only the decision to make it final. The draining and decision were infinitely soothing, like a good end to a story.

My relaxed nod appeared to satisfy Yihtor. "Good," he said. "Take up your cup. We need . . ."

The rest of his instructions whirled away as the sensation I'd experienced earlier returned, but now a thousandfold stronger. Numbly, my hand obeyed Yihtor, mimicking his motions while I tried to track down the source of the feeling. There.

Morgan was here!

I couldn't see him, not yet, but I knew he was close more certainly than I'd ever known anything before. And I knew the basis for that certainty. The blackness within me, the obscene mindless force, wasn't bound by Yihtor's drug. It was responding to Morgan's presence just as an echo reverberates the sound that produces it. My hair squirmed under its careful taming.

I felt more than heard Yihtor's angry voice urging me to some action. Through a haze, I saw his lips were ringed with red liquid, his cup already emptied. I stood and flung mine to the floor below—its bloodlike contents spraying in a great arc to stain a nearby tablecloth. A stillness spread through the hall.

My mind was anything but still. I struggled frantically to restrain that force in me. It stretched toward Morgan, drove at every level of my control with incredible power, seeking any crack or avenue to get to him. Somehow I curbed it, made my head turn so I could see Yihtor's livid face. "I can't Choose you." I looked back over the stunned crowd, ignored them, speaking to the man I couldn't see. "I've already Chosen. But I won't—" The surging dark battered at my control, resisted always, squirmed and heaved.

"I'll never let it hurt you," I gasped and gripped the tabletop—I couldn't control it—I had to. Yihtor was scanning the faces below, lips pulled back in a rictus of fury. "Go!" I warned Morgan desperately, knowing I was his greatest danger. "Go while you can!"

"No, Sira." A lean figure in spacer coveralls stepped gracefully from the shadows and began to walk forward, apparently oblivious to the heads that swiveled in comic unison to watch him. The fountain babbled in the silence.

Then Yihtor screamed. I cringed from the ghastly sound. "A Human? You—" spittle appeared at the corner of his mouth. "You Commenced for this—his feeble bastard power—" Yihtor was beyond reason.

I was almost as tormented—torn apart by my need for Morgan and my frantic effort to save him. Some of Yihtor's followers left their seats, closing on Morgan where he had stopped, his arms folded, calm eyes resting on me with a hint of a smile in their blue depths. "Stop!" Yihtor's command was harsh. "He's mine."

"Just us?" Morgan's question was enough to freeze Yihtor into a statue. "It's almost fair. Hardly your style, Clansman. Coercer of women. Murderer."

Yihtor summoned his power and lashed out at the lone figure standing below. There was a feeling of disorientation, of a twisting of the fabric of the air as if the real world was about to be sucked into the M'hir. Amazingly, Morgan stood, his shield holding. Abruptly, the assault ceased. The Human staggered, then collected himself with a smile full of mockery. "Not so easy as when we last met, Yihtor. Or did you have help, then?"

"Jason," I said urgently, my lips numb with the effort of speaking clearly. "I can't help you. Drugged me . . . Go—" Yihtor swung his arm. I watched it come in slow motion, felt it smash across my mouth, hurtling me backward to the floor.

"See what leads you!" Rael's voice rang out like a silvery bell over the uneasy murmuring beginning to fill the hall. I raised myself up, licking blood from my lips, and saw Morgan flanked by my sister, Huido, and a slender, young man who could only be Barac. "Brothers and sisters," Rael turned slowly, facing the gathered Clan. "See this evil for what it is!"

"Here's evil!" Yihtor countered quickly, pointing a shaking hand at me. "No *Chooser*. This thing is a traitor to our kind! She would bring an alien into the M'hir!"

"Sira di Sarc has done nothing wrong," Morgan answered steadily, his eyes ablaze in the paleness of his face. "Nothing except to fight for her life and the lives of those around her. What of you, Yihtor? What of your dealings with pirates to bring Sira here—against her will!" More shocked mutterings from Yihtor's followers.

"Hear me." Ossirus, it was hard to move my mind around words and speak; almost as difficult as the struggle to contain my power, to keep it from ending Morgan's valiant effort. Luckily, I had everyone's attention. "Some of you, maybe all, must be here because you wanted freedom, the right to make your own Choices." I paused, drawing as large a breath as I could, trying to project my voice, wondering how long I'd live. "That's not what Yihtor wants. He wants control." A looming force grew beside me, like the shadow of a sandstorm; I had little time left. "Yihtor needs me so his descendants will have enough power to rule you and yours forever. He plans to use my mindless body—"

Perhaps there was a roar of outrage, mental or vocal, imagined or real. I couldn't hear it. I was too busy fighting for my life. Soundless, unseen, Yihtor's awesome power sought to force me to stop breathing, to force my heart to cease, most of all to erase his shame in plain view of those he sought to command. *How ironic,* I thought as I died. This was the death I had planned to inflict on myself. It wasn't pleasant. A final weakness darkened my sight.

Out of nowhere, another's power filled me, driving my lungs to seek heaving gasps of air, speeding my heart to match the desperate need of my failing body. I grasped it as a drowning swimmer would reach for a lifeline, uncaring as to its source, only grateful to be alive for another minute.

The attack on me ended as quickly as it had begun; no longer necessary, my lifeline winked away at the same time. Gradually, I became aware of other lines of invisible force, they crisscrossed all around me, centering on Yihtor. I opened my eyes, saw the contemptuous curl of his lip. He was biding his time, playing with his attackers. They didn't know what he was. But I did.

Without stopping to think of the consequences, I reached down to the primitive force within me, the area untouched by the suppressing drug. I willed it to surface. The darkness rose eagerly, lapping toward Morgan. No! I was in command. My need was deeper, my will greater. Slowly, I bent the inner force to my determination. It was a thoroughly treacherous ally; I constantly intercepted tendrils trying to reach past my control.

I reopened my eyes and focused on my enemy. *Now,* I ordered: a barrier around *that* mind; cripple the power trying to destroy the one who was rightly mine. Drive *him* into the M'hir.

Yihtor looked confused as the edge of my weapon feathered against his mental shields. He shook his handsome head, then, realization dawning slowly, looked down at me. His widening smile was one of pure triumph. His eyes glowed with desire. "Oh, yes, Chooser. Come to me willingly." One hand reached down. I stretched my own hand eagerly to meet his. There was a shocked gasp from somewhere behind me. The crisscrossed lines of power faltered and died away. Yihtor's hot moist grip crushed my fingers.

That contact was all I needed. Refused any other outlet, my power lashed out, surging over the welcome of his mind like a black tide, smothering his power, driving him *out.* I couldn't tell if Yihtor fought to free himself or even knew what was happening before my trap closed utterly.

I was emptied of all but a weary relief. I would hold Yihtor's mind suspended in the M'hir; the rest of the struggle wasn't up to me. I closed my eyes and my thoughts.

*   *   *

INTERLUDE

"I'm here, Sira. I'm with you." Rael's whisper trailed away; she hated speaking aloud, even though it was safer at the moment. She gazed down at her unconscious sister, eased her arm to better cradle Sira's head and shoulders, and touched a loose strand of red-gold hair. After a second, the hair politely but firmly slid away from her fingers. Rael clenched her hand and sent Yihtor's crumpled body a look of pure hate. She was careful not to touch him.

"Barac," she said as he approached. "Look! What could have happened? What's she done?"

Barac opened his mouth to answer, then closed it when he noticed Morgan and Huido climbing up to join them. Barac refused to look at the two mind-erased Clansmen waiting in dull confusion at the edge of the platform. Kurr had been luckier, after all.

Morgan rushed forward to fall on his knees beside Sira, saying something incoherent.

"Don't touch her," Rael warned, one of her arms barring Morgan from any contact. "We don't know the consequences." She winced delicately. "To either of you."

"What's he done to her?" Morgan's eyes flashed from Sira's peaceful features to her small hand, clenched in Yihtor's fist.

"What has *she* done," Barac corrected him quietly. "We don't know yet. And if you don't mind, I'd prefer not to disturb whatever force is keeping Yihtor helpless." Barac knelt beside Morgan, resisting a strange impulse to put a comforting hand on the Human's shoulder. "Listen to me. Yihtor's mistake was in believing his followers would accept his attempt to force a Chooser. They are humiliated and angry. They don't know what to do—yet. We have to get out of here before they start thinking again."

"Barac's right, Morgan," Rael said, dark eyes imploring. "And there's great danger to you here. They heard Sira." She had trouble with the last words.

Morgan considered this for a moment. The Clan forced themselves to be patient, though Barac's eyes shifted to the cluster of Yihtor's people standing motionless and silent down by the fountains. For once he was grateful for the strict individualism of his kind. Without Yihtor's aberrant leadership, the Acranam Clan would need time to commune and argue before they could react.

Barac recognized faces among the group, dead faces come back to life. They weren't pleased to see him and he couldn't blame them. This new life of theirs was over once he reported to Council. Any unChosen among them would again be subject to the Prime Law.

Barac met Rael's eyes. She nodded slightly, indicating Morgan. Barac didn't need her inner sense to read Morgan's anguish, his struggle not to tear Sira from Yihtor's hold. Barac shrugged. What could they do about it now?

"We can't go to the *Fox*. Not with him," Morgan said steadily, though there was an undertone of violence in his voice. "There'd be no way to separate them without blowing Yihtor out the hatch." Huido immediately clicked his approval.

"Where, then?" Barac demanded hurriedly, moving closer to Morgan. "Here," Morgan said. Morgan placed his space-darkened hand lightly on Barac's forehead and dropped every mental barrier. For a shattering moment, Barac thought of eliminating the Human once and for all. It was his duty, wasn't it? Morgan waited, a hint of a challenge deep in his strange, blue eyes.

Barac relaxed, taking only the offered locate and courteously avoiding all else. The Human was no longer his or Rael's problem. The Council held authority over the Choosers—and their Chosen.

Morgan replaced his barriers, but not before Barac tasted the Human's rising self-confidence. Unfortunately, it was likely Morgan was as aware of the change in his status as the Clan.

Chapter 30

I RETURNED slowly, cautiously, working my way to consciousness like an animal roused from hibernation. First, I checked the force trapping Yihtor's mind and power in the M'hir. There was no sign of tampering, from within or without. The blackness heaved hopefully, and I slapped it down.

Good enough. I wondered if Yihtor would be any good as a hostage. I certainly didn't want him. I hoped my unlikely team of rescuers had conquered Acranam during my absence.

I traveled upward and outward, gathering the threads of my now functional power as I surfaced, weaving it into my own shielding. Hovering just at the point of consciousness, I paused, then heard a familiar sound and opened my eyes with relief.

A small fire crackled and snapped to itself a few feet from where I lay. I looked past its reassuring glow to Morgan.

I'm back, I sent gently, not wanting to startle him. His bowed heard jerked up, eyes glowing in the firelight, but he didn't move. I understood and reclosed my eyes. On a narrower, tighter band, I continued: *Are you all right?*

Warmth, deep and real, for me. *I thought I'd lost you.* My rising happiness was undercut by a sudden red current of loathing, anger, and was it also jealousy? from Morgan. *Must he hold you?*

Hold—? The word made me aware of a throbbing pain in my right hand and I looked down at it. To my horror, Yihtor lay close beside me, his hand clenched around my own, his rolled back eyes showing white under half-closed lids. I sat up, dragging at my fingers desperately.

Two brown hands reached past me and cracked open Yihtor's rigid hold. Then I was lifted into the air and held tightly.

Morgan carried me to the far side of the fire, cradling me in his lap despite my insincere protest. I laid my head back against his shoulder—content to shelter there while Morgan gently rubbed the circulation back into my whitened fingers. I watched the luminescent flowers above and smiled to myself, knowing this moment was worth all that had gone before.

After a while, I realized we weren't alone. Two slumbering forms, swathed in blankets, lay on the edge of the firelight. Reflections from two dozen shiny disks marked the spot under the trees where Huido stood, a silent sentry. I waved a greeting to the huge creature before asking Morgan silently: *Barac and Rael?*

I couldn't have reached you without them, Sira. Morgan's mental voice bubbled with the same joy I felt. Then a hint of something not quite so happy. *They're not a threat to you.*

No threat to me? I replied somewhat curtly, while at the same time nestling more firmly against him. *A threat to you, certainly. A threat to us, beyond any doubt.*

Light fingers stroked my hair, investigating its new fullness. I closed my eyes, not needing vision, feeling the living stuff quiver under Morgan's touch, winding in soft whirls around his hand, slipping up his arm to whisper across his cheek. "Sorceress," Morgan growled out loud, but very quietly, his other hand buried deep in the hair at the back of my neck.

How inevitable, that I should turn in his light hold to look up and see how his blue eyes darkened. Inevitable, that my aching right hand should search out and grip his warmly in the welcome Yihtor had thought to force. In answer to some echoing need of his own, Morgan's mouth lost its smile, coming down to press with infinite gentleness on mine. This was all there was, and should be, to life—a mutual comfort and excitement beyond any of my imaginings.

Soon I pulled away, wary of the growing restlessness within my thinly-controlled power, softening the movement with a smile from deep inside. *I mustn't lose my concentration, Captain,* I sent with a teasing note new to me. *Seeing as I'm all that keeps our prisoner in his current amiable state.*

Morgan shifted me rather unceremoniously to the soft moss, jumping up to walk rapidly to where Huido leaned sleepily against a tree trunk able to dwarf even his dimensions. Puzzled, but intrigued, I watched as the two of them conversed briefly, then came back to the fire, Huido's assortment of weapons and tools clattering with each hasty step.

The noise of Huido's approach was enough to disturb the sleepers; each in turn sat up with almost comic haste when they saw me sitting comfortably by the fire, hands stretched to its warmth. Rael recovered first and rushed to kneel by my side, reached to embrace me then stopped— perceptive enough to recognize my involuntary stiffening as a warning. "Sira. I'm so glad you're all right—" she began, beautiful eyes sparkling with tears.

"Is she?" Barac asked, his question aimed at Morgan. I bristled.

"Shouldn't I be the one to ask, Barac?" There was a fury in me I didn't quite understand.

"My apologies, *Chosen.*"

"Barac!" Rael exclaimed, her anger amplified by her aroused power.

He spread his arms wide. "Am I struck dead? By your outrage—or by the unleashing of a true Chooser?"

"Enough." Morgan's voice was quiet, but there was no mistaking its authority. He stepped forward, a small black case in one outstretched hand. "Huido's looked after this memento of the *Torquad* for me. I thought it might come in handy." A click and the lid opened, revealing contents with which I was regrettably most familiar. I smiled.

"A mind control drug—developed by Yihtor," I said for the Clans' benefit. "Its effect is temporary." Morgan sent me a flash of comfort; a vow of protection mixed with a plea for my approval. I gave it with a nod, appreciating the irony. Morgan knelt beside Yihtor's body and prepared the syringe.

"Human, we can't permit this," Barac protested. "It is forbidden—"

"I can't hold him forever," I snapped.

Barac frowned, looking from the unconscious Clansman to me in bewilderment. "But how are you holding him at all? I sense no output."

"Be grateful you don't, Cousin," Rael said slowly, comprehension warring with disbelief on her face. "Don't you see? Sira has mastered the Power-of-Choice."

"Impossible," Barac said, a humoring tone to his voice. "That can't be. Besides, she's Commenced—"

"Morgan, please," I urged him. They could talk all they wanted once I was free. Morgan reached for Yihtor's arm. His hand slowed as another tried to control it.

"How dare you!" I lashed out at Barac, severing his line of force. Before Rael could interfere, I expanded my shield to include Morgan, feeling him reinforce his own barriers. I relaxed, but glared a warning at my sister and cousin.

"There. Release him now, Sira," Morgan said, tossing the case back to Huido. The Carasian snapped it from the air with definite satisfaction. Rael and Barac looked ill. Well, they'd never been at Yihtor's mercy, or Roraqk's. I had no sympathy for them, their Clan morals, or Yihtor.

I closed my eyes to concentrate. There'd been no point telling Morgan I wasn't sure I knew how to pull my power's doppelganger out of Yihtor's mind. I needn't have worried. As I extended my thoughts outward and touched the Power-of-Choice tentatively, it snapped back to me like an elastic cord, burning and sharp on contact. In a panic, I withdrew deeper into myself. I felt it boil outward in search of Morgan.

I knew how to stop that. Fighting pain, I encompassed and buried the blackness, shivering as it rumbled and complained. Done. But my preoccupation kept me from withdrawing before Yihtor regained consciousness. Suddenly, I was aware of him at every level of my mind.

His emotions threatened to drown me. I barely flung one off when another hammered at my deepest shields: lust, hatred, pride, ambition. Overlying them all was need and triumph. He was free!

Then, I shared his horror as he discovered his power dwindled into its drugged coma. Or was I remembering my own despair? I was shaking, my head whipping back and forth, my teeth puncturing my lips. No. I was being shaken, that recognition enough to bring me completely back to myself.

When I opened my eyes and looked at Morgan, he released his bruising grip on my shoulders and gathered me
close, muttering something that was part apology and part
scolding. I tasted the blood in my mouth. My neck felt
like rubber and I ached from spine to forehead. But I was
free of Yihtor. I pushed myself back so I could meet Morgan's concerned eyes. "Was that the easiest method?" I
asked him, rubbing my head. He shrugged.

"It worked."

Yihtor sat hunched before the fire, eyes squeezed shut,
barely breathing. Huido stood behind him, close enough
that his sponge-toed feet were on either side of the Clansman. Yihtor didn't appear to notice. Barac stared at me,
an odd mix of resignation and longing in his firelit face.

"You don't need to be afraid of me, Barac," I said.
"Rael was right; I've learned to control what she called the
Power-of-Choice. You're safe. And so are you, Jason," I
added, holding out my hand. Ignoring Barac's choked
warning. Morgan wrapped his fingers around mine confidently, looking down at me with that warmth deep in
his eyes.

"No!" Yihtor's hoarse shout surprised us all. I felt a jolt
of fear as I watched him leap to his feet, power and grace
in every move. But Huido's clawed arms moved even
faster, the heavier, larger handling claws spanning Yihtor's waist and lifting him overhead as the two finer arms
clamped the Clansman's arms to his sides. Paired needle-
sharp points slid from the shadow of the Carasian's head
carapace, their tips aglitter in the firelight.

"No. Don't hurt him," Rael said quickly. "Please. He
can be helped by our people. We mustn't waste his
power."

The Carasian ignored her, busy turning Yihtor this way
and that, angling those killing fangs as if deciding upon
the best spot to strike. His movements were ponderous,
his violence inevitable rather than sudden. The Clansman
yammered something.

I watched, my first reaction of hot satisfaction dissolving. Were we no better than Roraqk now, to kill a helpless
prisoner? I eyed Huido's immense form dubiously. Convincing him wasn't within my ability.

Meanwhile, Morgan had slipped close to his friend. He
rapped his knuckles on one armored shoulder to get Huido's

attention. One eye bent to look at him, unwillingly, I thought.

"You know you always get sick afterward," Morgan said very calmly, though he had to shout to be heard over Yihtor's screams.

Huido shuddered, making a rain on tin sound. Morgan put his foot into the Carasian's knee joint, using it as a stair so he could reach over to grab the Carasian's fangs. Huido froze, all his eyes whipping down to Morgan. His claws opened slowly, dropping Yihtor to the ground where the Clansman huddled groaning, arms tight around his middle.

Morgan let go and jumped down. Huido's eyestalks parted, his fangs vanishing into shadows. With another shudder, he lurched away into the dark. "You'll thank me later," Morgan called after him.

Rael had watched curiously as Morgan bandaged Yihtor's broken ribs, then sedated the morose Clansman. She apparently could have healed him using her power, but, in her words, she wasn't a charity. Huido stood guard, Yihtor having been put into the escape pod once I'd finished changing into real clothes again. The Carasian seemed totally recovered from his killing frenzy, and spent his time transferring a nutrient broth Morgan had found for him from handling claw to mouth.

The flowers' light faded quickly in the predawn glow. We shared a breakfast of emergency rations with a false camaraderie, avoiding the arguments to come. Afterward, Morgan took Barac with him to scout the immediate area; the Human, despite his own abilities, carried an assortment of tiny detecting devices which Barac viewed with scorn.

Rael and I could see them occasionally through gaps between the trees. I stretched lazily, soaking up the peacefulness of the growing things around and above us. The air was fresh, scented, and warm.

"You know him better than we do," Rael said suddenly. I rolled over to look up at her.

"Morgan?"

She checked the ground before sitting on a corner of blanket. "His shielding is remarkable—for a Human."

I kept my grin to myself. "Frustrated?"

Rael's full lips curved in a rueful smile. "Totally. I'm used to our kind, to sharing emotions, reasons, arguments. With Morgan, I have to look at his face before I know if he's going to agree or disagree—and then I'm never sure anyway. Tell me, Sira. What does he think of us? And why has he helped you?"

I rolled onto my back again and studied the puzzle of leaves overhead. The flowers were closed into tight shiny globes. I watched as a furred animal hung by its tail to pick and chew one with relish. "Morgan's my Captain. Spacers take care of their own." Before Rael choked on that, I added: "I expect he thinks you're arrogant, self-centered, and beautiful."

She laughed. "And I think you're impossible these days, Sira di Sarc!" I peered at her, my peace of mind shattered by the name. Rael didn't seem to notice. She was gazing around the campsite and surrounding forest. "I can't wait to get back to Deneb," she said abruptly, giving an exaggerated shiver. "This overgrown garden is no place for civilized beings."

"I like it."

Rael laughed again, a sound like tinkling bells. "You've never been one to enjoy outsystem lifestyles, Sira. You'll know better once Cenebar restores your memories."

I made some excuse so I could move away from her. I didn't want to hear any more. I liked the sound of Sira di Sarc less and less. I was Sira Morgan. I would stay Sira Morgan.

I looked over to where Morgan and Barac were returning to the camp. Morgan found me immediately, seeking unerringly between the massive root buttresses to where I sat in their shade. A wave of understanding slipped across the surface of my mind, then away, leaving behind a companionable warmth. All this while Barac argued with him, his patronizing tone carrying, if not the words.

Rael stood and moved aside as Morgan came near, a graceful and, I thought, involuntary motion. She, like Barac, found Morgan's humanness almost intolerable.

Restore my memories? If they would make me see Morgan the way Barac and Rael saw him, if they cost me the smallest part of my feelings for him—I didn't want them.

Chapter 31

"I BELIEVE you believe what you say," I conceded, trying hard to sound interested.

Rael and Barac had finally brought their discussion of my future to a halt. Huido was apparently asleep standing up, though somehow I doubted the Carasian's inattention was as blatant as it seemed. Morgan was, to all appearances, engrossed in carving a piece of soft wood with a small knife; he leaned lazily on an elbow at my side.

"You're trying to ignore the truth!" Rael was close to exasperation. "I don't understand you. Why won't you let us discuss this with you properly?"

I didn't bother to answer that again. Rael and Barac were, or at least acted, deeply insulted by my insistence on verbal communication. Their reaction was understandable, though I disliked making them angry. In a way, it was their own fault. They'd convinced me of their desperation that I accept their decisions. So how could I trust them in my mind?

They'd abandoned hints or veiled meanings quite early, once it was plain I couldn't understand them. What I could understand as plainly as if it were shouted, was that both Rael and Barac had secrets, secrets they especially wanted to keep from Morgan.

"Come with us. You must return to Camos," Rael said, perhaps mistaking my long pause for wavering. "It's possible Cenebar can even do something about your condition." Her eyes flicked over my coveralls.

I see nothing to improve, a sly mental voice intruded. I glanced down to see Morgan's warm grin. A rush of blood to my cheeks brought an answering smile. The innocent exchange didn't escape Rael.

"How can you be so blind!" It was almost a shout. I faced her again, my own anger rising only to be quelled as her passionate outburst continued. "You haven't made Choice, Sira, either by Council sanction or by the realities of life. You're somehow hanging in the midst: kept from killing the unChosen—and your precious Human—by the most unnatural self-control ever conceived! How long can it last? Another hour? A day?"

Morgan impaled a flat sliver with unnecessary force. "You're forgetting something, Clanswoman."

Rael's lips tightened at Morgan's unwelcome contribution. "This isn't your affair, Human. You'll be paid—"

I bristled, but Morgan's low chuckle was more effective. "There's only one person who can send me away." The knife was thrust deep into the moss; the carved wood tossed accurately to join others in the growing woodpile beyond Barac. "And until this matter is settled to *my* satisfaction, not even you, Sira, could force me to leave." The sudden sternness of his voice was a more telling commitment than any flowery speech. I drew one hand in the air above Morgan's brown hair, watching the taut muscles of his shoulders and neck relax, enjoying my ability to affect him.

"What do you think we've forgotten, Human?" Barac demanded, an unusual heaviness in his tone and expression. "Your feelings?"

"Look past Sira and me for once, Barac," Morgan said, straightening. "And tell me something: Who invaded and so thoroughly blocked Sira's mind, despite her power? Who took Sira from her refuge and dumped her on Auord?"

"My father." They all looked at me. I was a bit surprised at myself, then continued: "I remember him taking me to Auord."

Rael and Barac looked from Morgan to me in comic unison. "Jarad?" Barac exclaimed with disbelief. "He's a member of Council himself. He'd be the last to disobey—"

"It was him," I kept my voice level. "I remember. But I don't remember why." Nor did I know why I was continuing to try and explain myself. To the two of them, I was damaged, not responsible. I could sympathize; certainly I wasn't behaving as expected. I should get rid of them both, simplify life again.

No, Sira, Morgan's thought intruded gently, his hand on mine. *We need them.*

. I didn't question his ability to know my thoughts. *We could take the* Fox. *I could block them from the M'hir until we were too far for Rael to reach.*

We could, he agreed. *And we may yet. But not now. There's more they're hiding. We need—*

A low-pitched whistle sounded, a startling interruption to the inner speech. Morgan drew a comlink from his belt, holding it close to one ear. He spoke into it briefly before restoring the instrument to its place.

"Terk," he said, aloud, looking at me with a small frown. "He wants me on the ship. Something wrong with the orbit stabilizer."

I stood with Morgan. He gave a shrug. "It's possible. Terk doesn't have the patience for the old girl."

Rael and Barac rose, too, their suspicion plain. "I'll take Morgan," Barac said to me. Their doubt scraped along my nerves.

"Fine," Morgan accepted easily. "Knowing Terk, he's probably annoyed with all the locks he's encountered while snooping." A flash of blue eyes to me, a quick whisper to Huido, and he and Barac disappeared.

Almost instantly, I was riveted in shock. Morgan's anger and surprise burned through my mind. A trap! Without a second thought, or heed to Rael's frantic voice, I *pushed* . . .

. . . and stood in the control room of the *Silver Fox* for the first time since Plexis.

"So you did find Fem di Sarc, Barac." The woman's brow lifted. "Or has she found you?"

"What have you done to Morgan?" I didn't look at the crumpled figure at my feet. I didn't need to—my other sense had already begun a thorough check.

"Took a stun," Barac answered, his tone implying a stupidity beyond belief. "How the trigger-happy fool missed me, I don't know."

A groan from Morgan made me bend down. Barac helped me raise him to his feet. "A misunderstanding, Clanswoman," the woman said smoothly, thumbs tucked into her belt, her eyes missing nothing of me, narrowing a bit at the outsized coveralls I wore. "Captain Morgan was regrettably swift in drawing his own weapon—"

I returned her stare, no longer intimidated by the insignia of a Trade Pact Enforcer. "What else did you expect, finding you on our ship!" I said furiously. "Who are you? What right—"

"This is Commander Bowman, Sira," Morgan said, his voice thick but clear. His attention was on a man standing to one side. This must have been the one who fired the stun. "And I think I told you about Russell Terk. I thought you'd call reinforcements." Morgan smiled. "Good."

Barac and I looked at Morgan as if he'd taken leave of his senses, or perhaps the mild stun hadn't quite worn off. Bowman scowled. "I've a few questions for you, Morgan," she said sharply, "beginning with the disaster on Plexis."

Morgan's tanned, regular features assumed the almost angelic innocence I knew signified full-speed plotting. "Let me explain," he offered. And did.

No place like home, I decided, turning the fresher to warm air, listening contentedly to the *Fox*'s throbbing engines.

True, I reflected, lifting my hair to let the air dry my back, it was somewhat crowded on board. But not as much as it would have been before the timely arrival of Bowman and her cruiser. Morgan had persuaded the rather testy commander to transport Yihtor to Camos—to be charged there with the murder of Kurr, among other things. Huido and Barac went along as his keepers. They were hostages for our good behavior as well; the latter a politely unstated condition. Fortunately, Bowman remained sufficiently intrigued by the Clan and Clan business to tie her ship to Barac's comet for a while longer.

The Clan enclave on Acranam had somehow never been mentioned as part of Yihtor's plot. Not only were the Enforcers woefully overmatched, despite their mind-deadening devices, the existence of so many Clan revolting against the Council was, to quote Barac, not Human business. I was glad, and maybe a touch sympathetic—Acranam was a beautiful world, especially with Yihtor gone.

"My turn!" I obediently slid into my cleaned coveralls

and opened the stall door. Rael smiled and rumpled my
hair. "I thought you were going to wash yourself away,"
she teased, sensing my relaxed mood.

"Nothing wrong with a little cleanliness," I said primly,
squeezing to one side in the small cabin to let her pass.
After the fresher closed, I paused a moment, brush in
hand, admiring the luminous white flowers Morgan had
somehow found time to paint along the ceiling's edge.
They might even have fooled the hapless insects of Acranam. I went forward to the control room, smiling to
myself.

It's good to be home, I sent to Morgan. He was busily
checking controls, obviously enjoying the feel of command again. My cheeks began to burn; why had I used
home, as though I had some right to stay here? Sitting on
the copilot's couch, I started brushing out my hair, sensitive to a tension that for once had nothing to do with my
tightly suppressed power.

Morgan's lean, brown hand took the brush from mine,
drawing it through my hair with long, slow strokes. He
hummed quietly to himself as he groomed the heavy stuff
lock by lock. I found the process almost unbearable and
wasn't sure why. "Stop it, Jason," my voice belonged to a
stranger.

Morgan immediately put down the brush, then sat beside me so that we faced each other across the seat.
"What's wrong, Sira?"

"Nothing," I said quickly, then stopped, confused. Why
should I feel uncomfortable with Morgan? He was my
friend and more. I hated to admit it, but Yihtor was right
about me. I was a half-thing, not Chosen or Unchosen, not
Clan or Human.

"Rael's quite beautiful," I said, rather than delve further in my own turmoil. The question brought back some
of my fierce jealousy and I instantly regretted it. Morgan
smiled.

"So are you," he replied softly.

"Now," I reminded him, feeling an odd pang. "I wasn't
before."

His smile grew, as if Morgan read more into my words
than I'd intended. "That's your opinion," he said firmly.
"You haven't really changed." A quick tug on a waving

strand of hair. "This." A downward gesture. "That. But you're still who you were, Sira."

"For how long?" I closed my lips tightly after the question, too many thoughts clamoring to be heard, too many fears waiting to pounce.

The bleakness in his face echoed the dread of my own thoughts. His mind touched mine. *Barac and Rael are right about one thing. You must recover what was taken from you, Sira. Even if it means I lose.*

I wished I could borrow some of Morgan's courage. I leaned toward him and he swept me close in an embrace almost painful in its strength, as if his fear was as great as my own.

Chapter 32

"PSST. Sira. You awake?"

The soft whisper startled me until I recognized the voice. "Rael? What's the matter?" I peered into the darkness of the cabin, trying to see her. I must be half-asleep. I ordered on the portlight.

Rael stood looking down at me. She was dressed, which I expected, since it was my turn to sleep. What I found unexpected was the pale and set expression on her face. "What is it?" I repeated.

"I have to talk to you, Sira. Please let me stay."

"You might as well," I said, trying not to sound unfriendly, trying to remember if ruining a good night's sleep was what sisters did to each other. I made myself comfortable in a corner of the hammock. Rael pulled out a crate from those lining the opposite wall of the galley cubby and perched on it, her whole body expressing a need for action. "Well?" I prompted, yawning.

Inside, I was awake enough. The past two days had gone by too calmly. I'd suspected Rael of biding her time, waiting for a moment when Morgan wasn't present, for a moment when I might be more approachable. I thought I'd be polite and listen; where was the harm in that?

"We've been contacted by Camos Port Authority. We're insystem, waiting for clearance." That news was enough to scour away the last remnants of my rest.

Rael continued: "By now, Barac will have contacted his superiors and they will report to the Council. There'll be a hearing of Yihtor's crimes—by Clan, not, as Bowman plans, by Human justice. The Council will learn everything when they scan Yihtor; the truth can't be hidden." Rael hesitated. "However, this takes time. Until then, Barac won't tell Council about you or about Morgan—we agreed on this. I trust him."

"What are you saying? I thought you wanted me to come to Camos—to this Council of yours."

"Yes. But." Her delicate fingers clasped and reclasped each other. "Barac and I have been troubled," Rael began at last. "What exists between you and that Human—"

"Morgan."

Rael nodded. "Between you and Morgan, Sira, is a closeness, a bond such as I've never seen before outside of heart-kin." She made a soft, sad sound. "You don't remember. Clan Joinings aren't like the life-pairings of other species, with affection or love as part of them. A few might turn out that way; most, like mine, appease a drive, no more. I despise my Chosen, and, to be honest, he isn't fond of me; at the same time our link is soul-deep and for life. When we're assigned children, he'll come to me and perform his function. Afterward, we can hope never to have to share a planet."

"I'm sorry—"

"Don't be," my sister said quickly, a proud flash in her dark eyes. "Once Chosen, a Clanswoman can go anywhere, do anything, and be answerable only to herself. My life's a good one. I'll return to it willingly once I'm certain you'll be all right." Rael looked at me for a long moment, as if she weighed some consequences in her mind. "Heart-kin, I can't bear to cause you pain. Barac and I have decided to take steps to hide Morgan from the Council."

My mouth went dry. "Why? What haven't you told me? What threat do they pose to us?" A faint alarm sounded deep in my thoughts.

Rael shook her head. "Don't be afraid, Sira. You're an innocent victim. The Council will help you."

The alarm grew louder, almost painful. I strengthened my barriers to prevent it from echoing into Morgan's mind. "But this Council is a threat to Morgan. That's what you're trying to say, isn't it? But why? Morgan's done nothing except help me, save my life, and more."

Another shake of Rael's head loosened anxious tendrils of black hair from their fastening. "Regardless of what Morgan's done or is, regardless of anything we say or do, the Prime Law requires his memory of us be erased and his power stripped." I don't know what Rael read in my face, but her voice grew defensive. "How else do you think we've survived on Human worlds for so long? Barac's already protected Morgan long after the Law should have been carried out." She leaned forward, eyes intent. "And how much worse if they so much as suspect a Human's connection with a Chooser."

"We must stop the *Fox*," I decided with a sense of unreality, pushing to my feet. "We can't take Morgan to Camos."

"Agreed," Rael said swiftly. "But what would our Enforcer escort do if the *Fox* changed course? What of Barac—and Morgan's friend?"

"What can I do, then?" I demanded. I stretched out a tiny portion of power, touched her shields only to find them gone, revealing her thoughts. "You want me to leave him," I said, recoiling. I sank back down.

Rael nodded. "You could return to Camos ahead of us, right to the Cloister itself, as if you'd never left. It separates you from Morgan before any Clan sense what you mean to each other. Bluff. Use up time. Confuse any who question you. Meanwhile, Barac will delay Yihtor's scan as long as possible. Morgan can lift from Camos and be systems away before Council suspects his existence."

"They'll hunt him down," I objected numbly, already halfway to accepting her plan of action, searching for holes with a sort of shocked calmness.

Rael spread her hands. "From what I've seen of your Morgan, he knows how to survive."

"So I must lose him in order to save him?"

She showed her discomfort but was frank in return. "What future had you anyway, Sira? You're doing Morgan a favor. Once your mind is restored, you'll understand why all this was impossible from the beginning."

I shook my head from side to side, wondering why I was unable to cry when every part of me was in so much pain. "No. Despite what you believe, I've made the Choice of my lifetime."

There was an inexpressible gentleness in her voice. "You must leave the Human. Go home, Sister."

Home? I swung my legs over the side of the bunk; I'd thought of this ship as my home mere hours ago. "I don't know where that is. Give me the locate. And promise me—" I hesitated, not knowing how to judge her.

"I'm yours, heart-kin," Rael's eyes were as moist as mine were dry.

"Look after him."

"I swear it."

Once dressed, I drew the locate from Rael and made ready. She embraced me tightly for a moment then backed away. "Draw on my strength, Sira. It's a long journey through the M'hir, even for you."

"You'll need your strength to handle Morgan," I said. "Make him understand. I don't intend this to be another trap for him."

Rael nodded, unable to speak. I *pushed* . . .

No! A mental shout ripped through my mind, almost dissolving the picture I had of my destination. *Sira—*

A barrier slammed between us just in time. I *pushed* again . . .

Nothingness. Its emptiness teased at me. Lances of force arched past, luring me after them in all directions at once. I fought to hold together . . .

. . . and then I stood in a room—no, a series of rooms. No particular luxury, but there was comfort and the oddments and personal effects of a long stay.

I sank down on the easi-rest under the barred window and leaned my head against the cool metal bars, listening to the echoes of Morgan's horrified cry.

* * *

INTERLUDE

"You were the one who kept saying you'd protect her. How could you let her go?" Rael wanted to flinch from each of Morgan's furious questions. "Why didn't she speak to me first?"

"She probably thought you wouldn't listen. You're not listening to *me*, Human." The Clanswoman's defenses were in place, but only by reflex.

"So. I'm listening." Morgan leaned back against the bulkhead, arms folded in a deliberately eased posture. His face, emptied of expression, was dominated by the piercing blue eyes which never left Rael's.

The Clanswoman rubbed her neck, trying without success to work out a knot of tension. "Camos is too dangerous for you—"

"And what about for Sira, especially alone?" Morgan's quick, heated rebuttal belied his outward calm. "Do you think she's safe now from whoever or whatever blocked her mind? Do you think she can just pick up her life as one of you, ignoring all that's happened?"

"No." Rael's quiet answer fueled Morgan's fury.

"Then why separate us now? On Acranam, you and Barac agreed I should come to Camos."

"Did we have any choice? You wouldn't leave Sira, and she wouldn't come without you." Rael shook her head. "The reality is that Sira has to be healed—you know that as well as we do. The Clan is scattered over a hundred different systems; only on Camos is there any concentration of us. I suppose that's more information you should be killed for, Human," Rael added in an absent tone. She continued, "There are those who can help her on Camos—"

"And those who used her."

"All in the throw, Human. They can't do anything more to her."

Morgan's lips twisted. "You're the most cold—"

"Don't presume to judge me," Rael warned him. "If I say Sira is safe, you have to accept my word. You don't know us, Morgan, even if you know more than you should. Sira is safe because of who and what she is."

"Those things didn't protect her before."

"I'll find out what happened. When the members of Council scan Yihtor's memories," Rael hesitated and changed what she wanted to say. "They'll take action. Our justice is more practical than yours—the current Council will be removed from power if they overlook any of this."

"None of this explains why Sira left the *Fox*."

"For your sake."

"Mine?"

"I'll be honest, Captain Morgan. You're a problem. Barac and I, well, we didn't have the stomach to deal with you after what happened on Acranam. We thought it would be easier to leave you for the Council. But we found we couldn't do that either."

"Forgive me if I seem unappreciative," Morgan said.

Rael smiled faintly. "I understand, Captain. I find it hard to believe I'm taking your side in this. I'm not sure how to convince you, but Barac and I are trying to help you. If the Council doesn't find out about you until you're outsystem again, there's a chance you can survive all this intact," Rael's smile was predatory. "Then you're on your own, Human. Barac and I are risking enough."

"What about Sira's risk?"

"Sira isn't your problem. She understands that you must go." Rael's lustrous eyes sparkled suspiciously. "I promised Sira I'd help you. You have to do what I say—to leave Camos and forever avoid the Clan." When Morgan didn't answer, Rael frowned. "If there were any future for the two of you, a way for you to stay together, I think I'd help." Rael shook her head with disbelief at her own words, her hair reluctant to lift as if her mood infected it with weight. "But all I see, all Barac can sense, is disaster unless you flee. For you and for Sira."

Morgan replied so softly Rael had to strain to hear. "Isn't this disaster enough?" He turned and walked slowly from the cabin, the measured tread of every step painfully eloquent.

"Morgan, wait!" Rael ran out into the short corridor. "Meet me on Deneb," she offered, hands outstretched. "It's a good world, new enough for opportunity and old enough for comfort. I'll arrange to cover your trail from Camos. After I'm sure Sira's safe, I'll join you."

Morgan lifted one brow. His eyes traveled over Rael's body in a studied gaze meant as an insult. "I don't require that sort of bribe, Clanswoman."

"And I can't offer it, Human," Rael replied in a low tone, not attempting to misunderstand him. "Choice means exactly that. Once made, no other partnerings are allowed by the force within us, the Power-of-Choice."

"What makes you think it's any different for me?" Morgan asked with a small smile that invited Rael to share the irony. Then a flash of pain, so fleeting Rael might have imagined it, tightened Morgan's lips. "I'll have to wait on Camos for Huido to board the *Fox*. I won't leave him stranded on your world. Can you arrange that, Clanswoman? Or will the hue-and-cry be out?"

Rael didn't hide her relief or concern. "I can do what I said; a di Sarc has power on Camos. As long as you don't delay until Yihtor's memories become public knowledge."

Morgan didn't bother to hide his pain this time. "Or Sira's?" he asked quietly.

"Or Sira's," Rael agreed sadly.

Chapter 33

EVERYTHING was so familiar, yet I didn't know where I was. I touched objects, opened closets, and almost caught the true meaning of what was around me. I spotted a brown jacket sprawled over a table. Had I tossed it there before leaving for Auord? I picked it up thoughtfully, rubbing the nubbly fabric between my hands, trying to remember. The effort hurt.

I tossed the clothing into a nearby chair, intrigued by the glistening surface of the table. Without knowing why, I pressed my right hand onto it, just forward of the center. Lights flickered within the tabletop, outlining a highly sophisticated computer interface. I glared at the machine, then kicked the nearest leg of the table. How many questions could it answer, if only I could remember how to make it speak?

The rest of my explorations were about as successful. I found a closet with changes of clothing, all of which pleased my taste, even if very little of it still fit. More proof, if I needed any, that these chambers had been Sira di Sarc's. *Mine,* I reminded myself.

It didn't help that Morgan's cry stuck to my thoughts like the cold sweat of a nightmare. I pushed the memory of it away as best I could, but it was difficult not to wonder what was happening on the *Fox.* Was Rael explaining? Was Morgan listening, or blaming her?

I thought about the Captain of the *Venture,* suddenly. She'd turned out to be a friend, if a self-serving one. How sure was I about Rael? Ossirus. What if I'd been fooled all along? What if she'd fed me a tale to get me here, leaving Morgan unprotected? What if . . .

"Sira?"

I whirled, then a ripple of memory transformed my alarm into something like relief. "Enora."

The older Clanswoman had come through the doorway leading from the living area to the bedroom where I'd started sorting through the contents of a chest. My memory of her assembled itself, complete except for the gaps where I should fit. But I remembered the dignified, graceful features of her face with its tiny laugh lines around mouth and eyes. She was taller than I and carried herself with unconscious pride, as befitted the First Chosen of the Freisnen branch of the Sarc House. Barac and Kurr's mother, not mine. There was nothing in my mind about a mother, I realized with an empty pain.

Run to her, whimpered some foreign part of my mind, bury my face against the shoulder which had performed that service many times before. I couldn't. For all I knew, she could be my enemy.

"It's so good to see you, Sira." Her bright, dark eyes ran over me quickly, as perceptive in their kindness as Bowman's in her suspicion. "Your father told me you'd be home soon." There was a pause, ended by a tactfully raised eyebrow. "Would you care to take supper on the terrace? The sunset will be exceptional." As she spoke, she went over to a closet door I hadn't tried yet. When she opened it, I could see racks of clothing, all of it looking brand new. So they had been ready here for my change, as well. I found the inevitability of it unsettling.

I sensed Enora's interest and concern, but detected almost no power from her beyond a feeling of empathy, of an ability to understand the emotional state of others. Mine must have been chaotic enough to warn her to restrain her questions. "On the terrace would be fine, Enora. I'm glad to be home." An untruth, but I tried hard to believe it. My reward was a brightening of her smile.

Funny kind of prison, I decided later, gazing out over the mountainside, savoring the lingering and familiar flavor of spice from the tea Enora had left me as the finish to my meal. The sunset had been everything she'd promised; long golden rays had sparked diamonds from the narrow lake below, then wrapped behind the mammoth peaks across the valley from where I sat in comfort. Now the light was a diffuse, rose-tinted glow. The pine-scented air began to have a bite to it and I was grateful Enora had brought my jacket.

The building behind me was smaller than I'd expected, and older, its aged stones softened by blue-green shrubs and wildly climbing vines. The terrace itself was fashioned into a prow that jutted out in exquisite defiance of gravity. A fortress, rather than a prison. A retreat, rather than a cage. I found, without intending to, that I liked it here.

I felt an odd sensation, deep inside, like a tickle in my head. Before I could decide how to react, the view in front of me abruptly changed. I blinked slowly, looking around a darkly paneled room. The Clan probably did this to each other all the time. I tried not to appear startled as I looked for the person responsible.

The room was lit by floating portlights, their globes confined at varying heights by rope tethers. It gave them a primitive look, as though their owner had disdained to have them programmed to stay put. I'd dreamed of this place, I remembered, or rather some other part of it. Here, instead of the artifacts and names I expected, were carvings, mostly in pale stone, displayed on wooden pedestals placed near each light.

The floor wasn't even, rising in steplike layers, irregular in shape. I was on the lowest. My chair hadn't been transported with me. I felt a hard cold slickness and realized I was on some kind of curved stone bench.

"I trust you'd finished your meal, Sira." A tall, almost gaunt man emerged from the shadows to stand within one of the small circles of light—a stranger my broken memory named my father, Jarad di Sarc, Clansman. His craggy, hawklike features refused to be softened by the dim illumination. One of his hands gestured a welcome. The other adjusted a pleat on his red robelike garment so it draped precisely like the others from shoulder to floor. "I have been waiting to see you since you've returned from your journey."

I felt no urge to embrace him, as I had with Enora. I didn't lower my mental defenses either. This deliberate distancing between us must have been customary; certainly Jarad di Sarc didn't appear concerned by my lack of warmth.

A memory rolled over without warning, exposing its sickly belly. I repeated it out loud, my lips gone numb. "On the way to Auord—I remember what you said. You promised me a candidate for Choice."

One of his hands stroked the carving nearest him, fingers lingering sensuously along a curve. "And has it been so distasteful? You appear to have met with success." I couldn't look away from his eyes. They were brilliant, darkly beautiful beneath incongruously long lashes.

My father moved forward and I drew a deep breath as the spell was broken. "What's wrong?" he said, stepping down from his level to mine. "Why does your stasis block remain in place?"

"Why shouldn't the blockage remain?" I snarled. "You put it there, didn't you! Why?"

Jarad put up one hand to silence me, then came close to where I sat and lifted both his hands to the top of my head before I could utter a protest. Instantly, I was afloat, suspended just like the lights glowing before my eyes. A breath later, I was freed.

Jarad paced in and out of shadows, flickering in and out of sight. I stayed still, holding the stone bench with my hands, checking my shields. They were intact. So what could he have touched in my mind to disturb him? What was happening?

Jarad stopped, only the edge of his dull red robe, three crisp pleats' worth, in the light. "Who tampered with you?" he said. "Who removed the initial layer?"

"A friend tried to help me," I said, careful and afraid.

"Helped?" The lights in the room dimmed then brightened. Jarad paid no attention; his eyes blazed at me. "What kind of help do you call it when it ruins everything! Sira, how could this happen after you convinced us! There were protections—" he choked, then went on: "Who removed it? No Clan would dare tamper with stasis—"

"No Clan did." The form of my life couldn't shift again like this, couldn't change before my eyes. "I convinced you?" I said faintly.

"Of course," Jarad said impatiently, bending forward. The light fought shadows for the right to reveal his expression and failed. "Do you think I'd have agreed otherwise? You argued Cenebar and me to the wall. Oh, he was easy enough to persuade, soft-headed old fool. I told you it was too great a risk, but you wouldn't listen. No one ever attempted to lock stasis release to Joining before, to bind a mind past the moment of Choice. Impossible to test, you said, how could you prove it, except by putting yourself—"

"Wait a minute. You're saying I helped block my own mind?" I said, playing out the dream, a stupor closing on all my thoughts. "I destroyed myself? Why? What drove me to this? I don't remember!"

"An interesting development, Jarad." The newcomer's voice hit with the force of a blow. Every portlight flared, scouring shadows and squinting the eyes of the white-robed Clansman who stood in the doorway at the highest point of the gallery.

"You aren't welcome in my home, Faitlen," Jarad said with a voice that shivered along my spine. "How dare you come in here—"

The shorter Clansman worked his meandering way around the carvings on their pedestals, his sandaled feet making loud slapping sounds as he stepped down each level. "I requested admittance, Jarad." Faitlen waved a disparaging hand at the unusual lights. "It's hardly my fault if you ignore your own alarms. As for your welcome, I don't seek it. The Council has its own interests to protect, in case you've forgotten—"

"You'd be wiser to protect yourself, eavesdropper. No one would grieve your passing from Camos."

I didn't need my father's barely-leashed rage to make me wary of the man. The narrow-featured Faitlen reminded me of Morgan's story of a shopkeeper he'd met on Plexis. The shopkeeper had had four arms, two of which he liked to use to sneak merchandise off the counter before it could be counted.

This Faitlen had two arms, both in sight, but I distrusted him. The power he'd broadcast in greeting was no match for what I sensed emanating from Jarad, and certainly couldn't explain his confident air. It was as if he held some leverage or threat no less potent for my father's refusal to acknowledge it.

Faitlen came to a stop at the end of my bench. Jarad glowered down at him from the opposite side. I had to slide back in order to see both their faces. "So good to see you freed from the heavy burdens of a Chooser at long last, daughter of di Sarc," the Clansman said graciously. "The Council will be pleased all went so very well. I assume by his absence that the Human failed to survive?"

The Human? I hadn't braced myself in time for another shock. I couldn't move or speak, even to demand answers. All the while, my inner warnings screamed of the danger of showing too much reaction before these two.

Faitlen drew his own interpretation of my silence. He tugged at the edges of the vest he wore over his robe with an air of satisfaction. "Just as well, though Cenebar will doubtless have some complaint or other," he said. "Didn't I say, Jarad, that the Human's death was the most likely outcome of Sira's Commencement?"

Jarad growled deep in his throat, his eyes fierce points of light. "Now is not the time for this, Faitlen. Sira must go to Cenebar immediately."

"An interesting development indeed, Jarad," Faitlen repeated. "A mind in stasis *after* Choice and Commencement must surely be unique. And must be discussed by Council. Which gives you little time, Jarad," his smile turned spiteful. "Council convenes at the third quarter." Faitlen shimmered and disappeared.

"How does he know about Morgan?" I blurted, unable to contain myself.

I wasn't prepared for my father's chuckle either. The lights gentled to a glow. "Poor Sira," he said almost sadly, sitting beside me on the bench, settling his robe neatly and dropping his arm onto my shoulders in a brief gesture of comfort. "I don't know—yet—exactly what's happened, or what you think has been happening, but the Human named Jason Morgan was the key to it all. I was about to ask you his fate myself before that misChosen fool interrupted us."

So much for Rael's concern about secrecy. Or was she part of this? "Morgan is fine—as far as I know," I said, torn between frustration at being so confused and a growing certainty that being confused might be vastly preferable to understanding.

"Interesting."

I stiffened. "I know, Father, how the Clan treats Humans who learn too much of its affairs. Jason Morgan is my Choice, if not my Chosen. I won't let you hurt him."

"Ahh." A cat's satisfaction, an audible purr to Jarad's voice, as if something in my quick speech had pleased him. The strange lights answered to his mood again, warming from yellow to rose. "Some success, at least."

"Success? You sound like this was all some kind of game," I said. "Whose success? Not mine."

"But it is yours, Sira." Jarad's smile widened as he looked down at me. "And so perhaps success for us all. Come. Let's go to Cenebar and see if he can pry those buried memories loose for us." His face tightened, its harsh lines suddenly grim. "We may need them."

"Wait a minute. You're pleased I've Chosen a Human?" I demanded incredulously. "What about Yihtor?"

"Yihtor. A problem we'd all believed dead and gone. From what little I've heard, he tried very hard, and unsuccessfully, to interfere. What other fantasies have you hidden under this stuff?" One of his hands smoothed the hair back from my forehead. A tendril lifted and clung to his arm for a fleeting moment. "Trust me, firstborn of my household. Surely you have some recollection of me."

I stood, accepting the hand my father offered to help, releasing it immediately. "Nothing that involves trust, Jarad di Sarc." I met his eyes and nodded more to myself than to him. "But I'll come with you."

I had to. I couldn't hide in Sira Morgan any longer. I had to know Sira di Sarc. It had nothing to do with curiosity or desire. What I was beginning to imagine was so unbearable, I had to prove myself wrong.

Chapter 34

"UNIQUE, Jarad, truly unique. You know I've been keeping the most careful records." From his glowing eyes to the restless movement of his extraordinarily long fingers, the Clan Healer, Cenebar di Teerac, radiated intense delight. His pleasure spilled over in power as well, pulling an answering smile from me.

My father was less amused. "Council convenes, Cenebar. You know how they'll react if you can't clear Sira's block."

The healer stopped circling me and dropped into a chair opposite my father. His gray-peppered black hair slipped in front of his eyes and he pushed it behind his ears absently. He seemed quite surprised by Jarad's harsh tone. "Why so grim, old friend?" he said. "Although I've never seen nor heard of a partial stasis—or partial Choice involving a *Human* for that matter," a conspiratorial wink at me. "The solution is straightforward. Sira's release mechanism was within the initial layer. This layer will have left its image in the mind of the Human, Morgan. He can restore it in Sira's."

"And what good will that do? If the total block is restored, Sira will lose what fraction of power and memory she's regained!" Jarad rose impatiently from his seat, towering over the slender healer. "Faitlen, that crasnig, is already drooling in anticipation of the disgrace to our House!"

"Tsh," Cenebar replied calmly. I sensed his confidence; I saw no reason to share it. "I wish you wouldn't jump to conclusions before I'm finished, Jarad. First, Sira must fulfill her Choice, no matter how she managed to prevent this from happening up until now. A remarkable achievement, Sira."

"I had to protect Morgan—" I started to say, but Cenebar dismissed my interruption with a knowing look at my father.

"Sira's Power-of-Choice must finish its attempt to Join with the Human through the M'hir. Then, with the block restored, Sira's own trigger will automatically free her mind and restore its normal full function, including her memory. Truly an elegant solution," Cenebar directed this last at me, his green eyes calm and reassuring under their bushy brows.

I'd wanted help. I was being offered my worst fear instead. "What happens to Morgan, if this Joining you want takes place and restores me?" I demanded, eyeing them both. "I want to know what happens to him."

Before Cenebar could answer, my father stepped in quickly—too quickly, I thought. "Don't you want to be whole again, to consummate your Choice?"

"Not if Morgan is the price!" I sought some sign of understanding on their faces, knowing it was futile. "Morgan isn't Clan. What you're talking about has nothing to do with him. That place, the M'hir, how can he survive there!" I lowered my voice. "What Morgan feels isn't based on some outlandish instinct. He loves me." *Which is more than you do,* I finished to myself.

"How Human of him," Jarad said quite seriously, as if to remind me to pity lesser species. "However, your Joining with Morgan has been planned and must, according to Cenebar, take place. By Ossirus, you selected Morgan yourself—he was the only telepathic Human to satisfy your parameters!"

"My parameters?" I repeated. I didn't like the sound of that, or what Morgan might have to say about it either. I looked away from Jarad only to be confronted by Cenebar's well-ordered garden, seeing its straight unwavering rows as another barrier to making either of them listen to me.

Jarad tapped once, smartly, on the metal tabletop. Reluctantly, I looked at him again. "Why do you think you were taken to Auord, Sira?" he said. "Why do you think you felt compelled to avoid anyone but Morgan, to seek out only his ship, to stay with him. Those implanted thoughts were the guarantees that you'd meet. They were yours!"

"Mine." I remembered how hard I'd struggled to escape the compulsions, to gain my freedom. It would be really easy to hate Sira di Sarc.

"I'm sorry you've somehow become attached to this Human," Jarad continued. He hesitated, then went on more softly: "You know this experiment means nothing to me compared to your health and well-being—"

"Morgan means nothing to you," I said flatly. Or to *her,* I added to myself. That night on Acranam, when Morgan had told me of his fear that Sira di Sarc's true nature would be the greatest threat to us—he'd been more right than either of us could have known.

My father shrugged. "That is irrelevant. You must be restored. Council won't accept your refusal to Join the Human when it's the only way to restore your full capabilities. You've no protection, no rights, as long as you remain neither Chooser nor Chosen."

Ah. So this was the source of Faitlen's hidden menace. And I'd been wrong to think Jarad impervious; there was a grayness to the stern features, a hollow feel to his power. I probed: "Rael said only Morgan was in danger from the Council."

"Your sister knows nothing of these matters. None of this could go beyond Council without disastrous effects."

"Sira," Cenebar said earnestly, breaking the tension binding me to Jarad. "It took two planet years to persuade the Council to take your ideas seriously."

"What ideas?" This came out somewhat shrilly. *Patience,* I told myself. These were reasonably intelligent men. "You're talking to Sira *Morgan,* Hom di Teerac," I reminded him. "I don't have any ideas, remember?"

Jarad and Cenebar exchanged glances. Perhaps they exchanged more than that, for after a brief second, the healer nodded with visible reluctance. Jarad motioned me to remain seated, then came to stand beside me. Cenebar explained: "Jarad will grant you access to his memories of what has occurred, Sira. Will you accept his touch?"

I hesitated, but there was no real choice. I nodded, then closed my eyes, lowering only the outermost of my mental barriers. Instantly, information flooded my surface thoughts, information sorted and presented with an

unemotional clarity that helped me absorb it without the
numbing shock I should have felt.

I saw myself, my former self, through Jarad's eyes. I
didn't know the quiet, bookish scholar, but the face was
familiar enough, even viewed from his taller perspective.
The computer under her/my hands paraded numbers across
its surface. Jarad observed without bothering to understand. His daughter's passion for numbers, for the obscure
sciences of populations and growth, was too unClanlike to
be generally acceptable, but harmless. After all, her exile
might prove permanent; any hobby would help.

A hobby? During those long years, that Sira had focused on the study of her personal curse: the deadly nature of the so-called "Power-of-Choice" and its place in
the life history of the Clan. When her research had exhausted all of the information she could access about living members of the Clan, she had started her quest to see
the records from the Stratification and before.

It had taken two decades of argument and persuasion,
as well as the convenient death of the most opposed voice
on the Council, to crack open the wall of secrecy the
Council maintained "for the good of all." The Sira-I-had-
been had devoured the records, much of what she found
confirming the predictions from her calculations.

The Stratification itself had been a deliberate attempt to
separate those bearing the genetic code for entering the
M'hir from those who did not. The Clan had always had
Choosers and mental linkage between mated pairs before
maturation. But the new breed of Chooser whose abilities
were amplified through the M'hir were deadly to any but
others of the same ability. It hadn't taken long for all to
realize that candidates for the new Choosers had to be
preselected for their own safety.

That Sira had skimmed past the arguments and discussions about the why and how of the separation. What mattered to her was that the Stratification marked not social
change among the Clan, but a major force in its evolution
as a species. By dispersing the new Choosers and their
mates, now calling themselves the M'hiray, from the
Homeworld, a new, incompatible species had arisen—a
species whose fitness had yet to be proved by time.

Among the information the Council had deemed worth

carrying from Homeworld was a detailed geneology for every member of the Clan that had left during the Stratification. They'd been a treasure trove of information to explore.

More years passed as that Sira added all of her research into her population models. The results were alarming. The trend to greater power in Choosers in each successive generation had acted to narrow the number of suitable Choices. Added to this, the Clan had never been a particularly fertile species; families of three children were unusual. The power to manipulate the M'hir was becoming concentrated: pooling in fewer, though stronger individuals, with the remainder of the population excluded from bearing children. Council policies regarding Choice and reproduction had only accelerated the process. And this process had one inevitable ending.

Sira dared to make that dreadful conclusion. Not only was there a theoretical limit to how much breeding for power within the M'hir the M'hiray could tolerate and remain viable, but this limit had already been reached. Her existence—my existence—was more than a warning. A Chooser who could not find a mate was the first step on a downward spiral of population decline. There was no escape. The crash was inevitable and the M'hiray was a doomed experiment, not a new species.

Or was it inevitable? This other me had also proposed a solution. Bring the unusable Choosers into the breeding pool. A return to the old ways, of Choosers assessing every unChosen male, was more than unthinkable: at best, it could only slow the decline, and at a cost too terrible to consider by a sentient species.

A dramatic new approach was needed and that Sira naively believed she had one: hybridize with a compatible telepathic humanoid species, Humans themselves perhaps or any species without the Power-of-Choice. The most favorable outcome could be a new race, retaining M'hiray ability to use the M'hir, but freed at last from the deadly consequences of Choice.

At worst, a means might have been found to bring Choosers to Commencement without costing more M'hiray lives. Before Stratification, there had been Commencement without Joining, Clan mates who knew each other only through reality and not through the M'hir. A scandalous, heretical thought to the M'hiray. But in the name of survival, the dwindling numbers could be offset by new breeders, Commenced by contact with aliens, breeders who would hold off the end of their species until a better, more lasting solution could be found. At the very least, the mothers and their offspring could continue to enhance the M'hir for the remaining M'hiray.

I was able to learn all this with remarkable objectivity. Indeed, I found it impossible to identify myself at all with the cold analytical mind Jarad remembered for me; I'd never been this woman who almost casually predicted the death of her kind, and as easily, suggested the potential deaths of others as a solution. Had that Sira been isolated so long that people marched in her mind like those numbers on the screen?

While that Sira went on to other concerns, minds accustomed to action and control began to worry away at her pronouncement of doom. She was believed by, or at least made uneasy, enough of those on the Council to set in motion a test of her proposed solution. And who better than the daughter of di Sarc?

But never to interbreed with another species—that heresy was too much for any of them. The Choice offered would be in the ancient manner. Knowing I would kill them, Council still suggested I be exposed to any and all unChosen males, one after another if necessary, in hopes of inducing Commencement. Once Commenced, Sira di Sarc would at least be physically capable of bearing young. Her incredible strength must not be lost from the M'hiray.

And the drive of the Power-of-Choice for a Joining through the M'hir? The Council proposal rushed from Jarad's emotionless and clear memory, to the horror-filled turmoil of my own. An erased mind can't heed the dictates of Choice.

My father had had barely enough warning. He'd come to her—to me—determined to outmaneuver his fellow Councillors and their plan. Together, he and that Sira selected a promising Human telepath, Morgan of Karolus. Then, to lessen the effects of training and prejudice, as well as to protect any unChosen she might meet by accident, Sira ruthlessly suppressed her power and memory beyond normal stasis—aided in the final stages by Jarad and Cenebar.

Suicide with no certainty of resurrection, I judged it, wondering if I could have made that choice.

A touch of the past—Jarad's, not mine: Barac, delicately probed for information; a programmed mob of overzealous cutthroats, intended to separate me from Barac's guardianship. And a last image of myself through Jarad's eyes: my face holding only a faint puzzling at the sound of thunder in the night air.

"I had to inform Council, once you were safely away, Sira," Jarad took up aloud. "Though displeased enough to bar me from the chambers, they were willing to await your return." Jarad stroked my hair again gently, thoughtfully. "But you must understand, Sira, that unless your mission turns out to be totally successful, they will order you erased and mated to their selection. You need Morgan. You must finish what you've begun."

* * *

INTERLUDE

"I don't like this," Huido grumbled, eyes close to tangling in their effort to scan every direction at once.

"You have received clearance for lift, Homs," the servo-gatekeeper repeated for the third time, a suspicious rise in volume suggesting an unmachinelike impatience.

"There they are," Morgan charged forward, snatching the proferred clearance disk from the machine's appendage and hurrying through the gateway. "Come on!"

The Carasian rocked his wide head in a shrug and followed the smaller Human. The being in line behind the alien moved up with an audible sigh of relief.

"I don't like this," Huido repeated when he caught up to Morgan. The Human was dodging through the crowd entering the spaceport terminal. The Carasian's path opened automatically as passersby registered his natural armament. "How do we know who's who?" Huido continued plaintively, eyes spread apart in a futile attempt to watch every face they passed. "Camos could be swarming with them. The grist is overwhelming. Can you tell Clan from Human?"

Morgan had stopped in the eddy between the main doorways. "Not unless I use power—which would gain us a quick and not so pleasant welcome. We'd best stay as inconspicuous as possible, old friend. No unnecessary inquiries—and no door-knocking. Barac will lead us where we must go." Cautiously, Morgan peered out, then signaled Huido to follow behind as the Human darted to the line of waiting transports.

An endless stream of vehicles was landing, disgorging passengers, and taking off with new fares. "There," Morgan said grimly, pointing to a transport just airborne. "And here we part. Take the clearance, and keep the *Fox* ready, Brother." There was time for no more than Huido's quick assent before Morgan pushed his way into the next-in-line transport and took off in pursuit.

Chapter 35

I WAS making some progress in the restoration of Sira di Sarc, despite the fact that I didn't like her. I'd begun to feel at home in my rooms, more a sense of comfort and knowing what was behind cupboards than really remembering. Unfortunately, every step closer to my former self pushed Sira Morgan further away, into some place that hurt when I probed it.

Like now. I tightened my arms around Rael again briefly, breathed in her clean warmth, truly glad to see her. It wasn't something Sira Morgan would have done. Rael pressed her cheek to my hair, her power enveloping us both for a moment, cutting off the world. More to the point, she deliberately excluded our father who stood to one side.

Morgan's safe, sister, her mental voice said, warm and comforting. *I kept my promise.*

I pulled away, turning to Jarad. "Morgan's gone, Father."

Rael looked aghast. "Sira!" She whirled on Jarad, taking visible notice of him for the first time since her appearance in the main room of my chambers moments before. "What have you done to Sira? I warn you, I won't stand by and—"

"Silence." Jarad looked more weary than angered. "Sira's attachment to the Human remains intact—just as when it convinced you to interfere with the will of Council. Regrettable, but true."

"They want me to find Morgan and bring him to Camos, Rael," I said. "Morgan holds the key to releasing my memory."

"And her power," Jarad growled. "Without Morgan,

there's no way to repair Sira's mind. If she remains this half-thing, she'll be erased by Council decree."

Rael looked from one to the other of us. "Erased? What in Seventeen Hells for?"

I seesawed for a moment between laughter and a curse of my own. "It seems, my dear sister," I explained, choosing neither, "that I was supposed to produce a fully Commenced and Chosen Sira upon my triumphant return from this adventure. Even if a Human were the Choice!"

"But why . . ." Rael's voice cracked. On her face, disgust warred with horror. Disgust won. "Council wants to bypass the Power-of-Choice," she whispered. "They hoped a Choice made with a Human—" her lips twisted around the word, "that such a Choice would induce Commencement without the linkage of a true Joining. But what if that hasn't happened? What if you're unable to— if you can't—" she turned red and stopped.

I politely filled the ensuing silence, since my father didn't appear interested in doing so. "The Council will eliminate the dangers of Choice by simply eliminating the Choosers. Of course, that means they need some way to retain the power contained in the Choosers' genes. Oh, Yihtor had the right idea."

Rael turned to our father. "Stop this!"

Jarad spread his hands helplessly. "I carry no other Councillors with me anymore. Sira's calculations have sent them scurrying for any shelter, any reprieve, no matter how repugnant. I can't influence or change their will in this."

"It doesn't help that there are no Choosers on Council," Rael spat almost viciously. "And as for your influence on Council, Jarad, how was it used seventy years ago when your firstborn was ordered imprisoned? What are you going to do this time except grovel?"

"You're unfair, Rael," I objected, having decided it was time to step in. Their feuding made me feel responsible, as if I'd once had a role in soothing their anger; I no longer knew how. "I'd have been erased already if it hadn't been for Jarad."

"Where is the Human?" Jarad demanded impatiently.

Before Rael could object, I spread my hands pleadingly. "Where is he?"

"Halfway to Deneb, maybe," she said with a sigh, drop-

ping into the nearest easi-rest. "Or halfway to anywhere."
Jarad took a seat also, the physical signs of a truce reflected in the mutual subsidence of their power.

"Sira, you must summon the Human now," Jarad's
voice was grim. I blinked, then regarded him narrowly.

"You heard Rael—"

Jarad looked exasperated. "You say this Human has
feelings for you. Humans are not rational thinkers, Daughters. I find it difficult to imagine him leaving Camos without making some attempt to see Sira."

Rael and I exchanged quick looks. There was enough
doubt on her face to arouse some in my own mind. Morgan's capitulation really wasn't in character. The only
surprise was that my father had seen what I should have
known.

"If I agree to contact him," I said, counting each "if" on
my fingers. "If Morgan is still on Camos; if he's willing
to come. Then what happens to him when he does?"
There was no answer from either of them, but the regret-
ful look in Rael's expression told me enough. I shook my
head slowly. "No. I have a better idea. Help me leave
Camos."

"You must reconsider, Sira." Jarad let me feel the pain
under his firmness. He leaned forward, liquid eyes pleading. "Your mind is in such a shambles now even the most
reluctant Councillor will be able to justify whatever they
plan. Your affection for this alien can only harm you."

"So I must use Morgan as they would use me?" I countered. "Why can't you understand one's as bad as the
other?"

Rael threw up her hands. "I've had my fill of arguing
with this Sira, Jarad. You know the defenses on Camos.
Can we get her offworld?"

Jarad's lips tightened and there was a heaviness to his
power. "Camos is our center. The M'hir dips deepest here
to form what we are—here the M'hir is watched at all
times. I'll help," he added quickly, forestalling Rael's
outburst. "I'll share your fate before condoning it with my
silence." I was uneasily aware of Rael's skeptical silence.

Our plotting began and ended in the same instant.
There was a sudden tug in my mind. A quick glance at my
father showed he felt it, too; the grim set to his face only

too revealing. I didn't need him to explain that Council had convened and that we were feeling its summons.

Where was Morgan? I was glad he was out of danger—that I'd been able to resist calling him back to Camos. Well, part of me was glad. The rest wished desperately to go to him, wherever he was, regardless of who or what would follow.

* * *

INTERLUDE

A final leafy branch hid the last traces of the rented aircar. Morgan eyed his handiwork critically. He had little hope of leaving as easily as he'd come. The hidden machine might make a difference, even against the Clan.

He turned and headed upslope, making his way cautiously but quickly through the bands of ornamental shrubs which encircled the busy scene below. The Human paused in the shelter of a clump of fruit-laden trees. The large ornate building before him, abuzz with activity on the ground and in the air, was nothing less than the Human government seat for the Camos Cluster.

Morgan checked the homing device in his belt and was reassured by its strong pulse. He was very close to Barac and so to Yihtor, but what were they doing here of all places on the planet? The government of Camos was Human. Why did the Clan come here? His mouth tightened in a thin line as he considered the possibilities. Bowman would be very interested.

But the only way to solve the riddle was to mix with the crowd. Morgan smoothed his dress tunic almost as carefully as he checked his mental shielding. Then he stepped nonchalantly onto the cream-colored pavement, immediately becoming lost in a stream of pedestrians.

Chapter 36

STEPPING off a cliff would be easier, I thought, staring from the windowless entrance chamber into the Council Chamber itself. Under my feet was a solid floor. Ahead was something perspectiveless, shifting, the only solid focus being a dais with seven hooded figures. The hall somehow existed both in the M'hir and in real time. The power needed to balance that existence was expended with a casualness even more intimidating than the fact.

I took the necessary first step, trusting my foot would find something solid under that whirling play of color, using my own awareness of myself within the M'hir—and a dose of healthy fear—to keep myself anchored.

Among those waiting, an indistinct head nodded slowly. I took another step forward. Then layer upon layer of anxiety and fear gently peeled away from me like pieces of too-tight clothing.

There was a welcoming here, a warmth that disarmed . . .

. . . until I found I had accepted betrayal without protest. Band upon band of unseen restraint enclosed me abruptly, tightening its hold upon my mind until my steps faltered and stopped. A cold wave of hostility flushed the last remnants of the soothing welcome from my thoughts. Lights brightened above the Councillors, whitening their robes to a harsh brilliance. The shifting boundaries of the hall solidified into real walls, ceiling, and floor. The magic was gone. It had, I told myself bitterly, never existed.

"Offspring of di Sarc. The not-Chosen." I couldn't decide which of the still faceless Councillors made the acknowledgment—or wasn't it more of an accusation?

I knew my father had followed me and now stood as

paralyzed as I did. Subtly, a pressure eased and I found I could speak. "You know me," I said. "Who—"

A different voice, deeper, broke across my words. "Answer our questions, not-Chosen. We have not yet decided as to your right to question us." There was a placating note to this voice, a humoring that sent a thrill of fear rippling through me. I'd been trapped so easily by their combined strength; they controlled me despite the power I was supposed to command.

The message under the voices was clear: I was theirs to deal with and there had never really been any doubt as to the outcome of this meeting.

"Ask your questions," I said finally, firmly enough. There was certainly no point in inviting any more drastic form of inquiry.

"Why did you refuse the Choice offered by Yihtor, son of Lorimar and Caraat?" a third voice asked.

A betraying heat warmed my cheeks. "Choice is my right! I didn't have to accept him."

Two hooded heads conferred noiselessly, then the one on the right seemed to look at me. "We rephrase the question, daughter of di Sarc. *How* were you able to refuse the Choice offered by Yihtor?"

Yawning open before me was the abyss Barac and Rael had feared. How ironic to know I'd designed the trap for myself. I wished fiercely to be able to move, if only to make a rude gesture, but my body was merely a sense of weight. "If you know to ask the question, you know the answer!" I responded furiously.

"Let's say we *suspect* the truth, not-Chosen," the first speaker said coldly. "Would you accept this Choice now?" Two figures appeared on the dais to one side of the row of seated Councillors. Barac's eyes widened slightly at the sight of me. My attention was on Yihtor. Why didn't he look at me? In fact, he seemed oblivious to everything, including his surroundings.

I didn't need the Councillor's gesture toward Yihtor, or Barac's immediate loss of color to understand the net the Council was weaving.

"You don't care if I kill either of them, do you?" I looked at my former foe, now seated on the floor, trapped as tightly as I was in their plotting.

"The House of sud Sarc would be lessened by Barac's

loss. He has learned to use his power well—if at times willfully."

I wasn't sure if this was as callous as it sounded, or merely the height of praise from one Clan to another. Could power and its use really be all they cared about in someone?

"What about him?" I said, unable to point at Yihtor, equally unable to explain the slack-mouthed expression on the renegade's handsome face.

"We value individuality. But we do not tolerate rebellion," explained the deep voice, still in that humoring tone. "This was once Yihtor di Caraat. His House is exiled. His mind has been dissolved within the M'hir. So you needn't waste your pity, not-Chosen. There is nothing in this shell to die under your power."

"There's nothing left to Choose, then," I said slowly, knowing deep within I was right. "You can't force me to release the Power-of-Choice."

"We're wasting time!" The robbed figure at one end of the row stood up, throwing his hood to the floor at my feet. Faitlen's face was fixed in a scowl. "Why argue with the pathetic remnants of her mind? We know what must be done. This talk, talk, talk is unnecessary." A toadlike figure materialized beside him, cloaked in mud gray. From the sudden rigidity of the rest of the Councillors, the identity of the widemouthed Retian was not unknown to them.

A voice from behind me, rough with emotion: "Remove your creature from our Council, Faitlen! Have you no decency!"

Faitlen leaped upon my father's words with obvious delight. "Who are you to dictate to Council, Jarad? Be glad we don't choose to punish you for daring to interfere with our great purpose!"

"Enough!" The centermost figure rose, removing his own hood and gesturing to the remaining Councillors to copy the move. No face was familiar to my blocked memory. No face looked other than determined, though to their credit most seemed uncomfortable. "You'll accord the House of di Sarc the courtesy due its power and lineage, Faitlen, or find yourself on the Contest Floor." A pause during which only Barac met my eyes; he was afraid, too, but I could see most of it was for me, not of me. I smiled at him, hoping he knew I understood.

"Jarad, we share your feelings. But what must be done shall be done. You're free to leave if you wish." There was an ominous tightening of the unseen bonds. "If you stay, we will tolerate no interference."

"I'll stay, Sawnda'at," my father's voice was thick but firm. "And record for all time the infamy you and your so-called 'Council' intend."

"Infamy?" repeated a dark-haired Clanswoman with features hauntingly like Enora's. "Are you equally prepared to witness our salvation, Jarad? We must gain control over the Power-of-Choice and over the destiny of our species. Don't you—"

"I thought you had questions for me, Councillors," I said flatly, repulsed. "If not, then I agree with Faitlen. This is becoming a game, and only you know the rules." For some reason, my gaze slid back to Barac's pale and troubled face. This chamber was no place to attempt mind-speech, but I thought there was some urgent message in his eyes.

Sawnda'at spoke as if repeating a lesson, his face donning a remote mask. "Sira di Sarc, we will not condone any further perversion. That your experiment was successful in initiating Commencement has absolved you and your kin from punishment, although you knowingly flouted the Prime Laws which guard our kind and the M'hir from alien contamination. The Human, Morgan, will be caught and his knowledge of us erased—as should have been done long before now." He pointedly refrained from looking at Barac.

Morgan. His name dropped so casually from the Clansman's lips sent an almost physical shock through me. How dare they try to make Morgan pay for their mistakes? I was no less to blame, I thought bitterly. What Morgan knew made him a danger, a source of humiliation, a potential threat that could ignite the vast numbers of his race against the powerful but scattered Clan.

I was Sira Morgan, not Sira di Sarc of the Clan. The price of being both was too high. I began to test the strength of the paralysis that held me.

"Sira di Sarc," Sawnda'at continued, "You will Join with our Choice for you, since you yourself are neither

Chosen nor unChosen. Following a successful Joining and pairing, you will be free to continue your life as a Chosen, no longer bound save by the Prime Law."

I'd have liked to raise an eyebrow at this, but had to settle for a cough. "Who have you *chosen* for me, may I ask?"

Faitlen vanished from his seat on the dais to rematerialize before me, but his attention was all for my imprisoned father. The triumph painted on his sly features was more than I could stand to watch, and I looked past his sneer to gaze sadly at Barac. I avoided Yithor's empty, drooling face.

Sawnda'at's voice was crisp. "We hope to salvage the power of Caraat's lineage as well as yours." Yihtor, of course. I didn't need to hear Barac's curse or to see Faitlen's taunting smile. "If the attempt is unsuccessful, Barac sud Sarc will be granted candidacy."

I raised my eyes to the remaining Council members and surveyed them one by one. Then I drew my eyes back to Sawnda'at. "I'd prefer the truth, Clansman, not more lies to grant you an easy conscience. Even I know Joining isn't possible with the mindless; perhaps the Power-of-Choice can't destroy him, but it would rebound and destroy me. If you're changing your own laws, at least admit it."

A Councillor who'd been silent until now broke the heavy silence that followed my accusation. "We are indeed changing the old Prime Laws." His voice shook, but a hint of strength underscored the words. "We intend to save your inheritance, Sira di Sarc, your progeny and *their* power, since, regrettably, we can no longer save you." He gestured toward the Retian. "Baltir's people have possessed the necessary technology for many years. He assures us he can provide a fruitful pairing."

I strained to move my hand. Had a finger responded? I wasn't sure. Barac smiled at me, a resigned look-what-you've-got-us-into-now smile. "How fortunate for you I was able to provide you with the perfect candidate." My voice dripped with acid. "But you'll need more than that!"

The necessary path was ready, I'd prepared it what seemed another lifetime ago on Acranam. I poured all of my available strength into its protection. Faitlen's smile faded and he looked to the rest of the Council with comical dismay.

"She prepares herself for self-death—" he began. Baltir, who had been a silent spectator, smiled, quite an impressive grimace on a face that was more than half mouth.

"Death is no obstacle," he said, his voice accentless and more precise than any Retian of my acquaintance. "In many ways, it makes things simpler."

A storm struck the interior of the chamber and sent the walls whirling away. Reality exploded into the M'hir. Reds, blacks, all the colors of rage and destruction blocked my vision. I fell to my knees as the restraint snapped. Deafened by sound more in my mind than without, I covered my head and tried to sense what was happening.

Jarad. Somehow in the whirlpool surrounding me I felt my father as a point of force. And a focus of all other forces. A hand grasped my arm, a physical contact pulling me up and dragging me through the maelstrom. I resisted, heard Barac's hoarse voice in my ear: "He buys us time, Cousin. Hurry."

How Barac knew where to go, I couldn't imagine. Certainly vision was useless in the play of illusion and reality warping the hall and adjoining chambers. Perhaps my father guided us. Perhaps he had deliberately chosen this type of contest in order to cover our escape.

Whatever the truth, I sobbed as I ran. Even without full memory, I knew the extent of my loss as the conflict behind us settled into an exhausted, ominous calm.

Chapter 37

BARAC didn't care for our current refuge; I thought it wasn't so bad, but kept my opinion to myself. We were in some sort of maintenance tunnel that twisted like an intestine through the depths of the complex. I liked the ship-like closeness of the walls and ceiling; the metal and oil tang to the air was comforting.

Barac shuddered again.

"We've got to keep moving." His shields were up, but some of his desperation spilled over. I nodded and stood.

"When can we use the M'hir?" I asked, making an effort to be helpful.

"Not here. The Council—" Barac's eyes were white-rimmed; his skin gleamed with sweat even though the air down here was chilled. I saw that his arrogance was gone, probably with it his confidence and faith in his own kind. The last hours had shaken loose everything he believed.

I was much better off, having lost nothing. No, I corrected myself guiltily. I'd lost a father. "The Council may be exhausted," Barac continued more calmly, "but there will be Watchers touching the M'hir, waiting for any disturbance or movement. Our only hope is to reach the Human portion of the building, wherever that is, and find some way through to it," he stopped, looking a bit more like himself, and shrugged. "Actually, there's no hope. I'd be lying to say there was."

"I don't need any hope, Barac." I tapped my fingers on a pipe, wondering how I could continue to feel this burning impatience when I was so physically and emotionally drained. "I'd be satisfied with a blaster like Morgan's."

"Would Morgan himself do?" An incredibly grimy head poked out from a crawl space, the covering grate falling to the floor with a clatter. Barac said something incoherent, rushing to help the Human wriggle his way out.

I stood, frozen with surprise as Morgan shook himself, dust flying from him in choking clouds. His hair was crowned with cobwebs. "Don't they clean in there?" I said at last, stepping back to avoid breathing the stuff.

"Guess not. It's an odd system, that's for sure," he muttered. The dust settled. His clear blue eyes met and kept mine. "Why didn't you say good-bye?"

"Good-bye?" I repeated, fighting to control my temper as well as the inner darkness that had begun squirming with need at his closeness. "I've been trying to save your life."

Morgan nodded a welcome to Barac before raising a brow at me. "Who needs saving at the moment?"

I brushed my hand over my eyes, behind the momentary blindness trying to sort out which of several conflicting feelings was closest to threatening my control. The effort was futile. I smothered them all and sat back down on the orange curl of pipe, moving my feet in time to allow one of the countless tiny cleaning servos to pass underneath. Where were rats when you needed to kick something? "I'd like to be glad to see you," I said. "But you've made a terrible mistake coming here."

"The Council's behind it all, Morgan," Barac explained bitterly, a bruised look to his eyes. "Rael and I were fools to think we'd find help for Sira here. All we found was death."

"Death?"

"Sira's father bought us time to escape with his life," Barac said when I didn't bother answering. "But if we don't leave Camos, now, his death will have been for nothing."

"All right," Morgan said. "Let's go, then."

I shook my head. "No," I said. "I won't leave. Not yet."

"Why?" This frantic and quick from Barac; Morgan allowed only curiosity to touch his eyes.

"You don't know the truth."

"There's no time—"

"It won't take long, Barac." I looked at Morgan, thinking each word out carefully; Barac was right, there wasn't any time to waste. But how could I take another step without telling them, telling him, what I was? That knowledge had crusted like a scab within my mind, the kind of scab you can't help but bump with every movement. "You've helped me because you think I'm the victim," I began. "You're wrong."

The pain of it burned away in me, hollowing my insides as I went on, listening to my own voice. I told them all of it, everything I'd learned from Jarad and Cenebar, everything I knew about the Council's purpose—and Sira di Sarc's. Barac, nervously watching the tunnel's entrance, slowly moved back toward me until, by the time I'd finished, he stood beside Morgan and stared at me. I looked only into Morgan's blue eyes.

I stopped at the end, which was almost the present, and waited for Morgan's judgment. The pain was almost gone. For that alone, it was worth whatever they now thought of me.

"You. You planned this!?" Barac spoke first, struggling to keep a note of accusation from his voice but failing. "You used me. You planned to break the Prime Law and you used me to help!"

Odd to defend the actions and motives of that other Sira. "Yes," I said. "But if I hadn't, the Council would have broken it their way—and at what consequence to me?"

"What of the consequence to Morgan?" Part of me cowered away from Barac's angry question; part of me echoed it. I couldn't speak. Something flickered in Morgan's blue eyes that I was amazed to recognize as amusement.

"Nice to have you on my side for once, Barac."

Barac looked startled, then shrugged it off with a shade of his old arrogance. "Don't get used to it, Human." Then to me, almost with revulsion: "What I can't believe is that you think you can justify what you tried to do—"

"What who tried to do, Barac?" Morgan interrupted, his eyes never leaving me. "I see two Siras here. Neither has to be justified."

"Barac's right. I planned—" I began, somewhat annoyed that he'd missed the point.

Morgan raised his hand to silence me, a gentle gesture.

"Neither one," Morgan repeated more softly. "Sira Morgan was born on Auord and has no part in this. The other? How can we judge Sira di Sarc? How can we imagine what it was like for her in exile? Could you, Barac, have smothered your own power and self to avoid hurting others? Could you have offered to undergo the most intimate act possible between two beings with a stranger, worse, a despised alien, having no idea of the outcome?" Mind-speech, warm and rich with emotion, filled my thoughts. *We can't change the past, Sira, but we can say we're done with it and go on. Please.*

I held myself stiff and unyielding. There was more to deal with than the past. Morgan's eyes narrowed. "Not done, after all," he said aloud. "What else, Clanswoman?" This finally with a touch of impatience.

"Nothing that can't wait, Morgan." I summoned all the earnestness I possessed. "If you can split me into different people and fates, so can I—for now. Both of me would like to survive."

Morgan brushed dirt from his coveralls then jerked a thumb at the small portal through which he had arrived. "I do know one tried-and-true escape route, if not where we are at the moment. From the looks of the system, whoever built this ductwork forgot it was there." He paused. "I take it you can't just go *poof.*"

"There are guards against using the power here, Morgan." Barac frowned. "But how did you find us without alerting the Watchers?"

Morgan shook his head sadly, then reached up to tug at the back of Barac's collar. "When will you listen to all my good advice, Clansman?" he chided. A tiny device shone dully between slim brown fingers.

Barac's astonished curse was enough to make me chuckle, but the sound was somehow harsh and I closed my lips over it. Morgan stored the device in a pocket on his belt before coming to me and reaching down a hand. I moved past it to press my face against his chest, extending my senses to encompass his breathing, the coursing of his blood, his determination, his caring. Only for a second.

A tendril of my hair lingered on his shoulder as I drew back and waved him onward.

Chapter 38

"STOP kicking it in my face!" Barac's rather frayed temper made his voice from behind me louder than was safe.

I stopped crawling long enough to whisper: "It's no better up here, Barac. Keep your voice down or we'll have more to worry about." The brightening within the duct was warning enough; we were passing another access point.

As before, I curbed my impatience and watched the silhouette ahead. Morgan snapped off his tiny, and to be frank, rather useless light. But this time he stopped and peered cautiously through the grating. I tapped his leg. In answer, the tiny light flashed on for a second to show me a cross scratched above the metal-clad opening.

There was a delay that gave every sore muscle in my back time to stab at me. At least my nose had stopped begging to sneeze. I didn't bother to complain; the other two must feel the same after our long journey on hands and knees. In one or two places, we'd had to lie flat and squirm around bends; I'd left a fair bit of skin behind. At junctions, where the sudden splitting of the duct into two or four would have left Barac and me hopelessly lost in the labyrinth, Morgan searched for his mark and led the way.

I grinned, feeling the grime crack on my face. He might be stubborn, but my Morgan possessed some admirable and unusual skills. His past would make very interesting conversation, granted that we survived to enjoy it.

Morgan hammered loose the finely woven grating. It fell away from the duct with a dreadful screech of sound.

I squinted in the sudden light. A hand shoved at my back as Barac practically threw me after Morgan and out of the duct.

"What do you—" I sputtered angrily at my cousin, only to burst out laughing at the gray apparition slithering out of the wall. Morgan chuckled.

"There are some odds and ends. It's better than walking around like this." Morgan pointed toward one corner of the room, which was more like a closet. Barac and I had to be careful of our elbows as well as a stack of cleaning tools as we rummaged through a basket of laundry, searching for the cleanest of the dirty coveralls. Morgan slipped off his own outer gear; underneath, his dress tunic was dust-free, if somewhat rumpled.

Moments later, and slightly cleaner, for there had been a low sink in another corner, I shook out my hair and was relieved to discover that it repelled most of the dust. Barac sneezed and glared at me. He'd put on some coveralls that more or less fit and was holding a sweeper—whether to add to his disguise or as an unlikely weapon, I wasn't sure. Sometimes it worked. I tied on a wraparound apron affair, trying not to notice the wads of lint clinging to my legs.

Once out of the closet, we found ourselves walking through corridors full of people, some hurrying as though their plas notes would melt, others taking their time and chatting like birds in a tree. I had the peculiar feeling the three of us were alone, all the people around us only existing for decoration, a disguise for the reality of the Clan and its ruling Council.

There were guards, Human, I hoped, at every junction and lift. "Was there this much security when you entered?" I asked.

Morgan shook his head, frowning slightly. "No. And I don't like the look of it. How many of these people are involved with the Clan, Barac?"

"None." Barac's surprise seemed genuine. "On Camos, we use Humans as camouflage; what good would they be if they knew of us? You're the only Human who knows the Council Chamber is in this building; barely a handful of your kind even know the Council exists."

"If you believe that, Barac, you're a fool," I said. "Care to bet there are Humans here who don't remember how deep the basement is, or how many floors they built, or where the ductwork really goes? How about the Humans in charge of climate control and ventilation? I'll take money, Cousin, that discrepancies here are conveniently forgotten. And you know who's best at that!"

"I have to agree with Sira," Morgan said, checking his chronometer. "The Clan could use these people against us—"

Barac thumped the floor with the sweeper, attracting attention. He smiled apologetically to onlookers, who shrugged and passed by. "The Clan doesn't need Humans to handle its problems," he hissed.

"Let's hope so," I said, sidestepping to avoid being stepped on by a preoccupied office worker. There must be thousands in the building. I could imagine them boiling over us in Clan-induced rage, like ants ripping apart crumbs. Silly notion, or was it? "How much farther to the exit—and your aircar, Morgan?"

A gesture ahead. "That doorway leads to the main reception area." The passage Morgan indicated was blocked by a gate, overlooked in turn by a pair of servos; even more threatening were the armed guards beyond. Morgan gave my arm a gentle shake. "Not to worry, Sira," he whispered cheerfully. "They're guarding against illegal entries—not exits."

"Then how did you get in?" Barac growled pointedly, dropping his sweeper behind a nearby planter and dusting his clothes once more. Morgan just smiled and led the way confidently. There was no choice but to trust his judgment, something I was sure Barac disliked intensely.

The moment we stepped between the servos, a soft bell rang, instantly making us the focus of attention. I was unpleasantly aware of the odd trio we formed. Morgan forestalled the approach of the guards by reaching into a pocket and drawing forth a striped card for the servos' inspection. A series of satisfied clicks and the gate opened.

"Where did you get—" Barac's question was cut off as one of the guards turned to watch us.

"Later," Morgan promised in a whisper. I began to breathe again as we made our way alongside the massive upward sweep of stairs that formed the core of the entrance hall. The rest of the room was equally impressive, with gleaming stone floors inset with designs and raised plantings of flowering shrubs. The murmur of voices was almost lost in the skyward-soaring ceiling. I craned my neck around and could barely make out the point at which the coil of inward-directed balconies ended.

People, Human and a few definitely non-Human, were everywhere. Small groups, possibly waiting to present their views to the local government, gathered around the base of the stairs; a couple of the more vocal clusters were being watched closely by security personnel. "There's our way out," Morgan said quite unnecessarily. No one could miss the row of sun-streaked doors along one wall. The constant swing-whoosh of their opening and closing sounded like breathing.

We'd barely started our walk out into the open when Morgan pulled me back into the shelter of the stair wall. Barac followed, looking nervously around for whatever had alarmed Morgan. "Trouble coming," Morgan said by way of explanation, but with a puzzled look in his eyes as he, too, searched our surroundings.

Barac hesitated, then closed his eyes tightly. "Yes," he said an instant later, glancing at the Human with a mix of disapproval and respect. "I taste it, too."

Obviously this wasn't part of my Talent, for I felt nothing unusual. Yet, perhaps in part due to their warning, I was alert enough to act immediately when the itching began in my mind. Someone was trying to pull us into the M'hir, to take us away from here. I resisted, somehow held us—more exactly, I continuously relocated us where we were. Barac's disciplined strength joined mine when, without thinking, I reached out and clutched his shoulder. Then I think I called: "Jason!" Raw power flowed to me through the grip of his hand, given without constraint.

I wasn't sure how long that battle lasted, if a battle it could be called. When the force trying to *push* us somewhere else ceased and I opened my eyes, I found to my dismay that it had been at least long enough to attract a curious crowd, including guards. One of them stepped forward cautiously, with the air of one who prepared to humor yet another group of oddities. The other guards began dispersing the spectators.

"Do you people need some help here?" The question was asked gruffly and certainly with the hope that we would rapidly take our eccentricities away from his post. I smiled at the ordinariness of it. Then my smile died.

A familiar figure had appeared behind the officer, pushing forward among the now saluting and respectful guards to stand before us. I heard Barac gasp.

"I'll handle this, Lieutenant," Jarad di Sarc said commandingly.

"Certainly, Lord Jarad," the officer said with barely hidden relief. I stared at my dead father, unwilling to believe the evidence of my senses, and equally unwilling to believe what it meant. "You must be Captain Morgan," Jarad said without ever meeting my eyes. "I've been expecting you."

I reached a hand to Morgan's; this time not for comfort or help, but for my father to see. I felt Morgan's wariness, knew he looked at me. "Stay away from him," I said, fear making my voice loud in the silence.

"Speak with respect to His Lordship," the lieutenant objected. Jarad waved one hand.

"My daughter, Lieutenant. Now, please clear this crowd. In fact, please clear this entire area."

"That isn't necessary, Jarad," I said quickly. "We were just leaving."

Jarad was unaffected by my feeble protest. The guards began to pull back. I readied my defenses, however futile they'd proved before, and felt Barac and Morgan do the same. Time was suspended as I searched Jarad's implacable face and tried without success to understand him. "You asked me to trust you," I said at last.

Jarad looked at me for the first time, his expression calm and detached. "I regret the deception, but it was necessary. You aren't responsible for your actions, dear daughter. Just like your mother. But this isn't the place for a discussion—there are too many ears."

"Doesn't bother me, di Sarc," the crisp statement made us all turn to look up at the staircase in surprise. Armed Enforcers in full uniform lined the banister for one full swing of the spiral. Morgan nodded a greeting to Commander Bowman as she came down to our level. "But I will agree that those not involved can go." Her smile was pleasant; the intensity of her bright eyes was anything but. Terk and a feathered creature stood at her back.

The Camosian lieutenant hesitated then backed away, signaling his underlings to continue moving spectators out of the hall. Jarad was speechless. Before he could recover the use of his tongue, Morgan stepped forward to take Bowman's hand in a quick clasp. "Cut it a trifle fine, Commander?" I heard him say under his breath. Bowman smiled thinly.

"We're here to protect your rights as a Sapient, Captain Morgan. Not to mention investigate your claim of Clan interference with Trading Pact species on this world."

"You're not authorized to interfere with me!" Jarad had recovered his voice, and backed his objection with a flare of power that made me wince. The Enforcers were unaffected; I looked at them with sudden interest. From the flicker of dismay in Jarad's eyes, I decided he wasn't used to this either.

"You're wrong, Lord Jarad. I'm fully authorized to interfere when Clan affairs spill over into the lives of other species." Bowman wasn't the least intimidated. "Your people may scorn civilized alliances but you'll not be allowed to abuse ours."

Suddenly Jarad was flanked by seven white-robed figures, grim and silent. Overhead, along the banister, there was a series of soft clicks as weapons were raised, and aimed. But it was Morgan who spoke next. "No one wants a confrontation, Lord Jarad."

"You would lose," my father said. "Despite your toys."

Morgan shrugged coolly. "Here and now, perhaps. But is it worth what you'd be starting?"

"What do you suggest, Human?" Sawnda'at demanded scornfully. "That we give up the work of generations, that we abandon the precious daughter of di Sarc to life as less than she was?"

"No. But I won't let you destroy her. There must be some solution we can all accept." I looked at Morgan out of the corner of my eye, uneasy for a different reason. He was plotting again.

Jarad smiled and bowed his head slightly. "I'm gratified by your concern for Sira, Human. You'll be the first to agree then that we must finish what has begun for her sake—"

"Leave Morgan out of this," I warned Jarad, taking a step forward. Morgan gripped my arm, pulling me roughly around to face him. I saw sudden comprehension widen his eyes.

"So. No wonder you didn't tell me. They want you to finalize your Choice, don't they? With me."

The Councillors, Barac, the enforcers were unimportant; it was as if Morgan and I were alone. I sighed. "Yes, that's what they want. You removed some key to restoring the old Sira when you lifted the blockage from my mind on Plexis. That key is now here." I touched his forehead lightly. "The Clan," I spat the word, "want me back as one of them, and are quite willing to gamble with your life. I'm not. Sira Morgan's enough for me."

Jarad and Sawnda'at exchanged meaningful glances, including a quick look at the line of Enforcers, then my father coughed. "While the use—the help of this Human was our hope, we do not want any disruption of our situation here on Camos. The Human may leave. We won't interfere."

Whether Bowman read the same message as I did in Morgan's one raised brow, or was already committed to further challenging the Clan, I never learned, but regardless, the Trade Pact Commander didn't budge. Her troops kept their weapons aimed. "Not enough, Lord Jarad. What about Sira Morgan? She's registered crew on a Trade Pact vessel—"

Jarad's eyes became hooded. There was a warning bite to his: "Now you interfere, Enforcer. The Clan does not recognize your authority. We are not members of your Pact. Sira di Sarc is one of us. You'd do well to remember that."

"There's no need for threats, Clansman," Morgan announced nonchalantly. "I'm quite willing to undergo your Choice ceremony."

Fool! I sent mind-to-mind with force enough to make Morgan stagger, uncaring about eavesdroppers. *They're trapping you with your feelings for me. I don't need you or want you here.* That didn't work; my feelings for Morgan flowed under the words in total contradiction. *Don't make me destroy you. You don't know—*

Morgan's answering mind voice was almost as violent, despite his carefully controlled features. *And you don't know either, Sira. We must take the risk. I can't take you from them—not without starting a bloodbath that could stretch through Human space.*

My despairing *Jason!* was overlaid by the sound of

Jarad's satisfied: "So be it. We're grateful to you, Captain Morgan."

Although most of the exchange had been silent, Bowman was quick to draw her own conclusion. "Not so fast, Lord di Sarc," she said, putting her hand on Morgan's shoulder. Her blunt fingers dug in, holding him in place. "There's a bit more to this bargaining than you realize."

Chapter 39

I PULLED my head out of the water, then held still while Enora struggled to recapture my hair to apply more soap. Blinking bubbles from my eyes, I tried to help her. The process was slightly hysterical in nature and she was breathless, not to mention soaking wet.

Cenebar stopped his flow of instructions with an irritated snort. I shrugged apologetically, dislodging most of the locks Enora had managed to grab. "You were telling me about the cup—" I said helpfully.

The Clan Healer tugged back the edge of his robe before it slipped down into the bathtub. "It would be helpful if you tried to listen to me, Sira," Cenebar said with unusual sharpness. His hands moved ceaselessly, betraying his own private distress.

Enora tapped the top of my head and I ducked under again obediently, hoping this meant she was finally done scrubbing. It did; she stood waiting with a large towel. The bath, and my present company, were traditions. I took their word for it.

"You've gone over everything twice, Cenebar," I protested, distracted by my hair as it vibrated, then squeezed itself dry. I stepped out, Enora skimming bubbles from my skin with a towel, tsking at the space tan that began at each wrist. "None of it tells me how to help Morgan."

Enora and Cenebar traded looks, probably sharing their exasperation. Well, I was a bit exasperated myself. I didn't like being scrubbed like a dirty pot, even if I had been filthy. Next time I washed, it would be in a fresher stall, where the water behaved.

Cenebar bowed to me, then to Enora, vanishing before he had straightened fully. Enora gazed at me, the composed

look on her face spoiled by a fluff of soap bubbles dripping
down one ear. She gracefully avoided the puddles my feet
had left as she gathered the white robe I was supposed to
wear and turned to offer it to me. "Your mother's," she said
to me, her voice carefully neutral.

She should have been a trader, I decided, swallowing
my first impulse. "Thank you," I said instead of "Never,"
taking the robe with an inner shudder at its cold weight. I
hesitated, holding it awkwardly. My emotions were awkward, too. I knew Enora wanted to comfort me, a gift
I could no longer accept, however much I could have
used it.

They had told me that I'd been fostered with Enora's
mother for years, that I'd attended Enora's birthing and
might have fostered her as a child in my own home had I
been Chosen. Instead, I had remained frozen in time,
while Enora went on to live a normal life. Once her sons
had grown and left, she had offered to be my companion
in exile, managing my affairs while I had buried my nose
in numbers.

It was a companionship that belonged in someone
else's life. "I don't mean to hurt you, Enora," I told her. "I
hope you know that."

"I know," she said gently, turning the robe to show me
where my arms were to go. "Where it matters, you
haven't changed."

I chewed on that doubtfully, giving up the effort to figure out the garment, letting her experienced hands take
over and pull it past my head. "I'm not Sira di Sarc," I
mumbled into the fabric, repeated it when my face was
free again.

Her hands were warm where they gripped the bare skin
of my forearms for a moment. She searched my face, her
own full of hope. "Don't worry about the past. Soon
you'll be whole and complete as never before, Sira."

I wondered which one of us had to die for that to happen: Sira Morgan, or Morgan himself.

Sawnda'at's voice rolled full and rich as he intoned the
first words of the Joining Ritual. "The Chooser has appeared. Bring forth the *duras,* so that all may witness."

Cenebar had been wrong; I'd listened to him, at least
between dunkings. So I knew the duras were cups con-

taining a liquid spiked with *somgelt,* a substance that enhanced the power for a brief moment, making each partner more appealing to the other. In Cenebar's words, somgelt's other benefit was that it eased the rational portion of the mind away from the turmoil of Choice. Great.

A young Clansman walked up to stand before Sawnda'at, lowering his tray to show the Head of the Clan Council a pair of carved wooden cups. Yihtor's had been exact replicas. And where had tradition gotten him?

"Witness the blending of power . . ."

I strengthened my mental shields automatically, but not because of what Sawnda'at was reciting. Someone on Council, I'd guess Faitlen, was leaking outrage again. There was little doubt Bowman and her guards were unwelcome, but a deal was a deal.

Bowman, predictably, looked perfectly comfortable, standing at ease near one wall. Her eyes were in constant motion, her attention flicking around the Council Chamber, assessing, recording, occasionally touching me where I stood beside Cenebar. I shifted from side to side, feet cold without shoes, the robe heavy and confining. Morgan—what was keeping Morgan? Maybe he'd changed his mind. Maybe he didn't want to come after all.

"Joining lasts forever . . ."

I didn't want to be here either. No, whispered a little, hot breath inside me, that was a lie. Not all my anticipation was fear for Morgan, was it? I shrank from the truth, then made myself follow the thought into the depths of me. I found it, felt the dark wet triumph there and recoiled. I had to have Morgan. How it was done mattered only to part of me, a part rapidly growing insignificant.

"Power seeks power through the M'hir . . ."

Bowman appeared fascinated by Sawnda'at's litany. Probably she'd be able to repeat it word for word to her specialists afterward, which would explain her easy agreement not to carry a recorder. I wasn't listening at all, too busy trying to remember every word of Cenebar's lecturing. Following the somgelt, came the Testing. In Clan, Cenebar had told me, the Power-of-Choice within the Chooser tried to master the power of the unChosen candidate. The battleground was the nothingness of the M'hir; the aim of the unChosen, to survive the assault of the

Chooser long enough to forge a permanent path—a Join-ing—through the M'hir.

Morgan? Cenebar had shaken his head. No one knew.

"And you won't help him," I had said then, aware that Bowman's bargaining with the Council hadn't included any survival guarantee. Cenebar promised to do what he could; we both knew that meant whatever Council allowed him to do. Most of them wanted Morgan conveniently dead.

A successful Testing ended with Joining, Cenebar had continued, carefully avoiding a prediction about ours. The linkage through the M'hir could only be broken by death. Having made a successful Joining, a Clanswoman entered the trancelike state during which her body would Commence, altering into its adult, reproductive form. I'd waved Cenebar past this definitely redundant part of the discussion; Enora, busy scrubbing the proof, had blushed bright pink. The physical act of mating took place when Council decreed, based upon predictions of which Clan bloodlines would produce offspring whose power would be advantageous to the whole. These predictions were based as much on guesswork as science, something most Clan had little interest in since they could do so much without technology or understanding.

Remembering that brought me back to the here and now, still not the least bit ready to consider the murky issue of mating—beyond a firm conviction that it was no one else's business, certainly not the Clan's. Then I forgot that, too, as the force within me surged expectantly.

"He's coming," I said, cutting into Sawnda'at's speech. I looked toward the entranceway, aware of the silent, watchful Clansmen at my back.

The Council Chamber, which had been a dull, muted gray, gradually warmed to more welcoming tones of amber and blue. *Hypocrites,* I sneered, but to myself. The space on the floor at the focus of the curved Council table glowed red. My father materialized to one side of it, clothed now in the same intricate garments as the remainder of the watching Council. There was neither remorse nor sympathy in his face. His eyes were ablaze with purpose. I looked away.

The assembled Enforcers snapped to attention as Morgan and Barac entered. At Cenebar's nod, I moved into

the red light and knelt. Out of the corner of my eye, I saw
Barac place his hand on the Human's shoulder for an instant, then all my attention was for Morgan as he came to
kneel before me. He reached out his right hand for mine.
Afraid if I hesitated, I would never take the risk, I placed
my hand in Morgan's.

Nothing happened. I used my left hand to take the
rough-hewn cup my father passed me, my fingers closing
on its worn stem, but I didn't lift it to my lips. "It's
drugged," I warned. Morgan glanced in his own goblet.

"Somgelt." The Human smiled at my look. "Old Barac's
thoughtfully told me something of what to expect, chit."

"I had the standard coaching, too. Not a vistape in the
place." Morgan's smile deepened at my weak attempt
at humor. For myself, I was empty, reflecting others'
emotions rather than my own: impatience, concern, a soft
underlay of bafflement that had to come from the Human
witnesses.

Then, answering involuntarily to the expectant thing inside me, I grew impervious to it all. My world narrowed
to the circle of red light, to Morgan's amused eyes as he
raised his cup with a salute and drained its contents.
Pricked by his unspoken challenge, I lifted my own and
drank.

Odd. I'd prepared myself for a bitter taste and the on-
slaught of the somgelt. Instead, I licked a last trace of
fruity sweetness from my lips. I raised my eyes back to
Morgan's and froze. His face was now made of flowing
color and line—only dark blue pits marking where there
should be eyes. It was as if I saw power rather than physical form. I realized we had passed into the M'hir together,
linked hand to hand as well as mind to mind.

I tried to focus on the witnesses outside the circle, but
the red light was a totally opaque dome. We were alone in
the emptiness. I made an effort and the confusing color
faded, allowing me to see a ghost of purple-white that was
Morgan's face.

His lips moved, but there was no sound. Morgan tilted
his head as if considering that failure, a thoughtful look
but unworried. Then a soft whisper in my mind: *So far so
good, witchling. It's up to you now. Let's finish with this
and get back to the* Fox.

The trouble was, it was up to me. I knew the location of

the Power-of-Choice—felt its heaving and straining. Yet
at the same time I knew I had control, despite the drug
and all the dire predictions. I looked over our clasped
hands to Morgan's calm face and shuddered at the change
I would witness there if I allowed that mindlessness to de-
vour him, to drag him deeper into the M'hir, to lose him
in its darkness. *Jason,* I whispered. *I can't—*

Wonder of wonders, his smile grew tender. *We're playing this table together, Sira. Trust me, not them.*

Something in me responded to his confidence, relaxing
taut bonds. Instantly, raw power coursed through my arm
to my hand. I looked down in amazement, almost expecting to see movement, so vivid was the sensation. The
spurt of power was gone.

No. Not gone, but accepted, unresisted, welcomed.
Morgan's eyes had taken on a luminescence. I relaxed
even further, feeling the sensation begin again. When
Morgan showed no pain, and I felt no conflict, I let the
draining continue. The force within me fought to reach
him all at once. After a moment, I wasn't sure which of us
truly controlled the Power-of-Choice, checking its passage to a safe, slow pace.

Time had no meaning in this place. A point came when
I felt strangely light, utterly free of the dark undercurrent
and the strain of harnessing it. Morgan glowed and crackled with power before my amazed eyes. It was done. And
not by contest, but as a gift.

I led Morgan from the M'hir to reality, watching the
colors of power settle into the more familiar tan of his
skin, the vivid blue of his eyes. It was right for him to release my hand and place his fingers feather-soft on my
forehead. I whispered good-bye to Sira Morgan, refusing
to admit my fear.

I was slowly being smothered. I smiled encouragingly
at Morgan as he carefully restored the original blocks in
my mind. Perception diminished as I lost my power. I began to feel confused and alarmed. Had it been a mistake
to let Captain Morgan into my mind, to try to assess
the damage to my memory? I blinked. Now I was sure
something was terribly wrong. I lunged to my feet and
backed away.

Lights brightened around me. I squinted, close to panic. This wasn't Plexis. "Captain—" I began.

"Sira?" A tall figure moved forward, not a spacer, a man wearing a robe that brushed the floor. I stared at his face; a memory flickered and I rushed forward to bury myself against my father's chest. Jarad's hands pushed me back so he could look at me. "It hasn't worked, Cenebar," he said with disappointment. "Not as we hoped."

Another figure spoke from among what I abruptly realized was a considerable number of people, several dressed in the same strangely formal clothes as my father, even, and I cringed, some Enforcers. Where was I? I listened more closely, trying to discover who was speaking. "—scan no strength. No matter. We shall care for her, di Sarc."

"What of the Human?" Another voice. Human? I pulled out of my father's loose grip.

Here, Sira. Words in my head. Why wasn't I surprised? Why was I sure it was—Morgan! I turned and stared at him, feeling my eyes widen.

"It's time for you to leave, all of you, if you recall our agreement." No trouble locating this speaker; he stood tall and solemn at the center of the dais. A sturdily-built Enforcer—surely I was losing my mind—stepped forward determinedly.

"Are you all right?" Why was she asking Morgan and not me? I thought, annoyed—something was definitely wrong with me.

Captain Morgan's eyes had a luster I didn't remember, but there was no mistaking the mischief in his grin. "I'm far more than all right, Commander Bowman," he said. "But first, to finish—come here, Sira." He held out one hand to me confidently. I looked from it to my silent father.

"What's going on here?" I demanded, intending this as a calm question; the result was regrettably close to a shout. I paused, embarrassed but resolute. "Where am I? What have you been doing?" This last with pure annoyance directed at Morgan, who regarded me with a strange soft smile before coming to stand before me. "Morgan?" I asked again, looking up at him, somehow knowing that he was the key—my link to what had happened.

"Stop, Human! Leave well enough alone and we shall allow you to go—"

Morgan's eyes dimmed as he lowered his head slightly. I shivered, wondering how I knew whoever had spoken had come very close to death.

No matter. Morgan raised now-smiling eyes to meet mine once more, reaching out with his tanned fingers to take my right hand in a light hold. "I think this is what you've been waiting for, Sira," he said softly. There was a sensation of something bursting in my head. I closed my eyes—losing all sense of where and what I was.

* * *

INTERLUDE

"Stop him!" Faitlen shouted. "Enough! There must be no Joining with an alien!"

"You wanted me to restore the block so Sira can trigger the release, Clansman. And I have," Morgan answered for himself, his obvious confidence in dealing with the Council reassuring a rather gray Bowman. "Ask Sira—when she's ready." Morgan leaned comfortably against the Council table, his eyes never leaving the Clanswoman he'd christened Sira Morgan.

She stood statue-still, totally absorbed, her face changing expression in flashes, no single change long enough to identify, the effect as if she was being rebuilt from within.

Who would she become? he wondered.

Chapter 40

AN awakening of a kind. But now I opened my eyes without fear, sure of my place and of the way things would be. I welcomed Sira Morgan; she had much to teach me.

"Council," I bowed politely, performing the requisite power gesture in recognition of equals. "Father," a deeper bow. "Cenebar, Barac—" For these last two, the configuration of heart-kin. They returned it immediately, but I saw and understood Barac's quick look to the Human.

"We see you and know your power, Sira di Sarc," Sawnda'at said graciously, adding power overtones of relief and pleasure to the bare words. I was touched by his sincerity, touched but not fooled into lowering any barriers in this place. "If all is well with you, we must also offer our thanks to this Human."

Morgan was leaning irreverently against one corner of the Council table. Others of the M'hiray could not read his waiting tautness, the tension in his deliberate smile; how blind they were, I thought with real pity. "My thanks also, Human," I said formally, hands sweeping the complete gesture of beholdenness. "I'm whole as I've never been—as I might never have been."

And it was true. My memory stretched clear and complete behind me; some memories less pleasant to recall than others, but that was the way of anyone's past. The future was the only place where one had choice.

"You have our leave to go, Morgan, you and the rest of your kind," Jarad said with a rude suddenness. "We will honor our promise to withdraw from Camos. We have what we want."

I gazed at my father's craggy cold features, aware of

more than enough memories there. Jarad's eyes took on a hooded look as he tried to scan me, a gleam appearing when he could not. "Welcome back, Daughter. We've much to discuss."

"Indeed?" I raised one brow. "It can wait, Jarad. I've more urgent business to take care of first."

An uneasy stirring from the Council behind us. Things were not as they seemed. How much, they couldn't begin to guess. "Are you leaving then, Chosen?" Sawnda'at asked ever so politely, very careful of my lawful status now, as befitted one whose individual power was inferior to my own.

"I'm not Chosen," I said to them, full of scorn. "How can I be, when there's been no Joining formed through the M'hir? The Power-of-Choice within me hasn't been matched in contest—I'm rid of it! Haven't you scanned *him* yet, in your arrogance?" I found it comical to watch the slow turn of heads, to feel delicate sensing beams reach to Morgan—reach and be drawn back in disbelief as they sensed the power hovering around him in the M'hir, like a static charge. Morgan ignored them, glowing eyes fixed on me in the same quiet waiting.

"I won't say I understand what's happened, but my congratulations, Fem di Sarc," Bowman said courteously. The creature to her left, a Tolian, was trying to stop panting; Terk dug his elbow into its ribs.

"Thank you," I smiled at the commander, extending the configuration of respect for the benefit of Clan senses. *What an exceptional Human,* I decided, though perhaps for different reasons than the Council. The stakes had been terribly high. Facing them to save Morgan, her own kind, was admirable but no more than her duty; trying to save me had taken a rare amount of sheer gall. I liked her.

"What will you do now?" Bowman asked, eyes full of bold curiosity.

"Do?" I echoed thoughtfully. "I intend to expand my horizons, Commander. Do you know, I've never played Stars and Comets?"

"Sas'qaat's tables are the best," Morgan asserted as one who should know, coming to my side.

"Wait!" Barac said roughly, almost leaping toward me, his face drawn white around nostrils and mouth. I noticed

the lines on his once-young features and grieved for him.
But I also stopped his speech with a flick of power.

"Cousin, we're done here," I stressed the last word as a
warning. There was little more I could safely say, in this
company. What mattered now was leaving the Council
Chamber with all of us intact. Morgan brushed my fingers
with his own, once, gently. I didn't need the reminder that
he and Barac were of one mind in this. "It's time to go," I
said, at risk with even so much.

"What of Kurr? Don't you care what happened to him?"
Barac's pain-filled demand was like a stone dropped into
a still pond. I could feel the waves of recently-eased tension begin again, a deadly stirring.

I dared a rapid mind send. *Stop, Barac. Stop now while
you have a mind to control. You can't reach past Yihtor,
but they can reach you. Don't allow your grief to waste
Kurr's death.*

He flinched as if I had struck him with a whip, eyes terrible. *You know . . .* a dark whisper in my mind.

And you may not, not and survive, I gave him. *It ends
here.* It was the truth, and cruel. Barac accepted it with a
shudder. Then he disappeared. I was relieved, yet faintly
surprised his escape had been so easy.

*Your wisdom has returned with your strength, my
daughter,* Jarad's mind voice was complimentary. I took a
breath, close to losing my own control as I looked at him
and knew the cost of saving Barac's life had been this—
that this monster believed I was his again.

Barac's under my protection, I sent very softly, just to
Jarad. *He doesn't know, as I now do, how you helped Yihtor and other discontents escape the Council. He doesn't
know, as I do, how you helped the renegade set up a little
kingdom—waiting only its queen. Barac doesn't even
know what I've just figured out: how the Council's decision about me rushed you into using any means to get me
to Yihtor, including using Kurr to unwittingly carry a
message about my coming and my plans for Morgan, a
service Yihtor repaid with murder. Barac doesn't know,
Father, but I do.*

Jarad might have been made of stone. We watched each
other, and the Council watched us, none willing to challenge, none willing to admit that lines had been drawn
and accepted. There was a moment of suspended motion.

Then a touch, ghostly light and familiar, brushed my forehead and the locate of a camouflaged aircar slipped into my thoughts. Willingly, I left both memories and the present behind, reaching for the future. I *pushed* . . .

Think you could teach me that, chit? I shared Morgan's smile deep in my thoughts as we winked out of reality together.

. . . and then was lifted joyously into the warm spring air.

C.S. Friedman

☐ **THIS ALIEN SHORE**   UE2798—$23.95

It is the second age of human space exploration. The first age ended in disaster when it was discovered that the primitive FTL drive caused catastrophic genetic damage—leading to the rise of new mutated human races on the now-abandoned colonies. But now one of the first colonies has given rise to a mutation which allows the members of the Gueran Outspace Guild to safely conduct humans through the stars. To break the Guild's monopoly could bring almost incalculable riches, and to some, it would be worth any risk—even launching a destructive computer virus into the all-important interstellar Net. And when, in this universe full of corporate intrigue, a young woman called Jamisia narrowly escapes an attack on the corporate satellite that has been her home for her entire life, she must discover why the attackers were looking for *her*. . . .

☐ **IN CONQUEST BORN**   UE2198—$6.99
☐ **THE MADNESS SEASON**   UE2444—$6.99

THE COLDFIRE TRILOGY

Centuries after being stranded on the planet Erna, humans have achieved an uneasy stalemate with the *fae*, a terrifying natural force with the power to prey upon people's minds. Damien Vryce, the warrior priest, and Gerald Tarrant, the undead sorcerer must join together in an uneasy alliance confront a power that threatens the very essence of the human spirit, in a battle which could cost them not only their lives, but the soul of all mankind.

☐ **BLACK SUN RISING** (Book 1)   UE2527—$6.99
☐ **WHEN TRUE NIGHT FALLS** (Book 2)   UE2615—$6.99
☐ **CROWN OF SHADOWS** (Book 3)   UE2717—$6.99

Prices slightly higher in Canada.   **DAW 140X**

OTHERLAND
TAD WILLIAMS

Otherland. A perilous and seductive realm of the imagination where any fantasy—whether cherished dream or dreaded nightmare—can be made shockingly real. Incredible amounts of money have been lavished on it. The best minds of two generations have labored to build it. And, somehow, bit by bit, it is claiming Earth's most valuable resource—its children. It is up to a small band of adventures to take up the challenge of Otherland in order to reveal the truth to the people of Earth. But they are split by mistrust, thrown into different worlds, and stalked at every turn by the sociopathic killer Dread and the mysterious Nemesis. . . .